LIKE EVERY ORPHAN, I had heard stories about Obernewtyn.

It was used by parents as a sort of horror tale to make naughty children behave. But in truth very little was known about it.

Some said it was just like another Councilfarm, and that the master there had only sought labor for an area too remote to interest normal laborers. Others said Lukas Seraphim was himself afflicted in some way, while still others claimed he was a doctor and wanted subjects to practice on.

Those Misfits taken there were never seen again.

ISOBELLE CARMODY

THE SEEKER

THE OBERNEWTYN CHRONICLES
Includes two complete novels
OBERNEWTYN • THE FARSEEKERS

BLUEFIRE

Obernewtyn copyright © 1987 by Isobelle Carmody
The Farseekers copyright © 1990 by Isobelle Carmody
Cover art copyright © 2007 by Penguin Group Australia
Map copyright © 2008 by Penguin Group Australia

All rights reserved. Published in the United States by Bluefire, an imprint of Random House Children's Books, a division of Random House, Inc., New York. The works in this collection were originally published separately by Penguin Books Australia Ltd, Camberwell, in 1987 and 1990. Published here by arrangement with Penguin Group Australia, a division of Pearson Australia Group Pty Ltd.

Bluefire and the colophon are trademarks of Random House, Inc.

Visit us on the Web! www.randomhouse.com/teens/strangelands

Educators and librarians, for a variety of teaching tools, visit us at
www.randomhouse.com/teachers

Library of Congress Cataloging-in-Publication Data is available upon request.
ISBN 978-0-375-87113-9 (tr. pbk.) — ISBN 978-0-307-97434-1 (ebook)

Printed in the United States of America
10 9 8 7 6 5 4 3 2 1
First Bluefire Edition 2011

✦ CONTENTS ✦

OBERNEWTYN

for Brenda

✦ INTRODUCTION ✦

IN THE DAYS following the holocaust, which came to be known as the Great White, there was death and madness. In part, this was the effect of the lingering radiation rained on the world from the skies. Those fortunate enough to live on remote holdings and farms were spared destruction, though they had seen the skies whiten and had understood that it meant death. These people preserved their untainted land and families ruthlessly, slaughtering the hundreds of refugees who poured from the poisoned cities.

This time of siege was called the Age of Chaos and lasted until no one else came from the cities. Unaware that the cities were now only silent graveyards on endless black plains where nothing lived or grew, the most powerful farmers formed a Council to protect their community from further siege and to mete out justice and aid. Peace came to the Land.

But time proved that the remote community had not completely escaped the effects of the Great White. Mutations in both man and beast were high. Not fully understanding the reason for the mutations, the Council feared for the community and decreed that any man or beast not born completely normal must be burned. To remove any qualms people might have about the killings, these burnings took on a ritual air, and were used to remind the people of their fortune in being spared in the holocaust and the time of Chaos.

The Council appointed a fledgling religious order to perform the burnings. The order, called the Herder Faction, believed that the holocaust was punishment from God, whom they called Lud. Gradually, religious dogma and law fused, and the honest way of the farmer was seen as the only right way. Machines, books, and all the artifacts of the Beforetime were abhorred and destroyed.

Some resisted the rigid lore, but by now the Council had provided itself with a band of militaristic protectors, called soldierguards. Any who dared oppose the order were tried and burned as seditioners or were given the lesser charge of being unsafe and sent to work on the Councilfarms.

After some time, the Herder Faction advised the Council that not all mutancies were immediately apparent at birth. Such afflictions as those that attacked the mind could not be discerned until later.

This created some difficulty, for while the Council saw the opportunity to further manipulate the community, accusing anyone of whom they disapproved of hidden mutancy, it was more difficult to proceed with a ritual burning of someone who had been accepted as normal for most of his or her life. The Council eventually decreed that none but the most horribly afflicted of this new kind of mutant would be burned and the rest would be sent instead to the Councilfarms. A new name was devised for anyone with an affliction not apparent at birth—Misfit.

It was a dark and violent age, though the untainted land flourished and even began cautiously to extend its boundaries as the effects of the Great White began at last to wane. New towns were established, all ruled by the iron hand of the Council from its seat in Sutrium. So great was the death toll under Council rule that hundreds of children were left orphaned each year. The Council responded by setting up a network of orphan homes to house those unclaimed by blood relatives.

The community regarded the inmates of orphan homes with an abiding suspicion, since most were the children of Misfits or seditioners, and as such were considered dangerous.

PART I

◆

THE LOWLANDS

✦ 1 ✦

BEFORE FIRST LIGHT, we set out for the Silent Vale.

It was a half day's journey, and we were led by a tall gangling boy called Elii, who carried a small sword and two hunting knives at his belt. These were the clearest visible reminders that our journey involved danger.

Also traveling with us was a young Herder. He represented the true danger that lay ahead. Around our necks we wore the dull graymetal circlet that denoted our orphan status. This would protect us from robbers and gypsies, for as orphans we owned nothing. Normally the presence of a Herder would be enough to frighten off robbers, who feared the wrath of the powerful order.

But this was a very young Herder, little more than a boy, with golden bum-fluff on his cheeks. His eyes held characteristic Herder zeal, but there was a nervous tic in one of his eyelids. I guessed this was his first duty away from the cloisters; he seemed as nervous of us as of any supernatural dangers he might perceive. It was rumored that Herders had the ability to see the ghosts of the Oldtimers flitting about as they had done in the terrible days when the sky was still white and radiant. This talent was said to be Ludgiven so they could warn of the dangers that lay in following the evil ways of the Beforetimers.

Our expedition to collect whitestick was considered perilous but important. The Council had ruled that only orphan homes could mine the rare substance, perhaps because orphans were the most expendable members of the community. Collection of the whitestick was fraught with danger, for the substance could only be found in areas verging on tainted, where the land had not long ago been untouchable. The whitestick was poisonous to the naked skin and had to be passed through a special process designed to remove its poisons before it was of any use.

Once cleansed, it was marvelously versatile, serving in everything from sleep potions to the potent medicines prepared by the Herders.

I had not been to the Silent Vale before. This was the Kinraide orphan home's area of collection, and it yielded high-grade whitestick. But the Silent Vale was considered dangerously close to the Blacklands, where the poisons of the Great White still ruled. It was even whispered there were traces of Oldtime dwellings nearby. I was thrilled, and terrified, to think I might see them.

We passed through a side gate in the walls of the Kinraide complex. The way from that door was a track leading steeply downward. Seldom traveled, it seemed a world apart from the neat, ordered gardens and paths within the orphanage. Bush creepers trailed unchecked from side to side, choking the path in places.

Elii chopped occasionally at the vines to clear the way. He was an odd boy. People tended to shun him because of his profession and because of his close connections with the orphan home, though he was no orphan. His father had worked in the same capacity and his grandfather before that, until they had died of the rotting sickness that came from prolonged exposure to the whitestick. He lived on the grounds at Kinraide but did not associate with us.

One of the girls in our party approached him. "Why not travel along the crevasse instead of going up this steep edge?" she panted.

For some way, we had been climbing a steep spur along one side of the rise. Northward the dale ran up into a glen of shadows.

"The path runs this way," Elii snapped, his eyes swiveling around to the rest of us, cold and contemptuous. "I don't want to hear any more whining questions from you lot. I'm the Lud of this expedition, and I say there'll be no more talk."

The Herder flushed at the nearly blasphemous mention of Lud's name, but the restraint in his face showed he had been warned already about the rude but necessary youth. Few would choose to do his job, whatever the prize in the end. Elii turned on his heel and led us at a smart pace to the crest of the hill. From the top, we could see a long way—the home behind us and beyond that the town center, and in front of us, far to the west, lay a belt of mountains, purpled with the distance. The boundary of untainted lands. Beyond those mountains, nothing lived. Hastily I averted my eyes, for no one understood all the dangers of the Blacklands. Even looking at them might do some harm.

The dawn came and went as we walked, a wan gray light seeping into the world. The path led us toward a pool of water in a small valley. It was utterly still and mirrored the dull overcast sky, its southern end dark in the shadow of the hills.

"I hope we are not going to swim that because it is in the way," said the same girl who had spoken before. I stared at her defiant face, still stained with the red dye used by Herders to mark the children of seditioners. Elii said nothing, but the Herder gave her a look that would have terrified me. A nervous young Herder is still a Herder.

We came to the pool at the shadowed end only to find the path cleaved to the very edge of the water.

"Touch this water not!" the Herder said suddenly in a loud voice that made us all jump.

Elii looked over his shoulder with a sneering expression. A little farther on, a cobbled border, crumbled in places and overrun with sprouting weeds, ran alongside the track. It was uncommon enough for me to wonder if this was from the Beforetime. If so, I was not much impressed, but the Herder made a warding-off sign at the border.

"Avert your eyes," he cried, his voice squeaking at the end. I wondered if he saw something. Perhaps there were faint impressions of Oldtimers fleeing along this very road, the Great White mushrooming behind them, filling the sky with deadly white light.

An eastward bend in the path led us around the edge of a natural stone wall, and there we suddenly came upon a thing that was unmistakably a product of the Oldtime. A single unbroken gray stone grew straight up into the sky like the trunk of a tree, marked at intervals with bizarre symbols, an obelisk of the ancient past.

"This is where the other Herders spoke their prayers to Lud," said Elii. "They saw no danger before this."

The young Herder flushed but kept his dignity. He made us kneel as he asked Lud for protection. The prayer lasted a very long time. Elii sighed loudly and impatiently. Making a final sign of rejection at the unnatural gray pedestal, the young priest rose and self-consciously brushed his habit.

The same girl spoke again. "Is that from the Beforetime,

then?" she asked. This time I did not look at her. She was dangerously careless and seemed not to think about what she was saying. And this Herder was nervous enough to report all of us because of the one stupid girl.

"It is a sign of the evil past," said the Herder at last, trembling with outrage. Finally, the girl seemed to sense she had gone too far and fell silent.

One of the others in our party, a girl named Rosamunde whom I knew only slightly, moved near and whispered in my ear, "That girl will be off to the Councilcourt if she keeps that up."

I nodded slightly but hoped she would not prolong her whispering.

To my concern, she leaned close again. "Perhaps she doesn't care if they send her to the farms. I heard her whole family was burned for sedition, and she only escaped because of her age," she added.

I shrugged, and to my relief, Rosamunde stepped back into line.

When we stopped for midmeal, Rosamunde sought me out again, sitting beside me and unwrapping her bread and curd cheese. I hoped there was nothing about her that would reflect on me. I had heard nothing of any detriment about her, but one never knew.

"That girl," Rosamunde said softly. "It must be unbearable to know that her whole family is dead except for her."

Unwillingly, I looked to where the other girl sat alone, not eating, her body stiff with some inner tension. "I heard her father was mixed up with Henry Druid."

I pretended not to be interested, but it was hard not to be curious about anyone linked with the mysterious rebel Herder priest.

Rosamunde leaned forward again, reaching for her cordial. "I know your brother, Jes," she said softly. I stiffened, wondering if he had sent her to spy on me. Unaware of my withdrawal, she went on. "He is fortunate to be so well thought of among the guardians. There is talk that the Herder wants to make him an assistant."

I was careful not to let my shock show. I had heard nothing of that and wondered if Jes knew. He would have seen no reason to tell me if he did.

Jes was the only person who knew the truth about me. What he knew was enough to see me burned, and I was frightened of him. My only comfort lay in the tendency of the Council to condemn all those in a family tainted by one Misfit birth. Jes might not be burned, but he would not like to be sentenced to the Councilfarms to process whitestick until he died. As long as it was safer for him to keep my secret, I was safe, but if it ever appeared that I would be exposed, I feared Jes would denounce me at once.

Suddenly I wondered if he had engineered my inclusion on the whitestick expedition. As a favored orphan, he had some influence. He was too pious to kill me himself, though that would have been his best solution, but if I died seeking whitestick, as many did, then he would be innocently free of me.

Elii called us to move. This time I positioned myself near him, where Rosamunde would not dare chatter. The Herder priest walked alongside, muttering his incantations. We had not gone far when a rushing noise came through the whispering greenery. We arrived shortly thereafter at a part of the path that curved steeply down. Here a subterranean waterway, swollen with the autumnal rains, had burst through the dark earth, using the path as its course until the next bend.

"Well, now," Elii said sourly.

The Herder came up to stand uneasily beside him. "We will have to find another way," he said. "Lud will lead us."

Elii snorted rudely. "Your Lud had better help us on *this* path—there ain't no other way."

The priest's face grew red, then white. "You go too far," he gasped, but Elii was already preoccupied, drawing a length of rope from his pack and tying the end around a tree. Then he slung the other end down the flooded path.

The Herder watched these movements with a look of horror.

Elii pulled at the rope, testing it, before swinging agilely down to the bottom of the small waterfall. Back on dry ground, he called for us to do the same, one at a time.

"We'll be dashed to pieces," Rosamunde observed gloomily.

The Herder gave her a dark look as one of the boys started to climb carefully down. Several others went, then Rosamunde, then me. The rope was slippery now and hard to grip. I found it difficult to lift my own weight. Two-thirds of the way down, my fingers became too numb to cling properly, and I fell the last several handspans, crashing heavily into a rock as I landed. The water soaked into my trousers.

"Get her out. The water may be tainted," Elii growled, then yelled up for the priest to descend.

I was completely breathless and dazed from my fall, and my head ached horribly where I had hit it on the rock.

"She's bleeding," Rosamunde told Elii.

"Won't matter. Running blood cleans a wound," he muttered absently, watching the priest descend slowly and with much crying out for Lud's help. I felt as though I were watching through a mist.

13

When the Herder reached the bottom, he knelt beside me quickly and began reciting a prayer for the dead.

"She's not dead," Rosamunde said gently.

Seeing that I was only stunned, the priest bandaged the cut on my temple with deft efficiency, and I reminded myself again that for all his youth, the Herder was fully trained in his calling.

"Come on," Elii said impatiently. "Though I doubt we'll make it in time now."

"Was the water tainted?" I asked. I ignored Rosamunde's audible gasp. There was no point in caution if I died from not speaking out.

The Herder shook his head, and I wondered how he knew—though I did not doubt that he was right. Herder knowledge was wide-ranging and sometimes obscure, but generally reliable.

We walked quickly then, urged on by Elii. My head ached steadily, but I was relieved that it was only a bump and not a serious infection. I had a sudden vision of my mother, applying a steaming herb poultice to my head. How quickly the pain had subsided on that occasion. Herb lore was forbidden now, though it was said there were still those who secretly practiced the art.

I nearly walked into Elii, having failed to notice he had called a halt.

"Through the Weirwood lies the Silent Vale," he said. "If we are too late today, we will have to camp here and enter the Vale tomorrow."

"The Weirwood?" said someone nervously.

"It is dangerous to be out at night in these parts," the Herder said, "where the spirits of the Beforetime rest uneasily."

14

Elii shrugged, saying there would be no help for it if the sun had gone. He had his orders. "Perhaps your Lud will cast his mantle of protection over us," he added with a faint glimmer of amusement.

We entered the Weirwood, and I shivered at the thought of spending a night there. It had an unnatural feel, and I saw several in our group look around nervously. We had not walked far when we came to a clearing, and in the center of this was the ravine they called the Silent Vale. It was very narrow, a mere slit in the ground, with steps hewn into one end, descending into the gap. The light reached just a handspan or so into the ravine, and the rest was in dense shadow.

I understood now Elii's haste, for only when the sun was directly overhead would it light the Vale, and it was almost at its zenith now.

We entered the ravine and descended the slippery steps fearfully. By the time we reached the bottom, I was numb with the cold, and we huddled together at the foot of the steps, afraid to move where we could not see. Moments passed and the sun reached its zenith, piercing the damp mists that filled the ravine and lighting up the Vale.

It was much wider at the base, and unexpectedly, there were trees growing—though they were stunted and diseased, with few leaves. A thick whitish moss covered the ground and some of the walls in a dense carpet. Where the moss did not grow, the walls were scored and charred, possibly marked by the fire said to have rained from the skies during the first days of the holocaust. A faint stench of burning still filled the air.

Elii handed out the gloves and bags for gathering the whitestick, instructing us needlessly to be quick and careful and never to let the substance touch our skin. Pulling on the gloves, we spread out and set to work, searching for the tell-tale black nodules that concealed the deposits of whitestick.

The bags were small but took time to fill, because the substance crumbled to dust if not handled carefully. Standing to ease my aching back once I had finished, I noticed that I had wandered out of the sight of everyone else. I could hear nothing, though the others had to have been quite near. I had noticed at once the aptly named Vale was oddly silent, but now it struck me anew how unnatural that silence was, and how complete. Even the wind made no murmur. It was as if a special kind of death had come to the Silent Vale.

"Are you finished?" Rosamunde asked, apologizing when I jumped in fright. "This place is enough to give even a soldier-guard a taste of the horrors," she said.

Returning to where some of the others had gathered at the bottom of the steps, we heard voices nearby.

"What do they use this stuff for, anyway?" one asked.

"Medicines and such, or so they say," said another voice with a bitter edge. It was the voice of the out-spoken girl marked with Herder red. "But I have heard rumors the priests use it to make special poisons and to torture their prisoners for information," she added softly.

Rosamunde looked at me in horror, but we said nothing. I was no informer, and I did not think Rosamunde was. But that girl was bent on disaster, and she would take anyone with her stupid enough not to see the danger. Better to forget what we had overheard.

I left Rosamunde with the others, going to examine a deep fissure in the ground. The Great White had savaged the earth, and there were many such holes and chasms leading deep into the ground. I bent and looked in, and a chill air struck at my face from those black depths.

Impulsively, I picked up a rock and dropped it in. My heart beat many times before I heard the faint report of impact.

"What was that?" cried the Herder, who had been packing the bags of whitestick.

Elii strode purposefully over. "Idiot of a girl. This is a serious place, not the garden at Kinraide. Throw yourself in next time and make me happy." I looked at my feet with a fast-beating heart. Twice now I had called attention to myself, and that was dangerous.

Suddenly there was a vague murmur from the ground beneath our feet.

"What was that?" the Herder cried again, edging closer to the steps.

"I don't know," Elii said with a frown. "Probably nothing, but I don't like it. After all, we are not far from the Blacklands. Come, the sun is going."

We ascended the steps in a single file. The Herder, who came last, kept looking behind him fearfully as if he expected something to reach out and grab him.

An air of relief came over the group as we threw off the oppressive air of the Vale. Fortunately, we had gathered enough whitestick, and we made good time on our return, reaching Kinraide early in the evening.

To my private astonishment, Jes was among those who met us, and he wore the beaten potmetal armband of a Herders' assistant.

✦ 2 ✦

"Elspeth?"

It was Jes, and I willed him to go away. He knocked again, then stuck his head in the door. "How are you?" he asked with a hint of disapproval.

Anger overcame caution. "For Lud's sake, Jes, they're not going to condemn me because of a headache. If you think it looks suspicious, then why don't you report me?" I retorted, staring pointedly at his armband.

He whitened and shut the door behind him. "Keep your voice down. There are people outside."

I bit my lip and forced myself to be calm. "What do you want?" I asked him coldly. I knew I was being stupid, but I didn't care. Jes was the only one I could strike out at. And that, I thought, looking at his stiff face, was becoming increasingly dangerous.

"Maybe you don't care about being burned, but I do. Much as you scorn it, caution has kept us safe until now. No thanks to you," he added, and I was bitterly reminded that our plight was my fault. "A headache is nothing, but you know how little things are blown out of all proportion. It is a short step from gossip to the Councilcourt in Sutrium."

"You have been made an assistant," I said flatly, and now he reddened. A look of pride mingled with shame came over his face. "How could you?" I asked him bleakly.

He clenched his jaw. "You will not ruin this for me," he said at last. "It is my sin that I do not denounce you. But you are my sister."

"You would not dare denounce me," I said. "Your own life would be ruined if it was known you had a Misfit for a sister. Don't pretend you care for me."

A queer flicker passed over his face, and I suddenly felt certain that this was the truth.

When he had gone, I lay back, my head aching dully, partly from tension. For all my bravado, I was afraid of Jes. There had been a time when we were close. Not so much when we were young, for he had been a dutiful son, and I too much of a wanderer to please anyone except my beloved mother. But after we had come into the orphan home system following the trial and execution of our parents, we had clung to one another. Jes had vowed then to have revenge on the Council and the Herder Faction for their evil work that day. He had wiped my eyes and sworn to protect me.

He had not known what that would entail. In those first years, we regarded our secretive behavior as a game. It was only as we grew older that we became increasingly aware of the dangers. Discovering the truth about myself made me more solitary than ever, while Jes developed a near obsession with caution. In those days, his one desire had been to get a Normalcy Certificate and get out, then ask permission to have me with him. But somehow we had drifted apart, till the bonds that held us were fragile indeed. I knew Jes had become fascinated with the Herder Faction and its ideas. But as an orphan, he would never be accepted into the cloister, so I had thought little of it.

Recently, we had fought bitterly over his explanations for why the Herders had burned our parents. I had called him a traitor and a dogmatic fool; he in turn had called me a Misfit. That he would even say the word revealed how much he had changed.

Aside from Jes, people thought my recent headaches and bouts of light-headedness were the result of my fall on the path to Silent Vale that day, and I let them. I'd intended to hide the pain altogether, but I had cried out in the night, and the guardians had come to hear of it. In the end, I told them of my fall, because I did not want them to speculate, and had been given light duties and some bitter powders by the Herder.

If not the fall, then the headaches might have been simply a reaction to a change in the weather, for winds from the Blacklands did cause fevers and rashes. But deep down, I knew they had nothing to do with either the fall or the weather.

I shook my head and decided to go for a walk in the garden, slipping out a side door into the fading sunset. Jes had called me a Misfit, and according to Council lore, that was what I was. But I did not feel like a monster. In a queer mental leap, I thought about my first visit with my father to the great city of Sutrium. We had gone all that way for the fabulous Sutrium moon fair, and we weren't alone. Everyone who could walk, hobble, or ride seemed to be on the road to the biggest town in the Land, bringing with them hay, wool, embroidery, honey, perfume, and a hundred other things to trade. They had come from Saithwold, Sawlney, Port Oran, Morganna, and even Aborium and Murmroth.

I had not known then that Sutrium was also the home of the main Councilcourt. That I had discovered on my grim second visit. There had been no fair then. It was wintertime, and the city was gray and cold. There were no gay crowds filling the streets, only a few people who had regarded us furtively as we passed in the open carriage, our faces stinging from the red dye. We had not known then that Henry Druid had only recently disappeared, fleeing the wrath of the Council, and that the entire community was fearful of the consequences, since many had known and openly agreed with the rebel. But what I did understand, even then, was the hatred and fear in the faces of the people who looked at us. I had felt the terror of being different that has never left me.

Shuddering, I thrust the grim memory away. Ludwilling, I would never see such looks again.

The time of changing was near, and I sighed, thinking it would be better for us both if Jes and I were sent this time to separate homes. The Herder told us that the custom of moving orphans around regularly from home to home had arisen to prevent friendships forming that could not be continued once leaving the system. But it was widely accepted that the changing was engineered to prevent alliances between the children of seditioners, which might lead to further trouble. And there was another effect, evident only when the time for the changing approached. No one knew where they might go and whom they might trust in the new home.

Even before the relocation, we learned to prepare mentally, withdrawing and steeling ourselves for the loneliness that would come until the new home was familiar, until it was possible to tell who could be trusted and who were the informers.

I looked up. It was growing dark, and soon I would have to go in. Fortunately, no one minded my wandering in the garden even on the coldest of days, but I never stayed out beyond nightfall—those dark hours belonged to the spirits of the Beforetime. I leaned against a statue of the founder of

Kinraide. Here I was hidden from the windows by a big laurel tree, and it was my favorite place.

The moon had risen early, and the darkening sky made it glow. An unnatural weakness coursed through me. I felt a sticky sweat break out on my forehead and thought I was going to faint. The pain in my head made me stagger to my knees.

I tried to force the vision not to come, but it was impossible. I stared up at the moon. It had become a penetrating yellow eye. I knew that eye sought me, and I felt the panic rise within me.

Then, abruptly, there was only the pale moon. My headache was gone, as though it had been only a painful precursor to what I had just experienced. I shivered violently and stood up. I would not let myself wonder about the vision— nor the others that had preceded it. Jes had told me long ago, when we could still talk of such things, that only Herders were permitted visions. "You must not imagine that you have them," he had said.

But I did not imagine them, either then or now, I thought, and walked shakily back across the garden. Yet though I did not try to understand what they meant, a few days later the meaning forced itself on me.

✦ 3 ✦

MARUMAN CONFIRMED IT in the end.

It had been a cold year overall despite the occasional muggy days that came whenever the wind blew in from the Blacklands. Most often even spring days were bitten with pale, frosted skies, which stretched away to the north and south and over the seas to the icy poles of the legends.

Sometimes in the late afternoon, I would sit and imagine the color fading out to where there was no color at all, as if the Great White again filled the skies, its lethal radiance leaching the natural blue. But unlike that age of terror when night was banished for days on end, I fancied the Land would be permanently frozen into the white world of wintertime, the sea afloat with giant towers of ice such as those in the stories my mother had told.

"Stories!" Maruman snorted as he came up, having overheard the last of my thoughts. I smiled at him as he joined me beside the statue of the founder. I scratched his stomach, and he rolled about and stretched with familiar abandon.

He was not a pretty cat nor a pampered one. His wild eyes were of a fierce amber hue, and he had a battered head and a torn ear. He once told me he had fought a village dog over a bone and that the hound had cheated by biting him on the head.

"Never can trust them pap-fed funaga lovers," he had observed disdainfully. "Funaga" was the thought symbol he used for men and women. "And I'd no sooner trust a wild one anytime; it'd bite me in half at one go."

Maruman possessed a dramatic and fanciful imagination. I thought perhaps that old war injury was to blame. Occasionally his thoughts would become muddled and disturbed. During those periods, he could dream very vividly. He had undergone such a fit shortly after we had begun to communicate, only to tell me that one day the mountains would seek me. I had laughed because it was such a strange image.

Another time he had confessed a Guanette bird had told him his destiny was twined with mine. This bird was used throughout the Land as a symbol representing an oracle-like wisdom or a preordained order of things. If there were meaning and reason behind the symbol, they were lost to me. The actual bird was said to be extinct. Yet Maruman quite often attributed his insights or notions to the direct intervention of the mythical wise bird.

Maruman was, he often told me, his own cat. Not so much wild, he would point out, as unencumbered. He once observed that life with a master was doubtless very nice, but for all that, he preferred his own way. Having a master, he said, seemed to take the stuffing out of a beast. I reflected to myself that this was certainly true. Despite this, and with a touch of cynicism, I thought that part of Maruman's devotion to me was because I fed him.

There seemed little to love in this rude, unbalanced cat with an ear that looked half devoured. Yet there was a kind of wild joy about him that I could only envy, for I was far from free. If he had been human, I think he would have been a gypsy, and in fact he quite liked to visit the troupes that roved about. He told me they fed him scraps and sang rollicking songs and laughed more than other funaga.

The bond between Maruman and myself had been the catalyst through which I had discovered the full extent of my telepathic powers. He said it had been destiny, but I doubted it.

I had been seated right next to the statue of the founder when it happened. A scraggy-looking cat was stalking a bird. I would have ignored them both, except that I was so struck by the carelessness of the bird. I thought it almost deserved its fate. As I concentrated on the pursuit, I suddenly had the sensation of something moving in my head. It was the queerest feeling, and I gasped loudly.

Startled, the bird flew off with an irritated chirp. I had saved the wretched creature's life, and it was annoyed! It did not yet occur to me to wonder how I knew what the bird felt. Instead I noticed that the cat seemed to glare indignantly at me with its bright yellow eyes. I shrugged wryly, and it looked away and began to clean itself.

I had the notion it was only pretending to ignore me. Then I laughed, thinking I must have sat too long in the sun. The cat turned to face me again, and for a moment I imagined a glint of amusement in its look. I wondered if maybe Jes was right and I was going mad.

"Stupid funaga," said a voice in my head. I somehow knew it was the cat and stared at it in shock. "All funaga are stupid." Again I had heard what it was thinking.

"They are not!" I answered without opening my mouth. Now it was the cat's turn to stare.

That first moment of mutual astonishment had given way to a curiosity about each other that had in time grown to an enduring friendship. Once we had overcome our initial disbelief and began to pool our knowledge, Maruman revealed that all beasts were capable of mindspeaking together as we did, sensing emotions and images as well as brief messages, though typically not so deeply or intimately. He said animals had been able to do so in a limited way even before the holocaust, which, interestingly, he, too, called the Great White.

I told him my one piece of knowledge about the link between animals and humans, gleaned from a Beforetime book my mother had read. It had claimed humans evolved from some hairy animals called apes, which no longer existed as far as I knew, but neither Maruman nor I could feel that was more than a fairy tale.

I had heard many stories about the Great White from my parents as a child, which were different than the stories told by the Herders once I entered the orphan home system.

I remembered little from my childhood, but Herder lessons about the Great White and Beforetime were driven into us during the daily rituals and prayers, exhorting us to seek purity of race and mind. The priest who dealt with such matters at Kinraide was old, with a sharp eye and a hard hand. His manner of preaching often reduced new orphans to screaming hysteria. He made the Beforetime sound like some terrifying concoction of heaven and hell, woven throughout with sloth, indulgence, and pride: the sins suffered by the Oldtimers. The holocaust itself was paraded as the wrath of Lud in all its terrible glory.

This fearful picture was tempered by the stories one heard from other sources, gypsies and traveling jacks and potmenders, who presented the Oldtimers to us as men who flew through the air in golden machines and could live and breathe beneath the sea. Those stories left little doubt that the

Beforetime people had possessed some remarkable abilities, however fantasized and exaggerated the details had become.

Maruman had little to offer about the Beforetime. He had more to say about the Great White. Dismissing the Herder version, Maruman said the beastworld believed that men had unleashed the Great White from things they called machines—powerful and violent inanimate creatures set deep under the ground, controlled and fed by men. Beasts called them glarsh.

I questioned him as to how inanimate things could be violent or fed, but he could not explain this apparent paradox.

Maruman said he "remembered" the Great White, and though that was impossible, he wove remarkably frightening pictures of a world in terror. He spoke of the rains that burned whatever they touched, and of the charnel stench. He spoke of the radiant heat that filled the skies and blotted out the night, of the thirst and the hunger and the screaming of those dying, of the invisible poisons that permeated the air and plants and waters of the world. And most of all, he spoke of the deaths of men, children, and women, and of the deaths of beasts, and when I listened, I wept with him, though I did not know if he had imagined it all or if he was somehow really able to remember something he had not seen firsthand.

According to the orthodox history of the Great White, only the righteous were spared. But Maruman said those spared had the luck of living a long way from the center of destruction and that was all. If he was right, then all that the Herders had told us were lies, and the Council, supposedly devised by Lud, was more likely man-made, too.

It was then I had begun to understand what my parents had been fighting for with more than blind loyalty.

Maruman bit me, bored with my musings; then he licked

the place as demanded by courtesy. I looked fondly at him, wondering where his wandering had taken him this time.

"Where have you been? I missed you," I told him.

He purred. "I am here now," he answered firmly, and I knew better than to question him further. He did not like to be questioned, and when he did not want to talk, the worst course was to press him. Gradually, over time, he would give me enough information to work out the rest, but for now I noticed a few places where his fur had rubbed off and assumed he had been to tainted land. If that was true, he would almost certainly undergo another of his mad periods. I resolved to feed him up, because he did not eat at such times and was already too thin.

"She is coming," he sent suddenly, and looking at his eyes, I saw that he was already half into a fey state, and his words were probably only raving.

Nonetheless, I asked, "Who is coming?"

"She. The darkOne," he answered. "She seeks you but does not know you." A thrill of fear coursed through me. His thoughts seemed to tally with my own persistent visions of being sought. "She comes soon. The whiteface smells of her." Maruman spat at the moon, which had risen in the daytime sky. It was full. I wondered why he hated the moon so much. It had something to do with the coming of the Great White, I knew.

He snapped at nothing above his injured ear, then yowled forlornly.

"When does she come?" I asked, but Maruman seemed to have lost the thread of the conversation. I watched his mind drift into his eyes. He growled and the hackles on his back rose, then he shook his head as if to clear it of the fog that sometimes floated there.

"When I was on the dreamtrails, I met the oldOne. She said I must follow you. It is my task. But I am . . . tired."

"Follow me where?" I asked. Then I gulped, for a horrible notion had come to me. "Where does the darkOne come from? Where will she take me?"

"To the mountains," Maruman answered. "To the mountains of shadow, where black wars with white, to the heart of darkness, to the aerie above the clouds, to the chasm underearth. To the others." Suddenly he pitched sideways, and a trickle of saliva came from his mouth.

I sat very still, because none lived in the mountains save those at Obernewtyn.

A keeper from Obernewtyn would come; if Maruman was right, it would be a woman who would find out the truth about me.

✦ 4 ✦

LIKE EVERY CHILD, I had heard stories about Obernewtyn. Parents and orphanage guardians used it as a sort of horror tale to make naughty children behave. But, in truth, very little was known about it.

In its early days, the Council had been approached by Lukas Seraphim, who had built a huge holding in the wilds of the northern mountains, on land ringed by savage peaks and only just free of the Blacklands. He had offered this holding as a solution to the problem of where to send the worst-afflicted Misfits and those who were too troublesome for use on the Councilfarms.

In the end, an agreement had been made to send some Misfits to Obernewtyn, where they would be put to work. A few generations later, the agreement still stood. Some said it was just like another Councilfarm and that the master there only sought labor for an area too remote to interest normal laborers. Others said the Seraphim family was itself afflicted in some way and pitied the creatures, while still others claimed they practiced the dark arts and needed human subjects.

Those Misfits taken there were never seen again, so none of these stories had ever been authenticated properly. But such was the legend of Obernewtyn, grown over the years because of its very mystery, and it was feared by all orphans, not the least because in more modern times, it sent out its keepers to investigate the homes, seeking undisclosed Misfits among us.

It was said these keepers were extraordinarily skillful at spotting aberrations, and that the resultant Council trial was a foregone conclusion.

If what I feared was true, Maruman's garbled predictions and my own premonitions could only add up to a visit by a keeper from Obernewtyn. In the past, I had been fortunate enough never to have been present at a home under such review, but it was an occasion I had dreaded, particularly as my abilities made me far more deviant than any Misfit I had ever heard of.

When official word of an Obernewtyn keeper's imminent arrival was circulated, my worst fears were realized. All the omens implied disaster.

Jes was worried enough to catch me alone in the garden and advise me to be careful. His warning itself did not surprise me, but he looked scared, and that made him more approachable. Impulsively, I told him of my premonition, but that only made him angry. "Don't start that business now," he said.

"I'm afraid," I said in a small voice.

His eyes softened, and to my surprise, he took one of my hands and squeezed it reassuringly. "She can't possibly know what you are unless she is like you." I stared because that was the first time in many years he had mentioned my secret without bitterness.

He went on. "Look, why do you think everyone finds out she's coming before she gets here? They do it deliberately, to scare people. If people are nervous, they're more likely to give themselves away."

31

Wanting badly to please him, I nodded in agreement. He looked surprised and rather pleased; we had done nothing but argue for a long time.

We smiled at each other hesitantly.

The keeper arrived three days later, and by then, the atmosphere in the home was electric. Even the guardians were jumpy, and the Herders' lectures had grown longer and more dogmatic. A keeper could not have wished for more.

Like me, many of the orphans had never seen an Obernewtyn keeper. I was amazed to see how beautiful she was, and not at all threatening. It was impossible to look at her petite, fashionably attired form and credit the Gothic horror stories that abounded in connection with Obernewtyn.

She was introduced to us at a special assembly as Madam Vega, head keeper of Obernewtyn.

The orphans who met her spoke of her beauty and sweetness and gentle manner. Nothing was as we had imagined, and nothing happened in those few days to cast any suspicion on me. I was even able to convince myself that both Maruman and I must have been mistaken. Even so, I greeted the morning of her departure with a kind of relief.

I was working in the kitchen when one of the guardians instructed me to prepare a tea tray for the Kinraide head and her guest. It was an innocent enough request, but as I wheeled the laden tray to the front interviewing chamber, I felt uneasy. I took a deep breath to calm myself.

The head was standing near the door when I entered and gestured impatiently for me to transfer the tea things from my tray to a low table. I did this rather awkwardly, wondering where Madam Vega was. I reached out with my abilities to locate her, an act that always made me feel oddly exposed because it required me to unshield my mind. Sensing that she was at the other end of the room, I turned to see her standing at the purple-draped window, her back to the room as she looked out over Kinraide's broad formal gardens.

Then, slowly, she turned around.

When she turned, it seemed she went on turning for an eternity, gradually showing more of herself. Struck with the dreadful curiosity of fear, unable to look away, I became convinced that when her movement was completed eons from now, I would be looking into the face of my most terrible nightmares.

Yet she was smiling at me, and her eyes were blue like the summer sky. She hastened to where I stood.

I swallowed, too scared to move until the Kinraide head gestured for me to pour the tea. My hands shook.

"My dear child," said Madam Vega, taking the teapot from me with her own lovely white hands, "you're trembling." Then she turned to the head with a faint look of reproach.

"She has been ill," the other woman said with a shrug. I prayed she would dismiss me, but she was sugaring her tea.

The keeper looked at me. "You seem upset. Now, why would that be, I wonder? Are you afraid?"

I shook my head, but of course she did not believe me.

"You need not fear me. I'm aware of all the silly stories. How they began, I really don't know. I am simply here to take away those children who are afflicted with mental problems. Obernewtyn is a beautiful place—though cold, I admit," she added confidingly. "But there is nothing there to frighten anyone. And my good master seeks only to find a cure for such afflictions. He thinks it is possible to do this before the mind is full grown."

"A noble purpose," murmured the other woman piously.

Madam Vega had been watching me very closely as she spoke. I felt as if I were drowning in the extraordinary blueness of her eyes. There was something almost hypnotic in them.

"I know a great deal about Misfits," she said.

I wanted to look away but couldn't, and an urge grew within me to find out what she was thinking. I let the edge of my shield fade.

In an instant, a dozen impressions pierced me like blades, but beneath the blue compulsion of her eyes, they faded.

"Well, well," she said, and stepped away from me.

I stood for a moment, half dazed.

"Well, go along, then," said the Kinraide head impatiently.

I turned on shaking legs, willing myself not to run. As I closed the door behind me, I heard Madam Vega's sweet voice utter the words that spelled my doom. "What did you say that girl was called?"

✦ 5 ✦

"JES!" I STUMBLED into the kitchen, sending out a cloud of panic and urgency. "Jes. Jes. Jes!"

I almost fell over the astonished Rosamunde, who was working there. "Elspeth?" she said disbelievingly.

Jes charged through another door, his face contorted with fury. "What are you doing?" he shouted. Noticing Rosamunde, he stopped to stare at us in confusion.

"For Lud's sake, Jes, don't yell at her. It's one of her fainting fits again." Rosamunde looked uncertainly at me. "That water must have been tainted, despite what the Herder said."

"Water?" Jes whispered incredulously.

"Of course," she said sternly. "And stop glaring at her. She's just been in with the Obernewtyn keeper. I'll get a powder," she added, and departed.

"Is it true?" he asked, fear in his eyes.

I nodded numbly. "I was only meant to serve tea. But she knows now."

"How can you be sure?" he pressed. "Tell me what they said. Did they speak of me?"

"They said nothing. But at the end, when I was leaving, she asked who I was."

He gaped. "That's all?"

I shook my head. "She knows, Jes."

The light died in his eyes. He might despise my powers, but he did not doubt them.

"Jes!" It was Rosamunde. She frowned at him from the veranda. "Don't stare her down like some idiot guardian. Help her outside. Some fresh air will revive her."

"She's all right," Jes snapped, but he carried me onto the veranda and set me on a couch. Ignoring him, Rosamunde handed me a powder. I swallowed it without demur, hardly noticing its bitter aftertaste.

"I am sorry," I told Jes, suddenly remorseful.

He made no reply. His face was grim. I could not blame his hatred of my abilities. At that moment, I hated them myself.

Rosamunde had noticed the look on Jes's face and sat on the couch beside him. "What is the matter? Tell me. You know you can trust me. I'll help if I can."

He looked at her, and to my astonishment, I could see that he did trust her. Lying to this girl would not come easily to him. I studied her properly. She was a plain, sensitive-looking girl, pale as most orphans were, with a mop of brown curls neatly tied back. I wondered how I had been so blind as to miss the thawing of my self-sufficient brother.

Jes turned to face me. "Are you all right, Elf?" he asked. That had been his pet name for me in happier days, but he had not used it for a long time. How odd that it had taken a disaster to show me that there was still some bond of affection between us. His face was thoughtful, and as I had often done before, I wished I could read his mind. He was not like me, yet his was one of the rare minds that seemed to have a natural shield.

Rosamunde gazed at us both in consternation. "Tell me, please," she urged.

"Elspeth will be declared a Misfit," Jes said tiredly.

"You poor thing," Rosamunde whispered.

"Elf . . . has begun to have unnatural dreams," Jes said slowly.

I stared at him. Occasionally I had true-dreamed, but that was the least of it. Why was Jes lying?

"It was the tainted water," Jes continued, his eyes evasive.

I gaped openly now.

"But . . . everyone knows that sometimes happens when someone comes into contact with tainted water," Rosamunde said incredulously. "She was normal before the accident, and I am sure that will temper their judgment. She might only go to the Councilfarms, and you could petition for her once you have your own Normalcy Certificate."

Then a look of concern passed over her features, and I knew what had occurred to her. If I was declared a birth Misfit, Jes would be stripped of his armband and privileges, and even his Certificate would be in doubt. On the other hand, if the Council judged that I had been affected by tainted water and declared me Misfit through misadventure, Jes's status would be unaffected.

I looked at my brother. I had never known what motivated him. But perhaps he thought of more than just himself as he weaved this tissue of lies. After all, it would go easier for me, too, if the Council thought I was a Misfit only by accident.

"Talk to them," Rosamunde urged Jes, but he shook his head. "You are no Misfit!" she cried.

"No," Jes agreed. His eyes were sad. "Leave us," he said to Rosamunde gently.

She burst into noisy tears. "No. I will come, too, if they take you. I could pretend—"

"Be wise," Jes said. "We don't know what the keeper will

do, or what happens at Obernewtyn." He paused, and I sensed the struggle taking place within him. "If things had been different . . . ," he began, and then stopped. He fell silent, his face troubled.

Rosamunde seemed to understand and dried her tears. Her face was wretched with unhappiness. "They might not take you," she said. "The tainted water is to blame."

I looked at her, and a plan came to me. I would have to be wary and delicate.

Carefully I directed my ability to manipulate thoughts into her reeling mind, seeking to create the chains of thought and action I needed, joining them carefully onto her own half-formed notions. I had not used my coercing ability so directly before, and I was curious to see how well the thoughts and decisions I had grafted would hold.

"You must go," Jes told her. "I want you to go. Never speak of this—or us—again. It is bad enough that we have been seen together. I will not let you be dragged into this mess."

"Oh Lud, no," she sobbed, and ran inside.

Jes and I looked at each other, neither of us having the slightest idea what the other thought.

"Elspeth Gordie."

I trembled at the sound of my name, though I had been waiting for it. At that last moment, there was a flare of hope that I had been wrong after all.

I waited, still trembling, as those around me drew back. The head of Kinraide went on to say that I had been affected by tainted water and was to be sent to the Councilcourt in Sutrium for sentencing. I knew then my plan had worked. I looked at Jes and caught his amazed look. He did not understand how the lie he had devised had come to be believed by the guardians. I prayed I knew him well enough to guess he would not protest or ask who had reported me. My eyes sought out Rosamunde, who would not look at me, and I hoped she would not be too badly affected by what I had willed her to do. I felt a self-loathing for having burdened her with a betrayal she would never have contemplated without my coercerthought.

Her denouncement had come too late to stop the proceedings under which I would be bonded to Obernewtyn, but it had saved Jes from any trouble and had categorized me as a very ordinary sort of Misfit. I prayed the knowledge that she had saved Jes would be enough to salve Rosamunde. I did not want her to suffer.

An awful lethargy filled me as I sat in the punishment room, where I would remain until the Council coach came for me at dawn. I could have picked the lock, for I had recently discovered that by concentrating fiercely I could exert a small amount of physical force with my mental powers. But were I to open the door, where would I go?

Maruman came to my prison window that night. I tried to explain that I was going away, but he was still under the sway of his fit, and I could not tell how much he understood.

"The mountains have called at last," he said dreamily. "Last night I dreamed of the oldOne again. She said your destiny is there."

"Oh, don't," I begged, but Maruman was merciless in his fey state.

"I smell the white in the mountains," he told me with drifting eyes that reflected the moonlight. I found myself trembling after he had gone and wished that now, of all times, Maruman had been his grumpy, sensible self, all too ready to scoff at my fears.

I slept fitfully until I heard movement at the door. It was still not dawn, and I wondered if the carriage had arrived already. But it was Jes.

"Forgive me," he said.

I gaped at him.

"I didn't tell them that business about the water. I swear. I . . . I thought of it, to save myself, but I didn't. I don't know how they came to know. I wouldn't blame you for thinking I had done it," he said wretchedly.

"It's better that they think I am only a dreamer and not a birth Misfit," I said earnestly, hoping he would not confess his anguish to poor Rosamunde, who might reveal her part in my denunciation.

"It shames me that when they read your name out I thought only of myself," he said in a muffled voice.

He seemed to feel he had betrayed me simply because the thought had occurred to him, and I sensed his rigid nature would crumble completely if I allowed him to break down.

"Soon you will have your Certificate. You will be able to petition for me," I said softly.

"But Obernewtyn does not release those it takes," he whispered.

Hastily I took his hand. "Oh, Jes," I said. "You saw the keeper. Did she look so awful? I'm not frightened. And I would have hated the Councilfarms," I added with a smile.

Wanly he smiled back.

There was a movement outside, and a voice called that the carriage was ready. I looked at Jes in sudden concern, fearing what would happen if he was caught with me. But seeing my alarm, he shook his head, saying the Herder himself had given permission for Jes to say prayers for my soul. I noticed he still wore the armband, but I said nothing.

He leaned forward suddenly, his eyes fierce. "I will come and get you one day. I promise."

But you are only sixteen, I thought, *with two more long years until you can apply for your Certificate.* Instinct told me this would be our last goodbye. Impulsively, I flung my arms around him. "Dear Jes, it really is best this way," I said. "Except for our parting, I am honestly glad it is done with."

"Time now," said the guardian. Jes nodded. Suddenly aware that he was being watched, he said the last few chants of a prayer.

"Goodbye," I whispered.

He did not wait to see me bundled into the dark coach, and I was glad for it.

I sat back into the stiff upholstery and wondered what destiny waited for me at Obernewtyn.

✦ 6 ✦

THERE WERE FEW people around to see me arrive at the Councilcourt in Sutrium. Even at the busiest hour, few tarried near those somber buildings. The white slate steps led up to the open double doors, and for the second time in my life, I ascended them, led by a soldierguard. The smell of wood polish made me vividly recollect my last visit. But back then, Jes had been with me, squeezing my hand.

"Sit and wait till you are called," said the soldierguard, peering into my face as if to ascertain whether I was capable of understanding. I nodded dully, and he went away.

A man and a boy came through the front door. There was something unusual about them, but I felt too numb at first to try working out what it was. Then it came to me. They were very tanned, as if they had spent their whole life outdoors.

The man followed a soldierguard through a door, while the boy looked around to find I was sitting on the only bench. He sat beside me.

"Hullo," he said.

I stared at him, astonished that he would speak to a complete stranger. And here of all places. "Who are you?" I asked, suddenly suspicious.

He looked amused, and his eyes crinkled in a nice sort of way. "Do I look like a spy?" he laughed. "My name is Daffyd.

My uncle is petitioning the council for a permit to trade in the mountains."

"The mountains," I echoed.

"Well, not exactly the mountains. After all, whom would we trade with? I meant the high country," he explained. He smiled again, and despite everything, I found myself smiling back. "Why are you here?" he asked.

"I'm a Misfit, or soon to be judged so," I said bluntly. "I am to be sent to Obernewtyn."

He didn't recoil. He only said, "Well, if you are like me, you will find the mountains beautiful. I don't have much patience for places like Sutrium," he added disparagingly.

Impulsively I tried to read him, but like Jes, he had a natural shield.

"Aren't you afraid to be seen talking to a Misfit?" I asked at last.

"Where I come from, they say Misfits are people who have been punished by Lud. I don't see how that is anything to fear. In truth it seems to me there are worse things than being a Misfit."

"Oh yes?" I asked sarcastically. "What could be worse?"

"These people, for one. This Luddamned Council," he said in a low, intense voice. I stared, for what he was saying was sedition. He was either mad or insanely careless.

Seeing my expression, he only shrugged. "These fools believe everyone who doesn't think and act as they do is evil. As for Obernewtyn, you need not fear it. It is merely a large mansion with farms. Not those labor camps the Council calls a farm. Real farms, with animals and crops and sowing and reaping. You might like it," he said reassuringly.

"Have you been there?" I asked.

His eyes were suddenly evasive, and though I did not press him, his unexpected reluctance angered me. "I might escape," I told him coldly, more for effect than because I meant it.

But he gave me a measured look. "If ever you do run away, you might seek out the Druid in the highlands. I have heard he lives still in hiding. He has no love for Misfits, but you need not tell him—"

He broke off his words at the sound of footsteps, and we both looked up to see his uncle reenter the room. "Come, Daffyd," the older man said, his eyes skidding over me.

Daffyd rose at once. He said nothing to me, but as they moved to the door, he smiled over his shoulder.

I watched them go thoughtfully. Henry Druid had been a Herder, forced to flee with some of his followers after defying a Council directive to burn his precious collection of Oldtime books. That had been long years past, and rumor was that he had died. Yet this boy implied otherwise.

I shrugged. The boy had surely been defective. He had been careless in talking to me at all.

A soldierguard stepped from one of the doors and waved impatiently for me to enter. I went slowly, playing the part of a dull wit.

The trial room was quite small. At the very front was a Councilman seated at a high bench, facing the rest of the room. Beside him at a lower table were two Herders. The rows of seats facing the front were occupied only by a few lounging soldierguards in their telltale yellow cloaks. The seats were theoretically meant for interested members of the community, but I could not imagine anyone would be curious enough to risk being associated with whoever was on trial. No one paid the slightest bit of attention as I was prodded to the front by the soldierguard on duty. I looked up at the Councilman, wondering bitterly what would happen to the daughter of such a person if *she* were judged Misfit.

"Well, now," said the Councilman in a brisk voice. His eyes passed over me with disinterest, reminding me that I was less than nothing to him. "I understand this is a routine affair with no defense," he said to a tall man in black who rose and nodded languidly.

The Councilman turned his attention to me. "You are Elspeth Gordie?"

I nodded.

"Very well. You have been accused of being a Misfit by Madam Vega of Obernewtyn. If so judged, you will be unfit ever to receive a Normalcy Certificate or to become part of the community of true humans. Corsak, you will speak for Stephen Seraphim, the Master of Obernewtyn?"

The man in black did not look at me as he spoke. "This orphan has been exposed as a Misfit by the Obernewtyn head keeper. She was also denounced by another orphan, who claims that she fell in tainted water and has from that time had unnatural dreams and fainting fits. This would normally mark her a Misfit by mischance, but there are several other points. May I expand?"

The Councilman nodded.

"In her first home, the girl was accused of giving an evil eye. Naturally we do not place too much credibility on these reports, but they do point to the possibility that she had Misfit tendencies even before this tainted water infected her." As he continued outlining various reports made about me in various homes, both by other orphans and by guardians, I began to feel truly frightened. I had never imagined my record would hold so much evidence to suggest I was a birth Misfit.

It was suddenly clear to me that I would never have been issued a Normalcy Certificate.

Suddenly the Councilman cut him off. "I do not see how any of this gossip is as significant as the fact that the girl came into contact with tainted water. Surely that is the cause of any mutancy. And is it not still true that your master has no interest in those made Misfit by mischance?"

"That is so, Councilman," Corsak said carefully. "But that evidence was not available at the time Madam Vega made her initial claim."

"And your master. Does he still feel there is some hope of a cure for Misfits?"

"Obernewtyn concentrates all its efforts on healing," the man in black answered somewhat defensively.

One of the Herders stood. "Misfits are not sick. They have allowed themselves to become habitations for demons."

Sirrah Corsak bowed. "My master feels it is the sickness that allows the invasion of demons, and that a young mind might be healed so that the demons could be driven out."

The Herder glanced at his companion, an older priest who also rose. He wore a gold-edged armband that denoted him the senior of the pair. "Driving away demons is Herder work," he said.

"Of course," said the Obernewtyn representative. "If a mind were to be healed, the subject would immediately be delivered to the Herder Faction."

"Yet where are your successes, Sirrah Corsak?" asked the first Herder aggressively. "Why should we keep sending Misfits to you, when none are healed?"

The Obernewtyn man cast an appealing look at the Councilman. "You are well paid for them," he said.

"That is not the point," snapped the Councilman. He nodded at the two Herders, who again sat down.

The man in black looked nervous. "I beg pardon, Councilman," he said. "It is true that Obernewtyn uses these Misfits for labor, but my master diligently seeks a cure as well."

The Councilman eyed him coolly. "So you have said, and so Madam Vega and your master have scribed. Even so, perhaps it is time for us to visit Obernewtyn and evaluate for ourselves what is done with the Misfits we send there."

His eyes flicked back to me. "Do you admit to being a Misfit?" he asked in a bored tone.

I cringed and gave him what I hoped was a convincingly, vacant leer. The Councilman sighed as if it were as much as he had expected, then asked if anyone knew whether I was able to speak. No one answered, and the Councilman scowled impatiently.

"Very well, I pronounce her Misfit by mischance. But you may take her, Corsak. Make arrangements to name her in the records when you make the bond over. And we look forward to an invitation to visit Obernewtyn and to see these healing efforts you have described with such eloquence," he added meaningfully.

Corsak nodded and indicated for me to follow him.

The Councilman forestalled him coldly. "If you please. Is the scribe here?"

"Yes!" said a cheerful voice.

"Ensure this reaches the people. Misfits are a particularly foul and insidious threat to our community. They often pass as normal for many years, since their defects are not obvious to the eye. We know this because of the efforts of our good and diligent Herders." The two Herders inclined their heads modestly. "They have lately informed me that their researches have revealed that Misfits are Lud's way of punishing our laxity. How is it, Lud asks us, that Misfits are permitted to roam and breed among us for so long? The answer is that we have failed in our duty of watchfulness. This attitude threatens to hurl us back into the Age of Chaos, and worse. Therefore, it is the order and decree of this Councilcourt that penalties for aiding and concealing Misfits and any other defective humans or beasts will increase. Each man must watch his neighbor. . . ."

He went on to explain the various new rulings and penalties, and I shuddered at the effect this would have on the community. Each time the Council sought to tighten its control, a new wave of denunciations and burnings occurred. Oddly enough, I fancied a look of surprise had crossed the face of the younger priest at the mention of Herder researches.

✦ 7 ✦

IT TOOK SOME time to reach the outskirts of Sutrium. I had forgotten the city was so big. The streets were completely deserted, and it was well into the morning before we reached the end of the town's sprawling outer limits, but toward midday, the city fell rapidly behind.

I had lived in urban orphan homes now for many years, but the curved road parting the soft folded hills and gullies brought back clear memories of my childhood in Rangorn, far from the towns and the ever-present menace of the Council. I realized I had not lied to Jes when I told him I was almost glad. There was an odd sort of peace in having got the thing done at last. I thought of Madam Vega and reflected that Obernewtyn was bound to be less terrible than the stories.

It was not hard to forget fear and to surrender myself to the peaceful solitude of the carriage. The morning burgeoned into a sun-filled day, and between naps I watched the country unfold.

To the east of the road, we passed the villages of Saithwold and Sawlney, and beyond them to the north were soft woodlands, where from the window I could see the downs sloping gently to Arandelft, set deep in the forest. To the west of the road were the vast hazy moors of Glenelg.

The road curved down to pass on the farthermost outskirts of Arandelft, where slate-gray buildings were framed by cultivated fields flanked by bloodberry trees. More than twenty leagues away and closing the horizon was the Gelfort Range—the mountains Tor, Aren Craggie, and Emeralfel. They marked the border of the highlands, and as if to underline this, the road began gradually to incline upward.

We passed onto the low westernmost slopes of the Brown Haw Rises, hillocky and undulant—I was astounded to discover how much I knew of land I had never seen. My father had talked a good deal of these places. He had traveled much in the Land before he bonded with my mother. Sometimes he had seated me on his knee and shown me colored pictures that he called maps. He would point to places, tell me their names, and explain what they were like.

We passed a small moor, wetter and more dense than Glenelg, and I peered through the leafy eben trees along the roadside at the mist-wreathed expanse. There had been no moors in Rangorn, but I recognized this from my father's descriptions. He had said the mists never went away but were always fed by some hissing subterranean source. He thought the moors were caused by some inner disturbance in the earth, yet another legacy of the Great White.

My mother had said good herbs always grew near the moors; she came from the high country and knew a great deal about herb lore. I thought of the great, white-trunked trees that had stood on the hillside around our house. Were they still there, though the house had long ago been reduced to ashes? I remembered my mother making me listen to the whispering sounds of the trees; the rich, shadowed glades where we collected mushrooms and healing flowers; and the summer brambles laden with fat berries, dragging over the bank of our favorite swimming hole. I thought of standing with my father and looking down from the hills to where the

Ford of Rangorn met the onrush of the Suggredoon, and the distant, grayish glint of a Blacklands lake.

And I remembered the burning of my mother and father, in the midst of all the beauty of Rangorn. Perhaps that was what Jes remembered most, what had made him so cold and strange in recent times.

As the late-afternoon sun slanted through the window of the carriage, we halted briefly at a wayside hostel, and a new coachman came to take the place of the other. The hostel was just outside a village called Guanette, and I felt a jolt at the name. It made me think of Maruman, and I wondered if he had understood that I really was going away for good.

We rode on, and I saw that the village consisted mostly of small stone-wrought hovels with shingled roofs. They looked ancient and had probably been erected during the Age of Chaos. Their stolidity seemed a response to the turmoiled past.

Laughter drifted in through the windows as we rode by children who scrabbled in pools of dust along the roadway. They looked up indifferently as we passed. I was once like them, I thought rather bitterly, until the Council had taken a hand.

The carriage jerked suddenly to a halt, and the coachman dismounted. We had stopped outside yet another hostel called The Green Tree.

After a long time, he came back, unlocked a window, and threw a soft parcel to me. "Supper," he grunted in a curious accent. Impulsively, I asked him if I could sit outside and eat.

He hesitated, then unlocked the door. "Out yer get, then," he said.

Thanking him profusely, I did as he bade, and he relocked the carriage, muttering about children. I stood blinking at him. "Go round th' back. Ye can eat there. Mind ye don't wander." Thanking him again, I hastened away, thinking many of the late-night callers at my father's house had spoken like this, with a slow, singsong lilt. They had looked like this man, too, gnarled and brown with kind eyes.

There was a pretty, unkempt garden out behind the hostel, and I scoured it for a spot under one of the trees.

"Least you/Elspeth could do is share food/meal," came a plaintive thought. I jumped to my feet in fright, dropping the food parcel. Maruman rushed forward and sniffed it tenderly. "Now look what you have done."

I stared at him, unable to believe my eyes. "What . . . how did you get here?" Maruman gave me a sly cat-look and fell to tearing at the parcel. I sat back, my own appetite forgotten.

"I came with you," he told me as he ate. "In the box with wheels, on the back. I am very clever," he added smugly.

I burst out laughing; then I looked around in fright, because my laughter had sounded so loud.

"You took a terrible risk," I sent. "What if you had been seen?"

"I had to come/follow," he sent. "Innle must be protected."

I looked into his eyes, but there was no sign of madness. "You won't be able to come all the way to Obernewtyn," I sent. "The carriage goes over tainted ground."

"I will stay here, and you will come to me."

I shook my head impatiently. "Obernewtyn is like a cage. I won't be allowed to do as I please."

Unperturbed, Maruman began cleaning one of his paws. "You will come," he sent at last. "Maruman does not like the mountains. I smell the white there."

"Well, how will you live here?" I asked him.

He gave me a scornful look; Maruman had, after all, lived a good many years before meeting me. Just the same, I reflected, he was not a young cat, and then there were his fits of madness. Finishing his ablutions, he curled in my lap and went to sleep.

I thought of what I had said to Daffyd, the boy in the Councilcourt. I had not meant it then, but now I seriously considered escaping. I could run off; it would be far easier here than it would have been in Sutrium. I could find work in some remote hamlet and keep Maruman with me. The thought of escape made me feel breathless.

My mother once had bought a wild bird from an old man who caught the poor things. We hadn't much money, but she had a soft heart. He had given her the oldest bird, an ugly creature he had had for some time. She had opened the cage to let it fly away. But it was a poor half-starved thing and would not go even when prodded. It died there, huddled in the corner of the cage. My mother had said it had been caged for too long. Neither Jes nor I had understood then, but I wondered if, like that bird, I had been caged too long to contemplate freedom.

A voice called my name. Maruman woke immediately. He leapt from my knee and melted into the shadows just as the coachman and a woman came onto the porch of the hostel. The old man blinked, and I sensed he had seen Maruman, but he said nothing. The woman turned to him. "Just as well for you that she did not wander away." She flicked her hand at me. "Get into the carriage."

I followed them to the road with an inward sigh, noticing the horses had been changed. The woman climbed heavily into the seat and glared at me as she settled herself.

"I am Guardian Hester," she said.

I waited, but she seemed to feel it was beneath her to say more. She yawned several times and soon seemed bored. Eventually she took a small vial from her pocket, uncorked it, and drank the contents. I recognized the bitter odor of the sleep drug. In a short time, she was dozing.

After leaving Guanette, the country grew steadily steeper. The road was still well cobbled, but it became progressively more narrow and winding. The coachman maneuvered carefully around the bends, for on one side was a sharp drop to a darkly wooded valley extending as far as the eye could see. It was slow going, and after about an hour, he pulled the coach over to the right of the road to fetch the horses water from a spring. I called out to him.

"Hey," he grumbled as he came to the window and peered in at me. "Is that my name, then?"

"I'm sorry. No one tells us names. Can I ride up there with you?"

Predictably he shook his head, peering in at the guardian's sleeping form. "If ye were alone, maybe I would let ye," he said softly. "But if she were to waken an' see ye gone . . ." He shook his head in anticipation of the coals of wrath that would be heaped on his head.

"But she won't wake for hours. She took some of that sleep stuff." I poked her hard to show him I spoke the truth.

He ruminated for a moment, then took out his keys.

"Oh, thank you," I gasped, astounded at my luck.

"Well fine of me it is," he agreed. "But she better not wake, or I'll be in deep troubles." He finished watering the horses while I capered in the crisp highland air. "Enoch," the coachman said suddenly.

"Pardon?" I said.

"Enoch, girl," he repeated. "That's my name." He helped

me up onto the seat beside him, and I felt a thrill as he clicked his tongue and the coach began to move.

"My name . . . ," I began to say, then stopped. Perhaps he wouldn't want to know my name. Misfits, after all, weren't supposed to be quite human.

"Your name?" he prompted; encouraged, I told him. He nodded and then pointed to the valley to the west. "That's the White Valley."

I stared, thinking that Maruman would not like the name. Enoch went on. "Many have gone to that valley in search of refuge, but it ain't a friendly place. Strange animals rove there, an' they don't love men."

"Maybe that's where Henry Druid perished," I said, to see how he would respond.

The old man gave me a sharp look. "Accordin' to yon Council, he died in the highlands, true enow, an' some say they have seen his ghost walk. Me, I dinna believe in ghosts." He saw my quick look of interest, and his expression went bland.

I looked at the wood and wondered whether the Druid still lived.

"That were a fine cat," the coachman said presently. "Some don't like cats. Reckon they're incapable of love or loyalty, but I dinna agree. A cat can love, fierce as any beast."

"He's not a very pretty cat," I said hesitantly.

The old man grinned. "All that's fine is nowt necessarily fair. Look at me. But as a matter of fact, I thought that cat a handsome creature." He glanced at me. "I've a good mind to have a bit of a look for him. Maybe he'd fancy living with me. Of course, he might not take to me."

"Oh, he will!" I cried. "I am sure of it."

The coachman grinned and nodded, and we rode for some

distance in companionable silence. Perhaps Enoch would find Maruman. I hoped so.

The valley was lost to sight at last as we wound into the mountains. "That stuff would kill a pig," said the coachman. He jerked his head back to where the guardian slept. "Now, me mam gave us herbs when we couldn't sleep. Good natural things. That were good enough for us."

"But herb lore is banned," I said.

He looked taken aback. "An' so it is. Damned if I didn't forget fer a minute. But it weren't so when I were a lad." He paused, seemingly struck by the oddness of something that had been a good thing in his youth but which had since become evil in the eyes of the community. Finally, he sighed as if the problem were unresolvable. "Things were different then," he said.

Looking around, he pointed again to where we had come back into the open. The mountains hid the White Valley from us, but there was a broad plain on the other side of the road. "Th' land hereabout is Darthnor, and th' village of Darthnor is that way," Enoch said, nodding to the east. I stared but could see no sign of any settlement. " 'Tis a strange place," he said, "an' I say so even though I were born there. None dwell in these parts but a few shepherds. Those in the village are mostly miners, but I reckon th' ground here is tainted, so I dinna go under it as me father did before me." He looked sad. Then his expression sharpened and he brought the coach to a halt.

"Ye'll have to get in now. Soon we come to tainted ground, an' the vapors are pure poison," he said.

Regretfully I climbed down and held the horses while the coachman tied rags around their noses and faces, and bags on their hooves.

56

"Won't you get sick?" I asked. He shook his head, saying that he would be all right for the short time we would be on tainted earth. Nonetheless, he tied a scarf around his face before leading me back to the carriage.

Suddenly he gave a shout and pointed up. I looked but saw nothing.

"That were a Guanette bird," he explained. "Ye missed it, an' that's a shame, for 'tis a rare sight."

"A Guanette bird?" I gaped, thinking I had misheard him. "I thought they were extinct."

Enoch shook his head. "Nowt extinct, but I guess it might be better to be thought so. They're rare, and rare things are hunted. That village back there were named after them by the first Master of Obernewtyn, Sirrah Lukas Seraphim. A grand queer man he must have been to make his home up there with the Blacklands all round. His grandson is master up there now."

There was a subtly different note in his voice at the mention of the present Master of Obernewtyn.

"Have you seen him?" I asked, hoping to elicit further information.

"He never comes down from the mountains," said the coachman. A strange look crossed his face, but it was so brief I thought I had imagined it.

"In ye go," he said. I clambered into the carriage. On the verge of locking the door again, Enoch hesitated. "Look, if ye be special fond of animals, I've a friend of sorts up there. His name be Rushton. Tell him I vouch for ye, an' maybe he'll find a job ye'll like."

But before I could thank him, he had locked me in, and the carriage lurched as he resumed his seat.

✦ 8 ✦

I DREAMED.

In my dream, I was somewhere cold and darkly quiet. I could hear water dripping, and I was afraid, though I didn't know why. I seemed to be waiting for something.

In the distance, there was a bright flash of light. A feeling of urgency made me hasten toward the light, stumbling over uneven ground I could not see. A high-pitched whining noise filled the air like a scream, but no one could scream for so long without stopping to breathe. I sensed danger, but the compulsion to find the light overrode my instincts. Again it flashed, apparently no closer than before. I could not tell what the source was, though it was obviously unnatural.

All at once, a voice spoke inside me. Shocked, I skidded to a halt, for it was a human voice.

"Tell me," the voice said. "Tell me."

There was a sharp pain behind my eyes, and I flinched in astonishment that a voice could hurt me, understanding at the same time that the whining noise and the voice inside me were connected. I turned to run, at last obeying the urge to escape. Then the ground beneath me burst into flames, and I screamed.

I woke and stared wildly about, my heart thundering even as the nightmare faded. I could feel perspiration on my hands and back. I lay there trying to think what such a dream might mean. I rarely dreamed so intensely.

It was dark, and bruised purple clouds scudded across the sky. A distant cracking noise heralded the coming storm, and within moments, a flash of lightning illuminated the barren landscape. There was a rumble of thunder, then another crack, and this time the scent of charred wood drifted in through the window. I pitied Enoch and hoped Maruman was somewhere safe.

I sensed the unease of the animals, and with each crash of thunder, their tension grew; yet I had the odd impression it was not the storm but something else that unnerved them. There was another loud crash, very close, and a log fell right alongside the carriage.

The horses' suppressed terror erupted, and they bolted, plunging along the road at a mad pace, jerking the coach after them like some doomed creature being dragged to its death. I could hear Enoch's blasphemous thoughts as he fought to control the maddened team.

Clinging to my seat, I looked down at the guardian, who continued to sleep. Branches scraped at the window; the road had suddenly narrowed, and we were in the midst of a thick clump of gnarled trees. I hoped none would fall, for they were big enough to crush the carriage.

A blinding gray rain fell as we passed from the trees and out into the open again. I could see very little because of the rain and the darkness, but the landscape looked barren and ugly. Then the rain stopped as abruptly as a tap turned off.

The silence that followed was so complete it was uncanny. The horses were under control again, and I heard a tired snort from one. The sound almost echoed in the stillness. It had grown fractionally lighter, and I could see sparse trees drooping wearily. I thought the land must indeed be cursed for the fury of nature to strike at it so mercilessly.

Then, before my eyes, the land seemed to transform itself from a barren place to the bleakest, deadest piece of earth. It was impossible to imagine a single blade of grass or even the most stunted tree growing in this place. A strange, terrible burning smell penetrated the carriage despite the thick glass of the windows. I could see vapors rising sluggishly from the earth and writhing along like yellowish snakes. In some places, the ground was as smooth and shiny as glass.

This, then, was the tainted ground, but surely it could not long ago have been true Blacklands.

Now I understood the tension of the horses. It was not the storm they had feared but the poisoned earth they must cross. It was a narrow stretch, and only a short time passed before we returned to a less desolate landscape, but the brief glimpse of the effects of the Great White seared into my mind.

I heard a faint rumbling sound and, looking around again, wondered what could happen next. The noise arose almost from the hills themselves, and a small breeze began to blow. The sky had the dull sheen of polished metal as the wind grew in force. All at once it was cold enough that my breath misted the air inside the carriage.

Then the storm burst over us again. This time there was no rain, just a fierce wind that tossed the cart around like a leaf. The long-suffering trees were bent almost double beneath this fresh onslaught, and I began to understand their ragged appearance. They did well even to survive in this savage land. There seemed something primitive and destructive in the wind, an evil intent I could nearly feel.

Like the rain, it stopped suddenly, and all at once I could hear only the slushy rattle of the wheels as they plowed through the new mud. The sound accomplished what nothing else had been able to do—it woke the guardian.

With a grunt, she sat up and blinked owlishly. "Have we passed the storms?" she asked.

"You mean . . . they're always like that?" I asked.

"If you went back there right now, the storms would still be going on," the guardian confirmed with a shudder of distaste. "They're caused by the Blacklands."

I looked out the window again.

The last stretch of the journey seemed endless, for Obernewtyn was some distance from the tainted pass. The country grew more fertile and ordinary, though very jagged and uneven, with great outcrops of stone rearing up here and there from the dense forest. It was still a hard, wild sort of land, but it seemed fair and rich after the devastated terrain.

My sense of time was utterly confused, but I realized now that night had given way to the early morning, for its dense blackness had transmuted into a frigid, dark blue.

"There," said the guardian suddenly, and I saw a sign swinging between two posts. In dark lettering, it read OBERNEWTYN. KEEP OUT.

The sight of it chilled me more effectively than all the Blacklands in existence. Just beyond was an iron gate set into a high stone wall. The wall extended as far as I could see in both directions. Enoch pulled the horses up and unlocked the gate. He walked the weary team through, then relocked it from the other side. I wondered why they bothered—surely Obernewtyn's remoteness barred the way more effectively than any locks. I tried to see the house, but thick, ornately clipped trees hid their secret well in the curving drive. Someone had gone to great lengths to keep Obernewtyn from prying eyes.

"Obernewtyn," whispered the guardian, looking out the other window. Her voice was low, as if the somber building that had come into view quelled her as much as it did me. Even the horses seemed to walk softly.

It was a massive construction and outwardly more like a series of bleak buildings pushed haphazardly together than one single mansion. It was constructed of large, rough-hewn blocks of gray stone streaked with flecks of darker stone. Aside from the stone itself, no effort had been made to make one section harmonize with the rest. In some places, it was two or three stories high, and turrets rose up at its corners, with steep little roofs ending in spires. Each wall was pocked with hundreds of slitlike holes that I realized must serve as windows.

The drive curved around an ugly fountain, from which rose a lamppost. Its flame flickered behind gleaming panels, making shadows dance along the walls of the building. Atop a set of wide stone steps, the entrance seemed to move in the shifting light, making me think of an opening maw.

The carriage had drawn to a stop at the foot of the steps, and Enoch unlocked the door. I climbed out after the guardian. The cold air gusted and made my cloak flap violently enough that I clutched at it, fearing it would be wrenched away from me. The branches of the trees were filled with the blustering wind, and the noise they made seemed a mad whispering that made my skin rise up into gooseflesh.

I shivered and told myself sternly not to let my imagination get the better of me.

Only when we reached the top of the steps did I see that the two broad entrance doors were deeply and intricately carved wood. The beauty of the carvings struck me, particularly because the building itself seemed so utterly utilitarian. I studied them as the guardian rang a bell. Men and all manner of queer beasts were represented, many seeming half man and half beast. Whoever had done the work was a true craftsman, for the expressions on the faces portrayed the essences of the emotions that shaped them. Framing the panels was a wide gilt border decorated with exotic symbols. The symbols seemed to me a sort of scribing, though I could make no sense of them.

At last the doors opened to reveal a tall, thin woman holding a candelabrum. The light shivered and twitched in the wind, giving her gaunt features a curious, almost fluid look. She bent closer, and I wondered if she found me as indistinct in the wavering light. I was too tired to pretend dullness and hoped weariness would do as well.

"You'll get no sense out of her," said Guardian Hester scornfully. "I thought Madam Vega did not intend to bring up any more dreamers. This one doesn't even look strong enough to be a good worker."

The other woman raised her eyebrows disdainfully. "If Madam chose this girl, she will not have done so without purpose," she said very distinctly, and peered into my face in much the same way Madam Vega had at Kinraide, but without any of her hypnotic power.

"Elspeth, this is Guardian Myrna," said Hester.

"You may leave now," the other woman told her abruptly.

"But . . . but I thought, since it was so late . . ." Guardian Hester hesitated and faltered before the gaze of the other.

"It is not permitted for temporary guardians to stay in the main house. You know that. If our arrangement does not please you, I am sure another can be found."

Guardian Hester clasped her hands together. "Please. No. I . . . forgot. I'll go to the farms with the coachman," she said.

Guardian Myrna inclined her head regally after a weighty pause. "You should hurry. So much talk has delayed you, and I think the dogs are out," she said. The other woman paled and hastened to the door. Guardian Myrna watched her go with a cold smile; then she took some keys from her apron pocket. "Come," she said.

We went out a doorway leading off the circular entrance chamber and into a long hall pitted with large doors. Clumsy locks hung from each, and I thought that if this was an indication of the security at Obernewtyn, I would have no trouble getting away. Distantly, I heard the bark of a dog.

The guardian unlocked one of the doors. "Tonight you will sleep here, and tomorrow you will be given a permanent room." She shut the door behind me and bolted it.

I stood a moment in the total darkness, using my mind to ascertain the dimensions of the room. I was relieved to discover that I was alone. It was too cold to get undressed, so I simply slipped my shoes off and climbed into the nearest bed. I drifted uneasily to sleep, thinking I would rather be anywhere than Obernewtyn.

✦ 9 ✦

THE DOOR BANGED violently open.

A girl stood on the stone threshold with a candle in one hand. With her free hand, she continued to hammer loudly at the open door with a peculiar fixed smile on her face.

"What is it?" I said.

She looked at me through lackluster eyes. "I am come . . . I have come . . ." She faltered as though her brain had lost the thread of whatever message she wanted to impart. She frowned. "I have come to . . . to warn you." There was a glimmer in the depth of her muddy eyes, and all at once, I doubted my initial impression that she was defective.

"Warn me about what?" I asked warily.

She made a warding-off movement with her free hand. "Them. You know."

I shook my head. "I don't know. I am new here. Who are you?"

She jerked her head in a spasm of despair, and a look of anguish came over her face. "Nothing! I'm nothing anymore. . . ."

She looked across the room at me and started to laugh. "You should not have come here," she said at last.

"I didn't choose to come here. I am an orphan, and now I am condemned a Misfit."

The girl giggled. "I was no orphan, but I am a Misfit."

Unable to make any sense out of her, I reached out with my thoughts. At once I learned that her name was Selmar and her mind was a charred wreckage. Most of her thought links did not exist, and little remained that was normal. I saw the remnant of someone I could have liked. But whatever she had gone through had left little of that person. Here was a mind teetering on the brink of madness.

Her eyes rolled back in panic, and cursing my stupidity, I realized she could feel me! She must have been one of those people with some fleeting ability. For an instant, her eyes rolled forward, and she looked out with a sort of puzzlement, as if she was struggling to remember something of great importance. But all too quickly, the muddiness in her eyes returned, and with it a pitiful, cowering fear.

"I promise I don't know anything about a map," she whispered.

I stared. What was she talking about now?

"Selmar . . . ," I began, throwing aside my covers and lowering my feet to the cold stone floor.

Before I could say more, a voice interrupted. "Selmar, how is it that you take so long to wake one person?"

It was a sweet, piping voice, high-pitched and querulous. Not a voice to inspire fear, yet, if it were possible, Selmar paled even further as she turned to face the young boy behind her. No more than eleven or twelve years, he was as slender as a wand, with delicate blond curls; slim, girlish shoulders; and large, pale eyes.

"Answer me," he hissed. Selmar swayed as if she would faint, though she was older and bigger than him.

"I . . . I didn't do anything," she gibbered. "She wouldn't wake up."

He clicked his teeth. "You took too long. I see you need a

talk with Madam to help you overcome your laziness. I will make sure to arrange it." The sheer maliciousness in his beautiful face angered me.

"It is as she told you," I said, stepping between them. "I had trouble waking, because I arrived so late last night."

Selmar nodded pathetically.

"Well, go on with your duties, then," he conceded with a nasty smile. Selmar turned with a frightened sob and fled down the hall, her stumbling footsteps echoing after her. Chewing his bottom lip, the boy watched her departure with thoughtful eyes.

"What did she say to you?" he asked, turning back to me.

"Nothing," I answered flatly, wondering by what right he interrogated me.

He frowned petulantly. "You're new. You will learn," he said. "Now get up and I will come back for you." He closed the door behind him.

Rummaging angrily through a chest of assorted clothes, I found a cloak. It was freezing within the stone walls, and pale early-morning light spilled in wanly from the room's sole window. There were no shutters, and cold gusts of air swept freely through the opening. I would have liked to look outside, but the window was inaccessible, fashioned long and thin, reaching from above my head almost to the ceiling.

The door opened suddenly. "Come on, then," the blond boy snapped.

As we walked down the hall, I noticed a good deal more than I had the previous night. There were metal candle brackets along the walls, shaped like gargoyles' heads with savage mouths. Cold, greenish drips of wax hung frozen from the gaping jaws. I eyed them with distaste, reflecting that whoever had built Obernewtyn had no desire for homely comfort.

We passed the entrance hall with its heavy front doors and continued along a narrow walkway on the other side.

"Where are you taking me?" I asked.

The boy did not answer, and presently we came to a double set of doors. He opened one with something of a flourish. It opened onto a kitchen, a long, rectangular room with two large dining arbors filled with bench seats and trestle tables. At the far end of the kitchen, almost an entire wall was taken up with a cavernous fireplace. Above it was set an immense mantelshelf, laden with stone and iron pots. From its underside hung a further selection of pans and pannikins. A huge, blackened cauldron was suspended over the flame, and stirring the contents was a woman of mountainous proportions.

Her elbows, though bent, resembled large cured hams, and a large white bow sat on her hips and waggled whenever she moved. The roaring heat of the fire had prevented her from noticing our entrance. Tearing my eyes away, I saw that there were several doors besides the one we had come through and a great number of cupboards and benches. A young girl was sitting at one of these, scraping potatoes, and they sat in two mounds on either side of her. She watched me with currant-like eyes buried in a slab-jowled face. The knife poised above the potato glinted brightly.

"Ma!" she yelled, waving the knife in agitation, throwing its light at me.

The mountain of flesh at the stove trembled, then turned with surprising grace. The woman's face was flushed from the heat and distorted by too many chins, but there was a definite resemblance between her and the girl. The thick ladle in her hand dripped brown gravy, unheeded.

"Ariel!" she cried in dulcet tones. Her accent was similar

to Enoch's but less musical. "Dear hinny, I have nowt seen ye in an age. Ye have not deserted me, have ye, sweet boy?"

She gathered him in a bone-crushing embrace and led him to one of the cupboards. She took out a sweet and gave it to him.

"Why, Andra, thank you." Ariel sounded pleased, and I wondered why the cook treated him with such favor. Surely he was only a Misfit, unless he was also an informer. Yet he seemed too arrogant for the latter. Most informers were clinging and contemptible, and even those who used them tended to dislike them.

The girl with the knife giggled violently, and again the blade flashed its silver light. The older woman glared ferociously at her.

"Ye born noddy-headed thing. Shut yer carrying on an' get back to work." The girl's giggles ceased abruptly. Catching sight of me watching her, she scowled as if I were to blame.

"Now, Andra," Ariel said. "You recall how I promised you some extra help? Well, I have brought you a new worker."

Responding with enthusiasm, the cook launched herself at him with much lip-smacking. I thought with suppressed glee that it served him right. He caught the amusement on my face. Disentangling himself, he ordered the cook to make sure I worked hard, as I was assuredly lazy and insolent. Andra promised to work my fingers to the bone as he departed with a look of spiteful satisfaction.

As soon as the door closed, her daughter leapt toward me, brandishing her knife. "Misfit pig. What sort of help will she be? Ye can see she don't have a brain in her," she sneered venomously, menacing me with the knife.

The syrupy smile dropped from the cook's face. She crossed the floor in two steps and dealt her daughter a resounding blow with the wooden spoon. "If she has no brains, then she'll be a good match fer ye, fool that ye are, Lila. If Ariel gives us th' gift of a fool, then ye mun show pleasure!" the cook snarled. "Oh, th' trials of my life. Yer no-good father gives me a fool fer a daughter, then disappears. I have to come to th' end of th' Land so ye won't be declared defective. I find a nice powerful boy to bond ye an' yer so stupid I got to do th' charmin' fer ye. Lud knows ye've little enough to offer without gollerin' an' gigglin' like a regular loon," she added succinctly.

With some amusement, I realized that the cook intended a match between her daughter and Ariel. It seemed he wasn't a Misfit. But what sort of power could such a young boy possess?

With a final look of disgust at her daughter, the cook turned to me. "As fer you, no doubt ye are a fool at that. An' work ye hard I will, if that's what Ariel wants. Ye've angered him somehow, an' ye mun pay. He'll see ye do. He ain't one to let petty angers gan away. Ye'll learn," she prophesied.

Turning to the sink, she explained that I was to wash the mountain of dishes and then scour the pots. I looked in dismay at the work ahead. In the orphan homes, there had been a great many of us, and a share in duties was always light. Yet there was nothing to do but obey.

I had been working for hours and had just managed to finish the dishes when the cook announced that the easy work was over since it was nearly time for midmeal. I felt like weeping. Already I was exhausted, but as Lila and I set the tables, I channeled my despair into fueling a growing hatred of Ariel, whom I regarded as the initiator of my woes. I was hungry, having missed firstmeal, but I dared not complain as I carried bowl after bowl of stew to the tables. Lila moaned endlessly and received endless slaps for her pains. I judged it wiser to hold my tongue.

Presently, the cook rang a bell. Young people of varying ages filed in through the double doors. Soon all the tables were full. The diners did not look at us at all but ate with steady concentration, then left, their seats soon taken by others. The meal consisted of a bowl of thick stew and freshly baked bread. The food smells made me feel dizzy with hunger. In town, food had seldom been this good or this fresh, but we had never had to work too hard. I wondered wistfully what the others did and regretted that I had fallen foul of Ariel.

"Ye gan eat now," the cook said finally, and thrust a generous helping into my hand. My stomach growled in appreciation. I sat at a nearly empty table and devoured the food. Only when I had spooned up the last morsel did I look up.

"Hello," said a soft voice at my elbow. I turned to look at a young blond girl sitting nearby. She smiled, and I was astonished that anyone would ever want to condemn her. Even her ungainly clothes could not hide the delicacy of her features and her slender bones. Her hair was like cream silk. She endured my examination without embarrassment, until it was I who looked away from her clear, naive gaze.

"I am Cameo," she whispered. I looked at her again, and such was the sweetness of her expression that I might have smiled back, but Lila, seated at the end of the table, was watching us.

"I am not interested in your name," I said in a repressive voice, worried that Ariel would punish the girl for her kindness toward me. But when the brightness of her face dimmed, I wished I had not been so terse.

A sharp cuff on the side of my head was the cook's signal

71

that my short respite was over. I rose and began to clear plates. The afternoon was spent washing all the midmeal dishes and scrubbing down the jagged kitchen floor, then serving stew and unwatered milk for nightmeal.

Every bone ached by the time Ariel took me to my permanent room, and I was too exhausted to care that I was not alone. At that moment, the Master of Obernewtyn himself could have been my roommate and met as little response.

✦ 10 ✦

My initial exhaustion wore off as I became accustomed to the hard physical labor in the kitchen, but it was replaced by a terrible mental despair. I could not endure the thought of going on in such a way forever, and yet there seemed no opportunity of finding Enoch's friend who might be able to help me move to the farms to work.

My sole comfort came from a conversation I had overheard at midmeal one day, which had implied that most of the house workers went down to work on the farms to prepare for the long wintertime. I prayed this was so, and that I would be among those dispatched to the farms. But I had arrived in the spring, and my calculations told me no extra workers would be required until the beginning of summerdays.

I shared my sleeping chamber with four other girls, including the strange disturbed girl I had seen on my first morning, Selmar, who now ignored me. Remembering the mess inside her mind, I thought it possible she had simply forgotten our meeting. She was, I noticed, permitted to wander more freely than the rest of us.

There were surprisingly few guardians at Obernewtyn. Most responsibility seemed to be taken by senior and favored Misfits, though none was so favored as Ariel. I had heard nothing of the mysterious master and had seen no sign of Madam Vega.

Altogether, life at Obernewtyn was a matter of grim endurance rather than terror. I thought a good deal about Jes. I had imagined myself a loner, never needing anyone, but now I saw that I had never really experienced loneliness. In Rangorn, there had always been my parents, and in the homes, there had been Jes and later Maruman. I had discounted Jes, but now I often found myself longing to talk to him, even if we spoke of nothing important.

One day late in spring, Ariel came to the kitchen to announce that I was to take a tour of the farms with some other Misfits. Even the knowledge that Ariel would lead the tour could not mar the joy that arose in me at the thought of even a few hours of freedom from the dreary kitchen routine. I had not been outside for so long.

Ariel had instructed me to wait for him in the entrance hall after midmeal. When I arrived, a boy ushered me down several halls and outside into a large enclosed courtyard. Three girls whose faces I recognized from the meal table were waiting already, and soon after a dark-haired boy with a limp arrived. With him was the pretty girl who had spoken to me at my first meal, Cameo. She smiled at me tentatively, but I felt her companion watching me and could not bring myself to respond.

Ariel arrived soon after accompanied by twins—Norselanders, judging by their height and blondness. There were few enough in the highlands for me to be curious about how they had ended up being charged as Misfits. I could not see anything out of the ordinary in their appearance, save that each lacked a hand. I was contemplating entering their minds when the hair on my neck prickled. Turning my head slightly,

I saw that the slight, dark-haired boy was still watching me. I scowled at him, suddenly remembering that I had seen him in the dining arbors and he had been watching me then, too. It occurred to me that he might be an informant, and I turned my back on him, resolving to have nothing to do with him.

At last two final Misfits joined us, and Ariel addressed the group. He told us we were being taken on this tour in preparation for working on the farms. I felt a ripple of delight at the news.

Like the kitchen courtyard, the one in which we had gathered was roofed, but now we followed Ariel through a gate into another courtyard that was open to the sky. The sun was shining brightly down on the cobbles, and I turned my face to it and breathed in warm mountain air and tasted the summerdays so soon to come.

Three sides of the courtyard were formed by the high walls of Obernewtyn. Windows pitted the gray expanse like hooded eyes. Above them, the roof sloped steeply so that in wintertime the snow would slide off.

Ariel led us to the fourth wall, beyond which showed the tops of trees. There was no mortar between the bricks of its gateway's arch; rather, it was held up by perfect balance of positioning. Certainly someone had possessed an eye for beauty, I thought, noting its graceful design and remembering the carved doors at the entrance.

I passed through the door beneath the arch expecting to find farms on the other side. Instead, before us rose a thick, impenetrable wall of greenthorn as high as the stone wall behind us. Peer as I might, I could not tell what lay beyond it, but a small grassy path ran to the left and the right. Ariel steered us to the left, and we followed the path a short way until it turned sharply to the right. We walked a few steps and came to a fork. Each way looked exactly alike, bordered on either side by the towering greenthorn hedge.

By now, the powerful exotic odor of the greenthorn and the sameness of the surroundings had completely confused my sense of direction, and I realized the shrubbery was actually a maze. I could not even use my powers to feel out the way ahead, because they were befuddled by the heavy scent in the air. Crushed, the thorn provided a painkiller, but in such concentration, the scent alone seemed to have a slight numbing effect on my mind. The maze was large and labyrinthine, and if Ariel had left us alone, I doubt whether we would have found our way out at all.

It was with some relief that we came around a corner to see the stone wall with its arched gateway. It was not until we had gone through it that I realized it was a different door than the one we'd entered. We had come right through the maze to the other side, and before us lay the vast farmlands of Obernewtyn.

I gazed around in amazement. Neat fields extended for leagues in all three directions, and there were barns and fences and livestock everywhere. Dozens of Misfits were working, repairing fences or building them, herding and raking. To the far left was an orchard, and there was the unmistakable scent of apples and plums.

Ariel led us along one of the many dirt paths from the maze toward a group of buildings. I hung back until the dark-haired boy went ahead of me, noting that he had a pronounced limp, though he seemed to have no trouble keeping pace.

"The maze door is always locked," Ariel said over his shoulder as we walked. "And there are few at Obernewtyn who know the way through. To stray from the path means death." The thought that anyone would choose to enter the fragrant green maze without a guide made me shudder. Ariel went on to explain that the buildings we approached were where the animals were kept during the wintertime, and those beyond were enormous storage silos.

"As far as you can see in all directions and much farther belongs to Obernewtyn and, as such, is contained within our walls," Ariel said. "We are almost completely self-sufficient here, as we must be, for in wintertime we are completely blocked off from the lowlands by snow. During that season, everyone will work in the house, spinning and weaving and preparing goods for trading when the spring comes. This enables us to purchase what we cannot produce. Before the wintertime, all the food in those silos must be transported to the main house."

We passed a massive shed that smelled strongly of animals. Ariel wrinkled his nose, but I breathed in deeply, because it reminded me of Rangorn.

"Those are the livestock storage houses. The grain and grasses in those must be enough to feed all the animals throughout the wintertime. Some of the cows and poultry are transferred to the house courtyards to provide meat and eggs and milk until spring."

There was no doubt that it was a highly efficient concern, and the surplus sold must more than cover the few things Obernewtyn wanted. I wondered what happened to the rest of the profits. No doubt some of it was used in purchasing more Misfits.

Far to the west, beyond the distant line of the wall around Obernewtyn, was a savage line of mountains. There were more mountains to the east. Busy with my own thoughts, I did not notice Ariel had been observing me.

"I see you are interested in the mountains beyond our borders," he sneered. "Look all you please, for you will never see them at less of a distance. Those mountains mean freedom and death for those who attempt to reach them."

A raucous squealing from behind us broke the tension. We followed Ariel toward a small shed, but before we reached it, a man came out carrying a small pig. As he approached, I could see that he was not a full-grown man at all but a well-built youth of about nineteen. He set the pig down in a small pen and wiped his hands on his trousers before turning to us. His greeting to Ariel was amicable but reserved; he seemed wary of the younger boy. I decided to probe him to find out why, when a strange thing happened.

He was telling Ariel about the pig he had just delivered when he broke off midsentence to stare at me with jade green eyes. Some instinct of danger made me fear I had betrayed myself, though I had only skirted the conscious thoughts that echoed his speech, and I had found no sign he was mindsensitive. I expected him to denounce me, but instead he seemed suddenly aware that he in turn was watched. He then let his eyes rove over our entire group, but I felt sure he did this only to cover the attention he had paid me.

Ariel's eyes passed from me to the youth thoughtfully. "This is Rushton," he said to the group. "He is our farm overseer."

Startled, I realized this was Enoch's friend. The dark youth did not have the air of a Misfit, but Ariel did not choose to tell us his exact status. The overseer gave us a description of the farms and crops and the animals thereon, before leaving us to Ariel. His eyes flickered at me once more as he departed, but I was careful to keep my expression bland.

That night, my dreams were full of shadowed green eyes

conveying messages I could not understand. When I woke the following morning, Selmar and one of the other girls eyed me oddly, and I knew I must have talked in my sleep, though I could hardly have said much to incriminate myself.

I told myself it did not matter if the overseer had dimly sensed my intrusion, for he would surely have forgotten me by the time I was sent to the farms to work. But that morning, Ariel was waiting for me in the kitchen and bade me sit down to firstmeal rather than serve it.

I was to begin work on the farms that very day.

✦ 11 ✦

THAT FIRST DAY working on the farms, I had my first glimpse of a Guanette bird. It was a surprising start to a surprising day.

I had been standing alone in the courtyard outside the maze when the bird flew straight up from behind the wall into the silver-streaked, dawn-gray sky. Uttering a long, lonely call, it flew in a graceful arc toward the northwest. I recognized the bird, though I had never seen a picture of one, by its massive wingspan and the brilliant red of its underbelly. As it crossed the line where the far mountains touched the sky, the sun rose in fiery splendor as if to welcome it. The enormous bird flew across the face of the sun, shimmered, and seemed to dissolve.

"Fair mazer it is," said a voice behind me. I turned to see the thin, dark-haired boy who had stared at me so unnervingly the previous day. But now all of his attention was fixed on the Guanette bird. I was startled to see the frank delight in his expression and wondered if he was an informer after all. Behind him was a slightly older boy with a tall, angular body, a rather big nose, and countless freckles struggling to cover his face. He was looking at me with such a peculiar intensity that I stiffened and glared at him indignantly.

Catching my expression, the thin boy turned to his companion and poked him in the chest. "Can't ye feel how uncomfortable she is, ye great gawk?" he asked him. He turned to me and said cheerfully, "Dinna worry about Dameon. He's as blind as a bat."

Horribly embarrassed, I was shamed to think of the icy look I had given him and was thankful he could not see me.

Dameon grinned apologetically. "I'm sorry if I seemed to stare," he said disarmingly, and held his hand out. Startled, I took his hand and wondered at his elegant manner and grace of speech.

"An' I'm Matthew," said the dark-haired boy. "An' you're Elspeth."

I did not know what to say, for his knowledge of my name suggested he had made inquiries about me, yet he did not act like an informant.

"What were you both admiring?" Dameon asked, before I could decide how to respond.

Matthew answered. "We saw a Guanette bird, an' ye know how rare those are. It came from near th' maze. Queer to see one here, though. They dinna usually come down from the high mountains."

The door to the inner courtyard opened, and a group of other Misfits arrived, most of them those who had come on the tour the day before. Ariel arrived last with Cameo in tow. He unlocked the maze door, then relocked it when we had gone through. As he took the lead, I moved to follow, but Matthew caught my arm and held me back until the others had passed. The twins went last, looking at us curiously. Furious, I shook Matthew's hand off and followed them, wishing that I had completely ignored him as my instincts had warned. Did he not understand the danger in doing anything that drew attention?

We walked in silence for a bit; then Cameo began to

chatter to Ariel. With her masking prattle, the twins began to talk in low, intense voices. Curiosity made me send out a probe. They were planning some sort of escape, so I withdrew smartly. I didn't even want to think of escapes, intended or otherwise.

Matthew came to walk beside me, and I glared at him, determined to snub any further attempt at friendship—if that was what he wanted.

"Can you hear me?" asked a voice in my thoughts.

Shocked, I stumbled. Righting myself, I fought to calm my clamoring thoughts. I told myself sternly that I had imagined Matthew's voice inside my mind, but now he reached out and put his hand on my arm. "I thought so," he said quietly. "I sensed you 'listening' to the twins. But I suspected ye before that." He was positively delighted.

I could only feel numb. Even surrounded by Misfits, I had never really thought there would be anybody else like me. "I . . . I don't understand," I said doggedly.

Matthew smiled again in an impish, knowing way. "I thought there was only me and me mam who could do it. Then for the last few sevendays, I began to feel like I did when me mam was about, and I started wonderin' if there was another. I felt it during meals, an' I was gannin' through everyone, dippin' into their minds to see if they could hear me. I couldn't reach ye, though, for ye've a powerful shield. I realized the only way I would ken for sure was to catch ye in the act of farseeking. So I waited, and now I know, Elf."

I shivered at the added proof of his intrusion into my mind, for how else could he have known Jes's nickname for me?

"It is dangerous to talk of such things here," I whispered, for I realized there was no point in pretending. It was too late to be cautious. But could he be trusted? I reached into his mind some little way, intending only to find out if there was any chance of betrayal. But before I could learn what I wanted to know, Matthew's eyes narrowed, and I sensed a slight withdrawal in him.

"Interestin'," he whispered. "Ye've just tried to deep-probe me like my mam used to do. I can't do that, and I couldn't stop ye if ye were determined. Ye mun be very strong." He looked suddenly pensive. "Now that I think of it, I can almost understand why those idiots from the village were afraid of me. 'Tis a queer thing to ken yer thoughts are on show. Dameon here has some power, too, but it is not farseeking or deep probing. It's something to do with being able to feel what people are feeling." Matthew shrugged as if he did not think it a very useful ability.

My mind reeled with the things he said. In a few moments, he had changed my life. I had so long believed I was a lone freak with the ability to read the thoughts of other people and of beasts. A strange, almost frightening thought came to me then: if there were three of us, there might be more. There must be more. Belatedly, it occurred to me that I had been rude to dip into Matthew's mind. This sudden desire not to invade the thoughts of another person was new and told me that I had accepted something I had previously thought impossible. I was no longer alone.

"We'll manage canny between us," Matthew was saying, still in that barely audible voice. "I'd be pleased, though, if ye'd teach me how to shield so well, fer I can't believe that shield of yours is any accident," he added humbly. I looked into his bright, intelligent face, and it was as if some wall in me crumbled.

"I will teach you," was all I said, but with those words it was as if I peeled off a layer of skin. Matthew beamed, seeming to understand the momentousness of sharing for the first time, and I thought of Jes and wished he could know what I had discovered.

"And Dameon?" Matthew asked anxiously, breaking into mindspeak.

I turned slightly to watch Dameon's graceful progress behind us and sent out a gentle probe. He flinched and stumbled, and I withdrew hurriedly.

"I'm sorry," I whispered, but he shook his head.

"I was just surprised. It's stronger than when Matthew does it," he said, and smiled. "I can feel your curiosity," he laughed. "It's almost as bad as his. I call my own ability empathy."

"He does that all th' time," Matthew reassured me aloud. "He picks up th' weirdest things. No words, though, an' he's deaf as a doorpost to other things."

"Quiet back there!" Ariel shouted, effectively silencing the entire group. I hoped Matthew would be careful, and to my relief, he said nothing more and dropped back to walk with Dameon. He sent a silent promise that we would meet again soon, when it was safe.

Busy with my thoughts, I cannoned into one of the twins, who had stopped in front of me. We had reached the end of the maze.

Ariel led us out and told us to wait by the maze gate until Rushton came to collect us. Matthew and Dameon made no move to join me, so I took their cue and stayed where I was. The sun had risen quite high now, and though the grass was still dew-soaked and the shadows long, the air smelled delicious with the mingled farm smells.

I glanced back at Matthew and, seeing his sober expression, I had an unaccountable desire to make a face at him. I was amazed at the warmth of my feelings, but as the farm

84

overseer approached from the direction of the sheds, I felt a moment of apprehension. Though this time he paid no particular attention to me, there was an aura of power about him, and I was reminded of something Maruman had once said about wild animals—that even the most gentle was not quite safe. That was how Rushton struck me—as if one might run a great risk in simply knowing him. Yet when he began assigning tasks, his apparent boredom reassured me.

Dameon, Matthew, and others were sent over to a large building that he called the drying shed. Cameo and the twins were sent across to the orchards. Then only two of us remained. The other girl was to feed the pigs, Rushton said, and I was to clean out the stables. He gave me an expressionless look with his bold green eyes and told me to wait inside until he returned.

A large dog lay against a wall just inside the stables. He opened his eyes as I entered and watched me sit on a bale of hay.

"Greetings," I thought on impulse.

His eyes widened, and he looked around before deciding I was the only one there. "Did you speak, funaga?" he asked with mild surprise.

I nodded. "I am Elspeth," I sent. "May I know your name?"

"I am called Sharna," he sent. "What manner of funaga are you?"

"I am a funaga like other funagas," I replied formally.

"I have heard your name before," he sent unexpectedly. "A cat spoke it."

"Maruman!" I projected a picture with the name, but Sharna was unresponsive.

"I did not see this mad cat who seeks a funaga. I heard it from a beast who heard it from another."

"Do you know where the cat was seen?" I asked excitedly.

"Who knows where a cat goes?" he sent philosophically. "The story was only told to me as a curiosity. Whoever heard of a cat looking for a funaga? I thought it a riddle."

Rushton entered the stable then. He looked about sharply as if sensing something had been going on, then he tersely told me to follow him.

If he had shown an interest in me the day before, today he seemed at pains to assure me of his total lack of interest. "The stables have to be cleaned every second day," he said in a bored voice as we entered one of the pens. A rich loamy smell rushed out to greet me. I watched as the overseer demonstrated how to catch hold of the horse's halter and lead it out. The horses were to be released into the yard leading off the stables, he explained, their halters removed and hung on a hook. Once a horse had been led out, Rushton gave me a broom, a rake, and a pan, taking up a long-handled fork himself.

"You have to lift the manure out in clumps and drop it in the pan, along with the dirtiest hay." Deftly he slid the prongs of the fork under some manure and threw it neatly into the pan. "When you've done all that, rake the rest of the hay to one side, then fork in some fresh stuff." He forked hay from a nearby pile onto the floor with economical movements. It looked easy.

"You lay the old hay over the new; if you don't, the horse will eat it." He handed the fork to me. "There are twelve stables in this lot, so you'd better get on with it. Come and get me at the drying shed if you have any trouble getting the horses out." I nodded, and briefly those inscrutable eyes searched mine, then he turned on his heel and left.

I turned and surveyed the stables.

"You would do well to mindspeak to them first," Sharna commented from his corner. Taking his advice, I approached the nearest box and greeted its occupant, a dappled mare with a large, comfortable rear. She flicked her tail and turned to face me.

"Who are you?" she asked with evident amusement. "I have spoken to many odd creatures in my time but never a funaga. I suppose you are behind this." She directed the latter thought to Sharna, who had ambled over to stand beside me. The mare leaned her long nose close to my face and snorted rudely. "I suppose you want to put me out? Well, I'm not having that thing on my head. Just open the door and I'll walk out."

I did as she asked, hoping Rushton would not come back and catch me disobeying his instructions. Sharna muttered about the mare's bossiness, but I ignored him and concentrated on copying Rushton's movements as I mucked out the box.

Except for a big, nasty black horse whom Sharna said had been badly mistreated by a previous master, the rest of the horses proved cooperative on the condition I did not use their halters. I had finished and was leaning on a post watching the horses graze when Rushton returned.

"You have been uncommonly swift," he said suspiciously. The smile fell from my face as I realized I had been stupid.

"Too quick to believe, even if Enoch did recommend you," he added.

And as I looked into his hard face, I was afraid.

PART II

◆

HEART OF THE DARKNESS

✦ 12 ✦

"WELL?" RUSHTON INQUIRED grimly.

"I . . . my father kept horses," I lied, hoping he did not know how young I had been orphaned.

"And you did not think to mention it during my instruction?" he asked. There was a speculative gleam in his eyes as I shrugged awkwardly. "All right. There are packages of food for midmeal out by the maze gate. Go and eat, and I'll find something else for you to do in the afternoon," he said.

I left as fast as I could to escape those curious, watchful eyes.

The packages lay on a piece of cloth on the ground next to a large bucket of milk covered with a piece of gauze. I scooped up a mug of milk but avoided the squashy packages I recognized from my days in the kitchen as bread and dripping. Propping myself against a rain barrel in the sun, I again berated myself for my foolishness in working so quickly. I could have been with Sharna and the horses all day, but instead Rushton was sure to give me some horrible job now that he thought I had wasted his time.

I turned my thoughts to Maruman and wondered if he had been in the mountains. I doubted it. He could not have crossed the tainted ground on foot, and I did not think Enoch's carriage had returned since my arrival, because I had noticed no new faces at meals.

I was so deep in thought that I did not see Matthew and Dameon approach, and I jumped as their shadows fell across my lap. They sat beside me, and I felt as though everything had changed in a matter of hours. Only yesterday this casual intrusion would have annoyed me, but I found I did not resent the company of this odd pair.

Nevertheless, I felt bound to point out to them that we made ourselves vulnerable by showing friendship openly. "I'm not saying I don't want your company, but maybe it's not a good idea to be so obvious," I ventured, looking around doubtfully at Misfits sitting nearby.

Matthew shrugged. "Elspeth, yer thinkin' like an orphan. We are Misfits now. What more could they do?"

Burn us, I thought, but did not say it, for that seemed unlikely now. And he was right. I *had* been thinking like an orphan. The two boys unwrapped their lunches. Dameon rewrapped his with a grimace, but Matthew ate his with a bored expression.

"Have ye come across old Larkin yet?" Matthew asked presently. I shrugged, saying I hadn't seen anyone but Rushton. "Nivver mind," Matthew laughed. "Yer bound to see him soon. Ye'll know when ye do. He's not th' sort ye could easily forget."

"Who is he, a guardian?" I asked curiously.

"There are only three permanent guardians up here," Dameon explained. "The others come and go. They don't last long, though." I thought of Guardian Myrna's treatment of the hapless Hester and did not wonder.

"Strictly speakin', Larkin is a Misfit, but he's much older than the rest of us," Matthew said. "Do you notice how there are no older Misfits? They send them to th' Councilfarms. But Larkin has been here forever, and probably the Councilfarms dinna want someone as old as him. But he's a queer fey old codger. An' rude as they come—I'm not even sure I like him exactly. But if ye can get him talkin', he has some interesting ideas."

"I don't suppose half of it is true," Dameon said with a grin.

But Matthew refused to be drawn. "I daresay he does make a lot of it up. But he knows a lot, too. An' some of th' things he says about th' Beforetime make a lot more sense than the rubbish the Herders put about. There's no harm in hearin' ideas . . . unless ye happen to be blind in more ways than one," he added with an oblique glance at Dameon. I thought it a rather tactless jibe, but Dameon only laughed.

"So where is he, then?" I asked crossly, somehow envious of their casual friendship.

"Well, he's nowt a man to blow th' whistle an' bang th' drum. In fact, I sometimes think he'd like to be invisible. But he works on th' farms, so ye'll meet him soon enough, doubtless," Matthew said.

I thought of something else. "Tell me, the overseer—is he a Misfit?"

"Nobody really seems to know," Matthew said. "I asked Larkin once, an' he told me to mind my business."

Dameon nodded. "He might work for pay, like the temporary guardians. But I don't know. Whenever I'm near him, I sense a ferocious purpose and drive, though to what I do not know."

"What about Ariel, then?" I asked.

"I hate him," Matthew said with cold venom. I was taken aback at his vehemence, and Dameon actually flinched.

"I'm sorry," Matthew said. He looked at me. "Ye have to be careful about what ye feel. Sometimes things hurt him."

"Burns," mumbled Dameon. "Hate always burns."

I thought that was true enough.

"Ariel is a Misfit, but he has great authority here," Dameon explained. "He is Madam Vega's personal assistant. I have heard that he started off as an informer and proved especially good at it."

"Do you . . . I mean, what do you feel when you're near him?" I asked.

"Lots of things, and none of them good. The ugliness is deep down in him. It's like being near something that smells sweet, and then you realize it's that sweet smell that rotten things sometimes get," he said, then he sighed as if annoyed by his vague explanation. But I found it a curiously apt description.

"And you say Larkin has been here for a long time?" I said, changing the subject because Dameon was looking pale. His powers seemed to demand more of him than mine did of me.

"Since this place was built," Matthew said extravagantly. "An' if ye want to know about people . . ."

I shook my head hastily. "Oh, it wasn't so much people as Obernewtyn itself I was thinking about. It seems such an odd place. Why would anyone build here in the first place? And when did it become a home for Misfits, and why? There is some kind of secret here, I sense it. I don't know why I should care. The world is full of secrets, but this nags at me."

"I feel that, too," Matthew said eagerly. "As if something is going on underneath all these everyday things."

"It makes me cold to listen to you two," Dameon said suddenly. "I don't deny that I have felt something, too. Not the way you two do, and not by using any power. But a blind person develops an instinct for such things, and mine tells me there is some mystery here. Something big. But some things

94

are better left unknown." His words were grim, and I found myself looking round nervously.

Dameon went on. "Sometimes I am afraid for people like you who have to know things. And there's no point in my even warning you that finding out can sometimes be a dangerous thing. Your kind will dig and hunt and worry at it until one day you will find what is hidden, waiting for you."

I shivered violently.

"Curiosity killed th' cat," Matthew said. I looked up, startled, thinking of Maruman. "That's what Larkin told me once. He said it was an Oldtime saying."

"And how would he know Oldtime sayings?" I asked, throwing off the chill cast over me by Dameon's words.

"From books," Matthew said calmly. "He keeps them hidden, but I've seen them."

"It seems like a silly sort of saying to me," I said, though I was fascinated at the thought of hidden books.

"Well, sayin' it cleared the ice out of me blood." Matthew looked at Dameon, who seemed preoccupied with his own thoughts since he had uttered his chilling little speech. "Ye fair give me th' creeps talkin' that way," he added.

"Do you know, I was just thinking," Dameon said. Matthew gave me a "not again" look. "I once thought it was the end of the world to be sent here, the end of everything. But here I sit, content, and with two friends, and I wonder."

"I know what ye mean," Matthew agreed. "I near died of fright when Madam Vega picked me to come here. But now I sometimes get th' funny feeling that this, all along, was where I was meant to come."

I said nothing but thought of Maruman saying that my destiny waited for me in the mountains.

"Yet, it is not freedom," Dameon added softly, and we both

looked at him. The bell to end midmeal rang, seeming to underline his words.

"Ah well. Back to work," Matthew said glumly, and pulled Dameon to his feet. With a wave, they went back across the fields.

Rushton came to stand beside me as I watched them go. "I see you accomplish many things quickly," he sneered. "I should have thought the orphan life would have taught you caution in choosing companions."

I said nothing.

"Well, this afternoon, you can show your talents at milking. I don't suppose your father had cows as well as horses?" he added.

I shook my head and fell into step behind him, hoping he was not to be my teacher for the afternoon. I was beginning to ache from the morning's work. We went to a big barn, which Rushton said was the dairy. A bearded man was sitting on a barrel near the entrance.

"Louis, this is Elspeth Gordie," Rushton told the man. "You can have her for the afternoon."

The old man's deeply weathered face twitched, but it was too wrinkled to tell if he smiled or not. "I hope she's quicker than th' last," the old man said abruptly.

"Oh, she's quick all right," Rushton said pointedly as the old man got to his feet and led me inside. I looked back, expecting to see the overseer's departing back, but he stood there watching me.

Louis instructed me on milking cows, thoroughly and at such length that I began to wonder if he thought me a halfwit. I understood what he meant long before he completed his explanations.

He reminded me of a tortoise. That is not to suggest, however, that there was anything foolish or absurd about him. Tortoises, though slow, are dignified and self-sufficient. On the other hand, I had the distinct but unfounded impression that his thoughts were not nearly as slow as his appearance would have me believe. He grunted his satisfaction when I demonstrated that I could milk the cow according to his instructions. Then he gave me terse directions on emptying the bucket into the correct section of a separation vat.

"Nowt like it," he said wistfully, and I jumped because so far, the only words he had spoken had been orders. He pointed to the milk, and I nodded, wondering if he was slightly unbalanced. "Ye don't gan milk like that in th' towns. Watery pale stuff tasting of drainpipes," he said, patting the cow's rump complacently. "Ye mun call me Larkin," he said.

"Oh," I said, startled at the realization that this was the man who Matthew and Dameon had told me about.

"Lead her out, then," Louis said easily.

Leading the cow outside to graze, I returned to find that Louis had brought in a second cow and was emptying the bucket of milk into a wooden vat.

"Dinna mix th' vats up," Louis cautioned me, and bid me get on with milking.

Sitting at the milking stool, I grasped the cow's udders. I apologized to her as I began to milk her, but she merely sighed and told me that it was a relief. Louis came to watch me, and I wondered if permission to use his last name was a good or bad sign. It was hard to be sure how he felt with that beard and his leathery face. As I milked, I took the opportunity to question the cow about him. Like most cows, she was a slow, amiable creature without much brain. But she was fond of Louis, and that disposed me to like him.

"Niver gan done that way!" Louis snapped, and I jumped.

I had fallen into a pleasant drowse, leaning my head on the cow's warm, velvety flank. As I sat up and went on milking, Louis pulled a box up and sat, scraping at a pipe.

"I suppose you've been here a long time," I ventured. He nodded, still busy with his pipe. "I suppose you would know just about everybody here. . . ." I looked up quickly, and he seemed unperturbed by my questions. But I decided it might be better to ask him about himself before questioning him about anything else. "Were you born in the highlands?" I asked daringly.

Louis chewed the end of his pipe and looked at me thoughtfully. "I were born here," he said. I stared but he did not elaborate. "After this place became what it is now, I went to work in the highlands, but I dinna fit there, an' soon enow they put me right back here." He gave a smile that was both sly and childishly transparent. "Them smart townsfolk think they know everything. They think they can keep things th' same forever. But change comes an' things have gone too far to drag 'em back to what they was. Every year there be more Misfits an' seditioners, an' one day that Council will find there's more in th' prisons than out." He chuckled.

Matthew had been right about the old man's interesting ideas. I wondered how I could get him to talk about Obernewtyn. "This place . . . it's been here a long time," I said.

He shrugged, hardly seeming to hear the question. I decided to try another tack. "Do you know Ariel? And Selmar?" I asked.

He nodded, but his eyes had grown wary, and I wondered which name had produced the change. "Oh, aye. I know them all, an' more. Selmar's a poor sad thing now. Ye'd nowt know her if ye could see how she were when she first came.

An' she were th' hope of Obernewtyn . . . ," he said bitterly.

I frowned in puzzlement, for the girl that had hammered at my door that first day seemed utterly defective. Apparently she had not been born that way. I was about to ask Louis what had happened to her when he suddenly stood up, knocked his pipe out, and ordered me tersely to get on with the milking and take myself back to the maze gate when I was finished. He stamped on the glowing ashes and walked away.

When I had finished the milking and washed the buckets, I came out of the barn forlornly, thinking I had a bad habit of annoying the wrong people. I had sat down outside the barn to rest for a moment when I heard a soft footfall.

"Don't tell me you are tired!" came Rushton's mocking voice. I looked up to find the overseer looking down at me, and suddenly anger surged through me.

"People like you are the worst sort," I said in a low voice that seemed to surprise him with its intensity. "You make everything so much worse with your sneering and snide comments. I do my work. Why don't you just leave me alone?"

For a moment, he actually seemed taken aback; then he shrugged. "I hardly think the opinions of one Misfit will trouble me too much," he said. "Now get up. It is time for you to return to the house."

I got to my feet, knowing I had been stupid to speak up as I had, for an overseer would certainly have power enough to make me regret my outburst. The weariness in my body had somehow crept into my spirit, and I said nothing as we made our way to the maze gate, collecting others along the way. Rushton left us with an older girl who unlocked the gate and led us through the maze.

I did not see Matthew or Dameon, and guessed they had gone back with an earlier group. I felt isolated and dispirited.

I thought of Enoch's warm recommendation of Rushton, wondering how they had become friends. Certainly it was impossible to imagine the cold, stern Rushton as anyone's friend.

Thinking of Enoch made me think of Maruman and wonder again where the story of a cat searching for a funaga had originated. If only he were safe with the friendly old coachman. Surely it must be so. The coach horses could easily have told one of the animals on the farm about Maruman when Enoch came to Obernewtyn. But again I remembered that I'd seen no new faces recently. And what other reason would Enoch have for coming to Obernewtyn save to deliver a new Misfit?

✦ 13 ✦

I WAS IN one of the tower rooms at Obernewtyn, a room I had not seen before. It was very small and round. There was a tiny window and a door leading to a balcony.

I was about to go outside when I heard voices and realized I had no right to be there. I cringed against a wall, seeking a place to hide. Then I heard a strange keening noise, a grinding sound like metal against metal, only more musical. There was a note in the noise not unlike a scream.

As I drifted out of the dream, the noise seemed to carry on into my waking state. It was a tantalizingly familiar sound, I realized, not something that I had ever heard in my life, but a sound that oft came to me in dreams.

Thunder rolled in the air.

I opened my eyes to see Cameo hasten into my room. I usually woke to the sound of the bedroom door being unlocked in the morning, but I knew I had overslept when I saw the other beds were empty.

"Are you all right?" Cameo said. "You yelled out, and I was passing. . . ." She faltered, unsure of her welcome.

I forced a smile. "I was having a nightmare that a horse was about to trample me," I said lightly as I climbed out of bed.

Uninvited, Cameo sat and watched me dress. She was

very pale. "I have dreams that frighten me, too," she said in a grave tone. I stared at her curiously, but she seemed lost in her thoughts.

"Nightmares," I suggested gently.

A tear slid down her nose and dripped onto her clasped hands. "True dreams," she said. "That's why they sent me here. But they are getting worse. I dream something is trying to get me, something horrible and evil." She dropped her head into her hands and wept in earnest.

I patted her shoulder awkwardly. "Perhaps it only feels like a true dream. I have heard it's hard to tell," I said.

She looked up, and a wave of exhaustion crossed her face, making her look suddenly much older. "I am so tired," she said. "I try not to go to sleep, because I'm scared of what I will dream."

I did not know what to say. She reminded me of Maruman in one of his fits, and there was never anything I could do to soothe him when he was under the sway of his strange dreams. Then the hair on my neck prickled, and I looked up to see Ariel watching us from the open doorway.

"What is going on here?" he demanded.

I glanced at Cameo, who sat white and silent, staring at her feet, and I remembered how she had happily chattered to Ariel when he had taken us to the farms. Yet now she would not look at him, and he regarded her like a hunter deciding when to loose the killing arrow. Perhaps he had appeared in her true dreams.

"What did you want?" I asked insolently, wanting to draw his attention from Cameo. He gave me a hard look, then told us to hurry up and assemble at the inner maze gate, for we had already missed firstmeal.

✦　✦　✦

Thunder rumbled all morning over the farms but no rain fell. The sky was a thick, congested gray with streaks of milky white clouds strung low in fibers from east to west. I ate midmeal with little appetite, despite having missed firstmeal. A foreboding feeling filled me. I could not talk to Dameon and Matthew about Cameo, because two other boys sat near us and engaged them in conversation.

Before we went back to work, Matthew did manage to tell me quickly that the boys he had been talking to were acquaintances of Rushton's. Matthew found their sudden friendliness suspicious.

"We'd better be careful," he warned. "I wouldn't like anyone to find out what we can do. I can just imagine the doctor wanting to experiment on us."

His words made my blood run cold. "Doctor?" I asked, the word unfamiliar.

"It is an Oldtime word meaning a person who studies healing," Matthew said.

I wanted to ask more, but there was no chance, for Rushton had arrived and was looking pointedly at us.

Since my outburst at the milking sheds several weeks before, the overseer had been curt, but he did not say anything to me apart from giving me instructions. I had expected some punishment, but nothing happened. That afternoon I was to spend with Louis Larkin learning how to make butter. I spent quite a lot of time with Louis and was looking after the horses and some goats. Best of all, I liked the time I spent alone with the horses. Sharna, who lived with Louis, usually spent that time with me.

I spent midmeals with Dameon and Matthew, and when it was safe, we talked, insatiably curious about the very different lives each of us had lived. Matthew had come from the highlands not too far from Guanette and had been able to hide his abilities under his mother's guidance. After she died, he had lived alone in her shack, poaching and fishing and generally living close to the bone, and he developed a reputation for being odd. A group of village boys constantly tormented him. Finally, several of the ringleaders in the gang came to harm. One fell from a roof, and another ate poisoned fish. The village called in the Council and claimed Matthew was dangerous. No one could explain how Matthew, with his lame foot, had hurt the boys, but the Council had been convinced, and he was declared a Misfit.

Astonishingly, Dameon was the son of a Councilman, who had left him vast properties upon his death. But a cousin had conspired to have him declared a Misfit. I was amazed at Dameon's lack of resentment. But he said he had never really felt like a Councilman's son. Because of his ability, he had always felt less than certain about his future. "And, after all, despite my cousin's lies, I *am* a Misfit," he had laughed.

Whenever Cameo came to work on the farms, she would join us. I had thought I would have to argue for her inclusion, since she had no abilities beyond dreaming true, but as it turned out, Matthew was quite fond of her, and Cameo swiftly came to adore him. I wondered what Dameon felt of what was growing between them, thinking it must be odd always to be feeling what other people felt. I was curious how he could tell the difference between other people's feelings and his own.

Midway through one afternoon later that week, Matthew came to the milking shed with a message for Louis and stayed on talking. Usually Louis discouraged gossip during work time, but that day he seemed inclined to conversation.

"Any news?" Matthew asked casually.

Louis was at times a fountain of highland news. It was hard to tell where he got it from, since he appeared to hate almost everyone. I suspected some of it came via Enoch, who was certain to know the old Misfit.

"Nowt much," the old man answered Matthew.

Matthew grinned at me and waited, and presently the old man went on. "Mind ye, rumor has it something is gannin on in th' highlands." Our interest quickened as he took his pipe out, for it was a sure sign he was in an expansive mood.

"I've known for an age something was up," he continued. "Too many strangers up in the high country, sayin' they lived out a way when it was a lie. 'Tis nowt enough just to listen to what people tells ye. Ye have to look in their eyes an' watch what they do. An' them folk belongs to th' towns."

I exchanged a puzzled look with Matthew as Louis relit his pipe.

"But why would they lie?" Matthew prompted.

"Think, boy," Louis retorted with sudden scorn. "What would towns folk be doin' up here to begin' with? They're up to some mischief."

"I heard Henry Druid lived up there still, that he wasn't dead. Maybe the Council is sending people to look for him," I suggested.

The old man looked at me sharply. " 'Tis nowt th' Council; I'll say that straight. They stay away from th' mountains. They get paid to stay out."

"I nivver heard the Druid was alive," Matthew said, looking at me curiously.

"A man like Henry Druid would not be easy to kill," Louis said, almost as if he knew the man.

Matthew looked at me, sending a quick thought that trouble in the highlands would detract attention from any escapes. We had spoken of escape, but not with any real intention. Yet there was a seriousness in his mind that told me he had thought of it more often than I'd realized.

Matthew persisted. "Th' last trouble in the high country was his defection, wasn't it?"

Louis frowned. "Aye. That'd be some ten years ago now. A long time ago past," he said after a pause.

"Maybe he's planning to attack the Council," Matthew said. "For revenge."

Louis shook his head. "Henry Druid must be over forty now. Not a hothead anymore. He was smart, I heard, and smart turns into cunning when ye get old. He'd never win in an outright battle against th' soldierguards. He'd find some other way. Though he would hate th' Council enough, to be sure. His son an' one of his daughters were killed in th' troubles," Louis added.

"What was it all over anyway?" asked Matthew.

"Nobody knows for sure what started it," Louis answered. "Ye'll hear th' Council say he was a seditious rebel settin' to take over an' drag the Land back into the Age of Chaos, but that's only one side to th' story, an' Henry Druid ain't here to talk in his defense. But he was a scholar, not a soldier. I dinna think he would even consider war. Not unless he were sure of winnin'."

"I heard he was a Herder," I said. "No wonder there was such a fuss. It was all over forbidden books, wasn't it?"

Louis nodded his head approvingly. "Aye. That's what began it. The Council decided to burn all Oldtime books. Henry Druid had a huge collection of 'em, an' he looked after th' Herder library, too. The Herders agreed with the Council, but Henry Druid refused. He was a popular man, an' he called on friends to help him. I dinna think he had any idea of what would happen. The soldierguards killed some of his friends and burned his whole house down, books an' all. The Herder Faction disowned him, and they were plannin' to execute him as an example. But he escaped with some followers, an' no one's seen them since. Leastways, no one who's talkin'," he added craftily. "It seemed a good idea at th' time, to burn all th' books that had caused th' Oldtimes to go wrong. But now . . . I ain't so sure." Louis's eyes were troubled, as if he recalled some long past battle with himself.

"He should have been able to keep th' books," Matthew declared, ever the advocate of the Beforetime.

"I dinna know about that either," Louis said sternly. "Maybe Henry Druid only wanted a look at th' past an' had no mind to seek trouble. Then again, maybe he was after some of th' power th' Oldtimers had."

"You mean th' Beforetimers' magic?" Matthew asked.

"Magic! Pah!" Louis scoffed. "I dinna think for one moment they was any more magic than us. Not th' sort of magic ye find in fairy stories, anyhow. Some of th' things they could do might seem like magic to us now. But 'tis my feeling they was just mighty clever people—too clever for their own good."

"Well, I think they were magic!" Matthew said stubbornly. "An' I think Lud would never have destroyed them."

That was as close as you could get to outright sedition—and to Louis, who we all agreed was interesting but probably not to be trusted.

But the old man only puffed at his pipe for a minute. "Boy," he said finally. "Ye mun be careful of what ye say. It ain't safe to be blatherin' out every crazy notion. As to what ye said, well, ye could be right. But if ye are, then who made th' Great White? Yer wonderful Beforetimers, that's who."

Matthew's face was stricken, and he did not answer. I remembered that Maruman believed much the same thing.

"However it happened, everything was changed by the Great White," Louis told him, almost gently. "Even th' seasons have changed. Once they were all a similar length. Nothing is like it was in th' Beforetime. The Great White killed th' Beforetime, an' it woke lots of queer things. It ain't th' same world now."

He puffed at his pipe again before continuing. "But maybe th' Beforetimers left some things hidden. Maybe there might be something left, and maybe Henry Druid's books were nowt harmless. Just in case Matthew is right an' th' holocaust were man-made, it might be better to leave that stuff hidden. After all, we dinna want to be finding out how they did it."

"But we wouldn't have to use the magic like they did," Matthew said at last.

Louis shook his head. "Dinna say it, lad. Ye dinna know what ye'd do. Power has a way of . . . changin' a person. In th' end, what would all that power do to yer good intentions?"

From that day on, thoughts of escape began to plague me.

Discovering I was no solitary freak had given rise to the notion that life seemed worth more than just endurance. Obernewtyn hadn't turned out as badly as I had feared, but any way you looked at it, the place was still a prison. And I wanted to be free. I wanted to find Maruman and make a home for us. I imagined a remote farm where we could live quietly with Dameon and Matthew. Cameo, too.

One cloud-filled morning that same week, I was thinking of how useful our abilities might be in throwing off any pursuit, when I was assailed by a premonition of danger as potent as the one I had experienced before Obernewtyn's head keeper had come to the Kinraide orphan home. I had such strong premonitions rarely, and they never revealed much—only that some threat loomed.

Later that day, the promise of rain was fulfilled with a vengeance. The dark skies opened, and the raindrops that fell were big and forceful. Everyone took shelter; those in the orchards ran for the nearest buildings, and even the cows and horses came under cover. I stayed in the shed, milking the cows and listening to the drumming noise the rain made on the tin roof. The disquiet that the premonition had roused gradually faded, and the downpour ended obligingly just before I was due to go back through the maze.

Ariel was waiting at the gate with the others when I arrived, and I was surprised by the air of gloom among them. I thought it was on account of the rain until, when Ariel turned to unlock the maze gate, one of the girls leaned near and whispered, "Madam Vega has returned. Ariel just told us." Her eyes were frightened, and I felt that old fluttery terror come back into my stomach.

It wasn't as if anything had really changed, but all at once I realized what had struck me about the atmosphere at Obernewtyn since I had come here. It had been waiting. . . .

♦ 14 ♦

I HAD THOUGHT I would be summoned by Madam Vega at once. But as the days passed much as before, I wondered whether I could have been wrong about the premonition.

Then I discovered something that drove my nagging worry over the head keeper to the back of my thoughts. Dameon told me he heard Cameo had been receiving "treatments" from the doctor since Madam Vega's return. No one knew precisely what the treatments were, but I remembered the talk at my trial concerning a "cure" for Misfit minds. I found it odd and rather frightening that so little was known of the treatments when Cameo could not have been the first to receive them.

Strangest of all was Cameo's reaction when I asked about her visits to the doctor's chamber. She just stared at me in surprise and said she didn't know what I was talking about. With anyone else, I might have thought they were lying, but not Cameo. She was not made for guile.

Dameon suggested that Cameo and perhaps all those who received the doctor's treatments had been subjected to an Oldtime technique called hypnosis, which could prevent them from remembering what had been done to them. Hypnosis sounded to me like a form of what I called coercion, and I almost said as much. But I had not explained my ability in this area to Dameon or Matthew, fearing they might react uncomfortably to a companion capable of tampering with their minds.

But we agreed, under the circumstances, that I should probe Cameo. To my astonishment, I found a series of blocks at different levels in her mind. They were not natural shields, and I did not see how hypnosis, as Dameon had described it, could have produced them. The worst thing about them was that they were clumsily made and had damaged her mind. This, I thought, might be the reason for both her nightmares and her physical weakening. I suspected I could have forced my way through the blocks, but to do so might hurt Cameo even more.

I withdrew from her, feeling confused and helpless. Most of all, I wondered why her mind had been blocked. What had this Doctor been doing to make him so determined to conceal the nature of his treatments?

It was a week before I saw Cameo again, at a nightmeal. She looked terrible, and Matthew went nearly as white as she was when he saw her enter the dining chamber. He hastened to bring her to join us. When Dameon asked gently where she had been, she would not meet any of our eyes, and said only that she had been ill and resting in a place where they kept sick Misfits. It was impossible to press her any harder. She was clearly happy to see us, and she talked and laughed more as the meal progressed, but there was a brittleness to her behavior, and she had lost a frightening amount of weight.

That night, I had a nightmare. Much as in the dream Cameo had once told me about, I was being pursued through the darkness by something terrible that hungered for me. When I mentioned it to Matthew, he gave me a haunted look and said he had had a similar nightmare, only it was not him being pursued but Cameo while he stood by helplessly.

Dameon said nothing, but it was obvious from the shadows under his eyes that he was sleeping badly, too, even if he had not had nightmares. I asked him if his empathy could give us any insight into what was happening.

"I don't perceive others' emotions as clearly as you and Matthew can hear their thoughts. Empathy is much hazier. I can sometimes even project feelings onto another and have tried to send calmness and serenity to Cameo, but her fear is like a wall I cannot surmount."

"Fear of the doctor?" I asked.

"Fear of something. I cannot say what," Dameon said, frowning.

Two nights later, Cameo was moved into my room, an extra bed having been put in to accommodate her. The reasons given were that a new group of Misfits would soon be arriving and extensive repairs were to be carried out in some areas of Obernewtyn before wintertime. Whether this was true or not, I was glad of the opportunity to spend more time with her.

On her first night, I was awakened by her scream. Sitting upright, I stared across at Cameo writhing in her bed. Then I looked in astonishment at the others, who were all still soundly asleep. Finally I realized that I had heard a *mental* scream, which I alone had been capable of receiving. I probed the others lightly to make sure they were truly asleep before getting up and padding across the cold floor.

Cameo was lying with her back to me now, whimpering softly. The moon fell across her pillow. It gleamed whitely in the light, but I could not see her face. She moved sharply and muttered something in an odd, deep voice. It didn't sound like her at all, and the queer thought came to me that it wasn't Cameo lying there, but some other person with soft blond hair.

She moaned and rolled over, and I could see of course it was Cameo. I sagged against the side of her bed, grinning like an idiot at my stupid fright. Then her eyes opened and my grin froze, for the eyes looking out of Cameo's face were the wrong color! They were a hot, sickly ocher hue and full of amusement.

"You'll never find it," she rasped in that same deep, strange voice.

I was petrified, but then I realized she was not actually speaking to me. She was in a trance, and it struck me that I might be able to question her in this state.

"Tell me about the doctor?" I asked softly after checking the others still slept. "What does he do to you?"

"Find it if you can. I'll not show you," said Cameo in the unfamiliar voice. She gave a sneering old woman's cackle of laughter.

I frowned. Her answer made no sense. Looking into her eyes, I wondered with a chill if a demon had taken possession of her. Louis insisted there were no such things, but seeing Cameo transformed like this, I wasn't so sure. All at once, she closed her eyes and dropped into a sound sleep. Returning to my own bed, I had to pinch myself to make sure I hadn't dreamed the whole thing.

"Poor Cameo," Dameon said the next day. "But I do not know what we can do to help her."

"Do you think a sleep drug would help, if we can manage to get some?" I suggested.

Dameon said he did not think sleep drugs were the answer. "She would still dream," he said. "We have to find out *why* she is having so many nightmares and take away whatever is causing them."

That brought us back to the doctor's treatments, but how could we stop them when we did not even know what they were? It occurred to me that night, when Ariel had again led Cameo away, that I could enter his mind. He might not know much, but he would surely know something.

But the next morning, Ariel did not take us to the farms as he usually did. When I asked where he was, one of the girls whispered that three people had tried to escape the previous night, and he was involved in the search. Later I heard the Norselander twins had been captured and were now locked up in cells beneath Obernewtyn. I was not surprised that they had attempted to escape. Had I not heard them plotting to do so? But I wondered who the other person was who had succeeded in getting away, and I hoped he or she would manage it unscathed, for it came to me that the only way to look after Cameo might be for us to escape with her.

Dameon and Matthew were as interested as I was in the identity of the escaped Misfit, and we spent midmeal and nightmeal that day speculating on who it might be.

Afterward, when I returned to my room, I found Cameo alone, sitting on her bed. Going to sit beside her, I asked her gently where she had been the previous night. She lifted her head as if it were too heavy for the slender stalk of her neck and said dully that she had been ill. I asked who had been treating her, but she only shrugged, though it seemed to me the shrug was as much a shudder as anything else. Then she burst into tears, and holding her, it occurred to me that sooner or later, her mind would crumble under the pressure of what was being done to her.

"I'm so scared," she whispered suddenly, turning her tear-stained face to me. "It didn't seem so awful at all when I came here. Not like I expected it to be. But now I keep dreaming of things chasing me and of an old lady laughing." That sounded like the persona that I had seen during her trance, and I wondered if the blocks were beginning to break down. I debated whether to press her but decided against it, because she looked so ill and exhausted.

The next morning, at firstmeal, I heard someone ask if Selmar had been caught. She had been missing from her bed for more than a week, and I had assumed she had been moved to another room or had been wandering at night as she had been wont to do.

"Caught?" I asked.

"Haven't you heard?" said the girl beside me. "She was with the twins when they tried to escape, but she got away."

It had never occurred to me that a defective might be the unknown escaped Misfit. Astonished at this news, it was a moment before I turned to Cameo, who had come to the meal with me. Her face had gone the color of dirty soap, and I wondered why the news that Selmar had escaped Obernewtyn provoked such a look of horror. Looking down at my food, I remembered suddenly what Louis Larkin had said about Selmar being different when she first came to Obernewtyn, and a terrible idea formed in my mind. What if the thing that had turned Selmar into a defective was the doctor's treatments? I was suddenly determined to question Louis about Selmar, and if he would not answer me willingly, then I would enter his mind and find out for myself what had happened to her.

I was shocked when Louis flew into a rage the moment I mentioned Selmar's name. He ordered me out of the milking barn, so there was no opportunity to probe him. I had simply to slink away, wondering why he reacted so violently. Only later did it occur to me that he had done so because he knew Selmar had escaped and feared for her. Hadn't there been real fondness in his voice when he had mentioned her before? Perhaps before she had become defective, they had been friends.

That night, no one knew whether or not Selmar had been caught, but there was a rumor that the twins were being sent to one of the remote Councilfarms that dealt with the cleansing of whitestick. It was no less of a death sentence that if they had been ordered burnt.

Ariel's absence continued, and more than once I heard it whispered that he was not just involved in the search for Selmar but was leading it. One boy told me that Ariel and his dogs—wolves, really—always chased anyone who ran off. And he always caught them. Remembering Selmar's reaction to Ariel, I pitied her, though I could hardly credit that he would use wolves to hunt her, for it was said that, unlike dogs, they would not be stayed from a kill.

I decided I would definitely deep-probe Ariel when he next showed himself. I would have tried again with Louis Larkin, but when Rushton came for us at the maze gate the next day, he said coolly that I had offended the old man and he had refused to have me in the milking barn. Therefore I would be mucking out stables that day. Rushton seemed to relish giving me the reassignment, and a cold anger filled me. I decided I would probe him instead. He might only be the farm overseer, but as such he might know something about the hunt for Selmar if dogs were used.

Then I thought of Sharna, and my heart quickened, for he might know something of these dogs Ariel was supposed to be using. But Sharna was not in the stables, and Rushton did not linger, so in a moment, I was alone. Even the horses had already been led out. In spite of everything, it was delicious to be entirely alone, and I lowered my shield and loosened my thoughts to let them fly and hover. It felt odd, since I had not done this since I was a child in Rangorn, and only ever when I was alone, roaming in the fields and on the edge of the forest, for to send out my thoughts in this way meant my body would remain motionless as a doll until I returned to it.

I felt almost light-headed as my mind floated free of my body; waves of thought and impressions washed over me. They came from every corner of the stable, flitting like butterflies, drifting like peat smoke. Idle thoughts about how to saddle a horse that had never been ridden or what to do with a fevered mare, a fleeting thought about a bitter wintertime when hundreds of animals had died. The barn was alive with memories now that I had opened myself to receive the imprints they had made. There was no telling how long the impression of a thought might last. It depended on the thinker and the time and the place and a dozen other things.

Remembering my intention to probe Rushton, I raised his image in my thoughts, seeking his mind in particular. The beauty of probing him at a distance was that even if he felt something, he would not associate it with me. But I would be very careful and reach only into the upper levels of his mind.

I pushed my thoughts farther afield, striving out to where Misfits were picking fruit, and beyond to where livestock grazed in far fields, into every corner of the farms. I was ranging too widely now to receive any individual thoughts; it was like traveling through a pool and getting deeper and deeper without ever touching the bottom.

I went out beyond Obernewtyn, forgetting Rushton and wondering how far I could go. If it was possible to go beyond the mountains, I might be able to reach Maruman. But before I could try, something brushed against my mind.

I recoiled, but curiosity made me withdraw only a little way. Foolishly, I ventured near again, and again my thoughts touched something. It was not a mind but some sort of force. I touched it again and felt it squirm. Then it reached out and enveloped me. Suddenly I was afraid. I began to withdraw, but the force grew stronger and held me tightly. Frantically, I pulled back, but whatever the force was that I had disturbed began to drive me back toward my own body. I fought, but I was like a leaf in a storm. I became aware of the nearness of my body. Dimly I registered that I had fallen to my knees.

Inexorably, I was forced into my body, and to my horror, it was my body as well as my mind that was now trapped. I could not move a muscle! A drumming sounded in my ears, and a wave of new fright washed over me when I realized that the force was summoning my body.

With a sob, I felt my legs tremble. Against my will, I began to walk stiffly toward the open door of the stable.

"No!" I screamed, but inwardly, since not even my mouth would respond to my will.

Then I sensed another mind. It was not like the mindless force that had taken hold of me. It was human, but there was something strange about it, too. But any curiosity I might have felt was swamped by my terror.

"O reaching girlmind . . . who?"

This other mind was far stronger than Matthew's, but there was something disjointed about it, as if a voice spoke in an echoing chamber. I felt the cool touch of the other mind, and its tendrils meshed gently with mine. Instinctively, I fought free of its embrace, knowing that such a connection would reveal me utterly to that unknown mind. Yet in that moment I had sensed its desire to help me.

"Who are you?" I asked.

"Trust me, sistermind. What is your name? My friends and I have sensed you before."

I struggled for a moment in the viselike grip of the inhuman force and realized I was about to walk out into the open.

"Help me!" I cried to the other.

"Perhaps if we help, you will trust. You are strong. But the machine that holds you is too strong for you to fight. Together we will be stronger. Meld with me, and when I signal, pull away as hard as you can. The machine has no mind to make a decision. It will not realize that to divide is to conquer."

"I can't meld," I said desperately, fearing the revelation that would result almost as much as I feared the terrible force that held my mind and drew my body forward.

"You must," said the othermind urgently.

I was in the doorway now, and I was suddenly fearful that whoever controlled the force that had taken hold of me was determined to make me reveal who I was. Terror gave me strength, and I swayed uncertainly, neither moving forward nor back as I battled the force with every bit of strength I could muster.

It was not enough. I stepped out into the sunlight.

"I will meld," I agreed in desperation. The othermind moved forward at once, and I felt a great desire to simply surrender to those soft tendrils. But as if it knew my fear of a deeper melding, the othermind held itself rigidly away from the center of my thoughts.

"Now!" it called, and we began a terrific tug-of-war. As predicted, the machine, if such it was, tried to keep us both but did not have the strength. The moment it slid off me, I slammed a shield into place.

I staggered back inside the stables, appalled to discover the extent of my weakness. My face dripped with perspiration, and I wiped it hastily on my sleeve.

A machine able to exert a force that could capture a mind!

I was astounded and frightened, and not only because some-one was apparently using a forbidden Beforetime device. It was the knowledge that whoever was using it might know about people like Matthew and me. And so, I thought, must the Oldtimers who had created such a machine. But I dis-missed that notion. My abilities, like Matthew's and Dameon's, were Misfit abilities that had arisen from the poi-sons of the Great White.

My more immediate concern was the identity of the strange othermind that had helped me.

There was nothing to do but to get on with mucking out the stables, and I did so slowly, because the battle with the machine had drained me. I cursed the stupidity that had led me to farseek. I would not dare attempt it again. In fact, I was now too frightened to use any but the most basic powers, for perhaps any use of my abilities would draw that malevolent force to me again. And the othermind might not be there to rescue me a second time.

My vague notion of escape grew into a determination to get away from Obernewtyn and all of its mysteries and dan-gers. Cameo must come, and Dameon and Matthew. I knew of no other I cared to trust. Fleetingly, I thought of my res-cuer. A man, I thought, but there was no way to contact him without arousing the machine. Anyway, he seemed smart and strong enough to take care of himself, and he had spoken of friends, so he was not alone.

Learning what had happened over midmeal, and agog with delight to hear of the othermind, Matthew disagreed. "If we really are going to escape, yer bound to take him an' his friends, too. After all, he saved ye."

"There is no way to learn who they are with that machine ready to catch any probe," I said.

"There must be some way," he insisted, entranced with the idea of my gallant rescuer.

I was less romantic. "He might not even want to leave. We don't know if he is a Misfit or if he is at Obernewtyn. I'm not even really sure it's a he. And the whole thing might have been a trap."

"Ungrateful Elspethelf," Matthew sputtered into thought.

"He helped me, and I am grateful he saved my life," I conceded hastily, forestalling one of Matthew's emotive lectures. "Which is why I am not going to throw it away trying to learn who he is. That would be truly ungrateful."

"Speaking of help," Dameon interjected quietly, "I have been thinking. If you really intend to escape, you should not take me. I would slow you down. And it is not so bad for me here."

"Of course yer comin' with us!" Matthew said firmly. "We've taken yer blindness into account."

Dameon smiled at his friend sadly. "Sometimes I think you have more heart than sense. Most times," he corrected comically, and we all laughed. Then Dameon grew serious again. "Well, if I am to come, then I will speak. This is a dead quest from the start if it is not planned carefully. Have you thought what will happen if we *do* get away? We have no Certificates, and we will stand out wherever we go."

I stared at him. I had not thought beyond escape, but he was right. We had to plan everything, otherwise we would find ourselves condemned to whitestick cleansing.

"What about dressing up as gypsies?" Dameon said.

"Wonderful!" I cried, for gypsies did not have Normalcy Certificates, and they moved constantly about the Land.

Suddenly Matthew stiffened, looking over my shoulder. "Look out. It is our surly friend, the overseer." I turned my head slightly to see that he was talking with another Misfit.

"He takes an interest in us," Dameon said softly, obviously empathising the overseer as he came closer. "He does not like what he sees."

"Maybe he's only interested in one of us," Matthew muttered with a sly glance in my direction.

Catching the gist of his thoughts, I scowled. "Don't be an idiot," I snapped. Rushton made no pretense of his dislike of me.

"He's coming over," Matthew said, and we all munched our food casually.

"You! Elspeth. I have a job for you," Rushton called. Nodding to the others, I got to my feet and went to the waiting overseer. I could not make out his expression, because the sun was behind him. He led me away.

"You are foolish to make your friendships so blatant," he said angrily. I stared at him in astonishment. "But I did not call you to say that. The girl Selmar sleeps in your chamber. When did you last see her?"

"She wanders at night," I said, suspicious at his knowledge of household matters.

"Did she sleep there the night before she disappeared?" he queried.

"I don't know. I don't know when she disappeared, I mean," I said, completely dumbfounded. "Why do you want to know?"

"You have no right to ask me questions," he said haughtily.

I saw red. "And what right have you to ask them of me?"

"I belong here," he said icily. I did not dare speak; he was so angry. "Fool of a girl," he snarled. "Go back to your cows."

Bewildered by the encounter, I went to the barn. Louis was waiting, and he seemed to have forgotten his anger with me. Recklessly, I asked him again about Selmar.

To my surprise, he did not lose his temper, but only sighed. "She were a lovely girl," he said sadly. I frowned, because he was talking as if she were dead.

"She is free," I said gently, now certain that they had once been friends.

"No," he responded, anguish in his face. "That devil-spawned brat, Ariel, has caught her, and no doubt he has taken her to the doctor, though what more he can do to the poor bairn, I dinna ken."

"That is what happened to Selmar, isn't it?" I asked slowly. "The doctor's treatments destroyed her mind."

"He never meant it to be so here, th' first master didn't," Louis said. I did not understand what he meant, but instinct kept me silent as he went on. "He were a good man, an' he built this place because he thought th' mountain air were a healin' thing. Two sons an' a wife he had buried already from the rotting sickness, an' another child burned. He wanted to make this place a sanctuary, and he took another wife to help him in his work. But she were no helpmate, an' when he died, their son, Michael, were too weak to fight against the yellow-eyed vixen. It was she that started buyin' Misfits from the Council."

I wanted to ask about the doctor, but Louis set me to churning, so instead I thought about the things he had told me. The first Master of Obernewtyn—Lukas Seraphim—had moved here out of grief and a desire to start anew. He had married again—someone Louis called a "yellow-eyed vixen," who must be the mother of Michael Seraphim, who had grown up to become the second Master of Obernewtyn. Though from what Louis said, his mother had been the true master. But who was master now?

That evening, on my way back from the farms, one

thought overshadowed all these others. Louis had confirmed my fear that the doctor's treatments could leave Cameo a ruin. It seemed to me that the only way to save her would be to make our escape, and soon.

I meant to speak to the others about it at nightmeal, but I had not long sat down before someone came to tell me the doctor wished to interview me the next day.

⋆ 15 ⋆

I woke early the next morning, feeling as if I had slept badly, though I could not remember any nightmare. Our rooms were always unlocked in the morning by one of the Misfits, and it was the only time we could really do as we pleased. Most mornings I readied myself for the day slowly, but today I was too apprehensive. I dressed swiftly and went straight-away to the kitchen. I was pleased to find Matthew had got there before me. He asked me about Cameo, and I had to shake my head and admit that she had not slept in her bed the night before.

We talked about what I had learned from Louis Larkin. Matthew was more worried than ever when I told him my theory that Selmar had been rendered defective by the doc-tor's treatments. He suggested that we talk seriously about escape at midmeal.

I swallowed and finally forced myself to tell him that I would not be going to the farms that morning because the doctor had summoned me.

He looked aghast. "Do ye know Louis once warned me to watch out for him? He said there was a dragon in the doc-tor's chamber. What does that mean, I'd like to know?"

"I hope I don't find out," I said.

The outside door opened with a gust of wind and a bang that made everyone including the cook turn and look to see who had come in. It was only a Misfit named Willie, whom Matthew nicknamed Sly Willie because he was a known informer. But just behind him came an older man who was a stranger. He was not a Guardian or a Councilman, but his clothes were so faded that it was impossible to tell if he wore the green of a traveling jack or the brown motley of a potmender. He must be one or the other, I thought. Who else would make the long, hard journey up to Obernewtyn?

"Who is that?" Matthew whispered.

I shrugged, but something about the stranger seemed familiar. He sat down at a table near us, and Andra gave him something to eat. He was very tall and tanned, and the knees of his pants were sturdily patched. He ate, shoveling the food down as Willie sat opposite him.

"So where do ye come from?" Willie asked.

"From the Lowlands," the man grunted. "I had to cross badlands on foot. No one warned me that pass is tainted like it is."

"As long as you kept to the path and didn't stop, you won't have been hurt," Willie said. "We don't get many visitors," he added

The stranger shrugged. "I came up because I heard there might be work for me. Potmetal is my specialty."

Hearing this, Andra came forward to speak with him. Most of the kitchen pots were in need of repair, and the potmender said he would do as much as he could that day and the next. The man spread out his tools to work, and the cook cuffed Willie and sent him about his business.

I had been told to wait in the kitchen after firstmeal when the others left to go down to the farms. I had thought Andra might decide to put me to work, but she did not, and so I watched the potmender at his craft. I was more convinced than ever that I had seen him somewhere before, but I could not remember where.

Then Sly Willie appeared again and, leering, bid me come with him to see the doctor and Madam Vega.

My mouth went dry, but I refused to let the informant see my fear as I followed him wordlessly from the kitchen and into a part of Obernewtyn I had not seen since the night of my arrival.

We passed through the entrance to Obernewtyn and into a windowless hall lit by pale green candles, which flickered and hissed as we passed. At the end of the hall was a small room with a single bench seat. Here, Willie told me to wait. My legs shook so much that I sat down and tried to make myself calm. I remembered all too well what had come of the last interview with Madam Vega, when I had let fear get the better of me. This time, I was determined to remain in control. If the woman did have some sort of sensitivity to Misfit abilities like mine, I must make sure I did not let her provoke me into using them. That way she might come to doubt her assessment that I was a birth Misfit and decide not to bother sending me to the doctor.

It was a slim hope, but I clung to it. I had one moment in which to wonder where the real Master of Obernewtyn was, and to think he was no less mysterious than the doctor, when Willie emerged from a door and gestured for me to go through. There was a sulkiness in his face that made me think he had wanted to stay while I was being interviewed and had been sent away. Willie was one of those informants who served his masters out of spite and slyness rather than out of fear or for favor.

Taking a deep breath outside the door, I pushed it open resolutely and reminded myself to stay calm no matter what happened. My first impression on entering was of heat. A quick look around revealed the source—a fire burning brightly in an open fireplace despite the warmth of the weather. Spare wood was piled high on one side of the fire, and two comfortable-looking armchairs were drawn up facing the hearth. The stone floor was covered by a brightly colored woven rug, and there were a number of attractive tapestries hanging on the walls. It was a pleasant, lavish room compared to the rest of Obernewtyn.

Against the back wall of the room was a desk, and behind this a wide window with a magnificent view of the cold arching sky and the jagged mountains. I stared, mesmerized, until Madam Vega stepped abruptly into my line of sight, the same stylishly attractive figure that I remembered. But her expression was no longer the coy, girlish one she had worn during her visit at Kinraide. Her blue eyes were cold and calculating, and she waved me impatiently to the chair nearest the fire. I sat down obediently, though a strange smell seemed to emanate from the fireplace, and I felt slightly sickened by it.

"You should have told me that you had only begun to show Misfit tendencies after being exposed to tainted water," Madame Vega said briskly. "I thought . . ." She bit off the words and drew a long breath.

"Still," she said after a moment, her voice now calm. "There may be some use in you. I am told that you have formed a circle of friends." I opened my mouth to deny it, but she held up her hand to silence me. "Do not trouble to lie. It bores me, and you do not want to bore me." There was a clear threat in her words, and I swallowed and said nothing.

"Well then," she said sweetly. She sat back and watched me through narrowed eyes. "Tell me about your friends," she said.

I thought of Rushton and damned him. It seemed he was an informer after all. "I only eat with them at meals," I said. "I won't do it again."

Irritation flicked over her features. "There is nothing wrong in your forming friendships. Indeed, it will suit me if you widen your group of friends. You will be my eyes and ears among the Misfits."

I stared. "I couldn't spy," I said stiffly. I would pretend stupidity but not that.

"I do not want you to report plots and petty misdeeds or even subversive gossip," she said so kindly that I was filled with suspicion. "All I want you to do is watch for any Misfits who seem . . . different. I am concerned that some of those brought here do not reveal the full extent of their . . . mutancy. That is most unfortunate, because it means we cannot help them." She performed this beautifully, and I even saw a hint of tears in her eyes. But I could only think of what was being done to Cameo. And what had been done to Selmar.

"What do you mean by different?" I asked, hoping I sounded dull-witted rather than frightened.

"I want to know of anyone with unusual or undisclosed deviations of the mind," she said. I could do no more than nod. "Good. I am sure you will be of much help to me," she purred. She smoothed her skirt and said very casually, "Cameo tells me you are her friend."

I felt the snakelike coil of fear in my belly. "She is a defective true dreamer," I said, but I wondered how much Cameo had said when she was hypnotized. We had not spoken to her about our undisclosed abilities, but neither had we been careful not to refer to them in front of her. Had she said something that had made Madam Vega want to look more closely at our group?

"She behaves as if she were defective, but that is something that can be made to seem so, rather than being so. And even true dreams may be a pretense." She said the last word with a coy, almost teasing smile that invited me to share the joke.

"I do not think she is pretending," I said stolidly, determined to make her think of me as a dullard.

"Very well," she said with sudden impatience. "I am going to take you to the doctor's chamber now. Get up," she added, coming toward me, her satin dress whispering to the rug. I rose, and she came to stand behind me. She stood so close that I felt her breath stir my hair. A moment of blind terror made me want to turn where I could see her, but I forced myself to be still.

"Come," she said at last, but she seemed to be gesturing to the fireplace. I went closer, only then seeing that one of the panels alongside the fireplace was an ornate door, so intricately worked in carving to match the panels on either side of it that I had not even noticed it was there. Opened, it led into a narrow hall, which smelled of damp. There was another door at the end of the short hall, and when Madam Vega opened it, a great wave of heat rushed out.

"The doctor's chamber," Madam Vega murmured, though she seemed to say this more to herself than to me. Despite its secretive entrance, it was an enormous circular room. There were no windows, but light flooded in from a huge skylight in the center of the ceiling. A fireplace almost as big as the one in the kitchen provided the nearly unbearable heat, but I paid less attention to this than I might have done, for there were books everywhere, not only those of recent origin— easily recognizable by their coarse workmanship and the purple Council stamp of approval—but also hundreds of smaller, beautifully made books that could only have been made in the Beforetime. Forbidden books, I thought, gazing around with amazement at walls lined with bookshelves, each full to overflowing. There were tables everywhere, and these, too, were piled with books as well as loose papers and maps.

"Doctor Seraphim?" called Madam Vega.

I was trying to understand what this name could mean, for surely Seraphim was the name of the Master of Obernewtyn, when there was a flurry of movement, and a rotund man emerged smiling from a dim corner. If this was the mysterious and sinister doctor responsible for what had happened to Selmar, his appearance was utterly unexpected. He greeted Madam Vega and drew up two chairs to the sweltering mouth of the fire. He bid us sit, and Madame Vega gestured to me to obey, but she remained standing. The doctor sat in the other chair and beamed at me.

"Another Misfit," he sighed, leaning over to peer nearsightedly into my face. Then he giggled suddenly and slapped his leg as if I had made a joke. It was a high-pitched, almost hysterical laugh, and I thought again that this could not really be the terrible and powerful doctor I had been so frightened of meeting.

"You are a cool one," he gurgled coyly, wagging his finger at me. I did not know what to say, and I glanced helplessly at Madam Vega, but she was gazing around the room with a distracted air. Without warning, she moved away purposefully between the shelves, leaving me alone with the doctor.

"You don't look like a Misfit," he said, peering at me closely again. "Vega tells me you are a dreamer and that tainted water caused your dreams, but the reports that came with you make me suspect that your exposure to tainted water only served to rouse latent Misfit tendencies. I am

131

interested in the idea that such exposure could be used to increase certain Misfit traits so that they could be more easily studied."

I said nothing, and indeed he seemed to be speaking to himself rather than to me. He sighed and shrugged. "Unfortunately, I do not have the time right now to begin a new research project. I have several important experiments to complete, and they will require all of my attention. However, I am going to write your name down for future research." He gave the same wide, encouraging smile, as if this news ought to please me, and then he got up and began rummaging through the contents on a cluttered table.

I glanced around, wondering where Madam Vega had gone. I noticed an enormous and very fine portrait of a woman hanging in a small alcove. I felt instantly repelled by the painted face, which seemed cruel and cold to me.

"I see you are looking at my dear grandmama," said the doctor. He gazed at the painting for a long moment, and several emotions flickered over his face: fear, awe, confusion. "Her name was Marisa," he whispered.

I saw the chance to ingratiate myself. "She is beautiful," I said admiringly, though I thought the face too sharp and cold for beauty. But she was handsome, and there was a fiery gleaming intelligence in the eyes. Yellow eyes, I noticed.

"She *was* beautiful," said the doctor. "It was such a shame she had to die."

This was such an odd thing to say that I turned to look at him, but the doctor had discovered a pencil at last. "Elspeth Gordie, wasn't it?"

I nodded, and he bent over a scrap of parchment and scribed laboriously, muttering, "Misfits are not always what they appear to be, you know. Often there are more demons that the treatment reveals. Do you know I once treated a girl who harbored amazing demons? Selmar was her name. Once I had forced the demons to reveal themselves, I was able to offer treatments that rendered her quite docile in the end. Presently, I am treating another who may be hiding demons."

The only demons you find in people's minds are the ones you put there with your treatments, I thought, all amusement at his foolish smile and dithering manner swallowed up in a surge of outrage at the knowledge that he was talking about Cameo. I looked at my feet, afraid the cold hatred of my heart would show in my eyes.

"Doctor, I do not think you should discuss such matters with a Misfit," said a voice as rich and smooth as undiluted honey.

"Alexi," said the doctor, looking over my shoulder with a flustered, almost guilty expression. I turned slowly and there stood a tall, beautiful man with shining white hair. His skin was pale and soft like that of a child, and his eyes were the coldest and darkest I had ever seen. As he stepped closer, I stood up, fighting an overpowering urge to back away.

"Of course, you're right. I was forgetting," said the doctor, talking too quickly, getting to his feet as well. He seemed afraid of the other man. Alexi flicked his unsettling eyes over me.

"Alexi is my assistant," the doctor said, and I fought the impulse to gape. "Would you like to examine her, Alexi? The tainted water may have acted as a catalyst—"

"I am sick of this," Alexi snarled, cutting the doctor off. "I have no use for yet another dreamer. Get rid of her. Where is Vega?" he asked imperiously.

The doctor looked around vaguely. "She was here . . . a moment ago," he said.

The other man turned his shadow-dark eyes on me. The irises seemed to be much larger than usual, with very little white visible around them. "Well, sit down. I might as well see if there is any use in you."

I sat down again, and Alexi sat in the chair vacated by the doctor.

"Her name is Elspeth," bleated the doctor, hovering nervously behind him.

Alexi ignored him and fixed me in his frigid black stare. "Your family were seditioners?" he asked.

I did not know if he was asking or telling me, so I nodded slightly.

"They were burned by the Herders?"

I nodded again, aware that he must have read my record, too.

"You dream true?" he asked.

"Sometimes," I said, but my voice came out as a croak.

"Are you able to know what people feel or think before they tell you?" he asked.

My heart almost stopped, but I managed to shake my head.

"Can you sometimes sense things that have happened before, in rooms or . . . or from an object?"

I shook my head again.

"What was the crime of your parents?" he asked. "For what were they charged?"

"Sedition," I said.

Without warning, he leapt to his feet, knocking the chair he had been sitting in to the ground with a great clatter. "She is useless. When will the right one be found?" he snarled.

"The blond girl . . . ," the doctor quavered, but Alexi shut him up with a poisonous look.

"My dear Alexi," said Madam Vega, emerging from behind some of the shelves. "I have been looking for you."

Alexi stalked over to her. "This one is impossibly stupid. I have enough idiocy to endure without your bringing me another fool. Why did you bring her here?"

"I already told you what happened. And she is here now because Stephen wanted to see her," Madam Vega said in a soft but steely voice, nodding toward the doctor.

It was all I could do to stop myself from gaping at the doctor, who hovered nearby, smiling too much and wringing his hands anxiously as he watched his so-called assistant rage. For Stephen Seraphim *was* the name of the current Master of Obernewtyn. But how could this ineffectual young man be legal master of anything?

"Does it not occur to you that stupidity is easily feigned?" Madame Vega was saying to Alexi now. "The one we seek would be clever enough to pretend stupidity or that she is no more than a dreamer and a defective. Have a care, someday you will make a fatal error in your impatience."

"Are you trying to tell me this creature is the one we are looking for?" Alexi snapped.

"Of course not. I have told you this one was a mistake, but there are others that might seem no less foolish," she added calmly.

"This last fiasco—" Alexi began, but Vega soothed him.

"We will speak of that matter later," she said, her eyes sliding pointedly to where I sat. She moved closer to me, her expression vaguely threatening. She studied me speculatively for a moment, and then crooked a finger at me. She waited until I had risen, then grasped my chin in hard, cold fingers.

"It is not wise to speak of this visit to the doctor, Elspeth. You will be most regretful if I hear that you have gossiped of

this visit. Indeed, it would be better if you forgot altogether."
She stared hard into my eyes, and for a moment her mind
seemed to brush against mine. I was shocked to realize that
she was not just sensitive to Misfit powers like mine—she
possessed a small ability herself. Though probably unaware
of her power, it was what made her such a good hunter of
Misfits.

I managed to keep my face bland. Finally, she released my
chin and said, "In the meantime, remember what I have said
about your friends." I felt a chill at the underlying menace of
her tone and did not doubt for one moment that she would
carry out the implied threat.

Returning with Sly Willie to work in the kitchens for the
remainder of the day, I understood the reason that people
were prevented from speaking about their visits to the doctor.
It wasn't to hide the truth about his treatments. It was to ensure no one knew that control of Obernewtyn had fallen to
Madam Vega and Alexi.

✦ 16 ✦

THE NEXT MORNING dawned warm and fair, but I woke with the memory of the previous day lodged inside my mind like an icicle radiating coldness. I dressed hastily and went to the kitchen, but before I could begin to tell Matthew anything of what had happened with the doctor, he told me Ariel had returned.

"Selmar?" I asked, thinking of what Louis had said.

He shook his head, saying there was still no sign of her. I noticed several people seated close were listening avidly to us, and I decided to save my own news until midmeal on the farms, where we could ensure that we would not be overheard. It had occurred to me the night before that I was unlikely to be the only person Madam Vega had set to spy.

In the fields that morning, we all toiled hard, bringing in the harvest. Every spare Misfit was on the farms now, and each of the sections was alive with activity. To my delight, later in the morning Matthew and I were among those sent out to bale a field of hay. Baling was a two-person job, and whenever we were at the end of our row, we were far enough from the other teams to be able to talk.

"Where is Dameon?" I asked, for although he had come to the farms with us, I had not seen him since.

"He was assigned to th' dryin' rooms," Matthew said.

"We're spread too thin over too many jobs. It was like this last year, too. It seems like a big fuss, but wintertime is really a killer in the mountains. Ye ken that stranger that Sly Willie brought to th' kitchen yesterday? Well, I saw him talking to Rushton later in th' day," Matthew said.

I scowled, certain the overseer had reported our friendship to Madam Vega. On the other hand, it seemed likely to me that his conversation with the stranger had only concerned the broken plow I had heard him mention to Louis some days before. I said so to Matthew, who looked disappointed. I could not help but think crossly that there were more than enough mysteries and plots at Obernewtyn without longing for more.

"So what happened in th' doctor's chamber, or don't you remember?" Matthew asked at last.

I drew a deep breath and told Matthew that I had only been questioned. "The doctor is too busy to be bothered with me at the moment, but he plans to get back to me later." I glanced around to make sure no one had come close enough to hear us, adding, "Madam Vega made it very clear that there would be unpleasant consequences if I talked about my visit. I think that must be how they shut up people who only go there once. As for those the doctor treats, well, maybe Dameon is right about hypnosis." In fact, I was no longer convinced hypnosis had been used on anyone. Madam Vega had told me to forget about my visit to the doctor, at the same time exerting her coercive ability. A normal person given that command would simply obey her and forget, but my own abilities had deflected her. I could not speak about any of this to Matthew without mentioning my own talent in this area. I would eventually do so, I promised myself, but not yet.

"What else happened?" Matthew urged.

"Madam Vega asked me to keep a watch for Misfits who were unusual."

Matthew paled. "Us?" he gasped.

"People like us. I'm sure she didn't suspect me. My being here is a mistake according to her. The doctor only wanted to see me because they believe my tainted-water ruse, and he was curious about the effect of the accident."

Matthew laughed incredulously. "What is he like?" he asked.

I frowned. "He is defective," I said. "And he is the Master of Obernewtyn."

Matthew stopped working and gave me a look of disbelief. "He can't be. It's against Council lore fer a defective to inherit."

"Exactly why they wouldn't want us talking about our visits to him," I whispered fiercely.

"But . . . then who is runnin' Obernewtyn?" Matthew asked.

"Madam Vega and . . ." I stopped, uncertain of the relationship between Alexi and Madam Vega. And she was careful to humor the doctor. Clearly she did not want to alienate him.

"Madam Vega an' who?" Matthew prompted impatiently.

I swallowed. "There was an older man in the doctor's chamber, called Alexi. The doctor—Stephen Seraphim—called him his assistant, but he didn't act like anyone's assistant. He acted like he was the master and he could barely be bothered with the doctor. Madam Vega fussed over him as if he was important. I think they are in league, and they keep the doctor as a sort of tame pet."

"But what about the treatments?" Matthew asked. "Surely a defective . . ."

"The doctor spoke of treating Cameo, and from what he said, he treated Selmar, too. But Alexi talked as if he was involved as well."

"Maybe they are both treating her in different ways," Matthew said. We fell silent as we passed another baling team.

I thought of the questions Alexi had asked me before losing his temper. Then I thought of Madam Vega instructing me to keep watch for Misfits that were more than they seemed, and a chill ran through me. "Matthew, what if they thought Cameo was like us and hiding it?"

"But why would they care?" Matthew asked. He gave me a quick warning look, and another couple passed behind us. When they were out of earshot, he leaned close and said softly, "We have to get away from here." I knew he was thinking of Cameo, and nodded.

The bell for midmeal rang, and I joined Dameon while Matthew went to stand in line for our food. I had time to tell the empath what had happened the previous day before Matthew returned, practically stuttering with excitement. "Ye'll never guess!" he cried. "Selmar is back! Sly Willie told me Ariel brought her back. He says a new Misfit has arrived, too."

"Was he telling the truth?" I asked cautiously.

"Oh yes, I think so. He said she was defective by mischance, and the Councilmen want her healed."

"Selmar?" I asked, puzzled.

Matthew shook his head. "The new Misfit."

"I meant was he telling the truth about Selmar?" I asked patiently.

"No gain in him lying," Matthew said.

I noticed Cameo standing in the shadow by the maze

wall, watching us. "Where have you come from?" I asked her gently, bringing her over to sit down. She did not answer, and when I saw her eyes I realized she was in some sort of trance.

"Something terrible is going to happen," she whispered. She looked straight into my eyes. "They are looking for you. They want you. They want your power. . . ." She slumped forward in a dead faint.

"Oh, Cam," Matthew whispered, and gathered her up into his arms.

I stared at them, my mind whirling.

"She is delirious," Dameon tried to assure me. "She does not know what she is saying."

But it was hard to believe it was a coincidence. Madame Vega had talked about looking for someone, and now Cameo said someone was looking for me. Suddenly I remembered that Maruman had talked of something waiting for me in the mountains.

Dameon shuddered violently.

"I'm sorry," I said, quelling the ripples of fear that ran down my spine.

Dameon looked pale. "It cannot be helped. You are in danger?"

"I think we are all in danger," I said. "They're looking for people like us."

Dameon's face took on a determined look. "Then we must get away from here before it is too late."

"What about Cameo?" Matthew asked.

"Cameo will recover, if we get her away," Dameon said decisively. "There is no time to lose. We must make our plans and act swiftly, lest we be trapped by the winter, for the pass to the lowlands is closed by the first blizzards and remains impassable until spring."

"We need to know more about the mountains, because we can't make straight for the lowland pass after we get away," I said. "It would be too obvious, and we would be captured even before we reached it." I told them about the maps I had seen in the doctor's chamber. "If we had a map of the area, there might even be another pass through the mountains that would keep us off the main road."

"Who will lead us if yer caught stealin' into the doctor's chamber?" Matthew interjected.

"There are those made to lead and those to follow," I said slowly. "And there are those who walk a lone path, to scout the way ahead. I am a scout at heart. We need someone smart and steady and wise to be our leader. Dameon would be my choice."

"But I am blind," Dameon said, visibly astonished.

"You are not blind when true seeing is wanted," I said. "You will lead us with those cautious instincts of yours and not be led astray by false paths."

"Oh, wise and tricky Elspethelf," Matthew laughed. Cameo stirred in his arms, and he looked down at her with quick concern until she settled. Then he looked from me to Dameon, his expression sober. "Ye know I'd follow either of ye, so maybe I am a follower. But if Dameon is leader an' says ye mun nowt go to th' doctor's chamber, ye mun obey him."

"Well?" I asked Dameon, somewhat defiantly.

Dameon shook his head slowly. "I will accept the role of leader for now, but I wish you had not given me the power of veto, Matthew, for I must disappoint you. If Elspeth can find a map, it would be worth some risk. Also, you might look out for an arrowcase. Do you know what that is?"

I nodded. "A thing of metal to point the direction," I said. "My father said the Beforetimers called it a compass."

"No good will come of this," Matthew said darkly as Cameo woke. She struggled from his arms and stood up, seemingly unaware of her collapse or her words prior to that.

Matthew watched her go sadly.

I worked alone that afternoon, cleaning and oiling bridles and saddles and other equipment for storage. I was glad of the time alone to think. No wonder there were so few permanent guardians, and temporary guardians were not permitted to stay at the main house. No wonder official visitors were discouraged. I wondered suddenly what would happen if a visiting party of Councilmen from the lowlands did come up to Obernewtyn unannounced, for they rarely traveled without an escort of soldierguards. Was that why Madam Vega kept Stephen Seraphim content? So he could be brought out at need? In a brief and artfully handled interview, his defective mind might not be apparent.

By the time I went to the evening meal, I had made up my mind to go to the doctor's chamber that very night.

Then I saw Selmar.

Ariel led her into the kitchens. She moved like a puppet, and when Ariel went away from her, she sat without moving. Her face was bloodless. Even her lips were white, and her eyes stared blankly ahead as if she was as blind as Dameon. But unlike the empath, her face was empty of all expression. She was like a body without a mind.

Cameo was sitting at the same table as Selmar, and her eyes were fixed on the older girl. She looked terrified.

· 17 ·

THE HALLS WERE chill and silent as I slipped along them in stocking feet. I encountered many closed doors, but their locks were simple enough to require very little power, and I did not let myself become discouraged by the amount of time it was taking me to get to the doctor's chamber. The sight of Selmar had been enough to make me absolutely determined to find a map.

At last I reached the entrance hall. Slipping across it, I hesitated, for there were several hallways leading off from it. But only one was lit by greenish candles. I hurried along it to the door at the end, then into the waiting room where Willie had left me. I listened at the door that led to Madam Vega's office before unlocking it. There was neither fire nor candles, but the room was bright with moonlight coming through the windows behind the desk. I crossed the room and felt for the latch that worked the door in the paneling alongside the fireplace. I would have liked to leave it open, but it was too much of a risk. Stepping into the musty hall, I closed it and was plunged into inky blackness. I groped my way along the short hall to the other door. This time I exerted a tiny farsensing probe to make sure the chamber beyond was empty. I could sense no one, but that did not mean the doctor or someone else was not there, sleeping. It was almost impossible to sense a sleeping presence.

I opened the door carefully and froze at the sight of fire-light flickering on the walls. But then I saw that there was only a dying fire in the enormous hearth, and no lanterns or candles. I glanced around the room and my eyes fell on the portrait of Marisa Seraphim. Closing the door behind me, I crossed the room to look more closely at it.

The dim, shifty light cast by the flames made it seem as if her eyes followed me. I thought she looked less cold than before. Indeed, it seemed to me now that there was a gleam of amusement in the set of her mouth and heavily lidded yellow eyes. Reminding myself that I had not come to look at a painting, I turned to scan the room, trying to remember where I had spotted the maps. The trouble was that there were so many books and papers. So many tables and shelves. A closer look revealed that I had been right in thinking many of the books had come from the Beforetime. Such books were forbidden now, but there had been a time when the ban had not been so strict and unilateral. This collection must have been amassed in that time. Impulsively, I reached out and took one from the shelves. As I remembered from the few tattered books my mother had possessed, the pages were thin and silky smooth and the scribing impossibly small and perfect. Who could guess how long it had taken to scribe it?

The book itself turned out to be uninteresting being filled with diagrams, symbols, and words that made no sense to me. On the book's spine I read "Basic Computer Programming" without comprehension. The next book I took up was much the same, except that the diagrams were beautifully colored.

Faintly disappointed, I moved to a different section of the shelves and took out more books at random. Many had been underlined and notated in a neat, sharp script in the margins, but none of them said anything I could understand. It seemed to me that there were as many numbers as words in them. Whatever they were about, I finally concluded, they were a far cry from the Oldtime storybooks and fictions my mother had read to Jes and me.

Suddenly I remembered where I had seen the maps. They had been on a table by the fire, where the doctor had rummaged for a pencil. My memory proved accurate, but the maps were of little use, being only badly tattered Beforetime maps. But on one I noticed that the spaces between places were covered in small faded ink notes in the same handwriting as in the Beforetime books. Maps of the Beforetime were nothing but curios, and yet someone clearly had been making an immense and determined effort to find some place that had existed in the Beforetime. A vain thing to attempt, for everyone knew the shape of the world had been changed forever by the Great White.

I wondered suddenly if these notes had been scribed by Alexi or Madam Vega. But when I looked at the scribing on the maps again, I saw that it was faded with age.

Suddenly a picture came into my mind of the potmender who had seemed so familiar to me, and I remembered where I had seen him before. He had been the older man with Daffyd, the boy I had met at the Sutrium Councilcourt. It seemed too much of a coincidence that Daffyd and I had spoken of Obernewtyn, and now here was the man that had been with him. I shook my head, reminding myself that this was not the time and place for solving such puzzles. At last, I found a book of modern maps. I opened it, but to my disappointment, they were all of the lowlands. I was about to replace the book when I noticed an inscription that read, "To Marisa."

Marisa! Impulsively, I opened another book to the front page and found the same inscription. It was the same in a

146

Beforetime book. Amazed, I understood that the collection had belonged to Marisa Seraphim. Then it struck me that the crabbed notes I had been reading were hers. I turned back to the painting, and Marisa's eyes mocked me in the light of the dying embers.

I began to search again, and this time I was startled to find that one set of shelves swung like a door. Behind it was another enormous chamber. I saw the unmistakable gleam of metal amid a pile of papers. And sure enough, it was an arrowcase. Delighted, I thrust it into my pocket. Then I noticed a square steel box standing on legs in a niche between two shelves. It was a metal cupboard with a lock built into the door. Curious, I knelt down and worked the tumblers with my mind. It was more complex than the door locks, but the mechanism was more delicate and therefore needed less force. In a moment, the door clicked open.

There were only two shelves inside, and both were stuffed with old papers and letters. I was disappointed, but I pulled out several pages. On top of the rest was a letter. It read:

My darling,

I have bitterly thought this over, and I have decided we cannot meet again. Mine is a strange family, tainted with madness. I do not want you to be part of that. I am the Master of Obernewtyn, and I belong here, but you do not. It would destroy you to be here. Forget what has passed between us. My mother has arranged a marriage. The lady in question does not love me. This is best, for, Lud knows, I do not love her. She bonds for gold, and I for convenience.

The letter ended suddenly halfway down the page, which suggested it had never been completed. I wondered why, and which Master of Obernewtyn had penned it. Not Stephen Seraphim, certainly, and not Lukas Seraphim. So it must be his son, Michael. And the mother he mentioned must be Marisa.

I found two more letters among the papers. Both had been opened and replaced neatly in their envelopes. One was a missive from Lukas Seraphim to his wife, Marisa, and the other was addressed to Michael Seraphim. I had no chance to read either, though, because I heard the sound of a muffled voice.

I quickly closed the door on the cabinet, the forgotten letters falling from my lap. There was no time to reopen the cupboard and replace them, so I thrust them in the narrow space beneath it and crept to the edge of the hinged shelves. My heart pounded at the knowledge that I was trapped.

But the voices faded without anyone coming into the doctor's chamber. Relieved, I waited until the voices had faded completely and then made my way back to my own room as fast as I could. Twice I had to conceal myself as older Misfits passed. By the time I was in my own bed, I was soaked with sweat and dizzy with fatigue. But even as I drifted to sleep, I seemed to see Selmar's dead eyes, gazing emptily at me.

I slept only two hours before being wakened. I had missed firstmeal, and there was no chance to talk to Matthew and Dameon, for they had already been taken through the maze to the farms. Nor had I any opportunity to speak to them at midmeal, for there were other people clustering about them. Too tired to eat, I stretched out in a patch of shade and slept, waking only when everyone was returning to their labor.

It was not until nightmeal that I finally had the chance to speak with them, but before I could whisper my news, Matthew leaned across the table and told me softly that the new Misfit was sitting at the next table. I looked where he had indicated, and my exhaustion fell away in my shock, for I knew that face.

It was Rosamunde! She seemed to sense my gaze and looked up. As I had expected, she recognized me. What I did not expect was the look of blank bitterness she gave me.

✦ 18 ✦

IT WAS SEVERAL days before I had the opportunity to speak to Rosamunde.

After that first meal, she did not come to the same sitting. I only saw her from a distance on the farms once or twice; then at last, one midmeal I saw her come out of a barn to collect her lunch. I followed and sat down beside her.

"What do you want?" she asked listlessly.

"Do you know me?" I said in a low voice.

"You are Elspeth Gordie," she said flatly.

Bewildered by her manner, I leaned closer and asked, "Is it Jes? Has something happened to him?"

"I don't want to talk to you," Rosamund said dully.

I bit my lip and suppressed an urge to shake her. "He would not have let you come here alone. He cared about you," I said. Her face trembled with some feeling, so I pressed her. "He's my brother. You must tell me if he's all right."

She looked away from me. "Leave me alone," she whispered.

"I know that you denounced me," I said, desperate to get a response from her.

Her face paled a little. "You knew?" Then the bitterness I had seen that first day in the kitchen returned to her eyes. "Of course you knew. You read my mind. I should have guessed you were like him," she said colorlessly.

I reeled at her words. "Are you saying that *Jes* can read your mind?" I said at last.

She gave a heavy sigh. "All right. I might as well tell you everything, though I wonder why you don't just read my mind and find out for yourself."

I glanced around uneasily, but no one was close enough to have heard what she was saying.

She looked up at me with sudden pathetic appeal, and for a second I saw the old Rosamunde. "You know, we were so happy in the beginning, before he found out what he was. It didn't matter about us being orphans, because soon we would get Normalcy Certificates. Then the boy came. Harald." The deadness returned to her features.

"Who was he?" I prompted.

"Just a boy, but somehow he was different from the rest of us. Nobody liked him much, because he would speak when he ought to have stayed silent, or he would refuse to do something or argue with a Herder. You could see he would never get a Certificate. Jes didn't like him any more than I did, to begin with. Then all of a sudden, they were the greatest friends. I couldn't understand it. But when I asked Jes about it, he just changed the subject. He became secretive and evasive. I did not see him as often, and there was a barrier between us when we were together.

"One day, he broke down and told me. He said, 'I have been afraid to tell you, but I love you and I must tell you the truth. I am a Misfit by birth.' I thought he was joking, and I laughed. But he wasn't. He wasn't!" This last was almost a sob. "He said Harald had shown him what he was. He said he could talk to people inside their minds and hear what people were thinking. He kept saying you were right about having to use the powers once you knew they were there. I knew then that you must have been the same.

"He showed me." Her voice had risen and again I looked around uneasily and saw that a number of curious glances were being directed toward us. I longed to coerce Rosamunde into calmness, but I dared not use my powers so close to where the machine had caught hold of me before. Rosamunde got control of herself and went on more calmly. "He said he had not wanted a rift to grow between us but that Harald had not wanted me to be told. But he told Harald that he trusted me with his life. I was terrified he would read my mind and learn that I had denounced you to save him. I made him promise never to invade my mind.

"Jes started to talk about escaping. He said that Harald knew others like them, in Kinraide and in nearby towns, and that we could all run away and live somewhere where no one would find us. If he had said just the two of us, I would even have gone, but a group of us? There would have been a massive search. He didn't care. He said the Herders knew something about Misfits like them and that they wanted to know more. He said the boy claimed some Misfits had been taken to Herder Isle because they had given themselves away."

She fell silent for a while, and I did not prompt her. Now that she had begun, I knew she would say it all.

"Jes told me one day that a group of orphans from the home in Berrioc had been uncovered and betrayed. Those taken were friends of Harald's. They had been taken to the Herder cloister in Kinraide to be interrogated, and Jes said he and Harald were going to escape and try to help them. It was madness. A nightmare! How could two orphans break into a Herder Cloister?

"Jes said I would never understand because I was not like them. He said he and Harald had heard the others calling out for help as they were taken to the cloister." She paused with deep sadness in her eyes. "I guess I knew then what I had really known since the whole thing started. Jes loved me, but it was as if I came from another race. In some ways, Jes was hard like a stone. He told me he had rejected you because you were different. He regretted that, yet now he did the same to me because I was different in another way.

"The night they meant to go, he came to ask me to leave with them. I loved him so much that I almost said yes. But I knew it would be no good. I refused, and he climbed out the window. Harald was waiting in the garden. And that is when the soldierguards got them."

My heart froze.

"They killed Harald. Then I saw Jes shot in the chest with an arrow. He tried to run, but he was too badly hurt. One of the soldierguards ran to where he had fallen. I heard him tell Jes the Herders would be pleased to hear they had taken him alive, for they knew there were others at Kinraide and he would be made to tell their names. That was when Jes did something to the soldierguard. I don't know what. The man just stopped laughing and fell down dead. Then another soldierguard shot Jes through the throat."

Rosamunde's voice was like cold death, and I wondered numbly if that was the end of her dreadful tale. But she went on. "I wanted to die, too. They knew he had been with me, and at first they thought I was like Jes. They wanted me to tell them who the others were, but Jes had never told me. I kept telling them I didn't know. But they didn't believe me. They took me to Sutrium. They tortured me. They wanted to know all about Jes. All he could do. I told them everything, and in the end I wanted to die. I tried to make myself die. Then they sent me here."

She saw the question in my eyes and shook her head. "I didn't tell them about you. Not because I was trying to save you. It just didn't occur to me. I would have told them if they asked. But I think they will figure it out in the end, and then they will come to question you as well." Two tears slipped down her cheeks, and she did not wipe them away. "They will come for you, because they are frightened of Misfits like Jes," she said. "Because of what he could do, and because he could pass for normal."

I stood up without a word and walked stiffly into the barn. It was empty, and I threw myself into a loose bale of hay and wept. I cried for the pity of Jes's end, and for all that had been done to Rosamunde, and for Jes's friends, who must now be living in fear of discovery. I remembered my prediction on the day we had parted at Kinraide. I had been sure I would never see Jes again, but foolishly I had imagined the loss to be his, not mine.

I sensed Sharna nearby, seeking entrance to my thoughts. "Sharna," I cried bitterly to him, "why is life so full of pain and danger? There seems no end to it. Where are peace and safety in the world?"

"It would take a wiser beast than me to answer that," he told me, nuzzling my arm sweetly.

"Then teach me to be wise, for I cannot bear this pain," I sent, and looking into his sad shaggy face, I opened my mind so that he would see what I had learned.

"It is a hard thing to lose a brother," he sent, and oddly, I felt he really understood what I felt. Then he told me with compassion that wisdom was not something one could teach, but a thing each person must discover for himself.

"I can't bear that he died like that," I sent.

"Death comes in a thousand forms," Sharna sent. "All who live, not only beasts, live with death riding on their back, though none knows what face it will show for them until the moment they face it. But beasts do not fear death or regard it as a burden. Only the funaga think death is evil. But it is nature. Evil exists only in life. There is much good and evil allotted to each life, and there is much that is neither good nor bad. Death is such a thing as that." He licked me roughly, then left me alone with my grief.

"What has happened?" came Rushton's voice.

I knew that I ought to get up and make some excuse for my tears. But anger flowed through me at the thought of him reporting to Madam Vega that I had made friends, and my pain became a raging fury.

I sat up and glared at him through swollen eyes. "Nothing has happened that you need to report to your mistress," I hissed. "I am not planning to kill anyone or burn down your precious farms. There is no dire plot in hand. Nothing . . . of any importance has happened. I have just heard my brother has been murdered." My rage died as quickly as it had begun, and I lay my head down and wept anew.

After a long moment, I heard the hay rustle and opened my eyes to see Rushton kneeling in the hay beside me. He reached out and touched my arm as gently as he had ever touched a hurt animal. "I suppose you will not believe it, but I am no informant," he said. "I am sorry about the death of your brother. You must think badly of me to imagine I have no compassion, though it's true I have cared for few since the death of my mother."

I was so astonished by his gentleness and his words that my tears stopped. Rushton went on in the same soft, low voice. "My life since my mother's death has been given to anger and cold purpose. I could almost envy your affection for your brother, though now it brings you pain. . . ."

His voice faded, and for a long moment he said nothing, only staring into my eyes with his searching gaze. Then he bent closer until his breath fanned my face, his eyes probing.

"Why do you plague me?" he whispered, as if I were a dream or a wraith.

I shook my head, bewildered by the tenderness in his tone, and he sat back abruptly.

"Come now. You must return to work," he said gruffly but not unkindly. "It is not wise to grieve too long. I am no tattletale, but there are many who are."

He was as brisk as ever, but strangely his manner no longer offended me. I rose, feeling empty of all emotion. Rushton sent me to a distant field alone to check the foot of a horse he said might be going lame and bade me walk him very slowly back to the stables.

As I walked, I realized that I believed Rushton when he had said he was not an informant. Any number of Misfits knew of my friendships and might have spoken of them to Madam Vega; Rushton had only warned me that it was dangerous making friends too openly. It was my resentment of him that had made me jump to the conclusion that he had spoken to Madam Vega.

Remembering that he was Enoch's friend, I considered asking him to inquire about Maruman. But even if my fear and hatred of Rushton were misplaced, I could not believe there was true friendship between us or any kind of easiness that would allow me to ask for his help.

Perhaps it was only because Maruman was so much on my mind, and I was still raw at the news of Jes's death, but the next morning I awoke with Maruman's dear grizzled face in my mind, his golden eyes clearly reflecting the jagged mountain range that lay between us. I told myself it was only the wisp of a dream, but what if I was wrong? What if Maruman was gazing at the mountains and longing for me as I was for him? What if he decided to try to find me?

✦ 19 ✦

THE FINAL WEEKS of harvest passed swiftly as everyone worked hard and long to complete preparations for the wintertime. The pain I had felt at learning of Jes's death had faded all too quickly; it was as if a memory had died rather than a person, because I had already accepted that I would never see him again. I had been nervous that Rosamunde would say something that would reach the ears of Madam Vega, but after that one conversation, she seemed to retreat into the silent blankness that I supposed was the reason she was sent to Obernewtyn.

I had finally, and with some trepidation, told Matthew and Dameon what Rosamunde had told me about Jes. Like me, they felt the soldierguard's death could not have happened as she had described. I could exert force enough to open a lock, and I had at last confessed my ability to coerce. But I could not possibly exert a force powerful enough to stop a person's heart or breathing. Most likely, having witnessed Jes's death and suffered torture, Rosamunde's crumbling mind had invented the vision of Jes destroying his tormentor.

No matter what had transpired that night, I feared it would eventually be discovered that Jes had a sister who had been convicted as a Misfit and sent to Obernewtyn. I was determined to escape before that happened.

But in the meantime, the doctor or Alexi seemed to have

lost interest in Cameo. She no longer disappeared, she slept more peacefully, and she grew stronger physically. A sly relationship grew between her and Matthew, and he and Dameon spoke less urgently of escape.

One midmeal, Dameon said, "It has occurred to me that if we organize our escape for the end of wintertime, just before the pass thaws, we would not have to survive the whole wintertime. I don't know how we would steal or carry enough food to sustain us for the entire season. And this way, we would only have to contend with Ariel and his wolves. With Elspeth's ability to speak with beasts and her coercion, I think we could manage to evade them."

Back and forth we talked, proposing plans, refining them, arguing, changing our minds and then changing them back again. But always Dameon was the one to make the point that ended a discussion. I had been right about him being the one to lead us.

One morning, there was a rumor at firstmeal that someone had broken into Madam Vega's chamber. I was immediately convinced that they had found the letters I had shoved under the steel cabinet in the doctor's chamber. There was no way they could trace the matter to me, but it meant I must wait a time before going back for a map. I chafed at yet another delay, but we were able to prepare for the escape in other ways. We were stealing and hiding food and supplies in a hole concealed beneath a loose board in one of the barns. We had two sacks of flour and some dried apples and potatoes, as well as two good knives and some coats and blankets.

During this period, Louis told us that things were becoming unsettled in the highlands. There were even rumors that the ghosts of the Oldtimers had been stirring restlessly on the Beforetime ruins at the edge of the Blacklands.

A ghost of a different sort, Selmar now drifted about Obernewtyn like a gray wraith, unsmiling, silent, and pale. After the initial shock of her appearance, nobody took much notice of her, and as before, she was permitted to wander freely.

Perhaps the strangest thing of all, though, was the relationship that arose between Rushton and myself. I could not like him, exactly, but his gentleness about Jes's death made me wonder why I had ever thought him a sinister figure. I had found out from Louis that he was a paid overseer who had been given the job by Madam Vega when he came to the mountains after his mother died, and sometimes I wondered at the purpose he had spoken of so fiercely.

For his part, Rushton no longer sneered at me whenever the opportunity arose. Ariel was another matter entirely. He had a queer mania that made him hurt people just to see them cringe—as though he wanted proof of his superiority. It had been even worse since he had brought Selmar back. As the days shortened, he took every opportunity to torment or hurt people, and everyone stayed out of his way as much as they could. He seemed to have forgotten about Cameo, but one day, near the end of the harvest season, he came to Cameo and bade her go with him to the doctor's chamber.

We watched her trail after him with dread.

That night, she was in her bed, but not the next night or the one following. Soon her nightmares recommenced. I tried again to make her talk to me about what was happening to her, as did Matthew, who tortured himself with dreadful speculations. He could not bear even to look at Selmar. But Cameo refused to speak.

One night, she woke me with her mental cries, but when I

went to comfort her as I had done before, I was appalled to see that her eyes were again the fierce eyes of a stranger.

"You'll never find where I hid the map." She laughed the rasping cackle of an old woman.

I stared at her. "What map?"

"Lukas said it was dangerous to think so much about the Beforetime, but I searched and I found it. I knew I would," said Cameo.

Suddenly, I realized what Cameo's altered eyes reminded me of—the yellow eyes in the portrait of Marisa Seraphim. Marisa, whose crabbed scribing was all over the Beforetime maps in the doctor's chamber.

She suddenly fell back into a natural sleep.

"It could be that she muddled our talk of needing a map with something she heard when she was in the doctor's chamber," Dameon said the next day. "If she was hypnotized, she would be very suggestible."

"You didn't see her eyes," I insisted. "They were yellow, like the eyes in the portrait. And she laughed like an old woman!"

"Are ye tryin' to say she's being haunted by the shade of a long-dead mistress of Obernewtyn?" Matthew asked bluntly.

I stared at him, knowing that this was exactly what I did think. "I know it sounds ridiculous," I admitted. "But I've been thinking: what if the reason Alexi and Madam Vega want a Misfit with mental abilities is they think it will help them locate something that Marisa Seraphim found and hid? This map Cameo mentioned might show where it is."

"A map to what?" Matthew wondered.

I looked at him helplessly.

Cameo's decline accelerated rapidly after that; she lost weight and color until she was as fragile and ill-looking as she had been before. One day Matthew said, "Every time we talk about Cam, ye shake yer heads an' look worried. But we're nowt doing anything. I say we should get away from Obernewtyn before it is too late for her. Maybe we can still make it to th' highlands before th' pass freezes."

Dameon shook his head. "Look at the skies. It could snow any day. We cannot take the chance of being trapped in the mountains for the entire wintertime without food enough to last. The wolves will grow hungry and daring, and Lud knows what other beasts will be on the prowl. We would have to endure cold, snow, hunger, and wild animals, not to mention pursuit. The mountains themselves would be nearly frozen solid, and the snow would keep us from being able to tell where the ground was tainted. Our only chance of surviving is to escape at the end of wintertime, as we have planned."

Regardless of when we would leave, we still needed a map. I resolved to go to the doctor's chamber again the next night. Whatever measures had been taken after the supposed break-in must surely have been eased by now, and if I had to, I would use coercion. It would not take much to prevent someone seeing me and surely it was far enough from the farms and the strange machine that had caught hold of me months before to risk it. I thought about the machine and wondered, as I had done before, if it was being used by Alexi and Madam Vega to try to trap a misfit like me. It seemed very likely. As for the machine itself, how had the Before-timers created such a thing before the Great White had begun to cause Misfits to be born? Or had Alexi done something to adapt a Beforetime machine to his purpose? Madam Vega had spoken of his ability at dealing with Beforetime machines.

I admitted to myself that beyond my desire to secure a map, I wanted to see if I could discover what Alexi and Madam Vega were seeking. I was convinced I would find the answers to all my questions in the doctor's chamber.

✦ 20 ✦

THE NEXT DAY, there was a story circulating that someone had tried to break into Obernewtyn. One of Ariel's wolves had been poisoned, and another shot full of arrows. It seemed incredible and insane. Whoever would want to attack a home for Misfits? Surely there was not enough of value to entice robbers over the badlands, and so close to winter!

Someone told Matthew the attackers had been the Druid's men and that one of them had been wounded in the clash. It seemed too far-fetched to credit, and yet I thought of Daffyd, who had spoken so knowledgeably of Henry Druid, then of his uncle's visit earlier in the year, disguised as a potmender. Was it possible that the events were connected? Given what I knew of the Druid, I knew he might covet the Beforetime books in the doctor's chamber. But how could he even know they existed?

I asked Louis what he thought, but he was in one of his reticent moods and answered all of my questions and speculations with shrugs and grunts.

That night, I waited until the others in my chamber slept, opened the lock, and slipped out into the halls. It was freezing cold, and I was shivering violently before I had gone more than a few steps. I had got as far as the circular entrance hall before I noticed a pungent smell in the air. I was moving along the hall to Madam Vega's waiting room when I stumbled clumsily, and all at once it came to me that the strange smell in the air was the same scent that came from the sleep candles my mother had created when Jes and I were sick. I held my breath and used my abilities to coerce the fog from my mind, guessing the precaution was the result of the break-in.

At Madam Vega's door, I forced myself to stop and listen carefully, despite the fact that my ears were beginning to buzz with my need for air. I could hear nothing, and I unlocked the door hastily. It was dark in the room beyond, for the moon was covered in a thick sludge of clouds, but the air was clear. I closed the door behind me and gasped in a great breath before continuing cautiously to the doctor's chamber. There was no one there, but the fire was burning brightly. Someone had been here not long ago.

This time I ignored the books. There were simply too many of them. I decided I would concentrate my search on the tables and their drawers. I set to work methodically, going from left to right.

In the second drawer, I found more arrowcases. Several were real compasses from the Beforetime. I pocketed a very small one with a cracked case, reasoning it would not be missed and that it would not hurt to have two.

Eventually, I came to a drawer containing a pile of modern maps. I took them out and began to leaf through them. There were dozens of them, and among them I found at last a map of the mountain region. It showed all of the mountains around Obernewtyn and even a sliver of the highlands, including a bit of the White Valley. I saw that the valley where Obernewtyn stood was only one of a series of valleys going high and deep into the mountains. I had not expected the area to be so big, and I felt a surge of relief, for surely we could find a place to hide. Resisting the urge to stand there poring over the map, I folded it and pushed it down my shirt, and I returned the rest to their drawer. Then I thought of the letters I had thrust under the metal cabinet.

I crossed to the bookshelf and entered the darker room behind it. I reached into the recess under the locked cabinet and pulled out the two letters I had thrust there in a panic.

I sat back on my heels, confused. If the report about someone breaking in had not been caused by the finding of the letters, then what? Was it possible that whoever had killed Ariel's wolves had also got into Madam Vega's room? There had been no specific mention of anyone gaining access to the doctor's chamber, after all, so perhaps my carelessness wasn't to blame.

Looking down at the letters, I decided on impulse to read them. The letter to Marisa from her husband was brief, a perfunctory inquiry after her health, then a list of books he had been able to obtain for her. At the end was a veiled suggestion that some of the books she wanted were dangerous, for the Herder Faction was becoming more stringent in its judgment against Beforetime artifacts.

The letter to Michael Seraphim was one page of what must have been a longer letter, and I gaped as I read it.

My friend,

I wish you would reconsider your notion to adopt young Alexi. Marisa finds him sly, and I fear I must for once agree with her. She is not motherly, of course, as you have oft said. She is too brilliant, too preoccupied with her books and researches, and seems to have little regard for her grandson, but she is still your mother. I think she knows that you never loved Manda and regrets your unhappiness. Now

that Manda is dead, can you not bond again? Stephen is
very young and would accept a stepmother, I am sure. What
of the village girl you loved? Can you not seek her out?

Slowly I pushed the letter back into its envelope and replaced them both in the cabinet, astounded that Alexi was the adopted son of Michael Seraphim, the second Master of Obernewtyn. No wonder Alexi had spoken with such arrogance. He was more than the doctor's "assistant"—they were legal brothers. How it must gall him to know that, by lore, only blood relatives could inherit property.

A slight scraping sound interrupted the thought, and I froze. The noise came again, and I crept across to the dividing shelf and peered into the main chamber. The door was closed fast, but to my utter amazement the entire huge fireplace suddenly swung open to reveal a descending staircase. I backed away and climbed under a table in a dark corner, my heart hammering. Hunched down as I was, I discovered that I could see the movement of legs and feet in the adjoining chamber. I could not tell if they were men or women, but there were four of them, and I saw the glitter of melting snow as they removed their coats. The passage they had used must lead outside.

The fireplace swung back into place, and when they spoke, I recognized their voices.

"I could have sworn I heard something as we came in," said Ariel.

"Don't be a fool," came Alexi's deep voice. "How could anyone come here without succumbing to the sleep candles?"

"Thank Lud we banked up the fire. It gets colder every time we go out, and now we have the snow to contend with," said Madam Vega irritably.

The fourth person said nothing, but I could see she was a woman. Was it Guardian Myrna?

"What are you going to do about the Druid's man?" Ariel asked.

"You can put his body out for the wild wolves," said Madam Vega. "I do not know what the old man hoped to achieve in sending him up here."

Alexi laughed. "I expect he fears that we are closer to the knowledge he seeks than he likes."

"We don't know for sure if the Druid is even alive. It could simply be his followers," Vega said.

"That's not what his man said," Ariel laughed unpleasantly.

"Either way, I don't like the competition. It's a pity we can't call the Council in to clear them up," said Madam Vega.

"Impossible," Alexi said coldly. "Soldierguards up here would make our search impossible. And imagine if they found out what we planned. It is hard enough to keep those nosy Herders from Darthnor out."

"Well, tonight was a waste of time as far as the search goes," Ariel said. "I told you she would be useless."

"I did not think to achieve anything. I merely wanted to try out the new configuration of the machine, and I don't want to ruin Cameo as we have this one," he added. I understood then that the silent fourth must be poor Selmar.

"I'm sick of her and all of these Misfits," Ariel said petulantly. "I am tired of guiding them through the maze and back and of listening to their idiocies."

"They keep Stephen happy, thinking he has some humanitarian cause," said Madam Vega. "And when the time comes, they will be good labor. Marisa thought the things we seek would be buried, and I have no intention of digging them up like a common farmer. Besides, it would have been impossible to suddenly stop purchasing Misfits without the Council wondering what was going on. And you must admit, the business of searching the orphan homes makes the perfect cover for our search for the right Misfit." She paused thoughtfully. "You really think it was Cameo who set off the Zebkrahn that day?"

"It would have taken a high level of mental power to engage the machine and then to escape it, and I would not have thought her capable of it," said Alexi. "But she has been dreaming about machines since it happened, according to our informant. It must be that she's hiding the true extent of her abilities. But once we use the Zebkrahn on her directly, the pretense will end."

"I'll be relieved when our search is done," Vega said.

"Damn that Marisa. If it wasn't for her, we would have had the map long ago," Alexi said angrily.

Madam Vega laughed. "Can you really blame her? It was she who discovered the location of the Beforetime weapon-machines, after all. A pity she was content to map their location and nothing more. Hiding the map from us was her sour idea of a joke . . . and I suspect she thought the knowledge would keep her alive," she said.

"She misjudged my patience," snarled Alexi. "I only hope she didn't destroy the map."

"She would never destroy knowledge," Vega said with confidence.

They stood with their backs to my hiding place, warming their hands and silent for the moment. I thought about what I had overheard. Alexi, Madam Vega, and Ariel were seeking Beforetime weapon-machines, and so too, it seemed, was Henry Druid. But why?

I thought of the machine they had spoken about—the Zebkrahn. This must be the machine that had caught hold of my mind. I shuddered at the thought of such a thing being used on Cameo. And yet maybe it would not harm her, since she did not have the power they sought.

Suddenly, I realized that Selmar had left the fire and was drifting toward the dividing shelves. To my horror, she knelt down and peered through the gap to where I was hiding. I doubted she could see me, but somehow she knew I was there. I held my breath.

"I'm so tired I can hardly keep my eyes open," Madam Vega said with a yawn.

"Get her away from the books," snapped Alexi.

Ariel came over and pulled Selmar to her feet. She went, unresisting as he led her away. To my relief, they all left the doctor's chamber, but I was so unnerved by what had happened that it was almost morning before I could summon the courage to come out of my hiding place and creep back to my room.

I hid the map behind a loose stone in the wall near my bed, and then I lay down and watched the sky lighten through the slot window.

In the end, I fell asleep, and woke a short time later wishing I had not. I felt heavy-eyed and sluggish, and I had to splash my face with freezing water to rouse my wits. Cameo tried to tell me of a dream she'd had, but I forestalled her, saying she could tell me later.

If I had known what was to come, I would have listened.

✦ 21 ✦

I ATE ALONE at firstmeal, having missed the first sitting, and was put to work at once by Rushton when I arrived on the farms. But when midmeal came, I hastened to sit with Matthew and Dameon, wanting to tell them what I had discovered. Before I could speak, however, Dameon asked coolly whether I had been out the previous night.

"Yes, but how did you know?" I asked, puzzled.

"You were careless," he said.

"No!" I said indignantly.

"You promised me that you would take care," Dameon said. "And now the decision has been made to release Ariel's wolf-dogs every night."

"Wait," I said. "Last night I went to the doctor's chamber. I heard Alexi and Madam Vega talking, but I'm sure they didn't see me. They had captured a man Henry Druid had sent here; he's after the same thing they are. *That* must be why they decided to put the dogs out."

"Henry Druid?" Matthew echoed, at the same time as Dameon asked what they were all searching for.

"Beforetime weaponmachines," I said. "I don't know why, but right now our biggest problem is that Alexi and Madam Vega are the ones who control the machine that caught hold of my mind that time. Tomorrow night, they are going to use it on Cameo, thinking it will force her to reveal hidden Misfit powers. Somehow, they imagine Cameo can help them find the weaponmachines—or at least Marisa Seraphim's map that shows where they are."

"But Cameo knows nowt of any map," Matthew said. He glanced over to where she sat farther along the bench, plaiting grass in her thin fingers, her eyes on the hazy line of mountains visible beyond the stark branches of the trees in the nearest orchard.

Dameon coughed, and we both looked at him. "I have been thinking about what is being done to Cameo. What if they think they can use Misfit powers to raise the ghost of Marisa Seraphim?"

"But . . . that is not possible," I said.

"No, but they do not know that."

"Wait!" Matthew said, eyes glittering with excitement. "What if it's nowt the ghost of her that they are seeking, but simply traces of her mind? Dameon, ye told me once that ye can pick up echoes of feelings from objects."

Dameon nodded, but said that feelings could not give them any useful information.

I nodded slowly, too. "If they are strong, thoughts leave an echo as well." I wondered if Matthew had hit upon the right answer. Certainly, Marisa's books and papers would be full of her thoughts and impressions, and I knew that if I desired it, I could probably read those thoughts. But how could Alexi and Madam Vega know so much about Misfit powers? Was it possible that Madam Vega divined it because of her own unacknowledged Misfit ability?

"We mun leave tonight," Matthew said urgently. "Perhaps if Henry Druid has a secret camp in the mountains, we can join him. Or at least raid his supplies."

"Perhaps we have no choice," Dameon said. "I just wish we had managed to get a map."

Triumphantly, I told them about the map I had found. That decided Dameon, who said the supplies we had collected would have to do. We would bring whatever of our stored supplies we could conceal and carry back through the maze that evening. I would come and unlock their doors that night and do any coercing needed, and we would then make our way to the front of the house and go out the same way we had come in—through the front gate. Despite everything, the audacity of the plan pleased me.

That afternoon, as we gathered to be taken back through the maze to the house, snow began to fall lightly and softly, whitening the world. Uneasily, I looked out to the mountains, my breath making little puffs of mist in the cold air. Their tips were white, too, barely visible against the pale sky.

"In case you have any notion of escape," Ariel said, so close that the hair on my neck stood on end, "I should warn you again about the mountains and the wild wolves. I have seen them tear rabbit and deer apart while literally on the run. No one has ever been mad enough to try to escape in this season." He ran his fingers through his white-blond hair, a languid movement that lent his cruelty a casual air.

I looked away from him, certain he must have been able to hear my heart hammering in my chest. Behind us, the imprints made by our boots were already filling up with a fresh drift of velvety white snow. I told myself that whatever Ariel guessed from my expression as I had looked out at the mountains, he could not possibly know we were plotting an escape that very night.

◆　◆　◆

But we did not go that night, for at midmeal, Sly Willie came for Cameo, and there was nothing any of us could do but watch as she was led away. Matthew looked so openly distraught that I kicked him under the table. There was no chance to talk until we got to the farms the next morning, and I was shocked to see they were covered in a thick white blanket of snow. We seemed to have gone in a matter of days from summerdays to wintertime.

"We mun help her," Matthew said, seeming not to see the transformation.

"Tonight I will see if I can find out where she is," I promised, just as Rushton arrived to send us off on our various errands. He seemed distracted, and it occurred to me that he had been that way for some time, but I was too worried about Cameo to ponder it deeply. I found myself among a group sent to round up the small herd of goats, which were to be led through the maze to a small yard adjacent to the house. I was in one of the farthest fields, having just found a lame goat, when it began to snow hard. It took me a long time to get her back to the stable, and when I'd done so, I was shivering with the cold.

Rushton heard me cough, took one look at me, and sent me up to the house with an older Misfit to see Guardian Myrna. By night, I was running a high fever, my voice was a painful croak, and I had been put into a sick chamber. There was no question of going out to look for Cameo, and I finally fell into a fitful sleep in which red birds swooped at my face and the ground opened up malevolently and tried to swallow me.

The first person I saw when I woke was Rushton. "You are awake at last," he said. "The horses missed you."

174

I frowned, wondering how long I had slept. Then I wondered why he was visiting me.

Before I could ask, Guardian Myrna came in. Rushton sat up slightly and said in a clipped voice, "Try to remember exactly what medicines you gave that lame horse." She went out again, and Rushton leaned close. "I told her I wanted to talk to you about a farm matter, but that isn't true. I came to give you this."

He held out a small cloth bag. I took it and opened it, and a wonderful summery smell filled the air. He closed my hands around the package and urged me to keep it hidden and eat it when no one was around. "It will help you regain strength quickly," he said, and then without another word, he left.

Later I drew the bag open and looked inside to find a moistened ball of herbs. My mother had made such things, and I pondered the fact that Rushton would give me medicine that was so obviously the product of forbidden herb lore. I came to the conclusion that he genuinely wanted to help me. Certainly the ball of herbs would do me no harm, and indeed that night, I slept deeply and well.

When I woke, it was night again and my head was clear. Guardian Myrna came in and, seeing I was awake, examined me and said brusquely that I might as well go back to my own chamber and sleep, for she needed the beds.

I arrived in my room as the others were changing for the nightmeal. There was a queer solemnity in their faces, and I asked with some trepidation if something had happened. I was afraid for Cameo, of course, for there was no sign of her. But one of the girls came close and whispered, "Selmar is dead. She tried to run again, but Ariel got her. He . . . shot her so she couldn't run, then . . . set his wolves loose."

"He couldn't . . . ," I whispered, sickened.

"Some of us saw it," said the other girl. Her face was ashen as she spoke, and I thought mine must look the same. I was still sitting on the side of my bed, alone and too shattered by what I had been told to eat, when Matthew came in. His face was haggard. I got to my feet at once, alarmed, and asked him if it was true that Ariel had let his wolves kill Selmar. He bowed his head. "He . . . he keeps boastin' about it like it was a good joke on her." Then he faltered and seemed to find it hard to speak.

I knew he must be worrying himself ill over Cameo, and I laid my hand on his shoulder. "I will go out and look for her tonight. I promise."

He shook his head, and when he looked at me, his eyes were full of compassion. A thrill of fear shot thought me.

"The Council have found out about ye, Elspeth," he said, answering the question he saw in my face. "That is what I came to tell you. I overheard Sly Willie tellin' Lila in the kitchen just now. Some soldierguards arrived about an hour ago an' they have been with Madam Vega ever since. She sent Willie fer a meal for them." He went on to say that two Councilmen were due to arrive the following morning, and I was to be ready for them to take away at once. "It seems they want to make sure they have ye down from th' mountains before the pass is completely closed. I came to tell ye that ye mun escape tonight, Elspeth," Matthew said. "Willie thinks yer still in the sick chamber, an' he told Lila that Madam Vega insists ye mun stay there fer the night. I've a bag of supplies an' a blanket and a tinder box stashed in the bottom of the linen cupboard for ye. It's not enough, but hopefully we will nowt be long after ye."

"But what about the rest of you? Cameo . . ." I stopped, seeing anguish flood his eyes. "Cameo?"

He shook his head and his expression grew bleak. "Ye ken as well as I do what they meant to do to her. Days have passed since Ariel took her away, an' no one has seen a hair of her since. I mun face . . . we mun face the fact that they have used th' machine on her."

"You can't just give up on her," I said.

"I will not. I dinna! But I am sayin' that there is nothing you can do now, Elspeth. Ye mun save yerself."

"At . . . at dusk each day, I will farseek you," I stammered, hardly able to believe that all our careful plans had come to this. I gathered my wits and got the map from behind the stone. Matthew tried to refuse it, but I insisted, telling him I had already looked at the map and I had a second compass. "This mountain valley runs up into another, and that runs into another beyond that. The valleys go much farther into the mountains than you would guess. I will go high and deep and try to find a cave."

Matthew nodded and pushed the map into his shirt, his eyes dark with apprehension. "Be careful."

"You too," I said. "Say goodbye to the others for me."

"Ye ken I will," he said. We stared at each other helplessly for a moment, and then he suddenly threw his arms around me and hugged me hard. "I love ye like a sister, Elspeth," he said gruffly into my ear, his accent very strong. Then he released me and strode away.

Deciding I had better not linger where I was, I slipped out into the hall and went to wait in an empty chamber I had noticed as I came from the healing room. The door stood open, and I sat on the floor behind it. I could feel nothing, not even grief for poor Cameo. I listened to the sound of people returning from their meal and then readying themselves for bed. I stayed still and quiet when one of the senior Misfits extinguished most of the hall candles and locked the doors. They did not trouble with the empty room. I waited until I could hear neither voice nor footfall, and then I stood up and got the supplies Matthew had left for me. I headed for the front entrance hall and the main doors, determined to coerce anyone who got in my way.

But all at once I heard the voices of Madam Vega and of Ariel. My heart gave a leap of fear, and I turned swiftly and ran down a short hall. Opening the first door I came to, I was startled to find a set of steps winding up. I ran to the second level and then to the third, slowing down when I saw light at the top, but it was only a lantern hung on the wall of a corridor. I decided to go along the passage and see if I could find other steps leading down, closer to the front door.

I had not gone far when, very quietly, a voice spoke behind me.

"If you make one sound, I will kill you." To my utter terror, I felt the tip of something sharp press into my neck.

PART III

◆

THE MASTER OF OBERNEWTYN

✦ 22 ✦

"Nod if you will not cry out," the voice said.

With a queer sense of desolation, I recognized whom that whispered voice belonged to. I moved my mouth to speak, but the hand over my mouth tightened. Limply, I nodded.

He unlocked a door beside us and propelled me into a small but lavish bedchamber. Candles were lit and a fire warmed the air.

I stared about me with a kind of despair, for this was not the room of any hired servant. Like the rest of Obernewtyn, the room was hewn of gray stone, but unlike those in the chambers of Misfits, the window in this room was wide and would afford a view, too, though now the shutters were pulled across to keep out the cold night air. The floor was covered in a thick, beautiful rug, and the table and chairs and the comfortable couch were enough to make anyone suspicious.

Forgetting my initial fear, I turned angrily to stare at my captor—Rushton.

"I thought you worked for pay," I said accusingly.

He shrugged, seemingly unashamed of himself. "My position here is . . . ambiguous," he said softly. "Keep your voice down," he added.

Outrage gave way to confusion. If he didn't want us to be heard, then he must not intend to denounce me. I watched him warily as he crossed to the front of the fire. He poked at the embers with a stick, and gradually I went closer.

He looked up at me, the firelight flickering over his grim face. "You don't seem frightened. Are you?" he asked.

"No," I said simply, because it was true. I felt too numb. He gestured for me to sit on the couch, and I shook my head. Uttering a growl, he moved swiftly, plonking me unceremoniously onto the seat.

"Then you are a fool," he said. I looked up at him resentfully. "Only a fool would not be afraid in your situation. I could have been one of the guardians. . . ."

My anger and bewilderment melted at his grave tone.

He sat down opposite me. "It is time for us to talk. Lud knows we should have done so before now." He shook his head as if at his own folly.

"Why were you sneaking around in the dark?" he asked with some of his old haughtiness. I bridled at his tone and gave him a sullen look that made him frown.

"I ought to march you off to Madam Vega right now," he said, but his tone was one of weary contempt, empty of threat. "You have caused me a great deal of trouble, and it might be the best thing to let them have you. I knew there would be trouble the first time I saw you," Rushton added. "And Louis warned me. . . ."

I stared. "Louis warned you about me?"

He actually smiled at that. "It is rather late in the day to become cautious, Elspeth. He said you were curious as a cat, and so you are. Perhaps I should tell you that I know Alexi is searching for a Misfit with particular abilities to help him find something hidden. I believe you have the abilities he seeks, and I suspect he finally knows that."

I gaped, my heart thundering. How could he know so much? "I . . . I don't know what you mean," I faltered.

He lifted his dark brows skeptically. "I am also aware that the Council has sent men to bring you to Sutrium. And I can guess that your friends have been unable to help you except to advise you to run, as far and as fast as you can. It is wise advice, for it appears the Council is very interested in Misfits like you—there are far more of you than most realize. The Council interrogates them, then burns them, or they are given to the Herders who carry them off to Herder Isle."

I looked at him dumbly, aware that I was shivering from fear. Seeing that I made no effort to deny what he said, he nodded slightly and continued.

"Your only option is to get away tonight, but I tell you quite simply that you have no hope unless you put yourself in my hands and do as I say."

"Who are you? Why would you help me?" I asked.

He gave me a guarded look. "It is enough for you to know that I am no enemy to you. Or to your suspicious friends, though you have jeopardized my own plans with your endless questions and curiosity. Rest assured I do not share the ambitions of Vega and Alexi to dig up the past. It is better dead and buried."

"Plans?" I asked, and unexpectedly he smiled.

"Even now you are curious," he said, his tone half amused and half exasperated. "I wonder if you really understand how much danger you face. Louis was right. You are curious to the point of foolishness." All at once, a sad sort of tenderness softened his eyes. "Selmar was curious, too, when she first came. Always asking questions and poking her nose into everything. She near drove Louis mad in the beginning. So hungry for answers, whatever the cost—and it proved dear."

"I can't help what life has made of me," I said defensively.

He stood abruptly. "Come. There is no more time for talk."

"What am I to do, then?" I asked.

Rushton handed me a thick gray cloak from a wall peg. "You'll need a heavier coat. It is impossible for you to leave the grounds tonight. The weather will get worse before it gets better and even an arrowcase would not help you, for the storms that run from the Blacklands affect the bearings. Nor can you go through the pass if you managed to find your way there, for it is white with snow, and though not yet completely blocked, it will be impossible to see where the ground is too badly tainted to cross on foot." He spoke calmly and deliberately. "I cannot let you stay here, either, because the house will be searched from top to bottom, and I am not exempt."

"Then there is nowhere for me to go," I said despairingly.

"You must remain on the farms until the weather clears. They will not be able to search there until the storm ends, and since the maze is snowed in, they are unlikely even to think of the farms to begin with. As soon as the moment is right, I will return for you, and I will tell you of a place where there are supplies enough to last you until the wintertime ends."

"But if the maze is impassable, how are we going to get to the farms?"

Rushton crossed restlessly to the window and peered through the shutter. "We will go outside the grounds and around. They won't imagine you would escape only to come back inside the walls." He frowned. "I thought I heard something. . . ." He shook his head and came back to the fire, pulling on his own coat.

"The wolves?" I asked, thinking of poor Selmar.

Rushton only smiled. "They are locked up." He looked at me searchingly. "You are pale. I hope you are properly recovered. You took the medicine I gave you?"

I nodded. "It was herb lore, wasn't it?"

"Yes," he said simply. "One of my friends has great skill in the art of healing, as did my mother. I know there is no evil in those old ways. The Council and Herder Faction are fools, frightened of everything. Now they have decided you are a danger because they don't understand you." He shook his head again and glanced out the window. "We must go now."

"Yes, I . . . ," I began, but Rushton waved his hand urgently. We both listened, and this time I heard something, too—the sound of running footsteps.

"Lud take it! I think they have discovered that you are missing. That was surely a coach I heard some while back. The Councilmen must have changed their minds about waiting in Guanette until morning. We have to get you out of the house *now*, or you will be trapped."

There was a loud knock on the door, and we both froze in horror. Rushton tore his coat off and gestured me toward the shuttered window, behind which lay a balcony. It was snowing hard outside. I pulled the door nearly shut and pressed my ear up against it.

"All right, all right," Ruston called grumpily after a second knock. "What is it?"

"Still dressed?" I heard Ariel ask him suspiciously.

"I was reading in front of the fire. I fell asleep," Rushton said casually. "What's going on? I heard a commotion."

"One of the Misfits has escaped," Ariel said. "Elspeth Gordie. Skinny girl with dark hair and a proud look. Sly bitch." There was a pause, and when Ariel spoke again, his voice was full of mistrust. "In fact, you must know her. She has been working on the farms."

My heart thumped wildly.

"I know the one you mean," Rushton said with a smothered yawn. "Quick with the horses but insolent. Anyway, why all the fuss over one Misfit? Lots more where she came from," he said coolly.

"The Council has sent some men here after her. She's wanted for questioning," Ariel said evasively.

"She'll be dead before morning if she's out in it. Storm's nearly on top of us."

"I don't doubt she will die," Ariel said viciously. "I have let the wolves out."

"A bit drastic, don't you think?" Rushton drawled through another yawn. "I suppose you want me to help look for her."

"You are paid to work," Ariel snarled.

There was a long pause. "I am paid to manage the farms," Rushton said at last, his voice cool. "But I might as well come. Otherwise I'll be up all night listening to your beasts."

"Good. It's snowing, so you'd better put on boots and a coat. I'll come back for you," he added imperiously. There was the sound of footsteps and the outer door closing; then I heard Rushton's voice.

"You can come in. He's gone."

I obeyed, shivering with cold. "He sounded suspicious," I said worriedly, but Rushton shook his head.

"He's always like that. But Alexi must want you badly to conduct a search while the Councilmen are here. Though I doubt very much that he has any intention of handing you over." Howling sounded in the distance, and he scowled. "We can't go out the front gate now, but there is one other way to get to the farms: pipes running under the maze. It is a foul labyrinth and hard going, but you are small enough to fit. The problem is there will be dogs in the courtyard, barring the way."

"Dogs or wolves?" I asked, my heartbeat quickening with hope.

"Half breeds and a few pure wolves Ariel has cowed

enough that they will obey him," Rushton said in open disgust. "Why?"

"I . . . I can control them," I offered hesitantly. "With my mind."

Rushton nodded slowly, and instead of the astonishment I had expected, there was a touch of humor in his eyes. "You can control these beasts? You know they have been tormented near to madness and only obey Ariel out of terror and hunger?"

"I can manage them," I insisted with more certainty than I felt, knowing there was no other choice but to try, and the longer I stayed, the more dangerous it was for Rushton. Yet I hesitated.

"Before . . . when you caught me, you said you would kill me if I didn't cooperate," I said in a low voice. "Did you mean it?"

Rushton looked at me with the same unreadable expression I had seen on his face that day in the barn.

"It would have been safer for me if I could have," he said at last. "Best for my friends and for yours. If you are caught, you will reveal my role in your escape, for no one resists Alexi. And if the Council gets you, the Herders will make you talk. Alive you are a danger to all I have planned."

"Is your plan so important, then?" I asked softly.

"More than you could possibly imagine," Rushton answered simply.

I stared at his troubled face and willed myself to be strong. "Tell me the way through to the farms. I will not betray you. And I will manage the wolves." *Or die trying*, I thought.

"The drains run from the courtyard to the farms and are like a maze themselves, but they were not designed to confuse. Remember to always take the right turn and you will be safe. To get from here to the courtyard, you will have to use the tunnels. I am not so certain about them. My mother told me of them, but she had never seen them herself, and I have had little opportunity to explore." He explained about the tunnels, then looked up warily as footsteps echoed past his door.

"When you get to the farms, keep to the walls. The storm will be much worse by then, and if you get lost, you will die. Follow the walls to the farthest silo. The door will be open. Hide there until I come."

"But . . . but is that all? For that I am to risk wild beasts and capture?" I asked.

"You risk no more than I," Rushton said coldly.

"But what if you don't come? Where is the refuge you mentioned?" I faltered.

He shook his head regretfully. "Understand this. I have already told you too much. If I tell you any more and you are caught, I will endanger others. It is my decision to risk my life for you. I will not decide that for them."

Chastened, I nodded, for what he said was surely the truth.

"You do not know what an irony it would be if you betrayed me," Rushton said cryptically, moving to the door. He pressed his ear against the dark wood and listened before opening the door and looking out. He motioned for me to go into the hall. "Go quickly. Ariel will be coming from the other direction. I will try to direct the search toward the front of the house." Rushton looked into my eyes, and I marveled at how green his were. Like deep forest pools.

"Perhaps someday we will have the chance to talk properly," he said. "There are many things I would like—"

He stopped abruptly. We could hear footsteps again. "Go quickly," he said urgently.

"Goodbye," I whispered as I slipped away from him and descended into the darkness.

✦ 23 ✦

I FELT MY way along the hidden passage, walking as carefully as possible, but there were several unpleasant crunches under foot that made me wonder what I was treading on. The smell and the veils of dusty cobwebs I pushed through told me that the tunnel had not been used for a very long time, and I wondered again how Rushton had known about it. The darkness was total, and I only hoped there was not a fork or turning I had missed.

Then I heard voices coming from the other side of a wall. I stopped and listened.

"She must be found," said a voice. "If it weren't for the Council . . ." It was Madam Vega.

"I am glad they came," said Alexi. "They have shown me that she is the one we have been seeking."

Ariel spoke. "She won't get past my hounds."

"I want her found, not torn to pieces. That affair with the other girl was quite unnecessary. You are a barbarian," Alexi added, almost as if he found that amusing.

"She will be found alive," Madam Vega promised soothingly.

It terrified me to hear her certainty. It did not enter any of their heads that I might get away.

"The beasts have been trained to mutilate," said Ariel sulkily. "They kill only on command."

"She must not be allowed to die," said Alexi in a flat voice that sent ice into my blood. "It might be years till another like her is found. A pity we wasted so much time on that last defective. I was so certain, but she had only minor abilities after all."

They passed out of my hearing, and despairingly, I knew they meant Cameo. What had they done to her?

I forced myself to continue. The tunnel seemed endless, but after some time I bumped headlong into a stone wall. I gave an involuntary cry as I staggered back, and then stopped to listen anxiously, fearful that someone might have heard.

"Greetings," came a thought.

My body sagged with relief and astonishment. "Sharna?" I asked incredulously.

"I dreamed you were in danger, so I came," he sent. "If you make yourself low, you can come through the wall."

I did as he suggested and felt a low gap in the wall. I reached my hand through it and brushed the soft scratchiness of a tapestry. I had never noticed it before, but when I crawled past it, I saw that I had come out in the kitchen pantry.

Sharna pressed his nose against my leg as I emerged, and I remembered what he had said.

"What did you dream about me?" I asked.

"I dreamed your life has a purpose that must be fulfilled, for the sake of all beasts," he answered.

It was late at night, and I squinted into the darkness of the kitchen, trying to see his face and thinking of the dreams Maruman had experienced in which I had figured. The old cat had always insisted that my life was important to the beastworld and that it was his task to aid me and keep me safe. But I had taken this as something he had imagined in his disturbed periods.

190

Sharna interrupted my reflections to ask how he could help. I explained that I had to get out of the kitchen and into the courtyard adjacent to the maze. From there, I could reach the farms.

"There are beasts in the yard," Sharna returned, projecting an image of huge doglike shapes moving about, sniffing at the wall and the maze gate.

"I know. I will talk to them and ask them to let me pass," I said.

"They will not hear you," Sharna warned. "They were once wild wolf cubs, but they were caught by the funaga-li and made mad with rage. There is a red screaming in their heads that stops them from being able to hear anything but their own fury. Best to come back when they are locked up."

"I have to pass them *now*," I sent. "Maybe I can find a way to distract them long enough for me to get into the drain."

There was a long pause while he ruminated. "I will go to them," he told me at last. "Innle must be shielded." I started, because "Innle" was what Maruman sometimes called me when he spoke of my appearances in his dreams. It meant "one who seeks" in beast thoughtsymbols, and I had always thought it some queer term of affection.

"Come," Sharna commanded, crossing the kitchen. I followed down a short corridor and unlocked the outer door, opening it only a crack. The chill of wintertime bit deep into my skin. Then I saw the glimmer of red eyes and heard a low, savage growling that filled me with icy fear.

"Greetings, sudarta," Sharna sent, flattering them with a title that applauded their strength. It seemed to have no effect on them.

Sharna turned to me, his own eyes gleaming. "Do not go until I tell you. While you wait, find with your eyes the place

191

you must go." Without waiting for an answer, he turned back to the door, nosed it open, and began to make an odd, low thrumming sound that vibrated in his throat. Beyond the door, I saw the red eyes withdraw.

"Sharna, what . . . ?" I began, but suddenly the old dog launched himself from the door and raced across the yard toward the wolves. Only then did I understand that he had not meant to persuade them to let me pass.

"Sharna!" I screamed. "Don't—"

"Go!" he commanded. The primitive snarling of the wolves sent a primeval shudder through my body. I heard Sharna taunting them, calling them away from my exit.

Trembling so hard I could scarcely walk, I stepped into the courtyard and stood for a moment, paralyzed with fear at the sight of the wolves falling on Sharna.

"Go!" he shouted again into my thoughts. A madness of terror roared through me as one set of red eyes turned to me and the beast uttered a growl. I flew across the courtyard, tore away the drain cover, and flung myself into the round opening behind it. Terrified one of the wolves would follow, I wriggled mindlessly along the pipe, imagining snapping jaws closing on my foot and dragging me backward.

I heard a howl of pain and stopped my mad flight. I was horrified to realize that I had left Sharna to his savage brethren.

"Go!" Sharna cried yet again, and I felt him weakening. I knew then that even if I could turn and go back, I could not help him. He had sacrificed himself for me, and I had not realized it until too late. Sick with shame and despair, I continued, but more slowly, for aside from the narrowness of the tunnel and the darkness, I was half suffocated by my tears.

In the end, I had to stop and gather myself before I could

go on. The crawl through the network of pipes was such a long, cold, exhausting journey that, by the time I reached its end, sorrow and guilt over Sharna had given way to sheer dogged determination to make use of the chance he had paid for with his life.

My trousers had shredded at the knees and my palms were so raw and painful that I did not even realize I had reached the end until I tumbled out into the soft, cold snow. Gasping, I lay in the drift for a long moment, panting and weeping, but it was too cold to stay there long. My tears were already freezing on my cheeks. I managed to stand and look about, but it was impossible to tell whether it was still night, for there was nothing to see but the blinding white of the flying snow, which was a kind of darkness, too. Squinting, I tried to make out the shape of the silo, but I could not see more than two steps in front of me, and I dared not move away from the wall.

In the end, I had no choice but to climb painfully back into the hated drain, wrap myself in the coat Rushton had given me, and wait until I could see the silo. It was only slightly warmer inside, and because I lay there motionless, the icy cold soon crept into my bones. I thought of the fever I had only just thrown off, and prayed it would not return.

After a long time, the snow seemed to lessen. I still could not see the silo, but made out a shape that seemed to be the back of the milking barn. Far better to be inside it than in the drain, I decided, and I slid out into the snow. My limbs felt stiff and unwieldy, and when I tried to step forward, my legs were so slow to obey me that I fell headlong into the snow. Cursing and weeping with frustration, I gritted my teeth and forced myself to rise again. Then I began to hobble carefully toward the barn. The snow slowed, and for a moment, eerily, the moon reflected on it. Or perhaps it was a veiled sun. I saw then that it was not the milking barn ahead, but another, smaller shed I did not recognize.

It began to snow hard again. I did not change direction, because I knew that I could not be outside for much longer without falling into a deadly lethargy that would have me lie down and die, imagining I was in a warm feather bed. Reaching the shed, I found that snow had blown against it in great drifts. I had stumbled all around it before I realized with despair that the door must be buried in snow.

"Who is there?" called a voice. I staggered in a circle, trying to see who had called out.

"Is someone there?" the voice called again, marginally closer.

"I am here," I called, all at once terrified of being left alone. I saw a flash of light and broke into a shuffling run toward it.

"Who is it?" asked the voice, much closer now. Suddenly a face appeared in front of me out of the swirling whiteness. I knew him. It was an unsmiling Misfit my age named Domick. I had sometimes seen him with Rushton, I remembered, and the thought reassured me.

"Elspeth Gordie?" He held the lantern up to my face. "What are you doing here?"

I stood in the midst of the storm, my mind reeling. What could I say? What possible reason could I have for wandering around on the farms? The silence between us lengthened, and I saw suspicion form on Domick's face.

At last he said, "Well, you had better come back with me. We'll talk where it's warmer."

He struck off to the right, and I followed him closely until we reached a squat, sturdy building I had not seen before.

"What is this place?" I asked through chattering teeth.

Domick bundled me through the door. "The watch-hut," he said shortly, and hustled me across to the fire. He hauled off my snow-crusted coat and threw a thick blanket around my shoulders, then he piled more wood on the fire.

"Are you numb anywhere?" he asked. Wordlessly, I pointed to my feet. He wrestled off my boots, grimacing at the bloody mess of my knees. Both feet were white and bloodless.

"Frostbite," muttered Domick, and he began to rub them vigorously. In a short while, sensation returned with burning, painful clarity. Only when I was writhing with pain did he stop.

"You were lucky. Don't you know anything about frostbite? You could have lost a foot if you'd left them that way," he scolded.

I shuddered.

He gave me a bowl of warm water to bathe my knees and palms, and when I had finished, he pressed a mug full of soup into my hand. Then he fixed me with a disconcerting stare. "Well, what are you doing out here?" he asked.

I sipped at the soup, then looked up at him. "I've run away," I said, for there was no other answer.

He nodded. "How did you get past the maze?"

I sipped again at the drink, trying to think what to say. Though I had seen them together, I couldn't risk giving away Rushton's part in my escape.

"I . . . found some drainpipes that go under the maze," I said at last, lamely.

Suspicion hardened in his face. "I will have to report you," he said coldly. "But there is the storm. I'll lock you in until someone comes from the house."

He put me into a small room and locked the door behind

him. I decided I would stay until the storm abated and Domick slept, then I would open the lock and find my way to the silo. In the meantime, there was a sacking bed in one corner. I climbed onto it gratefully, and not even my fear and despair at all that had happened could keep me awake.

✦ 24 ✦

I slept more deeply than I'd intended, but it was a healing sleep. When I woke, I felt rested and alert, and I lay still, enjoying a feeling of well-being and warmth. Outside I could hear the whirling roar of the wind. The storm had worsened, and though it prevented me from leaving, it might also mean I was safe for the moment.

I heard a knock at the hut's main door and sat up, terrified it was Ariel. Had I slept too long? Perhaps the soup Domick had given me had been laced with sleep potion.

"Who is it?" Domick asked from the other room.

"It's me. Roland," said another voice. I did not know the name. I heard Domick unlatch the door.

"Is Louis here?" asked the newcomer. I crawled out of the bed, crossed quietly to the door, and listened.

"He hasn't come yet," said Domick. "Where is Rushton?"

"He didn't turn up, though I near froze my eyebrows off waiting," said Roland, sounding aggrieved. "Alad says there is some sort of search going on at the house. Guess who has run away now?"

"Elspeth Gordie," Domick said. My heart began to thump wildly. There was a surprised silence.

"How could you know that?" Roland demanded.

"Because she's here," said Domick. "I was out getting wood when I saw her stumbling about like a blind ewe. I locked her in there. She says she came through the drains under the maze, but I don't know how she could know about them."

"She could not have come that way," said Roland. "Alad said Ariel's beasts are out, all around the house."

"From the look of her knees, it is true just the same," said Domick. "You might take a look at them when she wakes. They could use healing."

"We have other concerns," said Roland impatiently. "I want to know what we are to do about the Druid's man. He was supposed to meet with Rushton, but he turns up dead. How are we going to explain that?"

"Rushton will have to tell Henry Druid the truth," said Domick. "The man got himself caught. The question is, did he mention Rushton?"

Roland gave a grunt. "Fortunately, we won't have to explain anything to the Druid until spring, for tonight's snowfall will certainly close off the pass."

"I wish Louis were here," Domick said.

"That old nutter," Roland snapped.

"Well, he was the first to help Rushton," Domick said defensively. "And I know he has spent some time with her." I imagined him gesturing toward my door.

There was another silence.

I debated what to do. It sounded like these two and Louis Larkin were allies of Rushton. But where did the Druid fit in? Was Rushton working for him? He had told me that he had no interest in digging up the past, but Alexi had indicated the Druid was after the same thing he was.

"We ought to look for Rushton," Roland said.

"He said to wait and do nothing," Domick said.

"If Rushton's in trouble, I'm not going to sit back and do nothing."

"We don't even know if he *is* in trouble," Domick insisted.

A log in the fire cracked loudly, and I heard the sound of boots outside. There was a knock, and the outer door opened.

"Louis!" Domick sounded relieved.

"Where's Rushton?" Roland asked swiftly.

"They've taken him prisoner," Louis said in an angry growl. "Alexi and Vega and that demon's whelp, Ariel. They think he helped Elspeth Gordie to escape."

My heart plummeted. Impulsively, I unlocked the door.

For a moment, all was still, like a wax display. Louis, warmly clad with snow melting and dripping in a pool at his feet, and Domick and a man, Roland, near the fire. We all stared at one another, then Domick made a little warding-off movement that unfroze the tableau.

"I locked that," he said faintly.

"You!" Louis said, and to my astonishment, a look of anger filled his face as he stepped threateningly toward me. "You have some explainin' to do!" he growled. "Why do th' Council seek ye?"

"The Council?" Domick echoed.

Louis flicked him a quick quelling glance. "Aye, th' Council. Two Councilmen came up tonight. They have a permit to remove Elspeth Gordie. They said th' Herder Faction wanted to question ye as well."

I felt my face whiten. The Council wanted me, but I dreaded the fanatical Herders, who had burned my parents, far more.

But there was Rushton to think about. "I had a brother. He was involved in some sedition, and they think I can tell them the names of his accomplices," I said, leaving out a world of detail.

Louis squinted his eyes and looked at me skeptically, but I pretended not to see.

"You say they have Rushton? Where?" I asked.

No one answered.

"Look, Rushton *did* help me tonight," I said urgently. "He told me to hide in the silo, but I got lost in the storm."

"Why would he help you?" Roland asked sharply.

I looked at him helplessly, for I did not know that myself.

"She is not important now," said Domick. "We can deal with her later. I don't know how she undid that lock, but I'll tie her up in there and then we can talk."

"No!" I shouted. "Rushton helped me, and now I want to help him."

"Do you know what Rushton is doing here?" Louis asked very carefully.

I hesitated, and then shook my head. "He wouldn't tell me. He said it would put other people in danger. His friends—you, I suppose," I added soberly.

"Where have they got him?" Roland asked Louis.

"Somewhere outside Obernewtyn. It would have to be close," Louis said.

"How could they get outside Obernewtyn in this storm?" Roland demanded. "And why would they bother? They can interrogate him just as well in the doctor's chamber."

His words sparked my memory of the passage concealed behind the doctor's fireplace. Coming from it, Alexi and the others had been outside and they had spoken of the Zebkrahn machine. "I think I know where they have taken him," I said, trying to contain my excitement.

Louis looked at me, his eyes faded with age and watering from the cold but sharp as a knife. "An' where would that be?" he asked noncommittally.

Seeing that I must trust them if I wanted to be trusted, I told them nearly everything I had seen and heard that night in the doctor's chamber. The three men exchanged a long glance, and then Louis said, "Selmar once mentioned something about a track leading from a secret tunnel out of the grounds. The place is fair riddled with tunnels and hidden passages. And maybe it comes out close to a cave or rift where they found this Zebkrahn. The best way to find it would be to start in the doctor's chamber, but the house is in an uproar."

"We have to search outside the grounds for the other end of the passage," Roland said.

But Louis was still looking at me. "Perhaps you can find him," he said quietly.

The other two stared at him in bewilderment.

"You can ask him where he is and what he wants us to do," Louis continued.

My heart skipped a beat at the knowledge in his look. Slowly, I nodded. "It will be better if I can get outside the walls of Obernewtyn first. The closer I am, the better. And I won't be able to do anything until the snowstorm stops."

"My bones tell me that this storm has near worn out its malice. The minute it stops, I will take ye to the farm gate."

Realization dawned on Domick's face. "You . . . you are like Selmar was before," he said.

That was something I had not guessed, and it made what had been done to her even more of a tragedy. "I'll help," I said. "But I don't have much courage."

Louis spoke briskly. "There's strong an' weak in th' world. If yer born without courage, ye mun look in yerself an' find it. From what Selmar said, this place is a good step from here, so I'd say it mun be closer to the front gate of Obernewtyn. We'll head that way."

Roland stiffened. "What about the granite outcrops? No one bothers going near them because they are all jagged stone and brambles, but there could easily be a cave in them."

"It is the most likely spot for a cave," Domick agreed.

"Well then," said Louis, looking at me. "We'll start out walking in the direction of the outcrops as ye seek Rushton. I'll show ye when we get outside the gate, and from the sound of things, that won't be long, fer the storm is fading." We all listened a moment, and it was true that it was growing quieter.

"This is it, then, isn't it?" Domick said, bright spots of color in his cheeks. He grabbed his coat, then he handed me the one Rushton had given me.

Roland pulled on his own coat and said to Domick, "You get the swords and arrows from the weapons cache, and I will call the others together. Then we will come after you two." He nodded to Louis.

"Let's gan," Louis said to me, and hauled open the door. A few flakes of snow whirled in on the icy air, but the night was again still, the land glowing white and the sky black. We parted from the other two without any more words, and Louis took the lead, walking swiftly and unerringly over what the snow made a trackless, featureless terrain that went as far as my eyes could see. After some time, I saw the wall looming up in the bleakness, a gray band between the black sky and the white ground. As we walked along it, I asked him how he had known about me.

He glanced back. "Selmar told me just before she tried to escape fer th' last time. Most of her was long ago lost, but there were moments when she came to herself. She said you were like her, but stronger. She dreamed that you were coming, and that your coming would change everything."

I did not know what to say to that.

Louis stopped when we reached the farm gate. He unlocked

it with a key, and after we had gone through, he locked it from the other side. Then he looked at me expectantly. Knowing what he wanted, and feeling strangely self-conscious, I was about to farseek when I remembered what had happened the last time I had loosed my mind on the farms. The Zebkrahn machine had caught hold of me. On the other hand, if it was being used to interrogate Rushton, surely it could not also be able to entrap roaming minds. I shrugged, knowing I had no real choice but to try. I sent my mind out, but after a time, I breathed a sigh.

"I can't feel him. But maybe the cave wall is blocking me. I have to get closer."

Louis led me along a snowy track that followed the outside of the wall. After some time, he stopped and pointed. I saw the dim outline of several high stone mounds, gray against a slightly lighter sky. I tried again to farseek Rushton, and this time I felt something. The old man saw the look on my face and leaned forward eagerly.

"It was just the merest flicker, but I think the others were right. I think he's there. I need to go closer."

Louis nodded, then his face fell and he cursed. "I am a blatherin' fool! I locked the gate without thinking, an' th' others will not be able to come after us."

"Go back then," I urged. "I can see the outcrops now, so I don't need any guiding."

"I will, but ye be careful, lass. Find him, but dinna go close enough to be caught," Louis warned. "We'll need ye to guide us."

"You be careful, too," I said.

Louis nodded, and without ceremony turned to hurry back along the wall.

✦ 25 ✦

I woke to the dense whiteness of a blinding snowstorm. The events before my fall were tumbled together in a wild kaleidoscopic dream. The last thing I remembered clearly was that I had been walking toward the granite outcrops as the snow fell more and more thickly, until all at once I could see nothing at all. Then I was running. And now here I was, lying in a deep ditch, my head aching and a numbness creeping over my limbs.

I forced myself to sit up, and all at once I remembered what had made me run. I had seen the glimmer of eyes, and the memory of what Ariel's wolves had done to Sharna had sent me into a headlong, mindless flight. That was when I had fallen.

I climbed out of the ditch as carefully as I could for the sake of my aching head, only belatedly realizing that I might have crawled into the mouth of the very wolf that had sent me hurtling into the ditch in the first place. Fortunately, there was no wolf in sight. Brushing off the snow and stamping my feet hard, I looked around and wondered how long I had been unconscious. The fact that I had not frozen suggested it could not have been long. Then I thought of Rushton, and a sense of urgency filled me.

I heard a noise behind me and turned to find myself

looking into a pair of gleaming yellow eyes. I would have run, but terror drained the strength from my legs.

Then a familiar voice spoke inside my mind.

"Greetings, ElspethInnle."

"Maruman?" I whispered incredulously.

"It is I," he answered.

I burst out laughing, half in relief and half in hysteria.

"You fell," Maruman observed disapprovingly as he came closer.

I felt the laughter rise again but fought it down. "How on earth did you get here?" I asked.

"You did not come, so I/Maruman came," he sent. He sounded offended, but there was no time to soothe him.

"I could not come to you," I told him. "I have been a captive until this very day. But now I have escaped, and I have to help a friend who is in trouble."

He mulled that over for a moment, then sent in a less haughty tone, "This night I came over the poisoned snowy ground in the wheeled creature drawn by the equines. Funaga rode within. I came because I saw that your nameshape was in their thoughts. But when the horses stopped, I could not sense you anywhere. I slunk into the house, and then I slept and dreamed of you."

"You were clever to find me," I sent quickly. "But there is no time for mindspeak."

"Your friend?" Maruman inquired with pointed politeness.

"He helped me; now I must help him," I sent.

Maruman's thoughts showed he approved of that, at least. "Where is Innle friend?" he asked.

I explained that I did not know exactly where Rushton was. "He's in a cave nearby. I was walking to the mounds of stone, but I fell and now I don't know where I am."

"I will lead you to the mounds of stone," Maruman told me.

I told him cautiously that I thought it would be better if he stayed behind and waited for me, but he fixed me with a penetrating look.

"Innle must seek the darkness, and I/Maruman must go with her to watch the moon." I shivered and felt a mad impulse to forget everything and flee as fast as I could from the mountains and from all of the dangers and mysteries that lay within them.

But then I thought of Rushton and his cool green eyes, and knew there was a debt I must pay.

"Come then," I sent. "But we have to move quickly. I have wasted too much time here."

I had run right by the mounds of stone, as it transpired, and as we retraced my steps, Maruman proved to be an expert guide. Twice he prevented me from stumbling into holes filled with snow. Another time he stopped me from walking onto wafer-thin ice covering a frozen pool of water and camouflaged by a dusting of snow.

So when he stopped just ahead of me, fur fluffed, I froze immediately.

"What is it?" I asked.

He told me that his nose had caught the faint spoor of wolf. I picked up a stout stick before we continued, but saw almost immediately the large humped shapes of granite.

"That is where we will find my friend," I told Maruman.

Given my delays, I had no idea if Louis Larkin and the others had already come and gone, but I did not want to risk using the energy it would require to perform an open farsensing so close to the Zebkrahn machine. First I needed to locate Rushton, and a mental probe shaped to find him would use far less energy. I waited until we reached the bramble-covered rocks that formed a spiky barrier around the mounded stone humps, then I closed my eyes and loosed my mind. I strove about the granite hillocks and several times felt something, but the contact was too slight for me to know if it was Rushton.

"There is danger here," Maruman observed. Then he gave a low, eerie call, and his spine twitched convulsively. "Forever and forever is pain . . . ," he yowled, his eyes whirling.

"Please, not now," I begged. But it was a useless plea, for Maruman's fits were not his to control.

"Here is darkness, ElspethInnle, but it is not the same darkness you must seek out and end." He was trembling from head to toe now and I longed to gather him in my arms, but I knew from experience that he would attack me tooth and claw if I did.

I stared at him, wondering how I could look after Maruman and search for Rushton at the same time.

"The flies!" Maruman shrieked suddenly into my mind, then he swooned sideways and lay still. It was almost a relief to be able to wrap his limp form up in my coat. I laid him in a small hollow in a rock, fairly sure he would not wake until I returned. Then I clambered as fast as I could over the bramble-covered rocks, toward the larger hillocks in their midst.

Five minutes later, I was in a narrow flat space between the prickly scree and the mounds of stone. Almost at once, I found the entrance to a cave, though I saw no sign of any tunnel leading back to Obernewtyn.

✦ 26 ✦

THE CAVE ENTRANCE was hidden behind a rockfall. Its placement was too convenient, concealing the cave perfectly without blocking it off. I had no doubt that it had been purposefully placed, though only the machines of the Beforetimers could have shifted such weight.

Up close, I realized that the rockfall and the hillock itself were not true granite at all but some kind of smooth, hard stone the likes of which I had never seen.

I entered the cave and found that it was a tunnel burrowing into the largest of the mounds. I could see light ahead and approached with trepidation, but it was only a great shimmering cluster of insects gathered on a damp patch of rock. The light they gave out revealed the tunnel for some distance, and then I found a lantern hanging from a peg of wood that had been driven into a crack in the wall. It was the first certain proof that someone was using the cavern.

I continued, moving as swiftly as I could without making any noise, and keeping close to the walls. All at once, the walls and ceiling went from being something like raw stone to being smooth and perfectly squared, as if a stonemason had dressed and polished them. This and the machine Alexi had spoken of indicated that I was inside a Beforetime building—or what remained of one.

I passed another lantern and tried again to farseek Rushton. Now that I was within the mound of stone there was less interference, and for a moment I sensed him clearly.

He was in pain.

The tunnel began to slope down slightly, and here and there the smooth surface was broken. In one place, a thick pool of multicolored ooze was coming from a crack running up the wall. I kept well away from the slimy mess in case it was tainted. The tunnel curved, and I blinked at the flood of light ahead. Soon, the path swelled out and curved into an enormous, brightly lit cavern. The light came not from lanterns but from a round white sphere on top of a pole. It hummed faintly, and my skin rose into gooseflesh because this was a Beforetime artifact that *someone had brought to life*.

There was no one in sight. Entering the chamber warily, I saw that all around were silvery boxes of varying sizes, many higher than my head. Buttons and gleaming jewel-colored lights covered the surfaces of what must surely have been Beforetime machines. One had been forced away from the wall. It was very large, with a flat extension coming out one side and many thin colored strands running hither and thither. I wondered if this was the Zebkrahn machine. But if so, where was Alexi? Or Rushton? I looked closely at the machine, but I could not tell whether it was operating.

There were three open doorways in addition to the one I had come through. One way was smooth and perfectly shaped, but the other two were cracked and crumbling, both angling down. Hearing nothing when I listened at each of them, I decided to go through the undamaged doorway. The path leading from it was dark, for no lantern had been left hanging and there were none of the shining insects. I was on the verge of turning back when I thought I heard a voice ahead. Then a little farther on and around a corner I saw light again. It was another lantern hanging in an alcove, but as I reached for it I stifled a cry of fright and staggered back, for two eyes flared at me.

It took me a long moment to take in that the eyes did not move or glisten. My heart was still pounding as I went closer and took the lantern. I saw then that the eyes belonged to a stuffed Guanette bird mounted on a shelf of stone. Even in death, the massive bird's bright, round eyes seemed penetrating, and I wondered in disgust who would kill and stuff something so rare and lovely.

I heard a sound behind me and whirled, but I could see nothing. I went across to another alcove, where there was a bed set again the wall. Then I saw a movement and realized with a shock that it was occupied. "Rushton?" I whispered.

The person lying on the bed stirred and turned toward me. To my astonishment, I saw that it was Cameo!

The light bathed her face as I approached, and her skin glowed marble white so that the blackness under her eyes looked like crescents of ink. Her eyes flickered open. "Elf?" she murmured, but vaguely. It was strange and terrible to hear her using Jes's nickname for me, but I reached out and touched her face. She frowned and said more strongly, "Elspeth?"

"I'm here," I whispered.

Consternation crossed her features, bringing them to life. "No! You mustn't be here. He . . . he wants you. I heard him say it. You must go now."

"Don't talk," I begged.

She fell back and closed her eyes. "I knew you would come," she whispered.

But too late, I thought to myself.

"Not too late!" she protested, and I gasped, for she had

read my thought. Then I saw that she had heard my realization as well, for she said, "I don't know why, but somehow the pain made me . . . able to hear better. But I still couldn't do what they wanted. I'm not strong enough. But while they used their machines, I had a true dream. I dreamed there is something you have to do. You alone. I dreamed it was more important than anything else in the world. It has something to do with this place and with the map that Alexi seeks. The map that . . . shows the way to a terrible power. . . . He does not realize how terrible it is, and it would not stop him if he did know."

"A . . . terrible power?" I echoed, thinking of all the nightmarish stories I had heard of the capacity of the Beforetimers for violence and destruction.

"Worse," Cameo whispered. "Worse than you can possibly imagine. The map shows the way to the very machines that caused the Great White."

"No!" I gasped.

Her eyes fluttered, and I saw the effort it took for her to go on. "You have to stop them from finding the machines, Elspeth. You have to find them first and make sure no one can ever use them." The veins in her neck stood out like cords.

"I can't do that," I said, my mind whirling.

"You can, for you are the Seeker," she said.

"Please," I rasped, and discovered that tears were running down my face. For Cameo was dying. *It is my fault*, I thought. All along it was me they really wanted.

"You came," she whispered.

I fell to my knees by her bed and cried while she stroked my hair with a hand no heavier than a breath of air. Then her hand was still.

I wept bitter tears until a laugh echoed down the passages

and penetrated the fog of sorrow that had enveloped me. I stood up. I knew that laugh, and it dried all the tears and sorrow in me, leaving a rime of brittle determination. I set off down a hallway that led deeper into the structure, vowing that Ariel and the others would pay for what they had done to Cameo.

When I got closer to the source of his laughter, I saw there was light ahead. I extinguished my lantern and set it down before continuing.

I had been creeping along for several minutes when Madam Vega suddenly spoke, so near that it sent ice sifting over my skin. I inched forward until I could see into another room, and listened hard.

"You are collaborating with the Druid, aren't you?" Madam Vega asked. "You need not answer. What the Druid's man told us reveals that much. Did you really suppose we would allow you to come in and take what we have schemed and killed to gain? I suppose the old man promised to help you take Obernewtyn for yourself, if only to rid himself of us? As if he has the power for anything but skulking in the wilderness."

"The Council does not allow a defective to inherit, but it will allow a bastard son to do so," said Rushton.

My heart leapt at hearing him speak. I regretted that I had not tried to farseek Louis before I had entered the stone hillock, for I had clearly arrived before him. I decided to go back outside to wait for the others, but Madam Vega's next words froze me in my tracks.

"There is no proof that you are Michael Seraphim's illegitimate son," she said in an amused tone. "Your mother could easily have lied."

"There are my father's letters to her, and my appearance," Rushton said. "When my mother sent me here, she thought my father still lived. She thought he would see himself in my face, and so she gave me no letter or token to show the man she sent me to find. Nor did she tell me that he was my father."

"Too bad Michael Seraphim was dead before you arrived," Madam Vega sneered.

I had listened to what they were saying with growing amazement. That Rushton was Michael Seraphim's illegitimate son would explain much, but would he really ally himself with Henry Druid in order to make a claim for Obernewtyn?

"I will enjoy killing you," Madam Vega said softly when Rushton made no response. "As long as you were ignorant of your true status, it amused me to let you live. Even to indulge you. But you have proven troublesome and ungrateful. Now, there are a few questions I want answered."

"I will tell you nothing," Rushton grated.

There was the sound of a sharp blow.

"Have some respect," Ariel said silkily.

Creeping around a bank of machines, I saw Madam Vega, Ariel, and what looked to be the tip of Rushton's boot. He was lying on a metal tray before an immense machine, and my heart seized at the sight. *This* must be the Zebkrahn machine, I realized.

I was just summoning up a probe to reach out to Rushton when a voice spoke behind me, soft with menace.

"How obliging of you to come to us," murmured Alexi. Then something heavy crashed into the base of my skull, and a wave of blackness filled my mind.

Alexi and Madam Vega were talking when I woke. I was lying down and bound hand, foot, and throat. I kept my eyes closed and listened.

"Why did you have to hit her so hard?" the woman complained. "You could have killed her!"

"She will not die," Alexi said dismissively.

"What about *him*, then?" Ariel said. "He fainted, and you said he wouldn't. Now we'll have to wait till he wakes to finish questioning him."

"I'm not interested in him any longer," Alexi said coldly. "We have the girl."

"Nevertheless, I want to know how they are connected," said Madam Vega. "Rushton accepted pain rather than revealing the whereabouts of this girl, and it is obvious now that he *did* help her to escape."

"We will ask the girl," Alexi said after a thoughtful pause. "She will respond swiftly enough after we threaten him, if they are allies."

"He'll talk if we use her as a lever," Ariel said eagerly. "You should have seen his face when we came to that mess the wolves had made in the courtyard. At first, we thought it was her that had been torn apart. Rushton seemed to go mad. That's why I had to shoot him."

"I'm not interested in this," Alexi snapped. "I want that map."

"We will have it soon," Madam Vega said soothingly. "The girl will locate it for us. And what power we will have over the Council once we have Beforetime weaponmachines. They will refuse us nothing. And if they displease us, we will give them a demonstration."

I felt a caress on my face and opened my eyes.

"Awake . . . ," purred Alexi, his face close to mine, his eyes dark. I shuddered as far away from him as my bindings would allow, and he laughed wildly until Madam Vega took his hand and bade him calm himself.

"We don't want to make any mistakes. We cannot afford another Selmar."

"I will get the diaries," Alexi said, ignoring her admonition. He turned, addressing Ariel as he left. "She is sweating. That might affect the machine. Clean her."

"I am not his servant," Ariel hissed.

"Be silent and do as you were bidden," Madam Vega snapped.

Sullenly, Ariel wiped my face with a cool cloth. "Crazy as a loon, he is. Lud, but he's creepy with those monster eyes," he muttered under his breath.

"You forget yourself, Ariel," Madam Vega said. "Without Alexi, all of my plans will come to nothing. Only he understands these infernal machines. Now come with me."

I heard their voices receding in the distance and bitterly cursed my carelessness. I had practically given myself as a gift to them. And they meant to use me to find the weapon-machines that caused the Great White. Would it be any use to tell them what Cameo had said? I could not think so, remembering the relish in Madam Vega's voice when she had spoken of giving a demonstration of power to the Council. I knew I must not help them to find Marisa's map or I would be directly responsible for unleashing the horrors of the Great White on the world again. Bleakly, I prayed for the courage to keep silent, but the thought of being tortured terrified me.

I heard a groan and knew it meant Rushton was waking up. I decided I must tell him that his friends were searching for him, and that they had a good idea of his location. Now that I looked about me, I saw that I was strapped to the extended table of the machine I had seen earlier. I could not turn my head far because of the binding about my throat, but I could see a hand tied to a chair. It moved, straining against the bindings.

"Rushton?" I whispered.

"Elspeth?" he croaked. "I thought you were dead."

"It was Sharna the wolves killed," I said with a stab of renewed grief.

"I thought they had torn you apart," Rushton said again. "I wanted to kill Ariel. Instead, he shot me with a bolt from his crossbow." He stifled a groan, and I saw that he was again straining against his bonds.

"Rushton, I need to tell you . . ." I broke off, hearing the approach of footsteps. It was Alexi, and Madam Vega returned with Ariel a moment later. Among them, they had brought scrolled papers and maps and parchments, as well as several fat, battered-looking books.

"We will begin with the diaries," Alexi announced, taking one of the books and staring down into my eyes. "I wish you to use your Misfit abilities to learn where Marisa hid a map she made. I know you have the power to hear the thoughts she had when she scribed her notes. If you cooperate, I will not need to use the Zebkrahn."

"You will kill me, whatever happens," I said, thinking I had to give Louis and the others time to find us.

"You will tell me!" Alexi raged. He turned to the machine, and Vega hovered behind him with anxious eyes.

"Be careful, Alexi," she warned.

"I will teach her not to defy me," he snarled. He did something to the buttons, and several colored lights began to pulsate. The machine hummed very faintly, and Alexi took up a bowl-shaped helmet and fitted it over my head, his strange black eyes burning down at me.

All at once, I felt a faint buzzing in my head. It was only

slightly distracting, and my spirits lifted. If this was the extent of their torture, the secret of the map's whereabouts would be safe with me. I wondered suddenly if Marisa had even known the terrible capability of the weaponmachines she had located. I remembered that cold, enigmatic face in the portrait and thought it must be so.

"Even if you find what you want, the Council will not let you rule them," Rushton said.

"He's just trying to get you mad," Ariel sneered.

Alexi turned his hot, mad gaze on Ariel, who visibly quailed. "I'll kill you if you say anything else that annoys me," the man hissed.

"Concentrate on the girl," snapped Madam Vega, giving Ariel a warning look. Alexi came back to the machine and turned a knob, and the buzzing in my head increased sharply. The sensation was still a long way from being painful, yet I thought uneasily of Cameo and Selmar. Selmar, who had been more like me than I could have guessed. Was it this machine that had broken her mind?

Alexi took the diary, opened it, and held it in front of my eyes. I tried not to look at the crabbed scribing, which I recognized from the maps and books in the doctor's chamber, but the nearness of the diary was such that I could hear the faintest whisper of the woman's thoughts. I strengthened my shield.

"I have dreamed of the power that will come to me," Alexi said. "It is my destiny, and Marisa had no right to keep it from me." He moved a lever on the machine, and the buzzing increased. It was uncomfortable enough to begin eroding the solidity of my shield. Again I heard the whisper of Marisa's thoughts rising from the diary like a scent. Complex calculations. The desire for a certain book. An unkind thought about her baby son, whom she suspected of being dull-witted. Irritation with her husband.

"Open your mind to her," Alexi commanded, and again the buzzing increased. Now there was pain. I could tolerate it, but there would be more, I knew, and worse. What if I could not hold out?

Fear made me grope for Rushton's mind. If I could just speak with him, I might find courage enough to endure.

"Think of Marisa," Alexi commanded.

My mental probe found Rushton's mind, but it was blocked. I despaired for a moment, but then I realized that his mind was not consciously shielded. Nor had he a natural block. The barrier I encountered was unlike any I had felt. It was like a thick wall of cloud or mist. I gathered my strength and arrowed my way through it into his mind. Distantly I heard him moan.

"What is the matter with him?" Vega asked.

"He's fainted again," Ariel said contemptuously.

But he was wrong. Rushton had retreated into his thoughts to deal with my intrusion. Quickly I identified myself.

"It was *you*." I heard Rushton's thought and, with astonishment, recognized the mind of my rescuer. At least, his mind seemed part of the entity that had helped me get free from the Zebkrahn once before. But I could tell he had no Misfit ability.

Seeming to guess my puzzlement, Rushton explained. "There are many among my friends who have mental abilities like yours, and though none are as powerful as you, they are able to combine their strength. Somehow they use my mind to focus their energies, and carry me with them. If I had succeeded in making my claim on Obernewtyn, I would have made it a refuge for them."

I told Rushton he must not give up, for his friends were on their way with help.

"My friends?" he echoed.

Swiftly I shared with him everything that had happened since we parted last. It took but a moment, because I used mental pictures rather than words. I read in his mind that he was unaware that the weaponmachines sought by Alexi and the others were those that had caused the Great White. I chose not to burden him with the knowledge, though he asked if I could do what Alexi wanted.

Before I could answer, the effect of the Zebkrahn increased dramatically. I tried to withdraw from Rushton's mind, but he held me.

"Let me go!" I begged. It would have been easy enough to tear free, but he would be hurt.

"I can help you endure," he said. "Draw on me." I warned him that he would share my pain if I stayed inside his mind, but he insisted. "If you give them what they want, they will kill us both anyway, so I help myself in helping you."

"This is taking too long," I heard Ariel say impatiently. He reached up to adjust the machine, but this time there was no increase in the pain. Had the machine reached its limit? I prayed so, for on the other side of my mental barrier, I could sense Marisa's thoughts clamoring.

"Don't be afraid," Rushton told me. Then I heard him moan and realized with horror that he was shielding me from the worst of the pain. I did not know how it was possible, and yet he was doing it.

"What is wrong with him?" Vega snapped.

Alexi sprang forward and looked into my face. "He's helping her!" he screamed. "Kill him, Vega."

"No!" I cried.

His brows drew together in triumph. "Tell me where the map is or I will kill him," he whispered. I wrenched my mind from Rushton's with a scream.

"Vega, get a knife," Alexi instructed. He looked back at me. "Tell me or he will die."

"Elspeth!" Rushton shouted.

In that moment, the block that separated me from Marisa's thoughts was as thin as a web. I saw right through it and knew where the map was. It was hidden in plain sight, carved into the front doors of Obernewtyn. Then, as my mind began to buckle under the assault of the machine, I saw a vision of a dark chasm in the ground from which rose a thick brownish smoke, and I knew I was seeing the very place indicated on Marisa's map.

Terrified at what else I would see, I found the strength to block the vision and push Marisa from me.

"Very well, kill him," Alexi snarled.

I threw back my head and saw Madam Vega's hand raise the knife. "No!" I begged.

"Tell me," Alexi whispered.

"We come," said an unknown voice in my mind. Startled, I realized Rushton's friends must be within the stone hillock.

"Tell me!" Alexi shouted.

I hesitated. I could not tell him where the map was. That was too high a price for either my life or Rushton's.

Alexi's eyes narrowed, seeming to divine my thought. "All right. Do it."

Madam Vega lifted her arm slowly.

I heard running footsteps, and at the same time, the machine seemed to be overheating. There was the sound of an explosion, and a shower of sparks fell on my boot and onto my bare and grazed knees. I jerked and kicked as best I could.

Vega's hand paused before the downward blow. She looked at Alexi, and he nodded.

There was a terrible pain in my legs and feet, and I could smell smoke.

Then something inside my head crackled violently; a power stirred in me completely unlike any other ability I possessed. All at once, I knew that Rosamunde had spoken the truth: Jes had killed that soldierguard, *and I knew how.*

Whatever I had roused came from the deepest void of my mind, like a serpent uncoiling to strike. I felt a sense of exaltation at the knowledge that I could control such a terrible power. Madam Vega drove the knife downward, but I struck first, swatting her hand away and plowing a terrible furrow through her mind. She screamed horribly.

I felt flames burning my legs and feet. The smell reminded me of the day my mother and father died.

Dimly, I saw people running and shouting.

"Is she alive?" asked a voice I knew but could not recognize.

Am I? I wondered, and a dark wind swept me away.

✦ 27 ✦

"Yer nowt well enough!" Matthew said stubbornly. The look on his face told me what I already knew. I looked haggard even after all this time.

"It might be better . . . ," Dameon said diplomatically, but I would not let him finish.

"Stay here and miss this mysterious meeting? Not on your life," I said. I sat back after that outburst, feeling the now-familiar weakness roll over me. It was still incredible to think the machine had taken so much from me. That, and unleashing the strange power I had tapped in myself. I had been unconscious for days after.

"Ye look different," Matthew said. And I felt different, stronger somehow, despite my physical weakness and the scars. Even now I could feel the tingle in the depth of my mind that told me the power was there, waiting.

"So *you* would be different if some machine had been inside your head," I snapped.

He grinned.

"Where is Rushton?" I asked casually.

Matthew looked quickly at Dameon, but the empath's face remained as inscrutable as ever. I felt a stirring of resentment that Rushton had not come by to visit. Matthew had told me that Louis and the others had freed Rushton and he had beaten and smothered the flames that had engulfed my lower legs. Both Alexi and Madam Vega were dead—Alexi with an arrow to the heart and Vega without a mark on her. Louis guessed she had fallen and hit her head in the commotion. Ariel had fled, and had surely perished in the savage blizzard that had come that night.

It was known now by all those who dwelt at Obernewtyn that Rushton was its legal master and that the mysterious doctor was his defective half brother. None doubted the claim, and the new Master of Obernewtyn spoke openly of taking it to the Councilcourt to have the matter formally recognized.

I was amazed at how many different varieties of mental prowess there were among the Misfits at Obernewtyn, and at the fact that I had never realized it. But, of course, I had kept my mind tightly leashed after my first encounter with the Zebkrahn machine. And most of the Misfits had minimal abilities; Roland, Domick, and a few others were the exception. But type and strength of ability did not matter to Rushton, who had none save the curious ability to host a merge of minds. In a way, it seemed to me that his desire to turn Obernewtyn into a refuge echoed this ability. The meeting I wanted to attend was meant to outline his plans in detail.

Matthew and Dameon felt I was not fit enough to attend. I insisted that the numbness and pain in my mind had gone, but I was still very weak and the burns on my feet and legs were yet to heal fully. Rushton had left word that I was not to get up until I was completely recovered. And still he had not come to see me.

"He's the master here now," Matthew said, as if answering my thought.

"No doubt he is too busy to tell me himself that I must not come to his meeting," I said. I had meant to say it lightly, but

I heard a flash of anger in my voice and realized that I only wanted to go because Rushton wanted to stop me.

Dameon said gently, "He *did* come to see you several times, Elspeth. But you were always asleep, and he would not let us wake you."

"Of course," I said as casually as possible, ashamed to think he was privy to my pettiness when we all knew how busy Rushton was. And after all, Rushton did not know I had stopped Vega from killing him. In truth, I did not want anyone to know that. The fact that I had the capacity to kill with my mind was hardly likely to endear me to anyone.

"We've decided we're going to stay," Matthew said. "Rushton's going to make Obernewtyn a secret refuge for people like us. He has plans."

"I know that." I snapped. Dameon was staring at me with an odd expression on his face, and I felt a blush rise to my cheeks at the thought that he was sensing the muddled roil of my emotions.

"What about Henry Druid? Does he have a role in this great plan?" I asked. Rushton had met the renegade Herder several years before, when he had stumbled into his camp, on his way to Obernewtyn at the request of his dead mother. Instead of being killed or made prisoner, Rushton had been allowed to go free, on the condition that he aided the old man in acquiring some of the forbidden Beforetime books said to be hidden at Obernewtyn.

Once Rushton arrived at the mountain valley, he learned that Michael Seraphim had died. Still puzzled as to why his mother had insisted on him bringing news of her death to a stranger, he had accepted Madam Vega's offer of employment as overseer with the aim of finding out more about Michael Seraphim. Alexi had guessed the truth the moment he saw

Rushton, and they meant to keep him close in case the truth about Stephen Seraphim was ever revealed. Madam Vega had done her best to ingratiate herself with him, though she had not told him the truth about his father. It was Louis Larkin who had done that. Rushton had stayed on, hoping to meet his half brother, who was kept mysteriously out of sight. Finally, he had discovered the truth and knew that he had a legitimate claim to Obernewtyn.

But by now he had developed an alliance with Domick and Roland and other Misfits with forbidden abilities, and he had conceived of turning Obernewtyn into a secret refuge. So he had to be very careful about how he established his claim. He must control the process. He also needed to resolve his bargain with Henry Druid. He did not want to find himself at odds with the old man, so he had decided to provide him with several valuable books from the library before severing contact.

But would that satisfy the former Herder? If he was as voracious about forbidden knowledge as he sounded, he would not easily give up his search for weapon-machines. My thoughts shifted to the magnificent carvings on the doors to Obernewtyn. It was a great pity to destroy such craftsmanship, but I could see no other way to get rid of the map they concealed.

"What about the doctor?" I asked.

"I don't think Rushton is quite sure what to do with him," Dameon said in an amused voice. "He really is rather harmless. It turns out he was using garbled herb lore on the people he treated, and the worst he would have done is give someone a bad bellyache. Roland is trying to teach him some real herb lore, but the doctor is slow and Roland is so impatient."

Looking at my friends, I thought this business had wrought a change in them, too. Dameon seemed quieter and older, while Matthew carried the scar left by Cameo's death in the sadness I sometimes saw in his face. Yet they were more certain of themselves, more purposeful. Perhaps because Rushton had offered them a place in his world.

I found myself yawning and knew I did not really want to go to the meeting. I grinned at their relief when I said so.

"Will you stay?" Dameon asked.

"It will be some time before I can think of leaving," I said, sidestepping the question.

Dameon did not press me. In truth, I did not know what I would do. I did not think I would stay at Obernewtyn, for I had a yearning to travel, to see the great sea and the western coast. But it would be as difficult as ever to move from place to place in the Land, even if Rushton provided me with a Normalcy Certificate, as he had promised any of us who wished to leave the mountains.

"Ye mun stay!" Matthew cried, looking disappointed. "Rushton said you're stronger than all of us. He has the notion of starting his own council!"

Dameon nodded, sensing my curiosity and incredulity. "He wants to govern Obernewtyn with the help and advice of a council elected from our ranks. He wants us to work at our abilities and to train others to be better at what we do."

"He wants us to form groups, guilds organized by special abilities," Matthew added.

"And this council will be a sort of guild merge," I quipped.

Dameon's mouth twitched. "A good name. I will suggest it," he said.

I laughed. Then another question occurred to me.

"Speaking of councils, what happened to those Councilmen and the soldierguards that came up here?" To my surprise, Matthew only laughed.

"*There's* a story," he said with a twinkle in his eyes.

"Madam Vega made the mistake of leaving the Councilmen to Ariel's tender mercies. He fed them drugged wine and threw them in one of the underground storage chambers."

I gaped.

"By the time they were discovered, it was all over. Rushton got them out and told them what had happened—with a few omissions."

"A few omissions!" I gasped.

Matthew grinned widely, enjoying his audience. "He told them Madam Vega and Alexi had been plotting against the Council, and that they had organized to have the Councilmen knocked out and murdered in case they found out that Stephen Seraphim was defective and their prisoner."

"And they believed him?" I asked.

"With a little empathy," Dameon said with a sly, slow smile.

"Rushton gave them the impression the whole revolt had been meant to free them," Matthew continued. "They were sick to their stomachs from th' stuff Ariel had given them, and they were only too happy to believe anything they were told by the man who rescued them. Those with empath abilities have been preparing them to rush back to Sutrium after the thaw, and ye can be sure Rushton will have no trouble getting his claim accepted after they prepare the way."

I laughed aloud at the thought of the self-important Councilmen thrown into a storage cupboard. Then I sobered. "What about me?"

"What about you?" Matthew inquired pertly. "You're dead. You ran away during the battle and were almost certainly tragically devoured by wild wolves."

Domick poked his head around the door. "Rushton's coming up."

Dameon and Matthew moved to depart.

"Wait. Don't . . ." *Don't what?* I wondered. *Don't leave me alone with the person who risked his life to help me?* I shook my head at the absurdity, and they went.

Rushton seemed too tall in the turret room that had once been his own chamber. There were faint shadows under his green eyes that told of the long hours he had been spending at reorganizing Obernewtyn, but he looked remarkably content.

"I heard you want to come to the meeting," he said.

I shrugged. "Not really. It was a whim. I hear you have plans," I said.

He didn't seem to hear me. "I feared you would die or wake up senseless like Selmar."

I shrugged again, embarrassed at his intensity. "Well, I didn't," I said with some asperity. "I never thanked you for helping me with the machine that time."

He shrugged. "Will you stay?" he asked, rather as Dameon had done.

"I don't know," I said.

"Did they tell you my idea about the guilds? You could stay and help set it up," he offered diffidently.

"What guild would I belong to?" I asked, striving for a lightness I could not seem to feel.

"Choose whichever pleases you. You seem to have every ability save empathy." He smiled. "You are the strongest Misfit here by far, but we're going to bring others up here, too, you know. In secret. You could help to train them. And when we're strong enough, we will force the Council to accept Misfits." He paused. "Stay," he said again when I did not answer.

"I'll stay for a while," I said at last.

"That will do to start," he said cryptically. He glanced

228

through the unshuttered window at the pale wintertime sky. "It will not be easy, I know, to do what I want. But one day, Obernewtyn will be a force in this Land. I will see to that." He smiled down at me, and there was a fierce pride in his face that made it strangely beautiful.

He would be a good leader, I thought after he had gone. Guilds or not, he would remain the Master of Obernewtyn. There was a quality in him that inspired trust and a kind of love. He was born to lead.

People like Rushton never thought much about the past, I thought. It made them impatient. It was left to those like me to remember the past—and doubt.

Deep within, I felt again the tingle of the power I had wakened. Such power must have a purpose. I remembered my vision of a dark, smoke-filled chasm. I would destroy the map Marisa Seraphim had left showing its whereabouts, but the chasm would remain, as would whatever documents Marisa had used to create her map. Sooner or later, someone would find the chasm. Unless I found it first.

"The Seeker," Cameo had called me. Strangely, the name Maruman and Sharna had called me meant exactly that. Perhaps it was my destiny to find the weaponmachines and somehow disarm them. The thought lay in my mind, and all the restlessness in me seemed to flow toward it. A vague idea became resolve. One day, I would seek the chasm I had seen, and I would find a way to prevent the weaponmachines within from being used.

Cameo had believed I was important—that I had something important to do in the world—and so had Maruman and Sharna. What could be more important than making sure the Great White could never come again?

The Farseekers

for Shane

PART I

✦

REFUGE

✦ 1 ✦

ROLAND SHOOK HIS head decisively. "I can do nothing to hasten the healing, Elspeth. If you rested them more often . . ."

I sighed and rubbed the tender soles of my feet. "Kella said a warmer climate might help."

Roland nodded absently, returning satchels of herbs to his carryall. "It's true that cold doesn't help the healing process, but whatever miracles we healers can do, changing the weather to suit our patient is not among them."

I was startled at the unexpected touch of humor from the dour Healer guildmaster. Hefting the weighty bag onto his shoulder, Roland gave me a piercing look. "If you would stay in your room in wintertime with banked fires instead of wandering around the drafty halls—and beyond . . ."

"I *am* mistress of a guild," I said.

Roland was unsympathetic. "Garth finds no difficulty in remaining in his caves, and the Teknoguild works do not crumble because of its master's inactivity," he said.

The Teknoguild was concerned with studying the Beforetime and researching the effects—past, present, and future—of the Great White. I had little interest in such things, but I had met secretly with Garth only that morning. I wondered if Roland knew.

"Garth . . . is Garth," I said with a smile. Roland's lip twitched.

There was a knock at the door, and Kella entered, carrying a jug.

Roland waved his ward in impatiently as he addressed me. "Soak in that, then rub some of the salve into the soles. And stay off your feet!" he growled, slamming the door behind him.

Kella poured the liquid in a flat pan, smiling ruefully. "He's angry with himself, because your feet aren't healing properly."

I lowered my feet gingerly into the shallow pannikin. A sweet scent rose from the water. "Herb lore?" I guessed.

Kella nodded. "A recipe given to us by the Master of Obernewtyn himself."

I smiled, never quite able to accept Rushton's grandiose title. When I had first met him, he was an enigmatic farm overseer only a few years older than myself. No one had been more astonished than I to discover he was the legal owner of Obernewtyn.

Kella was staring into the fire, its orange glow playing over her cheeks. "Rushton has not come back yet from the highlands," she said, a faint line of worry between her brows. I wondered idly if the healer was attracted to Rushton. It would be a pity for her. His brooding singleness of purpose made him blind to anything but his complicated plans for the future. I smiled wryly.

"It's good to see you smile," Kella said. The old fear of revealing myself caused me a moment of panic, then I consciously relaxed. The need for hiding my expressions was past, at least at Obernewtyn.

"Yet there is not much to smile at, even here," I said somberly.

Kella's look sharpened. "You spoke to the newcomers?"

I nodded. "Their news is worrying. When I was in the orphan homes, torture was nothing more than a rumor."

Kella's face was pale. The deliberate infliction of pain was an anathema to any healer, but torture was doubly dreadful, involving as it did both mental and physical pain forged into one. She disliked even the mind-bending activities of the Coercer guild, and this was far worse.

As if reading my thoughts, she said, "Miryum claims there are times when the end justifies the means, but even a coercer could not condone torture."

Tactless Miryum was guilden of the aggressive Coercer guild, whose function was to defend Obernewtyn and prepare for battle with the Council, if it should come to that. There was a growing rift between the Healer and Coercer guilds. The members of each, along with futuretellers, could descend into the unconscious mind—we called it *deep probing*. But no two guilds used the ability to deep-probe in the same manner. The mind of a coercer was a weapon to suborn the will of other minds. By contrast, the healer used a probe, honed tendril-thin, for healing. It was little wonder the two guilds were at loggerheads—they used the same ability to opposing ends.

"Anyone would think you were a futureteller," Kella said resignedly, clearly referring to the habit futuretellers had of drifting into a dream in the middle of conversations.

I laughed. "It might be pleasant. You would never be surprised by anything."

"Not for me," Kella said. "I prefer to live in the present. I don't want to know the future."

Without warning, the door was flung open by a wild-eyed Matthew. Seeing me, his anxious expression dissolved. "Here ye are! I've been searchin' all over·for ye!" he said accusingly.

I blinked at him. "Oh? I must have forgotten to say where I was going."

Kella snorted, knowing I disliked the lack of privacy that went with being a guildmistress and often evaded such formalities as making my whereabouts known.

Forgetting his frustration, Matthew hurried over. "Rushton has just come back! An' he's called a guildmerge."

"When?" I asked.

"Now!" Matthew said.

My heart jumped. Rushton often traveled outside the mountains, for there was no danger to the legal Master of Obernewtyn doing so. But something serious must have happened for him to call a guildmerge so abruptly.

"Did he say why?" I asked. I dried my feet quickly and slipped on my boots.

"Nowt a word," Matthew answered, handing me my walking stick. "He was investigatin' a rumor that th' Council meant to establish a soldierguard camp in th' highlands. Do ye suppose . . . ?" he began, aghast at the thought of a camp so close to Obernewtyn. It had been bad enough when a soldierguard training camp was set up just below the lower ranges. If the Council meant to put a camp in the highlands, it could only be because they intended to tighten their control of the high country.

"It might be no more than gossip," I said.

Ceirwan would know what had happened, since he had gone with Rushton. As guilden of the farseekers, he would normally have reported to me at once, but Rushton's call for an immediate guildmerge had clearly made that impossible.

I wondered if any of the guilds would use the unexpected meeting to make requests. I had had no time to prepare a submission since meeting with Garth, but Pavo would be at the meeting and might fill in the gaps. If Matthew's speculations were right, it was important to act quickly in case Rushton decided to suspend all expeditions.

I shivered as we exited the outer doors of the Healer hall. As ever in the mountains, there was a chilly underbite to the air, and the old burn scars on my feet and lower legs ached. Roland had promised they would heal in time, but two years had passed and they still hurt at the first sign of cold weather.

My eyes went beyond the gray stone walls that surrounded Obernewtyn and its fields and farms to the horizon and the jagged line of the western mountains separating us from the highlands. Those mountains were our best protection, especially if soldierguards did set up camp in the highlands. In winter, snow cut us off from the highlands entirely, and even in the mildest season, the road to Obernewtyn was difficult. The mountains kept us safe, yet the sight of them never failed to disturb me in some deep, incomprehensible way.

Long ago, in one of his queer fits, Maruman had told me my destiny lay in the mountains. Battered and half mad, the old cat had been my first friend and had followed me to Obernewtyn. Expecting a grim existence there, perhaps a horrible death, I had found friends and learned I was not alone in my mutant abilities. Once Rushton had taken control of Obernewtyn from his defective half brother, who had been manipulated by the wicked Alexi and Madam Vega, I had accepted his offer of refuge and stayed on. Alexi and Madam Vega had been killed in their battle to keep control of Obernewtyn, and their young accomplice Ariel had fled to his death in the bitter mountain winter. I could hardly recall

Alexi's face or even Madam Vega's, but Ariel remained a vivid nightmare image. Of them all, he had left an impression, for his cruelty and his manipulative lust for power, hidden behind his angelic beauty, were evidence that evil might wear its own face.

To my surprise, I had been happy at Obernewtyn. Apart from his periodic wandering, Maruman also made Obernewtyn his home.

Yet I had the sudden chill premonition that the long time of healing and peace was drawing to an end.

"What is it?" Matthew asked.

"I was thinking of the past," I said. "Everything that happened in the caves with Alexi and Madam Vega, the Zebkrahn machine exploding, these . . ." I touched my scarred legs. "It all seems so long ago."

Matthew nodded grimly. "Sometimes I dream of Ariel an' I . . ." He shook his head. "I wish I had killed him. If he had nowt died in th' storm . . ."

I looked up, surprised at his vehemence.

When I had first met him, Matthew had been thin and frail-looking, with a pronounced limp and hungry, intelligent eyes. The limp had been long since healed with a reset bone, and Matthew now stood a head taller than I, with strong, wiry limbs. He had proven more than capable in his role as Farseeker ward. Ceirwan was convinced he was developing deep-probe ability, saying he often seemed to know our thoughts before we sent them. I had dismissed that, thinking it no more than the natural result of our closeness. But it might be so. There was so much about our abilities we had yet to understand.

Farseekers could converse mind to mind over varying distances, an ability that involved conscious rather than unconscious thought. I had believed myself the only farseeker also able to deep-probe. Yet multiTalents were not uncommon among us, and assignment to a guild was based on the dominant ability. In rare cases, two abilities were of equal strength.

As if to confirm his ability to know my private thoughts, Matthew said, "Maybe we should use this guildmerge to raise th' matter of Zarak changin' guilds."

Zarak had a strong Talent for communicating with animals, like his father, and he had chosen the Beastspeaking guild, only to discover that he had equally strong farseeking abilities. This had resulted in the desire to transfer to the Farseekers.

I shook my head decisively. "Now is not the time. Besides, I think that matter can be better resolved on a personal level. But something will have to be done soon, I agree. Zarak is proving to be a disturbing influence in the wrong guild."

Matthew nodded fervently. "Not that Lina isn't capable of gannin' up to mischief on her own. . . ." He trailed off as we approached the front steps to Obernewtyn.

The new doors were less imposing than the old, being too plain to complement the ornate stone scrolling of the entrance. I had a fleeting memory of watching the original doors burn, and with them the concealed maps that I alone knew showed a route to the Beforetime weaponmachines that had caused the Great White. To the others, the burning had been simply the easiest way to get at the inlaid gold we had used to make armbands for the guildmasters. That had been my suggestion, and Rushton had agreed. Perhaps my wounds had led him to humor me. He had been very kind and attentive then, I thought pensively.

As if conjured up by my thoughts, Rushton was waiting for us in the circular entrance hall.

He looked tired, and it was clear from his clothes that he had not bothered to change. I felt a rush of gladness at the sight of him, for though Obernewtyn ran smoothly even in his absence, I never felt as safe as when he was there.

He met my look with an ambivalent stare. It was almost a challenge. Before I could speak, he sent Matthew to find representatives from the Futuretell guild; then he ushered me toward the guildmerge, matching his steps to my own limping progress.

"What has happened?" I asked.

Rushton turned to look at me. "The Council is showing renewed interest in us. Two men were in the highlands asking questions about Obernewtyn."

"You think they were from the Council?"

He shrugged angrily. "I know nothing, except that I am tired of my ignorance. Do you remember when I went to claim Obernewtyn in Sutrium?" he asked.

I remembered. Sutrium was the center of Council activities. It had not been easy for him to convince everyone to wait for his return. Many had wanted to leave, fearing his trip would lead to their capture and burning. That we had chosen to wait had been an act of faith in Rushton. We had never regretted it.

"I remember," I murmured.

"I thought the Council had trusted me when I'd told them that Obernewtyn had been badly damaged in a firestorm but that I meant to rebuild slowly, using those who had survived for labor. I thought they would lose interest in us. Maybe I was wrong. With farseeker or coercer help, I could have made sure. But now . . ."

"Now?" I echoed.

Rushton looked at me, his green eyes glowing with sudden

excitement, as if he had resolved some inner doubt. "It's time we found out what the Council is up to. Time we made a move into *their* territory."

"Sutrium?" I whispered.

"Sutrium," he echoed.

⋆ 2 ⋆

As USUAL, GUILDMERGE was held in the circular room that had once served as the doctor's work chamber and library, but all of the tables and benches that had filled it were gone. Only the enormous fireplace and the enormous hinged bookshelf dividing the chamber remained, though the bookshelf was pushed back to allow for the enormous table and the chairs surrounding it.

The tunnel concealed by the pivoting fireplace was now used only for easy wintertime transport of firewood into the meeting hall and as a swift, hidden route to the complex of caves where the Teknoguilders worked. Like other hidden passages at Obernewtyn, it was no longer a secret, although the incorrigibly curious Lina was convinced there were others and was forever to be found tapping the walls and listening for telltale hollowness.

Obernewtyn's first master, the reclusive Lukas Seraphim, had been a morose and secretive man, and the great gray buildings reflected his personality.

Louis Larkin, the eldest of our number, had known the man who had carved Obernewtyn out of the wilderness on what was then the very fringe of the Blacklands. He said Lukas had possessed a mind that was as much a labyrinth as the greenthorn maze separating the main house from the farms.

As its current master, Rushton had made many changes to the main building to provide clear paths and better access to all parts of the rambling wings and levels. It had been his idea that each guild be allocated a certain section of Obernewtyn as its base and that the guild members make changes to their areas as they desired.

Though cavernous, the domed meeting room was kept warm by an enormous fire, and I seated myself in a chair near it, surreptitiously toasting my sore feet.

The buzz of talk was louder than usual, partly because of the abrupt way Rushton had called the meeting and partly because it was a full guildmerge, with almost all wards, guildens, and guildleaders present. Even the irascible Garth had come, though he looked impatient and bored.

On the other side of the table sat Ceirwan, guilden of my own guild, still clad in riding clothes. I felt momentarily irritated by the guildmerge rule restricting communication during meetings to the spoken word, but I did not try to reach him.

Matthew took a seat opposite me and next to Dameon, the blind Empath guildmaster, who smiled at me unerringly, sensing my attention. Empaths could read emotions the way farseekers read thoughts, though few were actually able to converse mentally. Some empaths, like Dameon, could also transmit emotion. The twin Empath guilden, Miky and her brother, Angina, sat beside him, deep in animated discussion.

Rushton had walked to the head of the table and was talking to Domick, the Coercer ward. Next to him, Maryon sat staring into the distance, a slight smile on her lips. No one could mistake her for anything but a futureteller. She had come in with Matthew, but the seat between her and the Futuretell ward was empty. I wondered what was important enough to keep the guilden, Christa, away.

Roland was alone in representing his guild. This was not unusual. The healers put their patients before anything else. Next, and completing the table, were the three members of the Beastspeaking guild—the master, Alad, looking unusually grim.

I was conscious of an expectant atmosphere among us as Rushton rose to speak, formally commencing the guildmerge. He invited those with business to raise their hand. Traditionally, Rushton spoke last. This meant that whatever had prompted the sudden guildmerge must wait until all other matters had been dealt with. His eyes widened speculatively at my hand among those few to rise.

Alad rose to speak, again raising the need for animals to be represented in guildmerge by one of their own. As before, no one could agree which animal should represent all animals and whether the animals should propose their own candidate. The increasing dominance of the volatile younger horses' attitude was raised. With a hint of impatience, Rushton suggested the matter be addressed at the next guildmerge.

The Beastspeaking guildmaster frowned. "This is the third time it's been put off. It's time we dealt with this once and for all."

"It will be dealt with. Next time," Rushton said tersely.

"The animals themselves requested a decision one way or the other. There will be trouble if it is left any longer," Alad said coldly.

Rushton lifted his brows questioningly. "Threats, Alad?"

The guildmaster shook his head. "Just a warning, Rushton. They have the right."

Rushton said nothing, and Alad sat, looking disgruntled.

I was surprised at his persistence. Everyone knew it was only a matter of time until the animals had a representative. But the mention of trouble from the horses made me decide it was time I visited the farms again.

The Coercer guild then proposed a competition, a contest of coercer skills, pitting one against another until a champion could be announced. Master, guilden, and ward would be excluded. This resulted in a heated discussion about the value of competitiveness. The Futuretell ward, Dell, argued persuasively against it, saying it would produce antisocial and aggressive tendencies in an already aggressive guild.

"The aim of Obernewtyn is to have all minds working together for a common goal, not to isolate winners from losers and devalue those whose skills are less violent," she said.

Roland was even more seriously opposed. Rushton interrupted what looked to be erupting into an argument to suggest the coercers draw up a plan for their proposed tournament. This would then be voted on by a full guildmerge.

At last he nodded to me, and I stood. "I request that the ban on Teknoguild expeditions be lifted," I said.

Rushton frowned. He did not like anyone to step outside the procedures that governed guildmerge and made it run smoothly. "This is a strange request for the Farseeker guildmistress to make, Elspeth," he said. "Surely it's up to Garth, especially since he graces us with his presence today."

There was a titter of humor, since everyone knew of the Teknoguild master's reluctance to leave his laboratory. Garth scowled.

"This request also concerns my guild," I said quietly.

Rushton's eyes bored into mine. "What interest could you have in the Teknoguild expeditions? If I recall, you were among those to vote for the ban."

I took a deep breath. "If the ban was lifted, I would propose a joint expedition."

Rushton shook his head emphatically. "If I refuse to let teknoguilders kill themselves roaming on poisoned Blackland fringes, I would hardly let farseekers replace them!" he said with impatient sarcasm.

The death toll among teknoguilders had always been high. The ban had been enforced after a disastrous Teknoguild expedition in which Henry Druid's people and the teknoguilders clashed over a newly discovered ruin on the edge of the Blackland. The argument had ended in a mysterious explosion that killed most of both parties. Either the Druids, as Henry Druid's men named themselves, had deliberately set off a forbidden weapon, or some ancient device hidden in the ruins had been accidentally triggered. Either way, there had been no further Teknoguild expeditions, and no more had been seen of Henry Druid or his followers.

Henry Druid had been a Herder novice until he had opposed the Council's book-burning laws. Cast out by the fanatical priests of the Herder Faction, the Druid had fled to exile in the high country and was assumed dead by most. And yet he lived. Rushton had even been befriended by the old ex-Herder, and for a time, their paths had matched. But the old man's fierce hatred of the Council was exceeded only by his hatred of mutations, and in the end, it had become too dangerous to continue the connection.

Sometimes it made me uneasy that we had not heard anything of the Druid for so long. Like Alexi and Madam Vega, the renegade Herder had wanted power in the form of Beforetime weaponmachines. What if he were to discover the machines that could set off another Great White?

I choked off that train of thought. "The expedition we propose will not be to Blackland fringes."

Rushton looked puzzled. "Then I don't see any difficulty. Teknoguild expeditions were banned because they never want to go anywhere but the fringes. But that still doesn't explain your interest. I would be surprised to find you had any aim in common with the Teknoguild."

It was true I had often opposed their interests. Of all those at Obernewtyn, the abilities of Teknoguilders were hardest to define, being little more than a vague empathy for inanimate things, a slight power to move things by will alone, and a passionate interest in the past. The Teknoguild was the only one that had established its base outside Obernewtyn because the caves that housed it were the remains of a Beforetime establishment and contained a number of ancient machines.

Pavo's request that I visit the cave network had been unexpected and unnerving. I had not been there since Alexi had tortured me with the Zebkrahn machine in his effort to force me to use my powers to locate an Oldtime weapons cache. In the end, I had gone, as much to lay my fears to rest as out of respect for Pavo, who was more concerned with understanding the Beforetimers than unearthing their mechanical secrets.

Also, I had been curious.

Returning to the cave had been a disturbing experience. The past had seemed to lie tangibly beneath the present, despite all that had changed. The passage into the cave network was now littered with boxes and sacks of Beforetime papers, books, and other relics unearthed in previous expeditions. The passage was well lit by candles set in sconces at regular intervals.

Coming from the sloping passage with its strangely

smooth walls into the main cave, I had been forced to stifle a gasp, having forgotten how big it all was and how bright the Beforetime sphere of light that lit the area. High up in the shadows, stalactites still hung, poised like spears. Yet it was also very different than I remembered. Woven rugs and thick mats softened cold floors, and the walls were almost covered with paper, scrawled with lists and notes and diagrams. Tables and chairs were occupied by busy teknoguilders, who barely registered my entrance.

Only the Zebkrahn machine had looked the same, though I knew it could no longer be used to coerce and torture, having long since been modified. Now it served as nothing more than an enhancer, enabling farseekers to double their normal range. Even so, my skin had risen to gooseflesh at the sight of it.

I thought of all this as I stood before the guildmerge. "Pavo asked me to come to the Teknoguild cave network this morning," I began in answer to Rushton's puzzlement.

The guilden gave a dry cough and rose. "It might be better if I explain, Guildmistress," the Teknoguild ward offered diffidently.

As in the cave that morning, I was struck anew by his pallor.

"I did not know Elspeth would raise this matter today, and so I have not brought my notes; therefore, you will have to take my word on some matters," Pavo said. "A while back, we uncovered evidence of an enormous book storage, which we believe might be untouched since the Beforetime. However, because of the ban, we set this matter reluctantly aside. Meanwhile, we succeeded in getting the Zebkrahn machine to penetrate the blocking static over tainted ground." He paused to remind everyone that the machine, like farseekers, had been unable to project through Blackland wastes; even the tainted ground at the borders of the Blacklands produced a static that limited our range to just beyond the mountains that surrounded Obernewtyn.

"It still only *locates* Talents—it won't help us to communicate with them. But the machine is now able to monitor areas previously out of reach even to farseekers as strong as Elspeth, whose range is otherwise better than that of the machine," Pavo said. "I thought it was necessary for Elspeth to see the machine—not to admire the new modification but so that she could see what it revealed." Pavo looked at me, and all eyes swung expectantly my way.

I said obligingly, "The Zebkrahn was registering a Talent at its outermost limit."

"But . . . that's impossible. Th' machine has to be focused through a farseeker," Matthew objected.

Pavo shook his head eagerly. "Only to detect ordinary or weak Talents. That is to say, in most cases. But the Zebkrahn would need no farseeker focusing to register, for instance, Elspeth."

"But . . . that means this Talent the Zebkrahn registers mun be as strong as she . . . ," Matthew said.

"Perhaps stronger," Pavo corrected gently.

"Such a Talent would be worth rescuing," interjected Gevan, guildmaster of the coercers.

"The two—the new Talent and the book storage Pavo told you about—are in the same region, and since it is so far away, we thought of a joint expedition," I said.

There was a buzz of excited talk, but Rushton ignored it. "'So far away' . . . ." he repeated coldly. "Exactly how far?"

My mouth felt suddenly dry. "Somewhere between Aborium and Murmroth."

There was silence, then someone sighed heavily. Aborium was on the west coast. The only known way to get there was to travel the main coast road, passing soldierguard camps and all the main towns, not to mention passing through Sutrium to reach the ferry that plied the Lower Suggredoon. And any expedition would be cut off from contact with Obernewtyn, as it would be far beyond the outer limits of even the most powerful farseekers.

Rushton's face was tight with anger; he must have realized his brief words to me before the guildmerge had prompted me to propose the expedition. He knew that he could not dismiss my proposal when he meant to propose his own equally dangerous expedition.

"That would mean traveling through Sutrium and crossing the river by ferry," Roland said brusquely. "A crazy, dangerous idea. Our false Certificates would not deceive the soldierguards for a moment."

Pavo coughed again. "It is not necessary to journey through Sutrium." He pulled one of the maps on the table toward him and spread it out. "I have a better map, but"—he pointed to the red circle denoting Obernewtyn—"the expedition would travel out of Obernewtyn and down the main road but would turn off to cut directly across the White Valley, then through an Olden pass between Tor and Aran Craggie in the lower mountain ranges and down to the lowlands. From there, it would be an easy trip across the Ford of Rangorn and down to the coast."

Rushton examined the route. "You are sure this mountain pass exists? I have never heard of it."

The teknoguilder nodded.

"T'would mean winterin' outside maybe, unless an expedition were to leave at once," Matthew said tentatively.

"It would be best to act at once," Pavo said anxiously. "Think of what we might learn from an untouched collection of Beforetime books. And who knows what ability this Talent will bring to us."

Rushton nodded for us to resume our seats, his expression inscrutable. His eyes swept the assembled faces. "Well," he said at last, "I called this guildmerge for a particular reason, but Guildmistress Elspeth has preempted me. I, too, meant to propose an expedition. While in the high country these last few days, I heard rumors of men asking questions about Obernewtyn. Strangers—perhaps Councilmen, perhaps not. They were asking questions about the damage caused by the firestorm, wanting to speak to anyone who had actually seen Obernewtyn. This means the Council may know I lied about the storm. If so, we will be investigated, probably after the next thaw."

There was a muffled howl of dismay.

"Or," Rushton went on, "it may mean nothing. The problem is that we have no idea what they know. Up until now, we have striven to avoid any contact with the Council, to hide and grow in strength until we were powerful enough to confront them. We are not yet strong enough for that battle, or any sort of open confrontation, but it is time we moved on to the next stage of our plans.

"I called this meeting to propose an expedition to Sutrium, with the aim of finding out if we are in danger and if the Council has any real knowledge of our existence. We can no longer hide in the dark, shivering. We must look, in the next year, to establishing a safe house in the lowlands, preferably right in Sutrium."

"What is a safe house?" Miryum asked.

"A refuge that will form the nexus of our inner defense. It

means we can move with more confidence among the low-landers. Most important, it means we will be in a better position to know what the Council is up to."

"What if someone is caught and . . . tortured into giving up its location or, worse, to tell th' truth about us and Obernewtyn?" Matthew asked. A few nodded fearfully at this.

· "Don't you understand that we are no safer hiding up here?" Rushton demanded. "Even if the rumors are just gossip, the soldierguards will come to hear of it, especially if they set up camp in the high country. The question is, do we wait until the Council descends on us before we act, or do we act now, while we can still move with relative freedom?"

A thoughtful silence greeted his words.

"Then, do you propose two expeditions to the lowlands?" Roland asked.

Rushton smiled slightly. "I vote that we accept the expedition proposed by Elspeth, with the addition of another person, whom I will choose, who will leave the main party after Rangorn and venture into Sutrium to investigate the possibility of establishing a safe house. An expedition that can have two purposes can as easily have three. Now we will vote on the expedition with its threefold purpose, and on the establishment of a safe house in Sutrium. Yes, first." He lifted his own hand.

I raised mine, hiding a reluctant smile. Rushton was as sly as ever. He knew Garth would never have agreed to the move on Sutrium without the lure of the coveted library. In the end, the vote was unanimous. Perhaps all felt that the time had come, whether we liked it or not, for a less passive strategy. At any rate, no one liked the idea of waiting like a lamb to be slaughtered.

Rushton rose to close the meeting but was interrupted by a commotion outside the doors.

Christa entered, her face betraying her worry.

Seeing me, the Futuretell guilden beckoned urgently. "Elspeth, it's Maruman. He's returned but is unconscious, and we cannot waken him. You had better come quickly."

✦ 3 ✦

MARUMAN HAD BEEN taken to the Healer hall. As usual after days of wandering, often on tainted ground, his fur was filthy and singed in places; dried blood matted the fur on one paw. But he looked no worse than he had on any other return. The wan afternoon light slanted obliquely from a high, slitlike window to lie across his body, making it seem insubstantial, while candles burning all around the hall gave the room a ghostly orange tinge.

In the bed alongside the old cat's was a girl, heavily bandaged. She had been literally wrested from the Herders' purifying flame and had been unconscious since her arrival. One of Christa's fellow futuretellers sat beside her, sunk in deep concentration.

I looked up to see Alad come through the door.

"He looks like he's asleep," I said.

Christa shook her head, then gestured at the meditating futureteller. "She can hardly think for Maruman's emanations. I don't understand how you can't feel them," she added.

"I have my shield up," I explained. I dissolved the protective mental barrier and almost staggered beneath the force of gibberish flowing from Maruman's mind. "I see what you mean."

I saw from Alad's expression that he had lowered his own

shield. "Usually I find the flow of beast thought soothing," he said ruefully.

"He was lying outside the Futuretell wing when we found him. It looked as if he had dragged himself there," Christa said.

"Can you reach his mind to find out what he's been doing?" I asked.

She looked down at the old cat. "The truth is, his mind is generally such a mess that it is a wonder he can think straight even some of the time. I can't imagine what caused the damage in the first place—perhaps a traumatic birth. For the most part, his mind seems to have adapted itself amazingly well. There are the most extraordinary links and bypasses—somehow it all functions. The fits he occasionally has are the result of some sort of upward leak in his mind, where material from the deepest unconscious levels rises to distort his everyday thinking, hence the wild futuretelling, but this . . ."

"What do you make of it?" I asked Alad.

He sighed. "I'm a simple beastspeaker. This is beyond me. I've sent for one of the few strong beastspeakers with a small Talent for deep probing. Christa suggested it since Maruman will not allow her to enter his unconscious mind. Perhaps he will permit a beastspeaker to deep-probe."

"I can deep-probe," I said.

Christa raised her brows, then she looked at the cat pensively. "You could try. He's less likely to oppose you. I'm afraid if it goes on much longer, he'll die of exhaustion. He looks calm enough, but this is pulling him apart."

I stared down at the battle-scarred old cat, tears pricking my eyes. He looked so vulnerable. He would have hated that. I stroked him, fighting for control.

"Is there no healer free to ease him?" I asked gruffly.

Christa shook her head. "They have done all they can. He's in no pain."

"What can I do?" I asked.

"Go into his mind," she answered. "See what you can find out. Make him wake if you can."

"I've never tried to deep-probe him before. What if he resists? I might hurt him."

Alad broke in impatiently. "He'll die if we can't help him. He is more wild than tame, and you know as well as I that the wild ones are hardest to reach, even in a normal communication. But you must try."

With a feeling of dread, I sat on the chair beside the bed. I stroked Maruman's coarse fur gently, willing him to wake. I was repelled by the idea of entering my old friend's most private mind. I could not have borne such an intrusion myself.

Alad squeezed my shoulder. I bit my lip, then closed my eyes. Loosing a deep-probe tendril gently into the first level, I forced myself to ignore the screaming babble that assaulted me. For a moment, I was swept along like a leaf in the dizzy maelstrom of Maruman's unconscious mind. I had a fleeting temptation to let myself go but concentrated on Alad's hand on my shoulder, forcing myself to the next level.

I slipped through effortlessly. Maruman was letting me in.

I drifted deeper, concentrating to avoid the forgetfulness that was one of the greatest dangers inherent to entering an unconscious mind.

Deeper still and suddenly the clamor of the upper levels ceased. It was very quiet and still.

"Maruman," I whispered. "Maruman?"

I sensed a ripple in the fabric of the cat's unconscious

mind. In a sense, I knew I was inside his dreams. I went deeper still. Again I whispered his name.

This time he responded. "ElspethInnle . . ."

"Come with me," I invited, hoping to draw him to the upper levels and wakefulness. I was buffeted gently by his refusal.

"Cannot. Must wait," he responded.

I was puzzled. "Wait for what?"

"Must wait until Seeker comes."

This was a name Maruman sometimes called me. More confused than ever, I said, "I am the Seeker."

"Deeper. Must come deeper," Maruman responded instantly.

"Why must?" I asked.

"The oldOne wishes it."

I shivered violently, becoming suddenly conscious of my physical presence in the Healer hall. I forced myself to concentrate, but I was unnerved. It struck me that Maruman had let me in easily, because he had wanted me to enter his deepest mind. Why? I could only know that by slipping deeper, but I was almost at my limit. The desire to rise was powerful, and my energy was running out quickly. Before long, I would have no choice. I would not have the strength to remain. If I wanted to go deeper, I had to do it immediately.

Yet I hesitated.

At the depths of the mind is a great unconscious mindstream. It was into this that the futuretellers dipped for their predictions. Without training, it was possible for a mind to literally dissolve at that depth. And I was already deeper than I had ever gone before.

I braced myself. Fighting an irresistible urge to rise, I

pushed my mind lower, fraction by fraction. All at once, the void seemed to brighten, and below, I was aware of the shining silver rush of the mindstream.

Now I felt an opposite tug from the stream, a siren call to merge. My innate fear of losing myself gave me the strength to resist.

"I have come," I grated.

"Deeper," Maruman urged. "Must come deeper."

I was truly frightened now, for it was possible Maruman did not realize the danger. I hesitated and felt myself begin to rise. Then I clamped on my probe and forced it deeper. I could feel the wind of the stream and its incredible cyclonic energy below. It seemed to sing my name in an indescribably lovely voice, willing me to join. Again fear helped me to resist. Then, suddenly, the pull to join the stream and the pull to rise equalized exactly, and I floated motionless.

I was on a high mountain in the highest ranges, the air around me filled with cold gusts of wind. I was inside the body of Maruman. I felt the wind ruffle his/my fur.

An illusion, but real as life.

He/I licked a paw and passed it over one ear.

Then I felt the calling. It was not a voice so much as an inner compulsion. Maruman/I rose at once and began to walk, balancing with easy grace on the jagged spines of rock leading to a higher peak. It was there, I sensed, that the calling originated.

Then I heard my own name, but the voice was not Maruman's.

I was so astonished that the mountain illusion wavered, and for a moment I saw the Healer hall overlay the mountain.

"Do you know me?" I ventured.

"I have always known you," came the response.

"Who are you? What are you?"

"I/We are the Agyllian," it answered in a tone a mother might use when speaking to a small child. "I have used the yelloweyes to communicate with you, ElspethInnle. The strangeness of his mind and his pain make him receptive to us and allow us to use him. He is weary to death, and it would be kind to let him join the stream, but he is not ready to go yet, and nor, I think, are you ready to let him go."

"So it's you who is making him sick," I said indignantly.

"Be at ease. He will suffer no harm, though he cannot sustain us much longer. I come only to warn you that your tasks have not ended, and to remind you of your promise. The deathmachines slumber, waiting to be wakened. While they survive, the world is in danger. When the time is right for you to seek out the machines, you must be ready to act swiftly and without doubt. You must not allow the concerns of your friends or your own needs to sway you. When the time for the dark journey is near, you must come to us, and we will provide you with help."

"Journey? What journey?" I cried, but I was alone.

The mountains dissolved, and I used the last of my strength to rise to where the upward drift would carry me to the surface of Maruman's mind. I was vaguely aware that the upper levels were now quiet.

"Are you all right?" Alad asked tensely as I opened my eyes. I was slumped in the chair, soaked with perspiration and vaguely amazed to find it was dark outside.

He reached out and touched Maruman gently. "He'll recover. He's sleeping normally now. What did you do?"

I was too tired to answer. Seeing I was nearly asleep in the chair, Alad and one of the healers helped me to my room.

Yet lying in bed, I found myself unable to sleep, so disturbed was I by what I'd experienced in Maruman's mind.

I told myself that my visit to the Teknoguild caves had caused a deep probe illusion based on the memory of the misfit Cameo, who had died there some years before, after she whispered to me that it was my destiny to destroy the weaponmachines that had caused the Great White. Or more likely, the dream was simply the product of Maruman's distorted mind, for he believed that I was a figure in beast mythology named Innle, or "the Seeker," destined to save what remained of the world.

It was foolish to dwell on what had happened as if it were real, yet the voice that had spoken to me had felt so real. And I knew, as no one else did, that the weaponmachines that had destroyed the Beforetimers were intact and might be used again.

The next morning, I came across Dameon and Matthew making their way toward the kitchen. I watched them approach, wondering what kept Dameon from running into things. His empath ability could not help him see, yet he was never clumsy.

"Elspeth?" he said unexpectedly in his soft, well-spoken voice. His father had been a member of the Council before his death, and Dameon had been a product of that privileged class before a cousin had arranged to have him judged Misfit in order to claim the deceased's estate. For the Council, one of the beauties of the Misfit charge was that it could not be absolutely proven or disproven.

"Are ye sure ye canna see?" Matthew asked the empath.

Dameon smiled sweetly. "I possess neither sight nor the wondrous magic of your precious Oldtimers," he teased. "I knew Elspeth was there because of your reaction to her."

"You empaths!" Matthew exploded. "I thought I had th' shield in place then. Ye'd think emotions at least ought to be private."

"You need to perfect that shield," Dameon admonished. "Do you think I want to be privy to your emotional turmoils, entertaining though they are?"

Matthew blushed to the roots of his hair. "One canna always be screenin' every thought," he muttered.

I bit my lip to conceal my amusement, but Dameon laughed aloud. He smiled in my direction. There was a touch of sadness in his face that had not always been there. Even as I wondered what had caused it, I caught Matthew's knowing look, as if he knew something I did not. I was tempted to deep-probe him when Dameon said pointedly that we ought to go into the kitchen before midmeal became nightmeal. He could not read my mind, yet I felt a flush rise to my cheeks.

Rushton always called the empath his conscience, and suddenly I understood why.

Dameon took my arm and said, with a smile in Matthew's direction, "I hear young Lina has been up to her tricks again."

Matthew scowled blackly. "That girl an' her pranks. She had me so flustered at nightmeal that I accidentally sat next to Miryum, who has as much grace an' wit as a lump of stone."

"Yet she is guilden," Dameon said with faint reproach.

Matthew looked put out. "She has Talent, I grant ye. But all she ever thinks about is the latest way to make people do things they dinna want to do."

The sound of cutlery clinking and laughter flowed down the hall from the kitchen to meet us. There had long been vague plans to open up another room as a separate dining area, but somehow the alcoves adjoining the kitchen remained the main eating area.

Guilds had gotten into the habit of sitting together for meals, but most of the guildleaders and some others sat at the table by the door with Rushton, who treated meals as another kind of strategy meeting. But Dameon went to join his guild members.

Though empath guildmaster, Dameon spent most of his time working with Rushton, and he had offered to forgo his place as master of the Empath guild to make way for Miky and Angina. The twins had refused emphatically, and their refusal had been echoed by the rest of the guild. No other guild had quite the same love for their master as the empaths. They made little official demand on Dameon's time, but at social occasions they were possessive.

Rushton and Domick were both absorbed in something Gevan was saying, and I noticed that Rushton's soup was untouched. I sighed and wondered if he ever noticed anything he ate or enjoyed a conversation just because it was fun.

I saw Louis Larkin hovering just inside the kitchen courtyard door, peering about nearsightedly. He hated coming up to the house, and I wondered what had been important enough to bring him up through the maze.

I sent a probe to Matthew, telling him to find out what Louis wanted. "He says he must talk with you," Matthew sent after a moment. "Ye'll have to come. I can't crack grouchy bugger's shield."

I sighed. Louis was just as hard to get along with as he had always been. His white hair stuck out like coils of wire on each side of his head but was sparse on top. His cheeks and nose were red with cold, but he insisted I come out into the maze courtyard before he would talk. Matthew came with us, closing the door behind him. It was growing colder, and my breath came out in little puffs of cloud.

"What is it, Louis?" I asked tersely.

"Hmph," Louis grumped. "I'm surprised ye've any time to spare for a beastspeaker." Though himself an unTalent, Louis had a natural affinity for animals and held an honorary place in the guild. He regarded my decision to lead the farseekers rather than the beastspeakers as the worst sort of traitorous defection.

"What is it, Louis?" I asked resignedly. Sometimes he reminded me of Maruman at his most difficult.

"No need to snap my head off," Louis said smugly. "T'were a bit of gossip I heard I thought might interest ye."

Louis was a remarkable source of odd bits of information. He hardly ever left Obernewtyn, but he always seemed to know what was going on in the highlands. And he knew everything that went on at Obernewtyn.

"I heard ye were wonderin' if th' Druid has left th' high country," Louis said, looking over his shoulder as if he thought someone might be listening. I was never sure how much of his eccentric behavior was affected and how much was genuine.

"Have you heard anything?" I asked.

He nodded. "Th' word is that th' Druid has nowt left th' high country. No one has seen a sign of his people in many a long day, but now an' then there are disappearances."

"That could be our fault," Matthew said. "Them missin' could be Misfits we rescue, despite th' trouble we gan to to make the disappearances seem natural."

"Ye'd be right, of course! It could nowt be that th' Druid is doin' his own recruitin'. 'Tis nowt possible the disappearances are the reason th' Council takes an interest in th' high country!" Louis huffed sarcastically.

"But if the Druid is taking people, where is he? An why haven't we been able to locate his camp in farseeking searches?" I asked.

The outrage on the old man's face melted into genuine puzzlement. " 'Tis strange enow. I would have said th' Druid had gone. But if he's nowt away from th' White Valley, yer expedition route mun be more dangerous than goin' th' main way."

"Have you mentioned this to Rushton?" I asked.

Louis gave me a look of sly entreaty. "Fact is, I only just heard it. Ought to tell th' master, but I've a yen to go on this expedition. I'd like to see th' lowlands once afore I die," he added. "Ye could put in a word for me."

"Ridiculous," Matthew said. "Ye'll live forever, ye ol' fake!"

"I will speak to Rushton," I said.

Louis's eyes were fixed on my face, and whatever he saw there made him smile sourly. "Ye do that," he said.

After he had gone, Matthew looked at me incredulously. "Why did ye let him bluff ye? Rushton'll nivver agree!"

"Because if Rushton heard this, he would be bound to cancel the expedition or at least delay it. And Louis knows it. Besides, he might . . ."

"What th' devil?" Matthew muttered, hearing a wild yell from the courtyard behind us.

Zarak and Lina of the Beastspeaking guild ran up to us. Both were white-faced.

"Guildmistress, we have to talk to you!" Lina gasped.

"Well?" I snapped, in no mood for their antics. Then Zarak

268

looked up, his eyes miserable and frightened, and suddenly I was filled with apprehension. "What is it?"

Lina answered, "We were sitting in the kitchen garden, and Zarak was . . ." She trailed off and glared at Zarak, who was now staring at his feet. I restrained an urge to shake him.

He burst out, "I know I'm not supposed to farseek, Guildmistress, but you don't know what it's like—being able to make your mind fly and not being allowed to do it. I only meant to go a little way, but it felt so wonderful. Then I bumped into someone. A stranger!"

I stared at him coldly. "You know even farseeker novices do not farseek beyond the mountains." He nodded. "Do you know why we have this rule?" He nodded again. "Tell me," I snapped.

"Because they might bump into a wild Talent . . . and not be able to shield well enough to stop them . . . tracing back to Obernewtyn," he mumbled. "But I swear it was someone as untrained as I am. He couldn't have traced me. He thought I was an evil spirit."

I felt a sneaking sympathy for Zarak, who was in the wrong guild because his father was a beastspeaker. But I showed none of these thoughts on my face. Zarak had to learn to curb his curiosity, for all our sakes.

"Then since you know the rules, it is not a matter of ignorance but of deliberate disobedience," I said coldly. Zarak hung his head, flushing. "You will go at once to Javo and tell him you will be available for heavy kitchen work until I say otherwise. You will be suspended from the Beastspeaking guild for the same period. I will speak to Alad and your father. Or do you want to lodge an appeal at the next guildmerge?"

Zarak shook his head.

Matthew nodded approvingly. "A fool who knows he is a fool is near to becomin' wise."

Lina fidgeted and looked at Zarak. "You'd better tell them everything," she advised.

Zarak bit his lip. "I might be wrong. It was so quick," he said, then floundered to a halt.

"What now?" Matthew asked.

Zarak said nothing.

"The person Zarak bumped into," Lina said with a sigh. "He thinks it was a Herder."

✦ 4 ✦

"Do ye think it were truly a Herder?" Matthew asked dubiously when the Farseeker guild met the following day.

"I don't know," I said. "Misfits have come to us from almost every walk of life. Why not from the Herder cloisters?"

Matthew frowned. "But would nowt they just burn any Misfit they found among themselves? They have th' right to do it."

I shook my head. "I don't know. The Council might, but the Herders are subtle enough to think of using a Misfit for their own purposes."

"You think this accidental meeting was no accident?" asked an older farseeker.

I shrugged. "Accidental on Zarak's part."

"Maybe Zarak was wrong about not being traced," Ceirwan said.

I shook my head. "I think he would have been able to tell, but we'll have to make sure, pending Rushton's approval. Have you traced the path from Zarak's memory?"

Ceirwan nodded. "Whoever he touched minds with was in a cloister, all right—in Darthnor, of all places."

"Darthnor. A town full of pro-Herder bigots and fanatics. Wonderful," Matthew said darkly.

✦ ✦ ✦

Later that day, I went down to the farms. Ostensibly, I wanted to organize wagons for the expedition to the lowlands. But I was also curious to talk to Alad about the horses. The Beast-speaking guildmaster was nowhere to be seen, but I noticed a dark stallion grazing nearby.

He looked up warily at my approach. "Greetings, funaga."

I was surprised at his guarded tone. "Greetings, equine," I sent. "Do you know where Alad Beastspeaking guildmaster is?"

The horse looked at me measuringly. "Who knows where the funaga go?" he sent coolly.

All at once, I realized whom I was talking to.

Alad had encountered the black horse in the town of Guanette. Half starved, he had been trying to pull a cart loaded with furniture, five plump children, and a fat, dirty gypsy man cursing and lashing out with a whip. Alad had told me the horse's imaginative mental curses had attracted his attention—that and his strength of mental projection.

The beastspeaker had ended up buying the horse from the gypsy troupe and bringing him to Obernewtyn. Despite a deep hatred of humans, the horse had chosen to remain, becoming almost at once the spokesman for his kind. He had arrived a dusty, bedraggled bag of bones. Now he was lean and muscled, his coat gleaming and sleek. Only his eyes were unchanged, still filled with anger and suspicion. Suddenly I was sure this equine was behind Alad's difficulties with the horses.

"I remember when you came to Obernewtyn," I sent gently.

The horse tossed his head, nostrils flared wide. "I was brought here a slave. I did not choose to come."

Taken aback, I sent, "We had to do it that way. It would

have looked odd to buy a horse and set it free. But you chose to stay."

"That is so, for there is no place in the world not infected by the funaga. Here is the same as anywhere else."

From the corner of my eye, I saw Alad approaching.

"We are not like the people who owned you before," I sent. "Here, all work together. We are equals."

The horse snorted savagely. "You talk like a fool. We have no place in the funaga conclaves."

"It's only a matter of time—" I began, but the horse cut me off with his own thought.

"Alad-gahltha asked that we be treated as true equals. Again this was set aside. 'Wait,' they say. We have waited long enough. Now we are tired of waiting. From now on, we work only for our food and shelter. We will carry no funaga, and we will pull no cart beyond these mountains. We will not risk our lives to help the funaga. We will not fight the funaga's battles unless they are also ours."

There was no doubt in my mind that the proud, bitter horse meant what he said.

"That won't make anyone like you or take—"

He snorted violently in my face. "Like! I care nothing for the likes and hates of the funaga. Allies we will be, or nothing. I have heard the funaga plan a journey to the lowlands. We will see how they fare with no equine to draw their carts or carry them in the dark lands."

I blinked. "But we're not going to the Blacklands."

"The places where the funaga-li dwell are dark," the horse sent bleakly.

"I tried to warn Rushton. And it's not just the horses," Alad said from behind.

I ignored this and addressed the horse again. I knew as well as Alad that no expedition could be undertaken on foot, especially one so far and through such terrain. We needed the horses. "What if the journey were a test—to see if your kind and mine could really be allies, working together, trusting one another?"

The black horse stood very still, but he did not respond.

"A way to find out if your kind and mine can work in accord," I went on softly. "A test in which we funaga must pretend to have no special abilities, and equines must pull carts, be ridden by funaga, and reined."

The horse reared violently, and Alad started swearing. I had expected the reaction, knowing the younger horses would not even tolerate a modified rein and would only work with beastspeakers.

For long moments he bucked and reared, driving blade-like hooves deep into the ground. At last he calmed and turned to face me, his coat dark with sweat. "What if all who journeyed were slain? What if this journey fails?"

"If the equines do their part faithfully, the test will be judged a success—regardless of the outcome. And one of your kind will sit at guildmerge."

I knew I was offering what I had no right to offer, but I had no doubt Rushton would concur. He knew we needed the horses.

"It shall be as you have stated, funaga," the horse sent finally. "I will find those to draw your cart for this testing. But I will join your expedition also. Not to draw a cart, but to bear *you*. Then we will see whose kind is best fitted to lead."

"Elspeth, you can't!" Alad cried aloud. "A guildmistress on an expedition? Rushton would have a fit!"

The black horse did not take his eyes from mine, and there

was challenge and cold amusement in his look. He was daring me to agree, certain I would refuse.

I took a deep breath, ignoring the horrified Beastspeaking guildmaster. "It will be as you say, equine. Together we will deceive the lowlanders into thinking I am your master."

The horse neighed his laughter.

✦ 5 ✦

"Who are you? Where are you? I know you're there. I feel you."

The probe was clumsy, its movements graceless and badly focused. "He's young," I assured Ceirwan. Even so, I was surprised he had sensed my presence, since I was tightly shielded. I let my probe brush against his fleetingly, testing.

His mind stabbed out in fright. "Are you the demon?"

Even while he grappled with my shielded probe, I entered him at a deeper level, deep-probing to find trace memories of his encounter with Zarak. The meeting had made a huge impact on his mind, for he thought Zarak a minor demon come to test his faith.

I decided to risk outright contact. If he reacted by calling out to his masters, I would stun him, and Domick would manufacture a coercive block.

Rushton had insisted Domick monitor the attempt after being reluctantly convinced we had to establish whether Zarak's probe had been traced back to Obernewtyn. I suspected Domick had orders to cripple the boy's mind if there was any risk of the Herders using him.

"Do your elders know of us?" I sent.

The boy's mind recoiled from my mental blast. I had deliberately made it harsh and even painful. While the boy believed he was dealing with demons, we were in no real danger.

"It is the way of a priest to undergo his tests in silence, demon. My master has warned me your kind would try to shake my faith," the young Herder sent proudly.

I had read from his thoughts that he was a novice, or apprentice, priest. After his initial training in the main cloister in Sutrium, he had been sent to Darthnor's cloister to serve out his apprenticeship in the highlands. It was only the town's proximity to Obernewtyn that had made it possible for Zarak to stumble upon the novice's thoughts. Ironically, he had become aware of his powers under the rigorous mental training of the priesthood. But Herder teachings said that anything outside normal abilities was a mutation. The boy had tried to refuse his abilities, refusing to accept that he might be a Misfit.

Despite all his reactions, he was no hardened fanatic. And the Herder boy's youth was a mark in his favor. We rescued few older folk, since most were unable to accept that their mutant abilities might not be evil. Those we encountered whom we judged a bad risk, we simply blocked, making it impossible for them to use their powers. This horrified the healers, but, in truth, the Misfits were happier to seem normal. Many believed Lud had cured them.

It was this boy's youth that stopped me from simply having Domick expunge the memory and block his mutant powers. That and an instinct that told me he was worth rescuing. But because he was a Herder, I had to be sure he would respond the right way. I had promised Rushton I would do nothing until I was certain he could be trusted.

"How do you know I am a demon?" I asked, curious to see how much dogma he had swallowed.

The response was immediate. "You are a greater demon. The other was a lesser novice. Only demons can talk inside a man's head. My master says many are driven mad by such things, but you will not find me easy to break."

I sensed Ceirwan's amusement. "A puppy," he sent in ardent relief.

"If we can bring him in, we would have an insight into the Herders' world," I said. "It's always possible those men asking questions about Obernewtyn were from the Herder Faction."

Ceirwan looked unconvinced. "He is a novice, unlikely to know their inner secrets."

"He is one of us," I insisted stubbornly. "If we leave him, the Herders might end up finding out what he is anyway, sooner or later. Then he might betray us at their behest. He is not fully committed to their way, and I believe he would do well among us."

"A rescue would have to be completely foolproof," Ceirwan warned.

"Are you still there, demon?" the boy sent.

The wistful inquiry in his voice reminded me of my own long-ago loneliness, thinking myself a freak, living in fear of disclosure.

"Do others of your kind speak to demons?" I asked.

There was a significant hesitation in his mind before he answered evasively. "Demons test many priests."

"They do, but I have not encountered any other human who could communicate with me," I sent, trying to sound like a demon.

Still probing his lower mind, I thought again of my childhood in the orphan home system. I had not known at once that I was a Misfit, but some instinct of self-protection had kept me silent about my developing abilities. My brother, Jes, had been even more frightened. His hatred of my mutant abilities had warred with his love for me. He had spent a lifetime suppressing, even from himself, the fact that he, too, was a Misfit. In the end, he had been killed trying to escape from an orphan home after I was sent to Obernewtyn.

"I want to bring him out," I told Ceirwan aloud.

The memory of Jes made me determined to rescue the boy before leaving for the lowlands. With this in mind, I contacted him for several consecutive nights, working on his buried fears. At last he broke down, confessing that he was a Misfit—and his fear that his masters had begun to suspect him.

"Surely such a small mutation would not matter," I said, at the same time evoking an old nightmare in the boy's mind based on a burning he had once witnessed.

I was startled at the strength of his reaction. He screamed.

The noise brought an older Herder. Fearing the worst, Domick struck to wipe the boy's mind clean. I deflected his blow with an ease that made him glare at me suspiciously.

"I said I'll handle this," I hissed aloud.

I was relieved to hear the Herder boy tell his master he had been dreaming, and I injected my own calm control over his outward expressions. The priest departed with a final hard stare. My own heart was thudding, reacting to the boy's fear.

"He knows," he sent forlornly. I had not meant to make an approach so soon, but the desperation I sensed in his thoughts decided me.

"You could run away," I suggested.

"Where could I go that they wouldn't find me?" he asked miserably. "If they suspect, they won't let me get away. They are interested in Misfits. They don't send them to the Council." I saw a fleeting thought that confirmed the rumors of the Herder interrogation methods and shuddered. What would happen to the boy if they guessed the truth?

"You know I am no demon," I sent gently, after a moment.

"Yes," the boy sent simply.

"Once, I was an orphan. Like you, I was different. I didn't fit in, and I was afraid of being found out and burned or sent to the farms. Now I live free, with others like me."

"Misfits," he sent, using the hated word.

"Other people like you," I sent. "You could join us," I added lightly.

Hope flared, swamped by a sudden regressive fear that I might, after all, be a demon tempting him to the loss of his soul. "The other one. The first one I met. Is he there?"

I called Zarak and shielded his beam while they talked. In the end, the young Herder agreed to join us.

"He wants to know if he can bring his dog," Zarak asked with a grin.

Zarak, Matthew, and Ceirwan brought him out. Officially, Zarak was still in Coventry, but the Herder boy trusted him and had insisted he be present.

Over a matter of days, the boy gradually gave his Herder masters the impression he was becoming increasingly homesick. He talked constantly about his family and refused to eat. He let his masters think he was having trouble with the mental disciplines of the priesthood. When he escaped, it was made to appear as if he had run away with his dog and had drowned trying to cross the Suggredoon.

It was a good scenario, one of the best we had designed. It had to be, or Rushton would never have approved it. It was artfully managed, even to the point of having clothes washed up on the bank and beastspeaking scavenger birds to hover ominously about the spot when the Herder search party arrived. It was one of the few rescues that had gone off without a single hitch.

The boy proved not only to be a powerful farseeker, which we had known already, but also a strong empath, which explained how he had sensed my presence when I was shielded. The joint ability was unusual. There were only two other farseekers among us with weak empath Talent. To my regret, the boy chose the Empath guild—little wonder, since Dameon had taken him gently in hand from the start. Within days, he had developed the empaths' traditional adoration for their gentle leader.

His name was Jik.

The expedition was due to depart in only a week when I met with Rushton to discuss the final plan. Discovering my name on the list of those to go, Rushton had exploded. He was furious to hear of my agreement with the black horse and even angrier that I had not spoken of it to him sooner.

"I won't be threatened," he said.

"It is an agreement," I said calmly. "We really don't have any choice. We need the horses. And I am the strongest farseeker and a perfectly good candidate for this expedition."

Rushton shook his head. "I will agree to this test in principle, but you won't be the one riding the black horse. I won't risk a guildleader on an expedition."

Using Alad as translator, Rushton argued with the black horse, but it was useless. "He asks why the equines should risk their leader if the funaga will not," Alad explained. "He says a test should involve leaders."

"Then offer *me* as his rider," Rushton said grimly.

The horse agreed this would be a fair exchange, but

guildmerge outvoted Rushton, saying he was more valuable than any other at Obernewtyn, being the legal master. Incensed, Rushton found his own rule, permitting a unanimous guildmerge to outweight his lone vote, used against him.

I was taken aback at his reaction. I understood his reluctance to risk a guildleader, but to offer himself as a replacement was senseless. Even he must see he was more important to Obernewtyn than I.

Ceirwan, along with two other farseekers, was to run the Farseeker guild in my absence, since Matthew had also been appointed to the expedition. Unspoken was the knowledge that Ceirwan would become guildmaster if I failed to return.

Rounding out the final list were Pavo, Kella, and Louis Larkin, with the Coercer ward Domick as Rushton's choice for our spy in Sutrium. The expedition was to be disguised as a gypsy troupe. The carts had been built by the Teknoguild.

The black horse snorted his loathing at the sight of the gypsy rig. He had appointed two older horses to draw the carts. "Finer horses will encourage robbers," he sent in terse explanation.

"What about you?" I asked.

The horse pricked his ears forward. "They will not find me desirable," he sent cryptically.

The night before we were to leave, Rushton came to my turret chamber, which had been his own room in his time as farm overseer. He had collected our false Normalcy Certificates. Written on old discolored parchment, they were good forgeries, but I hoped we would not need them.

"It's done, then," Rushton said. He stared into the fire. There was a drawn-out silence, and the fire crackled as if the lack of sound made it uneasy.

"Is something wrong?" I asked.

"Are you afraid?" he asked unexpectedly. I had a sudden vivid memory of him asking me the same question in that room when it had been his.

This time, I nodded soberly. "It will be dangerous, despite bypassing Sutrium and the main ways."

Rushton turned to face me, his green eyes troubled. "Don't . . . risk too much for this Talent," he said. "Whoever it is might not even want to join us. You . . . are perceptive, but you don't always see what is in front of your eyes."

I had the notion he had meant to say something else and shifted uncomfortably. I had never felt really at ease with him since the awkward intimacy of being forced into a mindbond with him two years earlier.

Rushton stood abruptly, shook his head, and walked across to open the window shutters, breathing deeply as if the air in the turret room were too thin. He turned, leaning back against the open window, his face in shadow. "You . . . are important to Obernewtyn. We can't afford to lose a guild-mistress. Even now it is not too late to change your mind. . . ."

I shook my head. "I want to go. Besides, I promised."

"You belong here," Rushton said sternly.

I wished he would come back into the room so I could see his face. There was an odd note in his voice that puzzled me.

"Have you been so unhappy here?" he asked.

I laughed. "I've never been more content in my life. But I am glad to go away for a while. It's as if I'm too safe and comfortable—like an old house cat. As Maruman would put it, I'm being tamed by comfort."

"And look at *him*," Rushton said darkly. "Someday you will have to come out of your ivory tower."

I shrugged, not understanding the reference. "Alad said Maruman is recovering, though he still sleeps."

Rushton nodded. "He will miss you."

Before I could answer, there was a knock at the door.

I was surprised to find Dameon and Maryon outside. Their eyes went beyond me to Rushton.

"What is it?" he asked brusquely.

"I have futuretold th' expedition," the Futuretell guildmistress announced in her soft highland accent.

"What have you seen?" Rushton demanded. "Will it be a success? Will those who travel return?"

I held my breath.

Maryon merely want on, looking grave and serene. "I have seen that th' boy Jik mun travel with th' expedition. If he does nowt go, many, perhaps all th' rest, will nowt return."

"Surely another, more experienced empath?" Rushton said.

Maryon shook her head. "The prediction deals specifically wi' th' boy, but it is unclear. I dinna see any direct action on his part. It is my belief that he matters in some obscure manner—perhaps something he will do or say will offer a turning point for the journey."

"That settles it; the expedition will have to be put off until Maryon can clarify the prediction," Rushton said.

Again the Futuretell guildmistress shook her head. "The boy was only part of the foreseeing. Th' fate of Obernewtyn hangs in th' balance of this journey, an' it mun proceed as planned. The expedition mun return to th' mountains wi' their prizes before winter freezes th' pass, else we will fall to our enemies."

Rushton shook his head. "I don't know what to make of this."

"You need not fear Jik will betray us," Dameon said.

Rushton looked taken aback. "I don't doubt his loyalty if

284

you vouch for him. But he's a boy! It's bad enough . . ." His eyes darted momentarily in my direction.

"I don't think we have any choice," Dameon said. "For some reason or other, Jik has to go on the expedition. There is no time to wait for clarification."

"Which might never come," Maryon added.

Rushton ran a hand through his hair and sighed. "I felt it was time to end our isolation, but I little thought what that would cost." He turned and nodded at the stack of Normalcy papers. "Jik will have to use the blank one I had made for the Talent you hope to find. It's too late to make another."

When they were gone, I went to the window and breathed in the cool night air, thinking how strangely things came about. A fortnight before, Jik had been a Herder novice. Now, suddenly, he was vital to Obernewtyn's future. If Zarak had not disobeyed me . . .

I shook my head. One could go mad thinking of alternate possibilities. Kella was right. The present was enough to deal with.

✦ 6 ✦

THE DAY OF the departure dawned, grim and unseasonably cold.

Gray clouds scudded across a metallic autumn sky. Wind blustered and rain fell in short, violent flurries.

I shivered, staring out over the gardens from my window. In that moment, I could imagine vividly the mountain valley blanketed in ice and snow, the mournful sound of wolves echoing across the frozen wastes. The lowlands would be much warmer than the mountains, even in wintertime. Perhaps at last the scars on my feet would have the chance to heal completely. I had avoided speaking to Roland about my feet for fear Rushton would hear of it and use them as reason to ban me from the expedition. Fortunately, Kella understood and had been treating me without telling Roland.

Thinking of the healer made me remember Maruman. I had gone to see him before firstmeal, but, though conscious, he was still dazed and barely coherent. I had wanted desperately to talk to him about the vision I had seen in his unconscious mind, but it was impossible.

As with all expeditions, no amount of forethought could avoid the last-minute rush as remembered necessities were rounded up. Feeling harassed with preparations, I looked up with relief to see Ceirwan and Matthew approach.

"See, I've been practicin'," Matthew sent on a tightly shielded probe. The momentary mischief in his eyes faded as he looked around.

"Until today, it hardly seemed such an important thing to be doin'," he said pensively.

Those who were part of the expedition knew we carried the fate of Obernewtyn on our backs, though the general population of Obernewtyn knew nothing of Maryon's prophecy. And Dameon had requested I tell no one, including Jik, of the part of the prophecy that concerned Jik. "It would not be fair to the boy," he insisted.

Jik was even younger than Lina and Zarak but was more serious and quieter of nature. He seemed bemused by the news that he was to be part of the expedition, though it seemed he would prove useful, for he had been to Sutrium more recently than any of us and would give Domick some idea of the present shape and disposition of the town as we traveled.

Jik had insisted that his companion, Darga, accompany us as well. A nondescript short-haired dog with a ferociously ugly face, he was one of a breed used by the Herders to guard the cloisters. Darga had been a miscolored runt in his litter, expected to die when Jik had volunteered to nurse him. No one had any objections to the dog's inclusion.

Zarak and Lina stood beside Jik, their faces openly envious.

The three horses to travel with us had been supplemented by another. I would ride the stallion, who had told Alad haughtily that he would answer to the title Gahltha, meaning leader. Domick would ride a newcomer, a small, wheat-colored mountain pony with doelike eyes. Named Avra, she had been brought wild to Obernewtyn the previous wintertime, having injured herself in a fall. Alad told me she was the black stallion's chosen mate. The two mares to pull the carts were Mira and Lo.

The horses stood together as Alad harnessed and installed the hated bit and bridles. Privately, Alad had warned me Gahltha had chosen horses that were completely loyal to him. It was clear where their allegiance would lie if it came to a choice between equine and funaga aims. They would follow me as leader of the expedition only under instructions from the black horse.

None of the equines seemed inclined to closer acquaintance, and I hoped I had not made a mistake in choosing Louis over a full Beastspeaking guilder. I could beastspeak, of course, but the animals were more receptive to those of the Beastspeaking guild.

With Kella, Jik, and Darga in one cart and Matthew, Pavo, and Louis in the other, the caravans were authentically crowded. Gypsies traveled traditionally in extended family groups, singing and dancing for money and providing amusing and impromptu plays. The descendants of those who had originally refused Council affiliation, they were little liked or trusted for all their variety of skills. In some ways, it was a dangerous disguise, but it was one of the few ways a number of us could travel about without drawing attention. Travel was not undertaken lightly, for people everywhere were suspicious of strangers in their midst.

To complete our disguise, we were unnaturally tanned and wore the layers of colored clothing favored by gypsies. The dark skin was the result of a powerful berry-based dye. I doubted anyone would have the slightest suspicion we were anything but a motley gypsy troupe.

Rushton stressed the need to maintain our disguise at all costs. We had all set up coercive blocks that would erase our memories in an emergency. These were Obernewtyn's safe-guard in case one of us was caught and tortured. Only Jik had been unable to prepare a block, being too untrained. Domick or I could wipe his memory should it come to that.

Rushton adjured us to work together and not to forget that each of the three aims in the expedition was equally impor-tant.

At the last, he wished us good fortune. "This journey is the beginning of a new stage for us. I wish you success, for your sake and ours." If anyone else noticed the slightly ominous note in his final words, it was not apparent.

All Obernewtyn turned out to see us go, but the festival air did not last long. We had barely finished preparations when it began to rain heavily.

I climbed awkwardly into Gahltha's saddle, ignoring his derisive whinny. He might not want to be ridden, but he knew an incompetent rider when he had one.

Wrapping an oiled cape about my head and shoulders, I nodded to Domick. We had decided he would ride in front of the carts and I at the rear, at least until we left the main road.

The rain had sent everyone running inside, but looking back, I had a final glimpse of Rushton standing alone on the top step, apparently oblivious to the downpour.

Even at that distance, I could see the same odd tension in his stance that had puzzled me in the turret room.

I wondered what he was thinking and impulsively lifted a hand to wave.

Instantly, he responded, raising his own hand. I stared over my shoulder until the gray curtain of rain came between us.

I felt an unexpected regret at the thought that I would not see him again for a long time, perhaps many months if we failed to make it back before the pass froze.

PART II

✦

THE LOWLANDS

✦ 7 ✦

I HAD BEEN nervous about riding and found it only slightly less traumatic than I had expected.

Gahltha began instructing me the moment we left Obernewtyn. Under his terse instructions, I tied the reins to the saddle. When I did not know what to do with my hands, I clutched at the saddle, hanging on for dear life. Gahltha forbade this, saying I must learn to ride by balance before we reached the lowlands. A gypsy did not rely on hands or stirrups. This seemed impossible enough, until he warned me that I would also have to be able to ride without a saddle, since gypsies rarely used them. And no gypsy would be so inept a rider as me.

It took great concentration to coordinate all the contortions Gahltha seemed to feel riding required.

"Heels out so you do not jab me in the ribs, or I may forget and buck you off," he sent. "Knees tight or you will be off the first time I stumble."

The first hours were punctuated by the horse's staccato instructions. He made no comment to me except to give me orders. I had the feeling he was enjoying every minute of my discomfort.

I noticed Domick casually slouched in his saddle as if it were an armchair and envied his skill and confidence.

The rain continued throughout the remainder of the day,

drumming steadily on my oiled coat and on the roofs of the caravans. The weather was so bleak that we traversed the tainted and storm-wracked pass almost without noticing. The last time I had gone over the stretch of tainted grounds, I had been journeying to Obernewtyn for the first time, filled with apprehension for the future. Now I was leaving, still full of apprehension.

We passed the area without mishap and soon after left the main road for the White Valley. Fortunately, the floor of the valley was flat, and there was little undergrowth beneath the trees, else the carts would have been useless.

I felt Jik clumsily seeking entrance into my thoughts. "Will the caravans be able to go through the Olden way?" he asked.

"Pavo thinks so. He believes it was once an important Beforetime thoroughfare," I sent.

"Why doesn't anyone else know about it?" he wondered. "I never heard any of the priests in the Darthnor cloister here mention it, and I never saw it on any of the maps."

The question had also occurred to me. "Pavo says it is probably because there has been no need of it, what with the main road. And no one much uses the White Valley. The highlanders believe it to be haunted."

When night fell, it was still raining. After a hasty conferral, we decided to go on as long as we could, since it would be impossible to make a proper camp or cook in the sodden valley.

In the end, Gahltha was the one to call a halt, saying the horses pulling the cart needed to rest. I was surprised at his consideration, then reminded myself his concern was for the horses, not the humans. But I was glad to stop just the same. Climbing down from his back stiffly, I was convinced every bone in my body was fractured and wondered if it could possibly be any worse to ride bareback.

Relieved of the hated trappings, the horses wandered off to graze, untroubled by the rain. Domick and I hung our soaking oil cloaks under an eben tree in the hope that they would dry by morning.

We all climbed into one carriage to talk. Darga had jumped out the moment the cart stopped; even so, it was too cramped to change my damp clothes, so I wrapped a blanket around my shoulders.

"We might as well close th' flaps an' keep out th' night air," Matthew said, tying the strings.

Kella had lit two candles in shielded sconces, and the interior of the van glowed dimly in the flickering light. It warmed up quickly with the flaps closed, and I felt myself drifting off to sleep watching Jik and the healer prepare a simple nightmeal. I felt so tired, it was an effort to eat, but Kella insisted.

I tried to shift my position, but my legs seemed to have set in their riding stance. Laughing, Kella produced a strongly scented green paste that she promised would ease the muscle strain.

I sighed regretfully and imagined sinking into my favorite chair in front of the turret-room fire when Jik interrupted my weary daydream to ask why he had been included on the expedition.

I had imagined Dameon would have provided some plausible reason, but it appeared he had left it to me. Trying to give myself time to think, I asked Jik why he had not asked Dameon himself.

He shrugged diffidently. "I thought somebody would tell me why eventually."

I nodded, deciding that I could not burden him with the true reason. "Your knowledge of Herder lore will be useful to us. We know so little about the practices of the priesthood or of their ambitions. They seem to be growing stronger and more powerful. And, of course, there is your knowledge of Sutrium."

Jik frowned. "I was taken by the priests when I was very young. I hardly remember it. I don't know any more about Sutrium than you," he concluded in a troubled voice.

I patted his arm reassuringly. "Don't worry about why you're here. Just concentrate on remembering everything you can about Sutrium and the Herder Faction."

I heard squelching noises outside just as Gahltha's cold probe slid into my mind.

I pulled aside the flap and looked into his dark, wet face, almost invisible in the night. Directly behind him, Avra was a pale blur.

"What is it?" I sent, matching his brevity.

"Avra found fresh equine tracks nearby, less than a day old. Funaga rode the equines," Gahltha sent. "They traveled the opposite way to us, making for the main road."

"Maybe someone else knows about the Olden way," Domick said when I told the others.

I sent a questing thought to Avra. "Do you know how many funaga there were?"

"More than here—two times more than here," Avra sent, as shy as Gahltha was arrogant. I bit my lip.

We had been incredibly lucky to miss the riders, but that did not solve the question of where they had come from. There were no mapped villages in the White Valley. But Louis said the highlands were full of small settlements unknown to Council mapmakers, made up of people who wanted to be free of Council domination without openly opposing it.

"Perhaps the riders came from such a settlement," he offered without conviction.

"Perhaps they were hunting," Domick said.

I weighed the options. "We'll stay the night here and leave at dawn."

I asked Gahltha to warn Darga and the other horses to keep an eye out for any sign of funaga that might give us a clue about why they had been in the White Valley. Then I dropped the flap, shutting out the bleak night.

"He doesn't like you," Jik said in puzzled wonder.

I nodded wryly. "Gahltha was badly abused by his old masters. I don't think he likes any human."

"But it's different at Obernewtyn. No one would hurt him there," Jik said indignantly. "It's not fair for him to blame us."

I smiled gently at his loyalty to his adopted home. "Not much in life is fair."

I realized Jik had not been able to hear Gahltha but had sensed the horse's dislike. Such sensitivity to a beast's emotions seemed to be a new use of empathising, or perhaps a new Talent altogether. I made a mental note to discuss it with Dameon when we returned.

"What do you think those people were doing here?" Kella asked.

"I don't know," I said. "But if they are in hiding, they won't want to see us any more than we want to stumble into their midst. I'm going to farsense the way ahead. If there is any sign of a settlement, we'll change course and bypass it." I closed my eyes.

For a moment, I was half mesmerized by my own exhaustion and the monotonous sound of rain on the canvas roof of the caravan. I had forgotten how storms could affect my range. Pavo's theory was that rain occasionally contained some sort of mild taint to which humans had adapted but which nevertheless acted upon Misfit abilities.

I forced myself to concentrate, and then my probe was flying swift and low along the path we had planned to take. I touched briefly on the minds of various nocturnal creatures but found no human mind. At one point, I was startled when a cloud of shadowy birds rose, flittering and shrieking indignantly, disturbed by my scrying. Finding nothing, I came back along the same path, swinging out on both sides.

My probe brushed briefly along the static barrier on the fringe of the Blacklands; then I went farther ahead, along the banks of the Suggredoon. I was surprised to realize we were less than an hour's ride from the river. We planned to follow the Suggredoon down to where it disappeared underground at the foot of the Gelfort Range. Not far from there, we would find the Olden way.

Making a last sweep of the area, I encountered a blank spot. I tried to penetrate it, but it was like trying to see in a blinding snowstorm.

Defeated, I withdrew and opened my eyes.

"Are ye all right?" Matthew asked.

"Did you find anything?" Domick asked.

I told them the result of my farsensing. "It sounds like Blackland static," Matthew said.

"It was like that but denser and cloudier," I said. "Maybe it was tainted water."

"But no settlement," Domick persisted.

"I couldn't sense even a single person, let alone a settlement," I said, feeling relieved. "Maybe it was a hunting party."

Matthew looked doubtful. "I dinna think anyone would come here to hunt. T'would be like takin' midmeal in a graveyard. Maybe it were soldierguards lookin' for escapees or robbers?"

I chewed my lip. "It wouldn't be possible to have a machine that would create that kind of blocking static, would it?" I asked.

Pavo looked thoughtful. "That would mean someone had found a way to modify another Beforetime machine. The Zebkrahn took years to modify—first Marisa Seraphim, then Alexi, and then the Teknoguild worked to change what seems to have been no more than a thing originally devised to measure brain waves. Besides, I think you would know if it was a machine."

"It must be some sort of taint, then," Domick said dismissively.

It was a cold night. I slept restlessly, dreamed of running through dark tunnels, and woke with the feeling that I had forgotten something important. After racking my brain, I pushed the nagging feeling to the back of my thoughts.

Pulling the flap aside, I was delighted to find sun streaming through the treetops. The others stirred in the blaze of light, blinking and groaning. The ground was soaking wet, and there was no question of lighting a fire, but it was lovely to stretch our legs and walk around. I was very stiff but suspected I would have been worse without Kella's healer wizardry.

Gahltha and the other horses emerged from the trees as we were finishing a scratch firstmeal. Darga accepted a bowl of milk with a polite flap of his tail. We tied the oilskins, which were still wet, on top of the caravans and washed our faces in a streamlet. Domick worried that the water might be tainted, but Darga pronounced it safe. He had an acute sense of smell and could tell when water was bad.

We set off far more cheerfully than the previous day. I felt happier despite Gahltha's insistence at my riding bareback. Mounting him was an awkward debacle, because my legs were too stiff to flex easily. But once up, I felt more comfortable than I had on the saddle, though less secure.

The sun shone in a golden autumn way, and Jik played a jaunty harvest song on his gita, accompanying himself in a surprisingly sweet singing voice. Even grim Domick appeared to enjoy the impromptu concert, and the horses perked their ears as if they liked the sound.

Later, I listened to a communication between Darga and Avra about funaga. I was amused to hear their interpretation of human parenting, but Gahltha snorted loudly at Avra's observation that the children of funaga seemed less dangerous than grown funaga.

"You do not know anything about the funaga and their ways," he told her icily. "They are all the same. I have been beaten savagely by a funaga child who laughed at my pain and jeered when I bled. Like poisoned ground, funaga bear poisoned fruit."

I shivered at the venom in his voice.

Gahltha's pace quickened after that. On a flat stretch, he broke into a trot without warning, and I fell. My only consolation was that the wet ground was soft. My anger made no impression on Gahltha, who insisted that I would not have fallen if I had been gripping with my knees the way I was supposed to. Louis laughed uproariously, and though the others restrained their amusement, my next fall sent them all into gales of laughter.

I kept my temper with difficulty, realizing Gahltha sought to goad me. And I knew he was right, however sarcastic he was. I had been sitting lazily.

By the time we stopped for midmeal, I was covered in mud. It was not worth changing, so I merely washed my hands and face to eat. The afternoon was worse than the morning, despite my forlorn hope for an easy walking pace. Gahltha decided I must advance to riding at a gallop. Only stubborn pride kept me from protesting that he was progressing too quickly.

So we cantered and galloped, and when the wagons moved too slowly for Gahltha, he would ride ahead, then turn and ride back. By late afternoon, I was beginning to feel the rhythm of his movements. Once or twice I even found myself enjoying the speed.

We had been traveling parallel to the Suggredoon most of the day, but soon after midmeal, the river broadened suddenly, swollen from the night's rain. The undergrowth thickened, too, slowing the caravans to a walking pace. Avra went slightly ahead with Domick, seeking the easiest path for the caravans. Later, Gahltha and I took over, leaving Domick free to range farther ahead.

We hoped to reach the foot of the mountains before nightfall, but Domick returned just as the sun fell behind the mountains. One look at his grim expression told us his news was bad.

"I found the place where the Suggredoon goes under the mountains, but I couldn't find any pass. We went a fair way up from the river, but there was nothing," he reported glumly.

"The distances on the map might be wrongly drawn, or the entrance to the pass might be sharply aslant so that you would have to be coming from the other way to see it," Pavo said.

"I hope you're right," Domick said. "But that's not all the bad news. Just ahead, there are great patches of swamp and wetlands. The wagons won't have a hope of going through, and it will take days to go round."

There seemed no point in pushing on in the darkness. We

decided to make camp on a high, grassy knoll beside the Sug-gredoon.

Louis, Jik, and Matthew went to forage for dry wood while Kella organized nightmeal. Domick unharnessed the horses and checked the wooden wheels for stress cracks. Pavo sat near the wagons and pored over his maps.

I went to bathe in the river, but just as I reached the edge of the clearing, I heard Kella and Domick begin a heated ar-gument. Sighing, I turned back. The last thing we needed was guild rivalry.

Before I could intervene, Pavo broke into a violent fit of coughing. Kella stared at him for a moment, then went over and commanded him to open his mouth.

"I swallowed a fly." He laughed and waved her away. But Kella's face was deadly serious.

"What is it?" Domick asked her.

The healer ignored him and laid a hand over Pavo's thin chest. The smile faded from his face, and suddenly I felt frightened.

"Why didn't you tell anyone?" Kella asked in a subdued voice.

Pavo smiled sadly. "What good would it have done, eh? I don't need a healer to tell me what the matter is."

"Rushton would never have let you come if he had known," Kella said.

Pavo turned away abruptly. "Don't you think I know that?"

"What is it?" I asked, coming back into the clearing.

Kella looked at me bleakly. "The rotting sickness. It's in his breathing."

"Are you sure?" Domick asked.

"It's not hard to feel, once you know. And the coughing is

always a sign. There's nothing I can do for him. Nothing," she said flatly.

Pavo still had his back to us, rigidly unmoving.

"You'll have to . . . ," I began.

"No!" The usually mild teknoguilder whirled, eyes ablaze. "I won't go back." He turned to Kella. "You said yourself there's nothing to be done. I accept that, but I'll go the way I want. I won't be a problem. Tell them."

She nodded. "He'll cough, and there will be bouts of pain. He won't be affected badly until near the end—three or four months, maybe less . . ."

I gaped. Pavo stared back, his eyes pleading and determined at the same time. "You will need me to get to the library."

I wished Rushton were there to decide. After a long moment, I nodded, and Pavo's shoulders slumped visibly as if he had been holding his breath.

"Thank you," he said.

I felt tears in my eyes and was relieved to see Matthew and Jik arrive, laden with dry wood. Jik froze and looked about, sensing the tangle of emotions. I sent a quick shielded instruction to Matthew, and he began to make a fire, diverting Jik's attention.

We slept inside the caravans again because of the sodden ground but left the flaps open for fresh air. Obernewtyn seemed very far away.

Near dawn, I was jolted awake by Domick poking his head into the wagon.

"Quick, there are people coming. Men," he hissed urgently.

I farsensed the area and almost fainted with horror. There were at least a dozen men approaching the clearing. "It's too

303

late to escape," I told him. "You get away. I'll send the horses away and contact you once I find out what this is all about. Quickly," I whispered.

He nodded, then melted silently into the gray predawn shadows.

My heart thundering, I farsent the group, warning them to let me do any talking. Then I urged the horses away.

Our only hope, I knew, was to be taken for the gypsies we appeared to be. I cursed my stupidity at not taking better precautions after Avra had found the tracks.

"Ho. What have we here?" called a gruff voice. I leaned out of the caravan. Three men stood in the open, illuminated by the dying embers of our fire. Behind them, the dark sky showed pink and gray traces of the dawn. I sensed the other men waiting in the bushes.

"Who are you? What do you want?" I shouted.

"Gypsies," sneered one, a fat, bristle-bearded man with a great pouting stomach and pale, glistening eyes.

"Perhaps," said the voice that had first hailed us. It belonged to a muscular young giant with ginger hair.

The third man appeared frail and was clad in a long, fine woolen gown much like the garb worn by Herder priests. I was terrified that we might have fallen into Herder hands. I prayed the priest would not recognize Jik and hurriedly warned him not to draw attention to himself. With his dark skin, dyed hair, and gypsy clothing, he did not look much like the Herder boy we had rescued.

"Who are you to be waking us in the middle of the night?" I demanded. Gypsies were not known for their manners.

"Get out of those wagons, all of you!" snarled the black-bearded man.

"This is a funny time to want your palm read," I grumbled. "If you mean to rob us, you'll be disappointed." I climbed out and put my hands on my hips as the others gathered behind me. I watched the man in the robe closely, but he did not seem to recognize Jik. "Well, you have us all out. Now what?" I asked.

The ginger-haired woodsman quirked his brow speculatively. "Is this all of you?"

"Enough for you," I said cheekily.

"Are you the leader of these people?" asked the man in the robe. He had a curiously colorless voice and very cold eyes.

"For now," I answered after swift thought. "My father is the leader of our troupe. We are to meet up with him in Arandelft." I nodded at Pavo. "My cousin here fell sick, and our party split in two. Though I don't know what business it is of yours," I added rudely.

"What are you doing here if you are headed for Arandelft?" asked the white-robed man.

My heart jumped. "We heard there was an Olden way through the mountains," I said. The best lies are the ones that are mostly true, Louis always told us. He was glaring belligerently at the men, and I hoped he would keep his mouth shut.

"There is no such pass." The robed man stepped forward, and I resisted the urge to step away. "Enough of this. We will bring them back to camp."

More men stepped out of the trees. I pretended to look surprised. "Find the horses and bring these vans."

"Where are you taking us?" I demanded.

The robed man did not answer, but the ginger-bearded woodsman grinned over his shoulder. "You are to meet the great man himself. The Druid."

305

✦ 8 ✦

THROUGH THE TREES, I could see a settlement. I realized we were headed for the blank area I had been unable to penetrate the night before. This and the knowledge that we had been captured by Henry Druid filled me with apprehension. We could hardly have gotten into a worse mess deliberately.

But more disturbing, as soon as we entered the area of blankness, my powers were useless. I could not even reach Matthew, who was directly behind me.

Mindbound for the first time in my life, I was nearly overcome with panic and the feeling of being trapped. Glancing over one shoulder, the look of rigid terror on Jik's face acted like a bucket of cold water on my own fear. I made myself smile reassuringly, and the stark tension in his movements subsided. Then I concentrated on calming myself. I had to find a way to free us, and that would only be possible with a cool head. Methodically, I tried reaching all the others, including Darga, who padded along quietly beside Jik. I could not sense a single thought. Then I tried to farseek outside the area—Domick, then Gahltha.

Nothing.

No wonder the Druids had seemed to disappear so completely. The block had to be a machine, modified like the Zebkrahn. There was something mindless about the static.

I was deeply concerned by what such a block must mean.

We had long heard rumors of Council and Herder interest in Misfits with special abilities, but to most of the Land we were thought to be harmless defectives who might occasionally have a meaningful dream. The Druid must know otherwise.

Somehow, Rushton had to be warned that he had mind weapons. What would happen if the rogue Herder discovered we were Misfits?

Or did he already know that, too?

Behind, Louis grunted in astonishment at the size of the walled encampment visible through the trees. The wall itself was no more than a barrier of thin, dark-stained striplings set upright in the ground, reaching high enough to obscure all but the tops of thatch-roofed buildings and a number of gently smoking chimneys.

Rounding the outer wall, we came to a wide gateway that was firmly bolted. A ruddy face appeared at an opening in answer to the red-haired woodsman's call. "Who is that wi' ye, Gilbert? I diven't know them faces."

Gilbert gestured impatiently at the door. "Open up, Relward."

"Bain't he a gypsy?" Relward inquired, staring doltishly into my face. He chewed his lip ponderously, then, unlatching the gate, planted himself firmly in the gap.

"Step aside, fool! You try my patience," Gilbert snapped.

Relward shook his head. "I canna let strangers in. Take him"—he nodded at me—"an' them others to th' compound. Her can come in," he added, nodding at Kella. Despite the seriousness of our situation, I felt indignant at being taken for a boy.

"I'll decide where they will be taken, Relward," Gilbert said through gritted teeth. "I'm not sure we should have a gatekeeper too blind to know the difference between man and maid."

The bumpkin's eyes widened. He stared at me accusingly, as if I had deliberately transformed myself to confound him. Then he gaped, seeing the robed man. "Master," he bleated. "I dinna know ye was there." He tripped over his feet in an effort to get out of the way. The robed man ignored him and swept into the camp.

Gilbert grinned covertly over his shoulder at me. "Do not think we are all such fools as that—or so blind," he murmured in a low voice.

There was nothing makeshift about what lay within the walls. It was a complete and settled village with graveled streets and stores. There was even a blacksmith and extensive holding yards and stables for horses.

People came out into the street to watch us pass, their eyes curious. Almost everyone seemed to wear arms, including the women and older children. The prospect of escape seemed dim.

At the very center of the settlement was a wide green expanse and garden beds. I was oddly reassured to see children playing on a swing, though they stopped their game to watch us pass.

Only one building edged on the square, a big stone house that reminded me vaguely of the main Councilcourt in Sutrium. Broad stone steps led up to the entrance, and double wooden doors like those at Obernewtyn stood open, revealing a long hall with a shining timber floor and a high sloped ceiling. Two young men emerged from one of the many doors leading off the hall. They smiled at Gilbert, but their good humor faded when they saw the rest of us.

"Gypsies," one spat. Gilbert frowned but made no comment, shepherding us through a door into an unadorned room.

The other men continued farther into the building, leaving

us alone except for Gilbert. I tried again to breach the block but with no success. It was incredible to think such mental blindness was considered normal.

"Gypsies, eh?" Gilbert said, leaning against the door. "Where were you really headed? The main road would be much quicker than any so-called Olden way."

I stepped up to him boldly. "I told you already, or are you as deaf as that gatewarden was blind? We are to meet my father in Arandelft."

Instead of becoming angry, Gilbert threw back his head and laughed with real amusement. "I wondered why a scrap of a girl was the leader over grown men, but now I see you carry the sharpest weapon in your wicked tongue."

"Why have you brought us here?" I demanded.

Gilbert smiled. "I am the one asking the questions. Tell me, where have you come from, if you insist you are going to Arandelft?"

I hesitated. "We have been in the high mountain country."

I heard a smothered gasp from Kella, but fortunately Gilbert was too intent on my answer to register it.

"Then . . . you must have seen Obernewtyn?" he said.

I shrugged carelessly. "Of course." From the corner of my eye, I could see Matthew looking at me as if I had gone mad.

"Why did you go up there?" Gilbert asked guardedly.

"Why does a gypsy travel anywhere? For silver. My father said there would be winter lodgings there and work to trade for it. He wanted to try trapping a snow bear. One sold in Sutrium last moon fair for a Councilman's ransom." I smiled as if the thought of such wealth excited me, then I let my face fall.

"But everything went wrong. There was a curse on that place, and we laid another in leaving. A firestorm had all but laid it to waste. There was nothing left but a few rough huts made of the ruins. The people remaining had no room or food to spare. Then my cousin fell sick, and I had to wait for him while the rest went on without us. And now this," I snorted petulantly.

"So, there *was* a firestorm," Gilbert murmured.

"We were supposed to meet the troupe at Arandelft in time for the harvest of eben berries," Matthew said.

Gilbert looked at him and grinned. "So, you *can* speak. I thought you were all mute, having this grubby wench speak for you."

I held my breath, hoping Matthew would have the sense to see he was being deliberately needled. He only shrugged sullenly and fell silent.

The robed man returned, and Gilbert spoke to him in a low voice. His pale eyes rested thoughtfully on me.

"Take the men to the compound, the boy to the other children, and the girl to Rilla," the robed man told Gilbert. "You will come with me," he instructed me coldly.

He led me down the hall to another door.

". . . but how can we have missed it . . ." A deep voice floated out as we entered. I blinked, dazzled by the sunlight streaming from a huge window. The room was an enclosed fern garden. There was a long table covered in books and papers and surrounded by chairs. A number of robed men and several dressed like Gilbert clustered around the head of the table.

"Forgive me, lord," said the man who had brought me there.

Those bending over the table drew back to reveal a white-bearded man seated in their midst. He wore a plain cream-colored robe like the others, yet there was an aura of authority about him. He had the thin face and body of an ascetic, but his features were curiously mismatched—a beaky nose, a jutting

310

chin, and beetling silver brows. His eyes were his sole visible beauty, dark and strangely compelling. Such eyes might easily see into a person's mind. I met his penetrating gaze uneasily.

"Who is this?" he asked in a low, sweet voice.

"This is the gypsy girl I mentioned a moment ago. But I had not realized then that she and her family have been in the high mountains," he added pointedly.

The old man's eyes glittered. "You have been to Obernewtyn?"

I nodded, wondering if I had made a mistake in mentioning Obernewtyn. I told them what I had told Gilbert. "Why have you brought us here?" I asked at last. I wanted to impress on them that I was a gypsy, interested in nothing but my own skin.

"Tell me what you saw at Obernewtyn," the old man invited.

"I've told you everything. They wouldn't let us stay because there was no room. Some of them were sick." I let distaste show in my eyes.

"My acolyte told me you were looking for a Beforetime pass."

I nodded.

"There is no pass," the old man said. "Now, what is the truth for your avoiding the main road? I suspect you were trying to leave the highlands without being seen. Gypsies are known for being light-fingered." I hung my head to hide my relief. He thought we were thieves trying to reach the lowlands without being arrested!

"What are you going to do with us?" I asked, hoping to encourage his assumptions.

"What was the name of the Master of Obernewtyn?" the old man asked.

A chill ran down my spine. "There was a youth in charge, if you would call him master. He seemed half out of his wits if you ask me. Kept raving about Obernewtyn belonging to him and wanting to restore it. Who would want to bother with such a ruin?" I chewed my lip as if trying to recall. "Rafe . . . Rushton, I think his name was."

An unreadable look flickered over the old man's face.

For a long moment, there was silence in the room, and I heard the muted sounds of children at play. The old man rose slowly and came round to stand in front of me.

"Do you know who I am?" he asked.

My heart sank. If he would tell that openly, he had no intention of letting us go. "Are you . . . the Druid from the old stories?" I asked shyly.

The old man gave me a quick, rather beautiful smile. "I am," he said. "It pleases me to know my name has not been forgotten. And what do gypsies know of Henry Druid?"

"My father told me the Council and the Herder Faction forced you into exile. He said you were not dead no matter what was said and that you would one day return."

A fanatic gleam flashed in the old man's eyes. "Your father is wise, for I do mean to return."

The door opened suddenly, and a pretty blond girl entered. She scanned the room lazily, her eyes stopping on the Druid. "Father, you promised to come to midmeal. We are all waiting." She pouted.

The Druid smiled indulgently. "I will be there very soon, Erin. In the meantime, take this girl to Rilla for me."

"Another gypsy?" she inquired disparagingly. Without waiting for an answer, she gestured languidly for me to follow.

The Druid's voice followed us into the hall. "And, Erin, tell

Rilla the two girls will attend nightmeal with us tonight. See that they have some suitable clothes."

Erin nodded and closed the door behind us. She led me wordlessly out of the building, across the green, and down a number of streets to a square building near the edge of the settlement. A delicious smell of cooking food flowed out the door. My mouth watered, but we bypassed the door, going round a narrow path to another building at the rear. The less appetizing smell of soapsuds met my nostrils. I cast a regretful look over my shoulder.

Erin glanced at me with as much interest as if I were a piece of cheese. Her eyes were hard and bright like pieces of blue glass.

A woman came out to meet us. Plump and pretty, she introduced herself as Rilla.

Erin looked bored at this exchange. "This one needs a good scrubbing. I don't wonder Relward mistook it for a boy. Still, do what you can. Both these gypsies are to come to nightmeal at the Druid's table tonight."

"Your friend is already bathing," Rilla said when Erin had gone. My stomach growled loudly as if defining its own priorities, and Rilla laughed. "Ye'd nowt be let into th' kitchen lookin' like that. But bathe quick and ye can have yer fill before yer tum gives up growlin' an' takes to bitin' ."

The bathhouse was filled with billowing steam. I squinted, making out a number of tin barrels all round the walls with fires burning beneath. In the center of the room were two vats. Kella's head popped above the rim of one, and Rilla pointed me to the other.

"There now," she said kindly, handing me a drying towel.

I turned to set the towel down and caught sight of myself

in the mirror. I gaped. My face was barely visible for filth—I scarcely looked human. My clothes were stiff with dirt, and my long hair was one lank rat tail. I had not bathed since Gahltha's riding lessons. With a grimace, I stripped off my clothes and slid into the soapy water. I scrubbed thoroughly, massaging gritty dirt from my hair and ears. Kella handed me a thick calico robe like the one she wore as I clambered out.

"Was it the Druid?" she asked worriedly.

I nodded. "Did you notice anything else since we came here?"

Kella sighed. "You too? I hoped your powers would be strong enough not to be affected. What do you think it is?"

"Some sort of machine, but no one mentioned it. Maybe this is how they test people to find out if they are Misfits. Yet I'm almost certain they believe we're real gypsies."

"Rilla won't be long. I think she's been told to keep an eye on us. What are we going to do?" Kella asked urgently.

"I'm going to try breaking through the barrier as soon as I have a moment alone. If that doesn't work, I'll have to get to the machine and damage it or switch it off somehow. If only Pavo were here. I wonder why we've been separated?"

"Didn't they say anything to you about this nightmeal?" Kella asked.

Puzzled at her tone, I said, "We're to eat with the Druid. What else should I be told?"

"We are to eat with the Druid and all unbonded men," Kella said pointedly. "Have you noticed how few women there are around here? Rilla let it slip. Tonight we are going to be looked over like batches of scones. For bonding."

Rilla returned carrying a green dress in one arm and a blue one in the other. "These will match your eyes," she said. Her own eyes widened. "Well, ye do clean up nice an' proper."

314

I had never seen such fine clothes before, let alone dreamed of wearing them. But where had such finery come from, if not Sutrium? And how would an exiled Herder priest obtain such luxuries?

"These will make ye pretty fer tonight," Rilla said, holding out the dresses.

"Pretty as lambs to the slaughter," I murmured sarcastically. I held mine up as if it were a shroud cloth. And well it might be, for I had no intention of being bonded to anyone.

✦ 9 ✦

IT WAS AN odd, strained occasion.

The Druid and his guests were formally attired, and the courses of food were lavishly presented. It was hard to believe we were in the middle of the White Valley.

The Druid's armsmen, as those of Gilbert's type called themselves, drank heavily, both red and white fements as well as a spicy warmed cordial. The latter could be made anywhere, but the highlands were no place to grow the delicate fement grapes. Like the dresses Kella and I wore, the fements could only have come from the lowlands, probably Arandelft.

The Druid had the head of the table, and his daughter, Erin, sat by his side, clad in a dazzling blood-red dress. Her long hair was elaborately plaited and beaded around her head.

Beside her, Gilbert smiled in welcome. "So, gypsy girl, how are you finding our rough-and-ready camp?"

Laughter met his words. All the Druid's captives were probably equally astounded at the lavish way the Druids lived. Gilbert was hardly recognizable in a fine white shirt and black velvet jacket, though he was less extravagantly clad than many of the other armsmen. None of the white-robed Druid acolytes were present.

"What? No words for us, gypsy girl? Have we disarmed

you at last? Perhaps the fire was quenched when the dirt was washed off," Gilbert teased.

Erin laid a dainty hand on his arm. "Dirt will wash away, Gilbert, but that particular hue of skin will remain the same grubby gypsy color, no matter how hard she scrubs."

The table fell silent, but before I could draw breath to respond, Gilbert laughed, smoothly drawing his arm from beneath hers. "I find that dusky tone more pleasing than the fashionable pallor of a fish underbelly," he said, smiling into my eyes.

I found myself seated some way down the table and apart from Kella. On either side, the men spoke only a few polite words to me. Their eyes said they shared Erin's attitude. It was funny, in a way. If they had known I was a Misfit, I would be far more despised.

A while later, Erin's voice rose above the buzz of talk. "Father, I am only saying that this desire to bond the armsmen is going too far. Surely you want to maintain some sort of standard. Yet you permit grubby gypsies to dine with us." I had no doubt she had raised her voice deliberately.

I stood abruptly. "Lord, my father told me enough to make me admire Henry Druid, but I will not be insulted by a painted doll!" There was a gasp from some of the men, and Erin's pouting mouth fell open in astonishment.

There was a long silence. I did not take my eyes from the Druid's, but I was not to hear his reply since someone had begun to clap.

"Well done, Lady Erin. I salute you for your wit," Gilbert said. He raised his mug to Erin. "I feared our gypsy girl had lost her tongue." He drank deeply, and a few hardy souls around him laughed.

Erin's face filled with rage, but the Druid laid a restraining hand on her arm. I wondered at Gilbert's recklessness. It was clear he had some rank in the camp, but now I wondered exactly what his position was.

He grinned at me down the length of the table, but I did not smile back. Beside him, Erin's eyes glittered with malice. Perhaps Gahltha's cynical comment that poisoned trees bore poisoned fruit was right, for I suspected the Druid shared his daughter's prejudice.

I finished my meal, ignored by my companions. I had a fierce longing to be back at Obernewtyn, where people were judged by their actions rather than their ancestry. Rushton would laugh to know how much I hungered to be home. With a painful lurch of my heart, I realized I missed him.

A young boy and an old man played a merry dance tune on a drum and a small flute. I was not surprised to see people rise to dance. I had never learned how. Orphan homes did not organize such frivolous pursuits. On both sides of me, the seats were empty, my dinner companions having deserted me for less controversial partners. My outburst had made me doubly an outcast despite my finery.

I looked up to find Gilbert standing beside my seat. "Come, let me see if you dance as well as you talk."

I lifted my chin. "I wonder you dare ask a gypsy to dance."

Gilbert frowned. "Hatred of gypsies is a foolish, unfounded prejudice that I do not share."

"It seems you are alone in that. Who are you, that you can safely voice such unpopular opinions?"

"I lead the armsmen. The Druid values my expertise. But I am known for my outspoken nature. It has not got me killed so far."

I smiled a little despite myself. Another place and time, I would have liked the bold armsman as a friend. But the knowledge that he was the leader of the Druid's fighting force made me nervous. His kindness might be no more than a strategy to put me off guard.

Gilbert slid into the seat beside me. "I am my own fellow. Dance with me," he invited softly.

I found I did not want to hurt his feelings with a plain refusal. I lifted the hem of my skirt and showed him my scarred legs and feet. His face tightened at the sight of the scars. "And I made you walk back to camp. Why didn't you say something?"

I smiled and shrugged wryly. "You didn't seem the sort to worry about a prisoner's feet."

"Then we will talk," he said firmly. "You may direct the course of our words."

The opportunity was too good to miss. "Tell me how you came to be here."

Gilbert smiled and obliged. It proved an unexpected tale.

He had been born to a seafaring family in Aborium, but his father had been taken by slavers and his boat sunk. As a child, Gilbert had worked as a harbor laborer to support his mother and sister, until they died of a plague that swept the coast one year. Weary of the sea and lonely, he had gone inland to seek his fortune as a hunter. He had been on his own in the White Valley when the Druid had recruited him. He smiled wryly at the euphemism.

"At first I was determined to escape, but where would I escape to? I had no home, and I loathe the Council. And, as you see, this is a pleasant enough life for one so skilled and useful as I."

"The Druid has a good supply of luxuries," I said.

He grinned. "He has a friend in Sutrium." He stopped abruptly.

I continued on, pretending not to have noticed his slip. "Are there really such things as slavers?" I asked.

He nodded. "There are at that, black-hearted souls. They prey on small fishing vessels like those belonging to my father, shanghai the crew, and sell them. I have also heard it said the Council sells seditioners they do not want brought to open trial. Those taken are never heard of again. Who knows where they end up? It is a wide, strange world."

"But . . . what do you mean? There is only this Land and the two islands," I said. "The rest is Blacklands."

Gilbert shook his head. "A myth spawned by the Council, who have a vested interest in ignorance. There are other places on the earth where the white death never reached or where the poisons have faded. My father always said so, and he had seen more of the world than most."

I stared. "But how is it no one talks of this?"

Gilbert smiled, not unpleasantly. "Any seafarer stupid enough to talk of such things disappears, no doubt himself sold to the slavers. After all, the Council do not want their subjects sailing off in search of greener pastures and freer lands."

I was fascinated. I had never dreamed of questioning Council teachings on the extent of the holocaust.

"Why not take to the sea yourself and go where there is no Council?" I wondered.

Gilbert sighed. "I could have done that, but a harsh lore is better than none. It is said that incredible mutations of plant and beast run riot beyond our horizons. And even lands untouched by the Great White must have suffered in the Age of

Chaos that followed. No, better to work here with the Druid to overcome the Council. Besides, unlike my father, I get seasick," he added.

I laughed, then sobered quickly. "You think the Druid and his acolytes are any better than the Council?" I hardly expected an answer to such a question, but he had certainly been forthcoming to this point.

"I don't know. I hope so. He is hard, but there is always hope of change. At least he has standards and rules to live by. He values order and normalcy."

I looked at him sharply. "You said the world is full of mutation. Who has the right to decide what is normal?"

Gilbert looked taken aback at the change in my tone. "I do not mind mutants; in my experience, those deemed Misfit are harmless. But the Druid was a Herder, after all. He is fanatical on the subject. And most of the others think as he does. Perhaps I'm not fine enough to distinguish between the smells of people as if they were so much spoiled meat."

I frowned, deciding whatever the Druid knew or guessed about Talents, Gilbert knew nothing. Perhaps only the Druid's acolytes knew about the machine blocking my abilities.

"And what about freedom? He would not let you leave here."

The armsman smiled. "No one keeps me where I do not want to be. But freedom is not a matter of that. You are a gypsy, so you think it is only the ability to move from place to place at will. Real freedom is a thing no one can take from you because it is of the spirit. I keep it here." He tapped his head, then rose. "I have promised a dance, but we will talk again."

I watched him go, surprised to find myself wishing we could have gone on talking, grateful that he had allowed me to question him without asking me questions in return.

I shook my head. He was an enemy, yet I liked him. And I was as certain he liked me. It had never occurred to me that I might be found desirable. Yet clothed in the fine dress, I had only been able to gape at my reflection as I'd caught sight of myself in a long mirror on my way to the dining hall. The girl who had looked back at me, with her cloud of dark silky hair and mysterious green eyes, had seemed a dazzling stranger. In that moment, I'd had the curious wish that Rushton might see me so transformed.

To my relief, the meal ended without talk of bonding. Like all farseekers, I knew bonding for me would mean more than a physical communion. A mindmeld would be far more intimate than any bodily merging. It would be an ultimate kind of nakedness with one of my own kind; to bond with an un-Talent would be like bonding to a statue.

I prepared for bed in a private chamber; Kella had been housed in a separate room. Dismissing all thoughts of the nightmeal from my mind, I concentrated my senses for a final, unrestrained attempt on the barrier of static.

The block lay like a wet blanket over my senses. I felt suffocated as I tried to farseek. I used more power, but the static seemed to respond, strengthening in direct proportion to the force I used.

Finally I lay back with a defeated sigh. It was no use. I would have to find the machine.

✦ 10 ✦

"WHAT ARE YE up to, Emmon?" Rilla demanded suspiciously of a slight boy with a lopsided grin who had entered the kitchen.

He looked exaggeratedly hurt. "Th' Druid sent me to bring the gypsy called Elspeth," he said in a wounded voice.

I had spent the morning with Kella helping to do the encampment chores. I had tried questioning Rilla, but she appeared to know no more than Gilbert about the existence of Talents, much less the blocking static. She also didn't seem to know where the rest of our friends were. I'd begun to worry.

Kella had learned that Rilla's dead bondmate had been one of the Druids slain in the last Teknoguild expedition, and the older girl's general ignorance of the incident confirmed that the Druid only told his people what he felt they needed to know. "Rilla knows that others were involved but has no idea that they were from Obernewtyn," Kella had said. "She did say the Druid believes the explosion had been caused deliberately with a Beforetime weapon. That and his interest in Obernewtyn must mean he suspects Rushton of treachery."

I wondered now what the Druid wanted of me.

As we left, Emmon stole a slice of meat and got a hard smack for his troubles. Outside, he rubbed his ear and grinned broadly. "T'was worth it. Come on." We had not gone far when I realized we were going in the wrong direction.

"Well, that's true . . . ," Emmon admitted. "As a matter of fact, I were nowt told to bring ye at once, so we've time to spare. I'd rather walk about than wash dishes or work at spellin' an' th' like. Wouldn't you?"

"Won't we get into trouble?" I asked warily.

He shook his head. "Ye won't. If we gan caught, I'll say ye knew nowt of it."

"Will you show me around, then? I haven't had much chance to see the camp," I said.

Emmon nodded enthusiastically. He marched off, at once setting out to describe the variety and uses of the buildings we passed. I tried in vain to lead him to talk of the Druid, in the hope of getting a clue about the location of any machine. Eventually, I concentrated instead on committing the camp to memory.

We passed a long series of windowless buildings, which Emmon identified as storehouses.

"Where do all the Druid's supplies come from?" I asked.

Emmon grinned. "From th' Council's own stores. Th' Council dinna know that one of their own trusted agents is oath kin to th' Druid."

Oath kin? That meant someone as close as blood without being related. The Druid was as canny a strategist as I'd ever encountered.

Emmon pointed out another building. "That's th' library." It seemed his dislike of spelling did not extend to reading. The Druid had obviously instilled his followers with his own love of books.

"I hear Erin dinna take to ye much," Emmon said.

"Who told you that?" I asked sharply.

Emmon smiled. "I'll take ye to visit a friend of mine."

Before I could question him, he ran off, and I was forced to follow. I found him knocking on the door to a small cottage.

"Who lives here?" I asked. I heard footsteps inside.

"Erin's twin sister lives here," he whispered. I gave him a furious look, but it was too late. The door opened, and a delicious odor wafted out.

"Gilaine, it's me. I've brought a visitor," Emmon announced. He sniffed and sighed, identifying the smell. "Honeyballs."

I stared at the girl who had answered the door.

There was no question whose sister she was. But they were as much alike as the sun and the moon. Where Erin's hair was spun gold and elaborately dressed, Gilaine wore her long, ashen tresses loose about her shoulders. Erin's eyes were bright blue, but Gilaine's were as gray as clouds lit from behind by the sun. The greatest difference, though, lay in their expressions. Erin's face was ever haughty and querulous, but Gilaine's was gentle, the smile on her mouth echoing in her eyes. I was immediately drawn to her.

"This is Elspeth. She's one of them gypsy folk," Emmon said, slipping behind her into the house.

I wondered why she did not speak. As if in answer to my thought, she raised a finger to her lips. At first I thought she was trying to tell me to be quiet. Then I realized she was mute.

"The honeyballs are burnin'!" Emmon wailed.

Gilaine smiled anew, gesturing for me to follow her. The cottage was tiny, consisting of three sections: a closet of a room with a bed in it, a front hall, and a cozy and relatively large kitchen.

The honeyballs turned out to be tiny, crisp sweets. My mouth full, I asked Emmon why I had not seen Gilaine at the nightmeal. He managed to look wrathful over bulging cheeks. "She is nowt asked," he said.

I could figure out the rest. The old Druid was a perfectionist. His hatred of Misfits extended to anything he considered flawed. And Gilaine was mute. Seeing my look, she smiled sadly and shrugged.

We stayed with Gilaine until it was time to go. I was surprised to hear Emmon confess his deception in retrieving me early, but she only shook her head helplessly and ruffled his hair with an expression of mingled concern and exasperation.

Crossing the green to the meeting house, I spotted Jik playing ball with some children and asked Emmon if I could talk to him.

"Well, yer nowt supposed to, an' ye know what a stickler I am for rules. But if I was to gan over an' wash my hands at th' spring, I'd nowt see what ye were up to. I'm a gullible fellow," he said with a smirk.

I called Jik away from his game. "Do you know where the others are being kept?" I asked him immediately. There was no time for greetings.

He shook his head. "I think they're someplace outside the walls."

"What about the block, can you feel it?"

He nodded, saying he had heard no talk of machines but that the Druid's acolytes worked in a shed forbidden to all others.

I nodded impatiently, frustrated that Emmon's tour had included neither this shed nor the compound I'd heard mentioned before. "Keep an ear out but don't ask any questions that will make anyone wonder about you. Remember, you're a gypsy. Where's Darga?"

"He's disappeared," Jik said miserably.

"Darga's a smart dog," I said. "He's probably gone to look for the others, or even to find Domick."

Jik's face brightened. "Do you think so?"

"Come on, Elspeth," Emmon called.

I patted Jik on the shoulder and ran to join Emmon.

I was taken in to the Druid by one of the acolytes. Struck again by his building's similarity to the Councilcourt, I wondered curiously if the Druid was indeed trying to start up his own opposing order. I had the feeling his order would be as bad as the Council's, whatever Gilbert believed. Entering the Druid's meeting chamber, I heard a tantalizing snatch of conversation.

A voice said, "If she is telling the truth, I don't see any need to waste more time on the mountains. I said all along it was your old friends in the Herder Faction that we bumped into."

"That may be, but it is likely too late to stop the soldier-guards from investigating Obernewtyn. And better to have them in the mountains than here." That was the Druid. I hesitated at the door, hoping to hear more, but the Druid looked up.

"Come in, Elspeth. I want you to tell me again all you saw at Obernewtyn. . . ."

I was there for the rest of the afternoon. Fortunately, my story was simple, and I resisted the temptation to embellish in case he asked me to repeat it again. I quickly realized what he really wanted to know was if Rushton were continuing Alexi's researches.

I was unsure how much he knew of the truth. It was common knowledge Alexi and Madam Vega had been involved in illegal research into the Beforetime and that Rushton had stopped that research when he had claimed Obernewtyn, as was his legal right. At one time, Henry Druid had befriended Rushton and had even supported him in his work to undermine the usurpers. But the Druid's motivations were less than admirable—he had sought for himself the same Beforetime weaponmachines that were the object of Alexi and Madam Vega's researches, and so far as I knew, he had hoped to eliminate his competition without getting the Council involved.

Rushton had severed ties without revealing his true plans for Obernewtyn, recognizing that the Druid's obsessive hatred of mutations was a danger to us. Ironically, this must have made the Druid wonder whether Rushton was continuing Alexi's search for Beforetime weapons, and our occasional exploration of the Blackland fringes would have only supported his suspicions.

The snatch of conversation I had overheard told me the Druid no longer saw Rushton as an enemy. Just the same, while taking care to present myself as an ignorant, self-centered gypsy, I made sure Rushton sounded as if he were verging on mania, committing all his resources to rebuilding the shattered Obernewtyn.

Dismissed at last, I went back to the kitchens. "What did he want?" Kella asked. "You've been ages!"

I told her of Emmon's antics, then recounted what I had heard.

"But it sounds like they now believe the Teknoguilders they clashed with at the ruins were Herders. How odd that they should jump to that conclusion, when Herders discourage any interest in the Beforetime," Kella said.

I nodded. "I think there is much about the Herders' activities that is secret. The important thing, though, is that the Druid now seems to believe Obernewtyn is a ruin. Even so, he seems to have set something in motion—there are soldierguards coming to the mountains. That means the rumors about renewed interest in Obernewtyn are true, and I'm almost sure this friend of theirs who works with the Council organized the investigation. It wouldn't be hard. The Council is so suspicious anyway."

Kella wiped her hands slowly on her apron. "We have to warn Rushton."

I nodded. "But first, I have to do something about this machine. Let Rilla think I'm still with the Druid. I think I can home in on the source of the static if I put my mind to it."

"Don't get caught," Kella said.

I climbed out the window at the back of the kitchen. Walking slowly, I let my mind explore the oddly pliant nature of the blocking static. Again I was reminded of a blanket and brushed my mind against it instead of using force. I had the eerie feeling it liked this, as if it were rubbing up against my mind like a kitten. I thought I could sense a core and moved in that direction.

Before long, I found myself in a part of the camp I had not seen before. I walked purposefully, trying to look as if I were running an errand, and avoided the eyes of the few people I passed.

Two men coming out of a doorway looked at me but made no move to stop me. As soon as I rounded a corner, I ran, keeping to the walls. I was determined nothing would keep me from at least locating the machine. A young girl looked out of a window curiously. I slowed abruptly to a walk, but her eyes followed me up the street.

I noticed a bank of ominous black clouds roiled along the horizon. An omen, though for good or ill I couldn't decide.

Suddenly I found myself on the very perimeter of the settlement. There was no one in sight. This part of the camp looked deserted. Uneasily, I wondered if the whole thing was some sort of trap.

I was about to turn back when, suddenly, I sensed the

source of the block was very near. I couldn't resist. It came, I was certain, from a long, low-slung building with a flat roof. There was only one door to the building, and no guard stood by it. My trapped powers prevented me from knowing if there were guards inside.

Pressing one ear against the door, I heard faint voices. Dry-mouthed, I made my decision. The door swung open soundlessly.

I gaped at the complete unexpectedness of what lay inside. The building was composed of a single, long, almost bare room filled with babies and very young children. On the far side of the room, a thin dark-haired girl wiped the face of a bawling tot.

In the middle of the room, playing with a group of happy children, was Gilaine.

She looked up idly, and her face registered my own shock.

I could not think of a single thing to say. The room was obviously a kind of communal nursery, but I was convinced it was also the source of the block. The machine had to be concealed somewhere in the room.

The dark-haired girl came over. "Yes?" she said pleasantly.

Gilaine touched her arm and made a few intricate hand motions. "Gilaine says you're a friend. Come in."

Gilaine made another agitated hand movement and the girl nodded. "I'll do it. You talk to your friend," she said kindly.

"What is this place?" I asked Gilaine when we were alone.

She frowned and pointed to the children. One of the toddlers waddled after her and lurched at my knees. Reaching out to catch him, my hand brushed against Gilaine's.

The baby gurgled in delight, oblivious to our stunned looks. The moment our hands touched, I had immediate access to her mind—and she to mine! Gilaine was a Talent. She had the same unusual combination of empath and farseeking abilities as Jik.

She pulled away almost immediately. I leaned forward slowly, not wanting to alarm her, and touched her forearm. Again contact was established. It seemed the block did not work if I was actually touching the person I wanted to communicate with.

"Gilaine?" I sent gently. She recoiled. I stood waiting, and she reached out, touching my shoulder with a tentative finger.

"Elspeth?" her mind responded. It was a weak signal despite the strength I had found in her mind.

I nodded. Gilaine sat on a chair as if her legs would not hold her and pulled the toddler onto her lap. I reached forward, pretending to look at the baby, and touched her. "We must not make ourselves obvious," I sent, at the same time wondering if Gilaine was the trap.

"You . . . are like us, but different," Gilaine sent timidly.

"Us? There are other Misfits here?" I asked, astounded.

She nodded almost imperceptibly. I sensed that she did not want to talk about them.

"Does your father know?" I asked.

She shook her head vehemently. "Must not know." The baby began to struggle to be put down. Gilaine jiggled her knees up and down, and he gurgled contentedly. "Father-druid thinks Misfits only feebleminds or dreamers. He does not know about us/you. He thinks Misfit/mutant evil," she stressed.

"And you? Do you think this is evil?" I asked.

She shook her head but without much conviction.

"It's dangerous for you and your friends here. Why do you stay?" I asked.

She shrugged, but I was startled to see a familiar face in her mind. It was the boy I had met in the Councilcourt in Sutrium years earlier, when I had been waiting to be sentenced to Obernewtyn. In her vision, he was older, but it was unmistakeably the same person. He had spoken to me of running away to take refuge in the mountains. He had even mentioned Henry Druid, saying the rumor of his death was a lie. Clearly, he must serve the Druid. I fumbled in my memory for the name he had told me. "Daffyd," I murmured aloud triumphantly.

Gilaine almost dropped the baby in fright. The startled child hitched in a breath and began to scream. When it was quieted, Gilaine touched my hand. "How do you know that name? Did you read my behindthoughts?" she asked suspiciously.

I shook my head without bothering to explain that I could have if I'd chosen to. People always thought I wanted to eavesdrop on their private thoughts, whereas the notion actually embarrassed me. "I saw his face in your mind. I met him once, in Sutrium. Is he a Misfit, too?"

She nodded, still wary.

"Where is he?" I asked, for surely I would have seen him if he were in the camp.

"Druid sent him to Sutrium/lowlands. Druidbusiness."

I noticed the dark-haired girl watching us curiously. We had been silent too long. In another moment, she would begin to wonder who I was and why she had not recognized me. I was putting Gilaine in danger and said as much to her in a low voice.

Rising, I sent a final, vital question. "Where is the blocking machine?"

She frowned. "Machine?"

"The block on our minds. Surely you can feel it?"

"Feel what?" Gilaine sent.

Confused, I sent a brief impression of the block.

"Oh, that," her mind sent, amused. "No machine. Lidge-baby." She pointed to a cot near one of the walls. "Lidge-babymind."

My mouth fell open. The incredible numbing effect blanketing the camp that had resisted all my strength was the uncontrollable mental static of a Misfit baby!

✦ 11 ✦

Something woke me.

It was a dark night, with no moon showing beyond the window glass. Rain was falling softly on the roof of the washhouse and its adjoining sleeping chambers.

Then I heard a voice, calling softly. "Elspeth?"

I sat bolt upright in bed, afraid to answer in case it was a trap. Trying to think how a real gypsy would react, I climbed out of bed and went across to the window.

"Who's out there?" My voice came out low and anxious, not quite a whisper.

"Shh!" the voice hissed urgently.

Apprehension prickled along my spine. "What do want? Who are you?"

There was a pause, as if the caller was wary, too.

"I come from a friend," the voice whispered at last, reluctantly.

I frowned. "I have no friends here."

Again there was a pause. "Gilaine," the voice grated, with a hint of irritation.

I bit my lip and peered into the rain-streaked night, wishing there was a moon. Whoever was out there had the perfect cover. I could see nothing.

"I have a key to unlock your door," the voice said.

I made up my mind. If it was a trap, I would blame gypsy curiosity.

A moment later, there was a faint click, and the door opened to reveal a man wearing a dark hooded cloak pulled low across his face. Pulling my own cape hastily over my nightdress, I padded out barefoot, closing the door behind me.

"Who are you?" I demanded.

"My name is Saul. And you don't need to know any more than that," he added brusquely.

We hurried along, keeping close to the walls, cloaks flapping in gusts of wind that blew along the dark, empty streets. Coming to a cobbled square, Saul stopped, intently scanning the square and the streets leading into it. Trees growing up through the cobbles flung bare branches about, sighing mournfully. After a long moment, he flicked his hand curtly and strode directly across the square.

On the other side, I stopped. "Wait a minute. This isn't the way to Gilaine's house."

"It is the way to mine," Saul answered.

His house proved to be as small as Gilaine's but looked dark and deserted. He opened the door, and light spilled out onto the wet ground. Dark heavy curtains had hidden the light from prying eyes. Reassured, I followed him inside.

Removing his cloak, Saul shook it and hung it on a peg in the wall. Studying him covertly in the light, I decided he was handsome in a cold sort of way. He was tall but too thin, and his skin was pale. His hands were as long and slender as a woman's, his facial features sharply defined beneath a fringe of straight light brown hair. He looked at me fleetingly with eyes the color of mud-stained ice. I smiled tentatively, but he

335

did not respond. I pretended to stumble as I followed him along the hallway, clutching at his arm to steady myself.

I had a brief impression of an intelligence bordering on brilliance, resting on a frighteningly unstable personality.

"Get out!" commanded an icy mental voice. He pushed me away with a look of revulsion.

I followed him wordlessly into the kitchen, knowing I had seen such stress before in people unable to tolerate the realization that they were Misfits. I guessed Saul had been ruthlessly orthodox before discovering his true nature. His very personality was disintegrating under the stress of being what he loathed. I wondered if the others knew how poorly he was coping.

The kitchen was almost the exact replica of Gilaine's but without cooking smells or flowers. It reminded me of an orphan-home kitchen before Council inspection.

Seated at a scrubbed timber table were Gilaine, the two musicians I had seen at the Druid's nightmeal, and an older heavyset man I had not seen before.

For a moment, they looked up at me with collective appraisal. Then Gilaine rose. Smiling welcome, she touched my arm. "I am glad you came. See? I am getting better at this strange way of communicating. But Lidegbaby does not like it. You know Saul. I think you have seen Peter and Michael." She gestured at the musicians. "And last is Jow, the brother of Daffyd."

"This is dangerous," I said aloud.

Gilaine nodded gravely. "You told me this afternoon that you meant to escape. We want to help, but you must answer questions first," she sent.

From the expressions on the faces of the others, I guessed they had been less eager to help than Gilaine. I wondered what she had said to convince them—especially to Saul, who made no pretense of liking my presence and was prowling back and forth like a caged animal.

"The others with you—Misfit also?" Gilaine asked.

I nodded, aware we would not get out of the camp without help. I had to take the risk. And I did trust Gilaine. I guessed she was reporting my answers to the others but could find no trace of their communication, though her hand rested on my arm. She seemed not to need physical contact to farseek with the others.

She looked back at me. "Have you really been to Obernewtyn?"

I nodded, and again told the story I had told the Druid, with one difference. I told her we had welcomed Pavo's illness as an excuse to split off from the rest of the troupe. "It was getting too dangerous for us to stay. Most gypsies hate Misfits."

"Then you never meant to rejoin your father?" Saul asked accusingly when Gilaine had relayed my answer. "You say Obernewtyn is a ruin. How can we believe you?"

I shrugged. "Believe what you want. Why would I bother to lie?"

It was odd how everyone seemed to know that the firestorm story was a lie, though no one but our own people had been up to the mountains since Rushton had staked his claim to Obernewtyn. I decided to ask my own questions.

"How did you discover your powers?"

Gilaine smiled. "It happened the night Lidgebaby was born," she sent.

The baby coercer had woken the entire group to operancy. Gilaine sent a graphic impression of the night the baby was born. She had been in bed asleep when the sound of a baby screaming woke her. She was in the street in her nightgown before she realized the cry she was hearing was inside her mind. She had gone back inside and dressed quickly, her mind reeling at the effort of fighting the summons. Only when she reached the street outside the birthing house did she begin to understand what had happened, for she was not alone. They had all answered the call: Saul, acolyte apprentice; Jow, an animal handler; his younger brother, Daffyd; and the two musicians.

Daffyd had sobered first to the peril of such a gathering, and they had dispersed at his urging, planning to meet again in less dangerous circumstances. It would prove the first of many such meetings. They all understood two things at once, though. They would never again be alone in their own minds, for Lidgebaby was with them constantly, linking them irrevocably to one another. And they were in terrible danger.

In that dramatic birthbonding, Lidgebaby had forged an indelible emotional link between himself and the group. None could ever consciously harm the baby. All were coerced to love and protect.

Little monster, I thought, keeping my mind shielded. No wonder I could not hear their communication. They talked through the baby, using their own powers only to maintain contact with Lidge. It was the combined network of minds, and the child's mental overflow, that was blocking me.

This incredible situation gave me a clear idea of Lidgebaby's mental prowess. A baby, his coercive demands were selfish but basically innocent. But what would happen when he grew up and became conscious of the power he wielded? I shuddered, seeing them smile in the collective memory of that first enslavement/wakening of their Misfit minds.

Seeing my eyes on him, Saul frowned and turned away.

"Where will you go, if we help you?" Gilaine asked.

"We hadn't thought that far ahead. We meant to use an Olden pass we'd heard about to reach the lowlands without going along the main roads."

Saul snorted. "No one can get through that pass alive."

I stared. "You mean there *is* a pass?"

Gilaine nodded. "But Saul is right. No way to go there. Dangerous."

Jow shifted in his seat and the others fell silent. For the first time, I glimpsed a hint of Daffyd's features in his face. "Where are you headed?" he asked aloud.

I shrugged. "To the west coast. We thought of getting a boat. I've heard there are places . . ." I hesitated.

"Over the sea," said the boy musician wistfully.

"I have heard there are places over the edge of the world, where there is no Council or Herder Faction," Jow said pensively.

"Why do you stay here?" I asked. "It's terribly dangerous."

Jow shook his head. "Better to wait until winter is over. And we must wait until Lidgebaby is weaned."

"Couldn't you get the mother to go with you?"

"The mother is bonded to an acolyte and has already had one babe burned. She denounced it," Jow said.

I stared at him in horror. "Why are you offering to help us?" I finally asked.

Jow frowned. "You are a danger to us as long as you stay. You are a danger to Lidgebaby. We'll help you, but you must understand we can't let you talk if you are caught. The acolytes are very persuasive."

I nodded, understanding what he left unsaid. "How can you help?"

"There are two things," Jow said. "First, we can absorb Lidgebaby's emanations so that you can communicate with your friends in the compound. Second, we will organize a diversion to give you all time to get away. The timing is good because soldierguards from the training camps below Gelfort Range will leave in a few days to witness the ordination of new Herders in Sutrium. That will mean the main road will be safe for a week or so, and you can cut right through their camp and make for the coast between the lower mountains and Glenelg Mor."

I bit my lip. It would take several days to go that way, but it seemed there was no choice.

At a word from Jow, Saul seated himself at the table, and the group linked hands. "Be quick," Jow said. "I'm not sure how long we can hold it."

They closed their eyes. For a long moment, there was silence. A log cracked noisily in the fire, spitting out an orange flame. Beads of perspiration stood out on Jow's face.

Then the block was gone.

I gasped in delight, realizing how greatly the restriction had oppressed me. I sent a specific probe tuned to Matthew's mind. There was too little time to locate him physically. He was asleep when I found him, and I woke him with an ungentle mental jab.

"Wha?" his mind inquired stupidly. "Elspethelf?" he sent.

"I don't have much time, so listen carefully," I sent. "Some Misfits here are going to help us escape. They'll create a joint diversion to give us the chance to get away."

"We canna use th' Olden way," Matthew warned.

I told Matthew about Jow's alternate route. "They still believe us gypsies—I can't let them know the truth about Obernewtyn if they intend on staying here. So I told them

340

nothing about Domick. I'm going to try to reach him now."

Matthew interrupted eagerly. "I was able to farseek with him." I was astonished. It was impossible to communicate over significant distance with anyone but another farseeker unless communicator and communicant each possessed some deep-probing ability. It seemed Ceirwan was right about Matthew's developing powers. But there was no time to think about that now.

"Are the horses with Domick?"

"An' Darga," Matthew sent. "Wait a minute! If ye haven't escaped, how can ye be contactin' me? We're in a compound, outside the settlement, but you—"

"The Misfits here helped me stop the block temporarily. It's not a machine. The static is caused by a baby with coercive powers."

"A baby!" Matthew echoed.

"Where is this compound? Show me," I demanded.

Matthew made his mind passive so that I could use his eyes. At once a ghostly vision unfolded in my mind. He was looking down a long, narrow rift between two mountains. There was a fence dividing a barren foreground from a heavily veg-etated background. I thought I could see patches of glowing gas in the faint moonlight beyond the barrier. It took a moment for me to realize what I was seeing.

"The Olden pass . . ."

Matthew confirmed it. "It's there, but so is tainted ground, poisoned air, an' gigantic growling beasts."

"Why build a compound there?" I wondered.

In answer, Matthew turned again. Dirt, rocks, and dispos-sessed trees lay in mounds on either side of a broad hole in the ground. A row of rough huts sat amidst the debris. "Th' ground here is safe enough. We're here to pander to th'

341

Druid's favorite obsession: Oldtime ruins. He thinks th' Great White was made by one of their machines and that th' machine is here somewhere. Mad as a snake is our Druid, to think it would still be workin' after all this time."

Not so mad, I thought with a feeling of cold dread.

"How is Pavo?" I asked.

"He says he refuses to die in a dirty, damp Druid hole," Matthew sent. "He's convinced you'll be along any minute to rescue us. 'Elspeth is a survivor,' he keeps sayin'."

"I wish I shared his faith. There's no hope now of getting to the lowlands and back before wintertime."

"If only we could farseek Ceirwan at Obernewtyn," Matthew sent.

I shrugged. He knew as well as I that it was impossible. But he was right—we needed to contact Obernewtyn. "I want you and Louis to take Mira and Lo and go back home as soon as you're free. Make sure you don't leave tracks or get caught. Someone has to warn Rushton about what the Druid is up to here." I made Matthew repeat the message back to me before bidding him goodbye.

Next I sought Domick. This was harder, and he instinctively responded by trying to repel me.

"You!" I saw him assimilate my ease in demolishing his defenses. "Have you escaped?"

I told him all I had told Matthew. "Then we are still going?" Domick asked when I had finished. "You know we can't make Maryon's deadline if we go that way. We are already cutting it too close because of the delay here."

"We dare not head back to Obernewtyn anyway, since the Druid would follow," I said flatly. "I'm sending Matthew and Louis to warn Rushton. The rest of us will continue, if only to draw the Druid's attention away from the high mountains.

I'll contact you as soon as we get outside the baby's static. In the meantime, stay out of sight. A group of armsmen went out this morning to hunt. Where are you now?"

Domick was unable to let me use his eyes, but he projected a picture with painful force into my mind. Cross-guild farseeking had its drawbacks. The coercer was right at the foot of the mountains. "Tor," he sent in explanation. "I've been hiding in the cave where the Suggredoon goes into the mountain. There's a good wide ledge. Pity it doesn't go right through alongside the river, or we could simply walk to the other side."

Severing the contact, I found myself back inside the room. The group was still hand-linked. Gathering my exhausted senses, I reached out to Jik. He was overjoyed to hear Darga was safe. I was in the middle of explaining the escape plans when the contact was severed neatly, and Lidgebaby's static filled the air.

I opened my eyes in time to see Gilaine pitch forward. Jow picked her up gently and laid her on the floor, using his coat as a pillow. She moaned, and her eyes fluttered open. I went to her side, stricken with guilt.

"She was the focus. Lidge likes her best," Saul said petulantly.

"Did you get through?" Jow asked.

I nodded. Gilaine reached out for my arm and projected a message to us all. "It will be difficult. Perhaps they should stay through the winter and leave when we go."

"They can't stay!" Saul broke in angrily. "They endanger the baby. They endanger us all. It was bad enough to reveal ourselves. . . ."

The older musician shook his head reproachfully. "Saul, we have already gone over this. Once Gilaine was revealed, it was the same as if we were all exposed. If the Druid forced her name from Elspeth, she in turn would be forced to betray us. I'm sorry, Gilaine, but it would be better for them to go."

She hung her head.

A queer expression flitted across Saul's intense features, and I felt certain he was thinking Gilaine's death would solve everything.

"We won't be staying," I said firmly. I looked at Jow. "You'll never have cause to regret this," I promised. "And someday you might be glad."

I vowed to myself that I would return to bring Gilaine and her friends up to Obernewtyn as soon as I had completed my quest to the west coast. By then, Lidgebaby would be old enough to travel.

I woke the next day to Rilla shaking me impatiently. "Elspeth. Ye sleep like th' dead," she scolded.

Outside, rain was falling steadily, and thunder rumbled in the distance. Hurrying across the gap that separated the washhouse from the kitchen, I glanced up at the drear gray sky with faint apprehension.

To my surprise, Emmon was sitting at the kitchen table with Kella. Seeing me, they both stood abruptly.

"What's the matter?" I asked.

"Gilaine sent me to tell ye," Emmon said. "Only ye mun nowt let on ye know, or she'll be in for it."

"I promise. Now what?"

"Yer to be bonded tomorrow," Emmon said, refusing to meet my eyes.

"To whom?" I asked in a strangely distant voice.

He made a warding-off gesture with his hand. "To . . .

344

Relward. The gatewarden. This is Erin's doin'," he added in a rush.

"But why?" I asked faintly.

"She's jealous. She thinks Gilbert means to request ye in bonding. He's gone off to hunt, an' by th' time he gans back, it will be too late for him to protest," Emmon explained.

I blinked rapidly, fighting off an unexpected rush of tears. I had always used Rushton's stern, dark face as a talisman against despair, but this time the thought of him only evoked a fierce pain in my chest and a bittersweet longing to be home.

Then the irony of it struck me, helping me gain a measure of calmness. Here was Erin, violently jealous of the fleeting and surely lighthearted interest Gilbert had taken in me, willing to go to incredible lengths to stop something I had no more desire for than she.

"I can't let it happen," I said, and in that moment, a daring idea came to me. With Emmon's help, I managed to speak privately with Gilaine. She agreed the bonding must be avoided and said she would talk to the others about an immediate escape. I also told her I had heard Pavo was getting sicker and that I wanted to make sure he would be able to walk unaided. But that night, when Gilaine and her friends damped Lidgebaby's emanations, I contacted Domick instead.

"Has something gone wrong?" he asked, responding to the agitation in my thoughts.

I told him of the intended bonding and that Kella would likely be next. I was surprised at the vehemence with which he said it must not be allowed to happen. "If I can help it, it won't," I sent. "Our friends here have set their plans for tomorrow night. But after we get away from here, I have an alternative to going round the mountains. It's dangerous. Rushton would never approve. But if it succeeds, we will be on the other side of the mountains in less than two days."

"Impossible. Unless your undisclosed Talents include teaching giant birds to carry us across the sky."

I ignored his sarcasm. "I want you to build a raft. A strong raft."

"A raft. But . . . you can't mean . . . ?"

"We're going to raft through the mountains on the Suggredoon," I sent determinedly.

✦ 12 ✦

ERIN SMILED.

"Wait in here," she said. She opened a door off the hallway, and I entered a small, musty-smelling antechamber.

Inside the Druid's house, it was unexpectedly quiet. The room was dark, though it was not yet evening. The day had been dreary, overshadowed by banks of foreboding storm clouds. A single candle burned in a sconce on the wall, offering meager light.

As soon as Erin's footsteps faded, I crossed to the window facing the street and pulled aside a gauzy pleat of curtain. I peeped into the windswept street. A brilliant flash of lightning gave the fleeting impression of a blighted daytime. Then it was dark again.

I hoped nothing had happened to delay the others.

There was another flash of lightning, and I wondered uneasily at the building storm. I did not mind the rain but thought warily of firestorms and of a theory of Pavo's that they were increasing in frequency in the lowlands. He had explained that they were not real storms, despite the lightning and thunder, but were an electrical imbalance in the complex forces holding the earth together—another legacy of the cataclysmic disturbance of the Great White. He could not explain why firestorm rain burned the skin, nor why that rain alone could extinguish the destructive flames that always preceded it. He was certain, though, that there had been no firestorms in the Beforetime.

The Herders also believed firestorms followed the holocaust but claimed they were sent by Lud and would continue ravaging the earth until the world was again pure. Naturally, the only way to achieve such a state of grace was to adhere to Herder doctrine. If there *was* a firestorm brewing, we could not think of escape. Firestorm flames burned even stone, but there would be more protection in the Druid encampment than in the open, at the mercy of the lethal flames.

Outside, the wind muttered sullenly, echoing my inner disquiet. Erin and her traditional lecture about the duties of a bondmate were the least of my worries. Though not yet told I was to be bonded that very night, I did not doubt it.

Scanning the length of the street visible from the window, I wondered anxiously if Kella had managed to get a message to Gilaine. She should have contacted her as soon as I was sent to the Druid's house. Jow had decided that was the best time to make our move. But if they did not come . . .

More lightning flashed, followed by a sharp crack of thunder. The time lapse between the flashes and the thunder was growing shorter. Rain fell in light flurries, but the heaviness of the clouds illuminated in the intermittent light indicated a deluge was coming.

Hearing a movement at the door, I dropped the curtain and moved quickly away from the window. Erin came in cautiously, as if she had thought I would be waiting to attack her. Her hand rested lightly on the hilt of a short knife she wore in a jeweled waist scabbard.

"You have been sent here so that I can tell you some wonderful news," Erin said, her eyes glittering vindictively. I was taken aback at the force of her dislike.

"Yes?" I asked calmly.

Her lips stretched across her teeth in a smile that looked more like a snarl. "You are to be bonded—to Relward."

Knowing took the force out of my reaction, and I was glad to see her look disappointed. "This is your news?" I asked sourly.

For a moment, Erin looked nonplussed; then her cheeks mottled with anger. "You are to be bonded tonight," she added viciously.

I shrugged. "I don't bother with such things," I said lethargically.

"You . . . w-what?" she stammered.

"What does it matter to be bonded or not? It is all the same in the dark," I added crudely.

Her face reddened, and she stepped away from me as if she thought I would contaminate her. "You dare speak of such things to me?"

I shrugged. "If you don't like such talk, why are you the one to tell me of this bonding?" Taking advantage of her loss of balance, I stepped toward her.

Her hand groped for the knife in her belt, and she held it up between us. "Stay back." There was a loud noise in the street, and we both jumped. "What was that?"

"The wind?" I said quickly, stepping forward again in my haste to distract her.

She lifted the knife. "What's going on?" she asked, suspicion flaring in her eyes. She backed to the door, holding the knife out menacingly.

Unable to think of a way to stop her, I stood still, heart banging against my ribs. If she caught the others and gave the alarm, we would all be lost. Erin groped behind her back, opening the door without taking her eyes off me.

My knees felt weak with relief. Blocking the hall behind her were Kella and Jik. I smiled at them in greeting.

"That is an old trick," Erin sneered. "Trying to make me think there's someone . . ." She stopped abruptly as Kella's knife pressed into her neck.

Jik reached round and took the knife carefully out of her fingers.

"Get inside the room," Kella ordered, her face pale but determined. I was momentarily astonished to see a healer waving a knife in such a businesslike way. Erin obeyed, shock turned to fury.

"You will all die for this. My father will burn you," she snarled.

"Did you bring the rope?" I asked Jik, ignoring her. He nodded. "Tie her up."

Erin stood rigidly erect as Jik bound her hands and feet. "What do you think this will get you?" she grated. "There are men in all the watchtowers and guards at the gate. And even if you *did* get out, my father will come after you. You will be caught, and then you will wish bonding was the only fate awaiting you."

I touched Jik's arm, sending a swift thought. The next time she opened her mouth to speak, he thrust a ball of cloth into it, then tied another round her head to stop her spitting it out. It was a relief to have her quiet. I checked the ropes. They were tight, and I guessed Erin's hissing threats had made Jik more efficient than he might otherwise have been.

I forced myself to face her. "Daughter of Henry Druid, we are gypsy folk and not meant for staying in one place. My father waits for me in Arandelft, and I mean to meet him. I bear no ill will to the Druid, but I cannot stay. That is why you have to be tied up. To stop you raising the alarm too soon."

"Perhaps we should kill her," Jik said, obeying my covert prompting.

I pretended to consider it, gratified to see the first sign of real fear in Erin's eyes. Slowly, as if reluctant, I shook my head. "I would be just as happy to kill her, but that might make her father annoyed. Besides, we will be long gone down the main road before they find her." I had no doubt Erin would faithfully relay all I had said, sending her father off in the wrong direction.

I nodded to Jik, and he opened a large chest under the window.

Erin's eyes widened with real horror. I did not like the idea of locking anyone in a trunk, even someone so detestable, but we had to make sure she was not found too quickly. If the Druid came home early, he was unlikely to think to look for his daughter inside a box in a spare room. With Kella's help, we lifted her into the trunk, leaving the lid slightly askew so she wouldn't suffocate. Then we went into the kitchen, where she would not be able to hear us.

"Phew," Jik said. "If eyes were knives, we'd all be dead."

Jik went to fetch Jow from outside. We gave the all-clear signal, and Jow came in the back door. "Where is she?" he asked in a low voice. I told him and, unexpectedly, he grinned.

"Do her good," he murmured. Then his face became serious. "Now, you know what you have to do?"

I recited the route he expected us to take, and he nodded.

"You'll be a bit ahead of schedule now. You might have to wait in the wilds until the soldierguards leave their camps. I wish we could give you more help."

"We'll be all right. Gypsies know a few things about hiding," I said, sorry to be deceiving him.

He opened a bundle and handed me boots, stout trousers, and a jumper and coat. I threw aside the silky red dress Rilla had made me wear, without regret. Fine clothes were no substitute for freedom.

Outside, thunder cracked loudly.

"This is an ordinary storm?" I asked Jow.

He nodded. "An ordinary storm, but bad all the same. Worse for the armsmen who will have to track you."

I pointed to the dress. "You could use that to lead them astray."

Jow shook his head. "You can't go in two directions at once. If he eventually found your tracks, the Druid would know for certain you had help."

"What are we waiting for?" Kella asked, looking round uneasily.

"A signal from Peter," Jow said. "He should have been here by now; I'll go and look."

A cold blast of wind swept through the back door as he left. I shivered, less from the cold than at what lay ahead. I prayed Domick could do his part in freeing Matthew and the others.

When the door swung open again, Jow had brought the older musician, Peter. With them, to my surprise, was Gilaine.

She took my hands in hers. "The others did not want me to come, because I am known to have associated with you. But I wanted to say goodbye. I wish you did not have to go," she sent wistfully.

I squeezed her fingers. "We'll meet again someday. I'm sure of it." I leaned forward and kissed a cheek that smelled faintly of honey.

"Come," Jow said impatiently. "There's no time to waste."

Gilaine gave me a gentle push and waved as we followed

Jow and Peter into the stormy night. Looking over my shoulder, I saw her disappear round the corner of the house.

It began to rain in earnest then, as if it had been waiting for us. To my consternation, the flashes of lightning lit up the streets. Anyone glancing through a window might see us.

I trotted to keep up, trying to ignore the pain in my feet. We stopped to rest in one of the alleys running between the dark storehouses alongside the gate. Peter left at once with a terse farewell.

"I live near, so it's safest for me to be seen here," Jow explained. "I've left two horses in the front yard nearest the gate. They've agreed to run the minute they're let out." Jow was a beastspeaker.

"Your job is to break the latch on the yard gate," he told Jik. "Wait until a crack of thunder and smash it with a rock. Then get out of sight. I'll come out and call the gatewarden to help me catch the horses. They're to run down to the other end of the camp. There'll be enough noise to attract the attention of the posted guards in the corner lookouts. Even so, you'll have to be quick. And don't leave any tracks showing which way you've gone. There must be no doubt you're making for the main road around the head of the river. Elspeth, you're sure you'll be able to relock the gate from the outside?"

I nodded. "My powers aren't blocked when there's physical contact. If I'm touching the door, I'll be able to lock it mentally."

Jow looked up as a flash of lightning lit the alley. "Count five and thirty once you're in position, to give me time to get back to my hut. Then bash away," he told Jik. Then he was gone.

We stared at one another, frightened and excited. "Go on," I prompted Jik after the time had passed. He darted off into

353

the shadows, and Kella and I edged closer to the main gate. The whole aim of Jow's plan was to give us a head start. Jow hoped no one would even realize we had gone until we were discovered missing at nightmeal. And even then, the locked gates would make them think we were hiding somewhere inside the camp.

But everything depended on our getting away unnoticed.

I jumped as a loud crash of thunder mingled faintly with the sound of splintering wood. Two horses thundered past us into the street, their hooves making a great clattering noise on the stones. We watched as Jow burst out of a door, shouting for help. Two other doors were flung open and men came out, wondering what was happening. A man poked his head out of the gatewarden's hut, and Jow called him to help catch the horses before someone was killed. He pulled on a coat and ran after the shouting group without looking back.

As soon as they were all out of sight, we hurried across to the gate, Jik running up behind us. My heart beat loud enough to drown the thunder. We were completely exposed, and my hand trembled as I reached for the lock.

But even as my fingers closed around the bolt, a hand shot out of the gatewarden's hut and fastened on my arm. Kella screamed and jumped back, knocking Jik to the ground.

Still holding my arm, the black-bearded man who had caught us in the first place came out into the rain, an unpleasant smile on his mouth. "What have we here?" His eyes ran over our bundles and dress. "Not running away, are we? And Relward so eager to have a maid in his bed." He laughed, and rain shook from the wiry beard hairs under his chin. "What a pity, since runaways here end up as bonfire fodder."

Kella moaned in terror, snapping me out of my own

trance. Anger flowed through me in a molten tide. If I did nothing, we would all burn. I gritted my teeth.

There was nothing subtle in what I did next. The armsman's bruising grip on me made him vulnerable, since the contact negated Lidgebaby's static net. I simply lashed out with all the frustrated power in my mind. Even so, it was less effective than it should have been. He recoiled in shock and, instinctively, tried to let go of my arm. My other hand snaked out and caught his wrist, keeping the connection. He fought me in earnest then, and when I clung like a limpet, he struck me across the face. It was too awkward a blow to have full force, but my ears rang and I suddenly felt a long way from my hands. I could feel my grip weaken.

Terrified of what would happen to us if I failed to get us away, I reached inside my darkest mind for the power I had once used to kill Madam Vega. I had not accessed it since the night we had taken Obernewtyn. I had tried to pretend to myself that it was gone. But it rose at my call like a great black snake, and only fear of that dreadful secret power gave me the strength to temper it. Even muted, the power of my attack on the armsman's mind was terrible. His mouth gaped wide in a soundless shriek, and he slumped half-dead at my feet. I slid to my knees behind him, retching and coughing.

Kella looked down at me, stunned. "What did you do to him?" Then her face changed. "Elspeth, you're bleeding."

I shook my head and climbed to my feet. "No . . . time. We have to get . . . away before they find him." I could taste blood and spat, but the taste persisted. Dazed, I wondered if it was my imagination that it was raining more heavily.

Kella visibly gathered herself, unlocking the gate and pulling us through after her. I put my hands on the door and relocked it. With luck, the locked gate would still throw off the search, and the Druids would assume the unconscious armsman had been struck by lightning.

We picked our way with careful haste across the spine of rocks Jow had said would hide our tracks. When we had gone some distance, I decided speed was more important. "Run!" I yelled over the noise of the rain. All around us, trees creaked under the weight of the downpour. It was like standing under a waterfall. I staggered after them, my head spinning and my feet hurting badly. I was too disoriented to know which way we should go and plodded after Kella, hoping she knew.

Then, abruptly, we were outside Lidgebaby's range. I sent a probe to Domick. Fortunately, he was waiting for me, because I had no strength left to fight his defenses or the interference of the rain. To my relief, Pavo was there already.

I stumbled over an exposed tree root and fell to my knees hard. Kella and Jik helped me up. The healer's hair was plastered to her head, and her face dripped with water. I struggled to stay conscious as they half dragged, half carried me between them. Crashing through the trees moments later, Domick ordered the other two to run and hefted me effortlessly over one shoulder. My teeth felt as if they were rattling round behind my eyes.

We reached the clearing where Pavo waited with Gahltha and Avra. Like Domick, Pavo was still clad in the ragged remnants of the clothes we had worn from Obernewtyn that first day.

"What's happened?" the teknoguilder asked. "Kella says you killed a man with your mind."

Domick gave me a startled look.

"Not killed . . . stunned," I said groggily.

"He hit her in the face. There was blood all over, but the

rain's washed it off. Wait . . ." Before I could stop her, Kella reached out and touched me, drawing my pain off into herself. At once the dizziness faded.

"Hurts . . . ," moaned Kella, white-faced.

I took her hands away. "That's enough. I can think now. You've stopped the faintness."

Kella smiled wanly.

We were all huddled under an eben tree, the only real shelter. Rain drummed down heavily on all sides.

"Matthew and Louis are on their way back to Obernewtyn, and no one at the compound pursued them. Did anyone follow you?" Domick shouted over the noise.

I shook my head. "No one will come after us until this storm is over. And even if they do, we'll be long gone on the raft."

Something in Domick's expression struck me.

"You *did* make the raft?"

Wordlessly, he pulled me to my feet and pointed through the trees to the water.

My heart sank.

Swollen by the phenomenal rains, the Suggredoon was a roaring torrent overflowing its banks, carrying whole trees and chunks of rock. Domick's raft was fastened to the bank by a thick, twisted rope and bobbed like a creature mad to be set free. Only a lunatic would set off on such a river.

Domick hauled the raft in and looked at me, panting. "What do we do?"

I took a deep breath. "We'll wait until daylight. Maybe the river will have calmed down by then?"

Before he could respond, I heard a bark and turned to see Darga pelting into the clearing. "Many funaga coming."

I translated. Domick's face hardened. "Then we've no

choice. We'll have to go now." He pointed to the raft. "There are ropes. Tie yourselves down."

"Quickly," I shouted when no one moved.

I helped Kella tie herself, and Jik tied Darga and himself down. Avra stepped into the large space in the middle obviously reserved for the two horses, and Domick bound her gently. I sat next to Pavo, trying not to look frightened.

My mind was reeling. How could anyone have followed so quickly?

Domick's cry broke into my thoughts. He was standing on the bank with Gahltha.

"What is it?" I shouted.

Domick waved his hand helplessly at the black horse. "He won't move."

I tried to reach Gahltha's mind, but it was as smooth and unassailable as a mountain of glass. I looked at Avra and sent an urgent query. Through the noise of the rain, I could hear men's voices and shouts.

"They come," Darga sent.

Domick threw his hands up and began to push the raft off the bank.

"Gahltha," I sent, forcing through his shield. He whinnied, a high quavering note, the whites of his eyes showing. But he made no move toward the raft.

"He's afraid!" Jik cried.

Domick jumped into the raft just as the water dragged it from the bank. There was a hard jerk as it reached the end of the tether rope. Still Gahltha stood on the bank unmoving, staring out at us.

"Gahltha!" I sent. "Go back to Obernewtyn."

He made no response. I saw figures running. "They're coming. Cut the rope!" I cried.

Domick lifted his small ax.

"Gahltha. Go now, or the funaga will trap you!" I sent forcefully.

He reared violently and plunged into the night. At the same time, Domick let the ax fall. It landed badly, and the rope was not severed. Several armsmen had reached the bank and were attempting to reel the raft in. Domick raised the ax again, and this time it fell true.

At once, the roaring water carried us swiftly away from the bank. Lightning flashed, and in that moment, I saw Gilbert among those who stood watching us. I knew he had been out hunting and realized our poor luck—we had not been followed from the encampment but had been found out all the same.

His eyes falling on me, Gilbert cried out something in evident dismay, but the sound of rain and rushing water made his words impossible to hear.

Then the raft carried us from his sight, and within seconds, we were speeding toward the dark bulk of the mountains. For a moment, it seemed we would be smashed to pieces against the side of the mountain. Then the black gape of a cave opened up before us.

I looked back and caught sight of Gahltha pawing at the raging water as if it were tongues of fire.

"Here we go," Domick said grimly, and we plunged into the heart of the mountain.

✦ 13 ✦

THE SUGGREDOON BORE us along its ancient course at the speed of a bolting horse.

Domick stood up on the raft, slipping his feet into rope loops, and took hold of the paddle, which gave him rudimentary steering. I was surprised to find a dim light in the cavern instead of dense blackness. The walls glowed gently and eerily, and only when a cloud of insects stirred and rose did I see that the light came from their tiny bodies. A stiff, cold draft blew in my face from somewhere ahead, but I knew we had far to go before we would see the sky again.

It was not long before the way narrowed and twisted, creating the first turbulent stretch of rapids. The water boiled savagely, sending the raft shuddering and careening through foaming torrents, barely missing jagged rocks. Luck as much as steering kept us from being overturned or having a rock smash the raft to splinters.

And there were many such stretches. Each time we began to breathe easy, thinking ourselves lucky to have reached calmer waters, we would hear the familiar hollow roar ahead and would tighten our grips on the raft.

At one point, the entire surface of the river seemed to tilt, and we were as much sliding as being swept by the current. The wind whistled past me, whipping strands of hair wildly in my face.

We knew the Suggredoon flowed down to the lowlands, but I had been secretly afraid that the tunnel it had carved through the stone roots of the mountain might become too narrow for the raft to pass. My heart sank when the walls began to close in around us, and for a moment, the mountain seemed to throb with brooding malevolence.

I tried to ignore the roof drawing steadily nearer and more dim, as if the glowing insects disliked the closeness as much as we did. Gradually, it became so low that Domick could not stand. I needed no empathy to sense Avra's fear. If the cavern became much more cramped, she would not fit. And we all knew there was no turning back.

But the way began to widen again, and I shivered with re-action. In my wildest fancies, I had never imagined the trip to the coast would be such a road of trials. I had worried only about soldierguards, yet in all that had befallen us, we had not even laid eyes on one.

Hearing a roar ahead, I prepared myself for another battering, but instead the raft flowed round a bend and through a natural stone arch into a vast, dark cavern. If not for the stalactites and stalagmites and the rock columns rising from the water to the roof where some had met and fused, I would have thought we had somehow got out onto the sea at night. The cave was lit by millions of the tiny insects.

The raft slowed but was still drawn along by a deeper current.

Our wonder at this great lake under the mountain dissolved into greater amazement as we drew near to what at first appeared to be strangely symmetrical rows of rocky mounds rising from the water.

Pavo realized first what we were seeing and gasped. I was struck by the wonder in his gaunt face. "This is a Beforetime city," he whispered reverently.

Squinting, I saw that he was right. The shapes were too square to be natural, but the height of them astounded me. These, then, were the skyscrapers of the legends.

I stared about me as the current carried us between two of the monstrous constructions, along what must once have been a street. There was no way of telling how far below the surface of the water lay the floor of the dead city. Out of the distant past, I seemed to hear Louis Larkin telling me there were certain to be rare niches in the world where bits of the Beforetime were preserved.

And what wonders lay inside these buildings with their thousands of dark windows?

Up close, the surfaces were badly eroded, especially at the water line. One day the currents' ebb and flow would eat the foundations, and the remnants of the ancient city would topple. Gaps in the rows of buildings suggested this had happened already in some cases.

Many of the smooth façades were crumbled, revealing the great black steel frames inside them, like the bones of some moldering animal. Much of the remaining walls were covered in a livid yellow fungus. The glowing insects either lived or fed on it, for wherever the fungus grew, they were clustered thickly, and their collective light was brighter.

I wondered if the city had somehow sunk into the mountain during the Great White or if the earth had spat the mountains on top of it like a gravestone.

I found myself wishing Matthew could see it. He had long worshipped the Oldtimers with a glib surety that had always troubled me, but the city told a story of people who were certainly great—but people just the same, with flaws that all their brilliance had not helped.

It was a somber and sobering experience. It was not hard

to think of the people who had built such cities as capable of any wonder—or terror. Looking around me, I had no doubt that such a people could create a weapon that would live far beyond their span. The stark reality of the brilliance and insanity of the Oldtimers struck me then as never before.

"This is a bad place," Avra sent uneasily.

As much to distract myself as the mare, I asked her about Gahltha's strange behavior.

She whinnied forlornly. "The funaga who owned him almost drowned him when he was first brought to them. It is a funaga way of breaking the spirit of an equine, to use water and fear. They did not break him, for he took refuge in a savage hidden hatred, but since that time he has a dread of water that goes beyond reason."

"I'm sure he's safely on his way back to Obernewtyn," I sent reassuringly.

"He is proud," she sent. "Too proud to bear such shame easily."

I stared at her, puzzled. "There is no shame in what happened. No one will blame him."

Avra sighed in a very human way. "He will blame himself. I do not think he will return to Obernewtyn."

Hours later, we were still gliding through the ancient city. The immediate wonder having worn off, we lapsed into silence for a time. I watched from the corner of my eye as Kella helped Domick to steer, thinking that the stresses and perils that had beset us since leaving Obernewtyn had eroded the old enmity between coercer and healer. I was imagining what effect their unexpected friendship would have on their guilds, when we suddenly passed out of the big cavern into a tunnel. Immediately, the raft picked up speed, and in seconds we were in rapids again.

Another hour passed with little respite from the ferocious white water, which seemed more frequent on this side of the underground sea. Domick was swaying on his feet with exhaustion.

Then we heard a noise. At first we checked our binding ropes, thinking there was another bout of rapids ahead, but as we came nearer to the source, the roaring became louder, taking on a curious vibrating quality.

I noticed that Pavo was listening intently. There was no fear on his face, only fierce concentration.

"What is it?" I shouted. "More rapids?"

"Let's hope that is all it is," Pavo answered.

I opened my mouth to ask what he meant when the raft tilted abruptly sideways. Being tied on was all that kept us together. I heard Kella scream, and then we were falling as the Suggredoon became a giant waterfall, plummeting us into a black void.

My face felt hot and damp at the memory of that fall.

I tried to open my eyes but saw nothing. I lifted my hand to feel if my eyes were open, wondering if I had gone blind.

"Shh, lie still," Kella said softly.

"My eyes," I croaked. My throat felt as dry as old paper.

"Your eyes are fine. They're stuck shut by blood from a cut on your forehead. Wait . . ."

I heard footsteps on a stone floor and the murmur of voices. It was strange to hear and not see; that was how it was for Dameon. Two sets of footsteps approached, and there was the sound of curtains being drawn. I felt a warm cloth on my face and gasped at the unexpected sting.

"There are lots of small cuts from the rocks," Kella explained gently. "Some of them reopened in the night. There now."

I opened my eyes. I was in bed in a small whitewashed bedroom with sun streaming through a window and birds chirping outside. Kella was sitting beside me on a stool, a bowl of bloodied water on her knees. Her cheek was badly bruised and her arm was bandaged. Behind her was a plump matronly woman I had never seen before.

"I am Katlyn," she said with a warm smile.

I did not know what to say and looked helplessly at Kella. "Katlyn and her bondmate, Grufyyd, found us washed up on the banks of the Suggredoon. They know we escaped from a Councilfarm," she said pointedly.

"Dinna worry about that now. Ye need to rest," Katlyn said, her highland accent strong. "That is the best healer of all, but first I will bring ye some food."

She went out, taking the stained water with her, and returned in a moment with a bowl of soup.

"That smells wonderful," I rasped.

She smiled. "It is an old recipe, a special healing mixture. Eat an' then sleep. Ye can talk later."

"Where are the others?" I asked Kella as soon as the woman had gone.

"Everyone is fine," Kella said, and pointed firmly to the soup. "Now eat. If Katlyn says it will heal, it will. She knows so much about healing and medicines. I've never seen such an herb garden."

"Herb?" I asked sharply.

"Katlyn is an herb lorist. She learned it from her grandmother. Apparently people came to the woman's village from all over the Land, and they used to come see Katlyn before herb lore was banned. Many still come. I wish Roland could meet her.

"Does she not fear the Herders?"

Kella smiled. "She talks about the Council and the Herders as if they were a collection of naughty boys. She knows what she does is dangerous, but she says it's her job."

"How long have we been here?" I asked, anxious that we had stayed too long in the house of a woman who cared so little for her safety.

"Only a day, but without her help, we would have taken much longer to heal," Kella said sternly, seeing my disapproval.

"I'm grateful for her help," I said. "But it's my job to keep us safe and finish this expedition without getting caught by the Council or the Faction—who are a lot more dangerous than bad boys. Now, tell me, where are we?"

Kella shrugged. "We're not far from Rangorn and the Ford. It's only the two of them here. There's a son, but he's a seaman. They seemed to think we might have heard of him when I'd told them we were runaways. I thought it best not to pry."

"Good. How did you come to tell them we had escaped from a Councilfarm?"

"We had to tell them something. There was no way of hiding that we had been in a boating accident, but no one would have crossed the Suggredoon this far north unless they were trying to avoid being seen. Gypsies would hardly travel by water, and besides, our coloring has all but faded now. The Councilfarm runaway story seemed most plausible."

"It's risky," I said. "You are certain they didn't send word to the Council? There is a reward for information leading to the capture of runaways."

Kella shook her head emphatically. "I don't think it occurred to them."

I frowned. "I suppose if Katlyn is an herb lorist, she wouldn't want soldierguards here. So we're probably safe enough for now."

A flicker of anger crossed Kella's face. "You're too cynical, Elspeth. It makes you blind to things right under your nose," she added obliquely.

"What about the others?"

"Everyone's fine except for a few bruises and bumps. Pavo is not too good, but that has nothing to do with the accident."

"Jik?" I asked.

She smiled. "A cracked rib. He's milking the goats with Grufyyd. Domick has gone off to scout the area. Once a coercer . . ." I was astounded to see her eyes soften and wondered if friendship was all that had developed between them.

Kella stood, taking the empty bowl from my fingers. I could not even remember drinking the soup.

"Sleep and get better. The world will wait," the healer said.

Weary as I was, I could not rest easy. The expedition seemed to be in tatters, without disguise or papers, two all but unfit to travel. I wondered if we would ever get home again.

Domick returned late that night.

"Elspeth?" he whispered outside the window.

"I'm awake," I answered softly, sitting up. "Come in."

He climbed through the window. "I am sleeping in the stables with Jik and Darga, but I wanted to talk to you while it was quiet. Katlyn and Grufyyd are good people," Domick said. "Kella believes it, and so do I. I don't like lying to them."

I hid my amazement at these uncoercer-like sentiments. Domick went on. "They seem . . . accustomed to people like us—people on the run, scared, and without anything but a flimsy cover story. The medicines, the food, the lack of questions . . . it makes me think they have done this before—sheltered runaways."

"Are you sure? How do you know?"

He shrugged. "Instinct as much as anything. But Jik can sense their sincerity. If we were forced to leave him or Pavo behind, I think it would be safe for them here."

I did not respond to the question in his voice, knowing that Jik must accompany us however dangerous the expedition had become. "You're right to think of leaving soon, or we'll waste the time we gained coming through the mountain. You scouted ahead?"

Domick's face was impassive. "Yes. We're above Rangorn, but we can easily get to the ford without passing through the town. The ford is unguarded, though Grufyyd says there are guards at the ferry terminal. You will need papers to cross."

"We'll have to manage without them until we reach Sutrium. We need to try to get hold of another cart. That way we should be able to leave together—all of us." I touched his hand. "Go to bed now."

He slipped out as soundlessly as he had entered.

The next morning, Katlyn came in to change the bandages on my feet. "Poor ill-treated feet," she said gently, unwrapping them. "I put on a salve to numb them so you could sleep. The scars are deep and have not healed well, though they are old."

"I have to be able to walk," I said.

Katlyn nodded. "If you must, these will carry you. But walking will increase the hurt. If they are ever to heal properly, you must rest them completely for many months, perhaps even longer."

Katlyn looked up at me, her expression serious. "Child, there is something I want to say to you. Kella told me you are making for the west coast, in search of sanctuary. But I dinna think you will find any safe place on the coast. I want ye to think of staying here with us."

"Here?" I echoed, astounded by the offer.

Katlyn reached out and touched my hand. "This is a safe house, a refuge for runaways . . . and for others. You could help us in our work. Help others like yourself . . ."

I stared at Katlyn, my heart beating fast, for her eyes told me clearly that she knew we had not told her the truth about ourselves.

"Think on it," she said softly. "Talk with the others. Let us know tonight what you decide."

✦ 14 ✦

"WHAT WILL YOU tell her? Won't she find it odd that runaways refuse refuge?" Pavo asked when I told the others of Katlyn's offer.

"I will tell them the truth," I said. "As much of it as we can. I think we owe them that."

Grufyyd turned out to be a big, silent man with a brown beard and somber, smoke-gray eyes. After we had eaten nightmeal, my first out of bed, I asked the couple if I could retell our story.

"We have so often had to lie that it's hard to see where the truth can be told," I began. "It is true we are escapees, in one sense, but that was a long time ago. Now we, and others, have a secret . . . place in the highlands. There are a lot of us there now, mostly no more than children and many runaways. Some came to us, more we helped get away.

"Until recently, we thought our existence a secret. Then we started to hear rumors that the Council meant to investigate the highlands, so our leader decided to send down a delegation to see what we could find out. And at the same time, we came to find a . . . a friend who is hiding somewhere near Murmroth and Aborium."

Katlyn and Grufyyd exchanged an odd, tense look.

"How did you come to be half-drowned on the banks of

the Suggredoon?" Grufyyd asked in his rumbling voice.

"We were in the White Valley looking for an Oldtime pass through the mountains. We didn't want to use the main roads. But we stumbled on a secret camp run by Henry Druid. He takes prisoner anyone who gets too near. He uses the men for labor or else makes them join his armsmen."

Katlyn cast an appalled glance at Grufyyd. "Armsmen. Then he still means to get revenge?"

Grufyyd shook his head sorrowfully.

"We escaped, but the Olden way proved impassable. We were desperate with the Druid's armsmen close behind us, so we rafted the Suggredoon through the mountain."

Katlyn gasped. "But is it possible?" No one answered, since we were the living proof of our story.

"Looked overmuch damage for an overturned boat," Grufyyd observed dispassionately.

I continued. "Now . . . all I have told you is true, but I have not told everything, mostly to protect the ones we left behind. But I would not have said this much unless I trusted you and because we want you to understand why we can't stay here."

"We are no strangers to necessary secrets," Katlyn said gently. "But since you will not stay, then we would like to offer you further help, in return for a favor."

"What favor?" Domick asked.

Grufyyd rose suddenly and decisively. "Our son, Brydda, does not live strictly according to Council lore. In short, he is a seditioner. He helps people who are to be burned—helps them to get away an' start afresh. Our problem is that we have lost contact with him. Brydda has neither visited us nor sent people to be hidden for two moons. We are afraid something has happened to him. We are too old for intrigue, and

371

we ask that you will go into Aborium to give Brydda a message from us."

"Aborium," Jik said and paled.

Domick looked at me. "No," he said decisively. I was startled at his brusqueness after his words the previous night. "If I was coming with you, it might be different, but . . ."

"We mean to part before Morganna, you see," I explained. "Domick will remain in Sutrium. The rest of us will cross the Suggredoon, and on the other side we meant to stay away from the towns. Especially Aborium, for it does not have a good reputation, even in the highlands."

Grufyyd nodded. "It is a bad place. Yet all west coast cities are the same. Ye will have to enter one for food and fodder. And it may be that we can help."

"I do not see how asking us to deliver a message to your son can help us," Domick said belligerently. He stole a glance at Kella, and suddenly I understood his agitation.

Grufyyd nodded with a grave courtesy that made Domick seem rude and brash. "I meant to offer you the use of a cart. Ye will travel more swiftly and safely that way. And I can provide you with some false Normalcy Certificates."

"We will be happy to deliver a message to your son," I said. "It is the least we can do."

Grufyyd's face broke into a beguiling smile. He crossed abruptly to the door, gathering up his coat. On the threshold, he turned. "It will be best for you to go soon. I will ready the cart for tomorrow morning." Without waiting for a response, he went out, leaving a startled silence behind him.

I looked around to see Katlyn giving Domick an apologetic look. "He has been frightened for Brydda; we both have. But dinna fear for your friends, Domick. No one checks papers, save at the main entrance to Aborium. And it is even possible Brydda can help you find th' refuge ye seek."

Katlyn looked at me and smiled. "Now . . . food and drink to travel." She turned to her store cupboards.

"How are we to find your son?" Jik asked timidly.

Katlyn smiled over her shoulder at him. "Ye mun go to the Inn of the Cuttlefish and ask for Brydda Llewellyn—that is the name he calls himself. Wait then, and he will come to you."

"And if he doesn't?" Domick asked.

Katlyn's back faced us, but it seemed to shrink. "Then that will mean he cannot come. The journey takes two days. If you leave very early tomorrow morning and travel steadily, you will arrive at Aborium at daybreak. That is the best and safest time to enter the city. Tradesmen from outlying regions come then, when the gates are opened."

"It is a walled city?" Domick asked sharply.

"The gates are open freely and unguarded in the daylight hours," Katlyn assured him.

She turned to us suddenly, her face serious. "I dinna think ye will come to harm seekin' Brydda out, but take care just th' same, for there are other dangers on the west coast besides the Herders and the Council soldierguards. Those Brydda helps to run away do not account for all the disappearances from the city."

"Slavers . . . ," I murmured.

Katlyn's expression altered subtly. "You have heard of such things?"

"I heard a story while we were in the Druid camp. A man whose father had been to sea. I didn't know if it was the truth or not."

"Many things that seem impossible are true of Aborium. In its own way, it is worse than Sutrium. There the Council rules, but Aborium belongs to the Herder Faction, for that is where ships from Herder Isle and Norseland dock." Katlyn was silent for a time, her eyes anxious. She shook her head and said, "Dinna linger there, is all I'm saying."

✦ 15 ✦

WE ARRIVED AT Aborium two days later.

Bypassing Morganna on Grufyyd's advice, we traveled on a lesser road. Only when we were near Aborium did we venture near to the coast.

From a distance, the city was curiously ugly. Sprawled along the shore, it seemed to be made up of smaller versions of the square skyscrapers we had seen under Tor. Above the rooftops hung a dense, bleary mire of smoke.

"I don't like the look of this place," Kella murmured.

"All such places where the funaga live like rats in a nest stink," Avra observed with a disparagement that would have pleased Gahltha.

The mare was more interested in the sea, which truly provided a dazzling setting for such a grimy jewel. Being mountain bred, she had never seen so much water and was fascinated by it.

We had meant to arrive outside Aborium at dawn, but the loss and slow repair of a wheel delayed us. By the time Kella, Jik, and I had repaired it, the day was drawing to an end. I did not want to enter the city by night, so we made camp on the shore. We would enter Aborium as Katlyn had suggested—at dawn with the tradefolk.

We used the last of the wood Grufyyd had provided to build a small fire in the dunes above the high-water line in the sand so it would not be seen by soldierguards in watch-huts along the top of the city walls. Kella began cooking pancakes from the coarse flour Katlyn had given us while Pavo reorganized the cart, concealing the all-important maps that were to lead us to the Beforetime library in a concealed pocket in Avra's halter. I had brushed down the mare and was putting out grain and a bowl of water for her when the sun fell into the sea in a blaze of colored glory.

Avra went down to the water's edge, and on impulse I followed her and took off my boots. Stepping into the water, I sighed with relief as the cold soothed my scarred feet.

"There is a story among the equines that there is a land beyond the sea where there are no funaga, and beasts rule themselves," Avra sent. We stood for a time in silence, half-mesmerized by the murmurous sighing of the waves on the shore.

Returning to the fire, I found the others seated, staring into the flames with the dreamy expressions a fire always seems to evoke.

We ate the pancakes slowly and fell to talking of Katlyn and Grufyyd.

"I wonder what their son will be like," Kella said.

"Like Grufyyd. Big and soft-spoken. A man of few words," I guessed.

"Perhaps he will be like Katlyn, short and plumpish and always smiling and singing," she suggested.

Pavo smiled. "More like a bit of both. And what will he make of us? I doubt he'll be as free and easy as his parents. He can't afford to be." We all looked at the city behind its wall.

I felt my own smile fade. "I trust them, but we know nothing of this son. I'll keep my judgment until we meet."

Kella bridled angrily. "If he is Katlyn's son, how can he be other than honest?"

Pavo gave her a reproving look. "The guildmistress is wise to be cautious," he said with a faint emphasis on my title. I caught his behindthought that the trip had made Kella too outspoken.

Jik shifted uncomfortably beside me, disturbing Darga, whose head rested on his knee.

"I wonder if Domick has found lodgings yet?" Kella asked.

I was tempted to tell her what I had seen in Domick's mind when he had bid us farewell, despite his coolness with her. Then I realized the knowledge would only intensify her regret at his loss. Better not to meddle.

"Much better," Darga sent laconically.

I stared at the dog in amazement. He had passed through my shield with an ease that astounded me.

"My mind grows stronger," Darga sent.

I was about to answer this when a blinding realization struck me. In my excitement, I shouted, "What if the Talent is not human?"

"What?" Kella asked, looking at me as if I had gone mad.

"I meant, what if the Talent that registered on the Zebkrahn isn't human? What if it's a dog or an equine?" I said.

"Does it matter?" Avra inquired coolly.

I was taken aback. *Did* it matter? If we were to accept animals as equals and allies, this must lead eventually to animal rescues. Sobered, I shook my head.

"I'm an idiot. Of course it doesn't matter," I sent.

"Gahltha hoped it would be a beast, to break the funaga prejudice," Avra sent, mollified.

"Prejudice?" I said.

"The worst prejudice is that which goes unrecognized,"

Darga explained. "You think you treat us as equals, but in your deepest heart, you regard the funaga as superior. In part, this is because you yourself are powerful. But that does not make the race of the funaga better than that of dog or equine." Darga's gentle criticism cut like a knife. I was not certain I believed the funaga admirable as a race, but there was some truth in his accusation. And how could one fight such an insidious prejudice?

"You are less prejudiced than most of your race," Darga sent. "But Gahltha hoped we would find a beast mind to rival yours. He believes that is the only way to alter the funaga's deepest attitudes, even at Obernewtyn. Perhaps he was right."

"It might be a girlfriend for Darga," Jik sent with a shy grin. The others had not been part of our silent beastspeaking.

"We'll know soon enough," said Pavo.

"How many hours do you calculate from here to the hidden library?" I asked.

Pavo considered. "Half a day, if the distances shown on the map are consistent. I hope we will not be delayed too long in Aborium."

Coming to the side gate of the city just after sunrise, I was startled and unnerved to see how many soldierguards were posted. There was no mistaking the yellow cloaks they wore as a badge of office. But though they looked searchingly at our faces, they neither spoke nor sought our papers. Just as unexpected as the guards were the huge crowd of people and carts clamoring to be let in the gate. Many of those waiting were laughing and singing, and one girl did a cheeky jig to the calls and encouragement of her friends. I was puzzled by the crowd's high spirits but reassured, too. Surely a city that had so many eager visitors could not be such a bad place.

The sun was well risen by the time our cart was allowed to enter, and we made directly for the seafront and the Inn of the Cuttlefish. Grufyyd had given us directions, but it was harder than we had expected to follow them, for we were swept along by the crowd past the turns we had wanted to take. The city was of a tortuous design, so there was no working our way back. Streets ran off in all directions, bisecting, curving, and turning back on themselves.

"If we can find the water, we can work our way along," Pavo suggested. We were loath to mark ourselves strangers by asking the way, but morning passed into afternoon and still we were lost. I did not even remember how to get back to the gate. "No wonder people come in and never come out," I said wearily. "They probably can't find their way."

"We'll have to ask," Kella said.

I asked a woman, then a boy and another woman. All claimed not to know the inn. That struck me oddly. Aborium was large, but Grufydd had said the inn was big and well known. Still trying to decide what to do, we continued to be carried along within the milling crowd. Jik warned us that Avra was on the verge of panicking at the way people were pressing all around her.

"Let's get out of this," I said, and directed Avra to force her way to the edge of the crowd and take the next turn away from the throng.

"I didn't know there were so many people in the Land," Kella said in a shaken voice, when we had reached a quiet side lane.

I looked at Jik, who wore a puzzled air. "There were not so many when I was here."

We came to the end of the lane and stopped in dismay, for

it ended at an enormous central square. Here people swirled and butted one another like goats in a pen. I could hear laughter and strains of music, and the smells of food and warmed drinks wafted to our noses.

"It's a moon fair!" Pavo said, slapping his forehead. I laughed aloud in relief. That was the reason for the number of people waiting to come into the city. And the people of whom we had asked directions were strangers, too.

Avra managed to take a turn just inside the square, and we halted the cart in a quiet byway. A foul stench filled the air.

"What is that?" Kella asked in a disgusted voice.

"Seaweed," Jik said with a grin. "We must be near the wharves."

"Fancy having an inn near such a smell," Kella muttered. Then she noticed me climbing down. "Where are you going?"

"I'll have a look for the inn on foot. It will be easier than trying to maneuver the cart."

"I will go with you," Darga offered, and jumped down.

"Darga will come back alone if anything goes wrong. If he does come back without me, go back out of the city and wait for me where we camped last night," I said.

Kella and Jik looked aghast, and I laughed. "Nothing will happen, but we must have a plan just in case." They looked only slightly reassured.

I set off, ignoring the slight pain in my feet. The gypsy caravan, the raft, and the cart meant I had done little walking, and they were much better, though still tender. I hoped I would not have to walk too far on them. I was glad of Darga's company, though once or twice I noticed people looking at him so oddly that I wondered if I was breaking some city law, letting him walk unchained.

I looked around, trying to see someone who appeared to

belong in Aborium. Spoting an old woman struggling with a load of washing down an alley, I hurried to catch up, hoping kindness would beget kindness.

"Mother, let me help you," I offered.

She gave me a long measuring look before letting me take one of the handles. " 'Tis good of ye, sure enough," she said. "I dinna mean to be so slow at takin' yer offer, but a moon fair dinna improve manners, an' a helpin' hand is rare at any time. What be yer name, lass?" she asked, squinting at me.

"Elspeth," I said.

"Well, I'm Luma," she said cheerfully. "I live just round th' next corner. I went out to gan th' wash an' were near swept away wi' moonies. It gans worse every year," she added despondently. She prattled on as we walked, complaining bitterly about the damage done to the city during the fairs. At a narrow door, she set down the basket to find her key.

"No doubt it's been picked from me," she said, searching all her pockets and folds in a haphazard way. "I'm from th' highlands. There ye dinna have to lock yer door, but in a city, leavin' it open is a right invitation to any robber." At last she found the key. Bidding me help her a little further, she told me to call Darga in.

"Things have a way of disappearin' in Aborium," she said confidingly.

Stone steps led down directly from the front door. We carried the basket awkwardly between us, down the stairs and into a large, rustic kitchen.

"What an effort," gasped Luma, panting and fanning her red face. "Ye'll have a glass of cordial to wet yer whistle?" Taking a squat jug from the cooling cabinet, she poured two mugs. " 'Tis me own brew I'm givin' ye, though I'll thank ye nowt to speak of it after. We are bound by lore to buy th'

Herders' bitter cordials, an' makin' it is an offense." She drained her glass with relish and watched me drink mine.

"Ye be a moonie? I'm sorry for all that I were sayin' of them, but it gans on a body's nerve to have so many at once."

"I'm a traveler on my way to Murmroth. I only called into Aborium to deliver a message," I said.

Luma beamed. "An' I might ha' guessed it. Ye look to have too much sense to be part of that nonsense. Who do ye carry a message to? 'Tis nowt of my affair or care, but I know most folk hereabout, an' might save ye some trouble."

I took a deep breath. "He's staying at the Inn of the Cuttlefish."

She nodded thoughtfully, her eyes on Darga. "A fine creature that, for all he puts me in mind of th' Herder breed."

"I've heard they use dogs to protect the Isle," I said.

"An' th' cloister here in Aborium. But who in their right mind would want to break into one?" She looked at Darga again with faint unease. "Yet he's a match, though small an' th' wrong shape. Well, th' inn ye seek is just a step from here. Ye dinna say who ye were lookin' for."

"A seaman," I stalled.

She cackled. "A seaman? Ha! Well, what else would ye find a man doin' in a seaport? I myself ha' two strappin' sons, an' my bondmate were a seaman, too, Lud rest his head."

"The man I'm looking for is called Brydda Llewellyn," I said.

The color drained from the washerwoman's face.

"What is it?" I asked quickly.

She smiled, a horrible false twist of her lips. " 'Tis naught. I were thinkin' somethin' else for a minute. I hardly heard ye. I dinna know th' name."

"She is afraid," Darga sent as the old woman took me onto

382

the street and pointed the way to the inn. I felt her eyes boring into my back until I was out of sight.

"What happened?" Darga asked when we had gone out of her sight.

"I don't know. One minute we are talking like two sisters, and the next she looks as if I murdered her best friend. And all after I mentioned the name of Katlyn's son."

"He is well known?" Darga suggested.

"I don't know what it means, but I don't like it."

The inn was not far from Luma's house, and rather than being the grand place I had half imagined, it was a modest establishment with a faintly dingy air and peeling paint. Along the front was a stone veranda where men sat in the fading twilight talking in low voices. Wishing I had reached the inn before dark, I told Darga to wait in the street. "If I don't come out within an hour, go back to the others."

"Better not to go in," he sent.

I glanced down at him, wondering what he sensed. "I don't want to, but I promised."

The men on the porch fell silent as I approached. I asked for the manager of the inn in what I hoped was a confident voice. One of the men jerked his head toward the door.

"Thank you," I said.

The reception room was dim and cool. For a moment, I could see nothing and blinked, trying to accustom my eyes to the lack of light.

"What do you want?" asked a sharp voice. I jumped and heard a snicker of laughter. A woman and two men were sitting near the window, silhouetted against the fading pink sunset.

I swallowed dryly. "I'm . . . looking for a man. I have a message to deliver."

"What is his name?" the woman asked coldly.

I made myself speak, though I was regretting not listening to Darga. "Brydda Llewellyn."

A match flared and a lamp was lit on the table, illuminating the narrow, ratty face of the manageress and the hard, wary faces of the men.

The woman smiled, a folding rather than a curve of thin lips. "Brydda lives at the inn, but he has been on his boat this last moon. He will be here tomorrow morning. I can let you have a room for tonight."

Again the sour smile, and as she rose, dark satin skirts rustled around her feet like a nest of snakes. "Come with me," she commanded, and I dared not refuse. The inn was larger than it looked, and I was filled with unease as she took me downstairs where there were a number of bedrooms. The room she gave me was halfway down a hall and had a narrow window, level with the street. It was sparsely furnished.

"This is the only room we have free. Best if you keep to it until morning. The men who stay here are not used to having women around. I'll send water for you to wash and some supper."

Forcing a smile, I went across and tested the springs of the bed. "It's been a while since I've slept in a bed," I said casually. "I don't mind a bit of rest."

"I'll lock the door so you're not disturbed. Ring the bell if you want anything." She nodded smugly and departed.

My false smile fell away the minute the door closed, for I had no doubt I was a prisoner. The moment I tried to leave, the thinly veiled pretense would end. I pushed a bench to the window and climbed up to peer out. There was no possibility of getting out that way. I could fiddle locks, but I could not magic myself through the ground. I sent a call to Darga.

384

"Can you get out?" he asked as soon as he appeared at the window.

"I can open the lock, but I will have to wait until everyone goes to sleep. I want you to go back to the cart and get the others out of the city."

"Why have they locked you up?" Darga asked.

"I don't know, but I think it was because I asked for Bry-dda Llewellyn." I wondered what Rushton would do in such a situation.

"He would not risk you," Darga sent.

I stared. "What do you mean?" I shook my head. "Look, there's no time for this. You have to get the others out of the city before the gates are closed for the night."

An hour later, I could wait no longer. The door lock was a simple device, and I tampered with the mechanism so it would seem to be broken. Then I wrapped a towel round my hair and stuck my head out into the hall. The man outside started in astonishment at the sight of me. "How—?"

I interrupted him. "I've rung the bell three times, and no one comes. I was promised some water for a wash," I complained. Amazement gave way to confusion and then indecision. He had obviously been told to guard the door, but I was not acting like a prisoner. My querulous demand for water and the towel on my hair had confused him, and I sensed him wondering if he had somehow got his instructions muddled.

"Go on, then, tell her," I snapped, and shut the door.

I listened to his footsteps receding. Then I threw off the towel and slipped out into the hallway. I had barely taken two steps before I heard voices coming. I dared not go back to the room. Turning, I hurried in the other direction, trying every door I passed. A locked door had to mean the room was occupied.

My heart leaped as I recognized the manageress's voice. "What do you mean the door was unlocked? I locked it."

The last door was also locked, but I had no choice. If there was someone in the room, I would have to coerce them. I bent my mind to the lock, but before I could do anything, the door opened and a young, bearded man looked out. We stared at one another in surprise; then the voice of the manageress came clearly down the hall.

"Find her! She can't have gone far. She has a limp. Search all the rooms on this level."

Without saying a word, the man reached out and pulled me through the door, shutting it quickly. He made a sign for me to be quiet, and we listened intently. I heard the manageress shriek in rage at finding me gone.

The young man turned to look at me. He was not much older than Rushton, and his skin was the clear smooth brown of a seaman. He wore trousers, but his wet face and bare chest told me I had caught him in the middle of a wash.

"You are the girl who asked after Brydda Llewellyn?" he asked in a low voice.

I nodded, dazed that he should know.

There was a loud knock on the next door, and I looked at him in a panic.

In two strides he crossed the floor and flung open the lid of a big trunk. "Get in."

There was a knock at his door. I climbed in the trunk and heard him turning the key slowly.

"Why did you take so long to answer?" It was the manageress. I held my breath in terror.

"I was washing. What's going on?" he asked crossly.

"Ah . . . well, we have had a girl staying, as a favor to her father, who is a seaman. She is subject to manias and brain-

386

storms. For her own safety, she was locked in, but she has got away."

"Is she dangerous?" asked my rescuer seriously. Despite my fear, I grinned at his convincingly anxious tone.

She grunted.

"Well, I heard this was a respectable place, but with all the noise and murdering madwomen running around, I am glad I am heading out to sea this night. Send someone to bring up my trunk."

My heart thumped in fear that she would demand to see what was in it.

"Carry your own trunk!" she snapped rudely, slamming the door. There was silence and some movement, then I felt myself lifted. I slid to the bottom of the trunk, half-suffocated by clothes.

"Don't make a sound," he hissed in a strained voice that told me he had hoisted the trunk—and me—onto his back.

In the hall, I heard enough to chill my blood. "The Council won't like this," said one voice.

" 'Tis nowt th' Council troubles me but th' priests. They're th' ones he's plagued," said another voice. The two voices faded, and I realized we were climbing the stairs.

Suddenly there was another voice. "Ho, Reuvan. Where are ye goin' at this hour?"

"I'm for the sea tonight," said my rescuer.

"Tonight?" There was an edge of surprise in the other's voice.

"The Herders have given permission to my master," Reuvan said. "But I don't know why he can't wait till a civil hour to set sail."

I wished he would get moving. The air in the trunk was beginning to foul. I felt sweat trickle down my spine.

At last the other laughed. "Better you than me. I'll see you."

"Not here you won't," Reuvan said easily. "It's a damn sight too noisy, and that sharp-tongued manageress is no enticement."

The other man laughed, and we moved on. At long last, I felt myself being set down, and the distinctive sound of hooves scraping over cobbles told me we were in the street.

The chest jerked, and I realized I was in a cart. It set off, and after an eternity, the latch was undone. "Stay down. It's not safe yet," the seaman whispered softly.

"Why are you helping me?" I asked in a low voice.

There was a pause. "You wanted to talk to Brydda Llewellyn, didn't you? Well, I'm taking you to him."

· 16 ·

BRYDDA LLEWELLYN WAS a giant of a man, towering head and shoulders above the men around him. His face, illuminated fitfully in the guttering candlelight, was as stern and craggy as weathered rock.

Reuvan gave me a slight push. "Brýdda, here is the girl who asked for you at the inn. I caught her trying to escape the old crow's clutches."

The buzz of talk from the men in the room ceased. My heart thumped unevenly under their hostile scrutiny.

"You have taken your time in coming," said Brydda, for all the world as if he had expected me.

"If you were where you were supposed to be, I would have been quicker," I said.

An astounded silence followed my words, then the giant roared with laughter. "Well, well, so they have sent a kitten that snarls and spits. I could crush you with one hand, little sad eyes, but I don't. Let that be a sign of my good faith. Now, what do you have to tell me?"

I was less intimidated by his threats than reassured by his laughter, for I had seen Katlyn in it. "I come from Rangorn. I bring a message from your—"

To my surprise, Brydda's smile disappeared and he held up an imperious hand. "Speak no more of that for a moment." He glanced around, and silently the men filed out, giving me curious looks. Then we were alone except for Reuvan, who went to stand by the door.

"Don't be afraid," Brydda said in a softer voice. "I thought you were a messenger from Sutrium. I did not think . . . You come from my parents? Are they well?"

I nodded. "They are worried because you haven't sent word to them in so long. I think they feared something had happened to you."

Brydda ran a massive hand through the dark, springing curls on his forehead. "So it has. I suppose they told you about me?"

"They said you help seditioners."

He smiled faintly. "Well, that is as good a way as any of putting it. How did you come to meet my parents? You are not from Rangorn."

"We had an accident, and your parents helped us. We offered to bring a message to repay their kindness."

"You are with friends?" Brydda said sharply.

I nodded, hoping Darga had got the others away. "When I left them, they were in an alley not far from the inn. I'm not sure whether they made it out of the city before nightfall."

Brydda started, a look of concern on his face. "Quickly, Reuvan, go and take some of the others. Bring them back." He turned to me. "What do they look like?"

"A girl and a boy not much younger than I am, and a much younger boy," I said. "A wheat-colored mare is pulling the cart."

He nodded, and Reuvan hurried away. "It is dangerous to be out in the streets at night, though less than usual because of the moon fair. Is there no one full grown among your companions?"

Slightly indignant, I told him we were perfectly able to look after ourselves. Changing the subject, I asked why I had been locked up at the inn. "Your parents told us to mention your name. I didn't reckon on such an unfriendly reception," I said resentfully. Brydda only laughed and gave me a slap on the back that winded me.

"Much has happened since I last spoke to my parents. I was betrayed by one of my men. Once I could go to and from the inn openly, an ordinary seaman, but now I am known to be the notorious seditioner they call the Black Dog. You are lucky I had friends keeping an eye out at the inn for the messenger I mistook you for. Once she comes, I will leave Aborium. I dared not send word to my parents while I am here, because I was afraid of having their connection with me exposed. But I am glad to hear they are safe."

"Those soldierguards at the gate," I said in sudden realization. "It was you they were looking for."

He nodded. "The Council would like to catch me, and so would the Herder Faction. But I will slip through their fingers like snow during the moon fair."

"Where will you go?" I said unthinkingly.

Brydda looked at me for a long moment. "Few would expect an honest answer to such a question. But I believe I can trust you. Does it seem strange to you that a wanted man trusts his instinct over caution?" He smiled when I did not answer. "I have a kind of infallible knack for judging people."

"Yet you say you were betrayed . . ."

He nodded grimly. "By a man I loved like a brother. But I did not misjudge him. He was tortured and made to speak, and there will be a payment for that. Come, tell me the truth. Are you not a seditioner or a runaway yourself, that my mother should tell you my secrets?"

I stared at him in fright.

"I told you. I have a knack at guessing. But don't look so

unnerved. It makes us allies, not enemies," he said.

I nodded, shaken, entertaining an odd notion about this uncanny "knack" of his. "My parents were burned by the Council as seditioners, and my brother was killed by soldier-guards," I said.

Brydda nodded triumphantly. "I thought as much, though I think there is more to your story than that. But it is enough to know we fight the same fight. It is my aim to rid this land of the Herder Faction and its tyranny. I have many allies who think as I do, and for now we oppose the Herders in a thousand small ways. But the time is not too distant when we will challenge them openly."

I was filled with excitement, for his words were almost identical to Rushton's, except Brydda seemed to think the Herder Faction worse than the Council.

He continued. "The message I wait for is to ensure there are no Herders waiting for me in Sutrium. It is too dangerous for me here now, so I will go elsewhere and harass them anew. Sutrium. They will not expect me to be so bold."

Reuvan came in, grim-faced. He bent and spoke into Brydda's ear.

"What is it?" I asked.

"Your friends are gone," Reuvan said.

I sighed in relief. "They will have gone outside the city when I didn't come back. That was what we planned."

Brydda said, "Reuvan means they have been taken prisoner. I have allies who let me know who has been taken by the Herders and the soldierguards. It seems your friends were among today's intake."

I shook my head in disbelief.

"Rumor says the boy was a runaway Herder novice," Brydda went on.

"No!" I whispered in horror. "Where have they been taken? Who has them?"

"The Herders," Reuvan said. "They'll have been taken to the cloister for interrogation."

"I have to help them," I cried.

Reuvan shook his head. "No one escapes the cloister cells. There are priests everywhere and killer dogs. And the place is built like a labyrinth."

Brydda scratched his head. "Only a madman would attempt such an impossible rescue."

There was a commotion at the door, and a girl entered. Weary and travel stained, she half staggered into a chair. "You are the messenger?" Brydda asked.

The girl nodded. "Sutrium and all the other branches are safe. It seems he died before they could make him tell any more. . . ."

Brydda's shoulders slumped. "I should be glad. . . ."

I did not wait to hear any more. Taking the chance offered by the momentary confusion, I slipped into the street.

It was dark and very cold, the moon obscured by clouds. I shivered and wished I had not left my coat on the cart. I had delivered my message, I thought bitterly, but at what cost?

When I had gone a safe distance from Brydda's hovel, I stepped into a darkened doorway and closed my eyes, sending my mind to the other side of town. My mind played back and forth, seeking Jik's familiar pattern. It seemed ages before I spotted a dull glimmer at the farthest edge of my reduced lowland range. I sent a farseeking probe gratefully.

"Elspeth?" Jik's thoughts were faint.

"Jik, are you in the Herder cloister?" Lightning flashed, making it a strain to communicate at such a distance.

"Yes," he sent.

"What about the others?"

"I'm on my own in a cell. Kella and Pavo are here somewhere. Avra is in the stable," Jik sent. I was filled with loneliness and apprehension but realized Jik was empathising his own emotions to me.

"What happened?" I asked.

"One of the priests recognized me from Darthnor. I tried to tell them Kella and Pavo didn't know about me, but I don't think they believed me. They want to know how I got here and how I made it look like I died. They want to know where I've been and if I had help. I'm scared. I think they mean to take me out to Herder Isle." Jik's terror spilled over into my own mind, and for a moment, I saw his nightmarish vision of the interrogation methods awaiting him.

"I won't let that happen. I'm coming," I sent, but the contact had begun to fade.

I found myself slumped in the doorway, gritty water seeping through the knees of my trousers. Sweat was freezing on my cheeks, and my teeth were chattering violently.

I had meant to try farseeking Darga as well, but that would have to wait. I needed to reach the cloisters as fast as I could and get Jik away from there. Get him away, or erase his mind, a darker voice reminded me. I shuddered and walked faster.

I was limping badly by the time I reached the area of the city nearest the cloister, certain that all Kella's good work on the scars had been undone. It was not hard to tell which building was the cloister. Set apart from the other buildings, it had its own high wall. Branches of trees and leaves visible at the top told me there was a garden inside. I made my way carefully around the perimeter, looking for a weak point. There were two small gates, barred and guarded, and one larger gate, open but heavily guarded. The contact with Jik had left me too depleted to coerce a guard, let alone more than one. Somehow I had to get in without being seen. I decided I would have to climb over the wall.

Leaning against it to gather my energy for the climb, I realized a dog was pacing on the other side. He had sensed me and was about to bark. I sent a quick greeting, and his urge to bark diffused into curiosity.

"Who/what are you?" It was a dog named Kadarf.

"I am a funaga. I mean no harm. I want to come over the fence and visit a friend," I sent. Fighting a wave of nausea, I gave his mind a coercive push. I climbed the fence with the help of a spindly tree growing by the wall. Sitting on the top, I could see the Herder cloister through the trees, a dark, squarish building with few windows and no visible doors.

At the foot of the wall, a muscular, brindled dog watched me slither awkwardly to the ground. He bore a strong resemblance to Darga, and I remembered how the townspeople had eyed him warily.

I closed my eyes and reached out with my mind for Jik. When I farsought him, he almost overwhelmed me with a wave of emphathised terror.

"Elspeth!" Jik sent. "They're taking me to the Herder Isle tonight!"

"I'm right outside. Now, how long before they come?"

Jik made a concentrated effort to control his panic. "In . . . in an hour, they said. But that was a while ago. Is Darga with you?"

I sent a gentle negative. "I was delayed at the inn and sent him back to the cart, but you must have already been taken. He's a smart dog. Remember when he disappeared in the Druid camp? He'll turn up."

I left Jik for a moment to locate the others. Kella and Pavo were in a cell together, and I let Kella know I was coming. Avra was in a stable near the perimeter of the grounds.

She responded with relief to my probe, and I realized she had been afraid we would abandon her. Quickly, she outlined the arrangement of the stables. I told her Kella and Pavo would come to get her shortly.

Returning to Jik, I was glad to find him calmer. "I've found Kella and Pavo. I'm going to free them first, because they're on the top level, and they can free Avra," I sent.

"If the Herders come for me . . . ," Jik sent fearfully.

"I'll get back in time," I sent.

"Promise you won't let them take me to the Isle," Jik urged.

"I promise," I sent.

I looked down at Kadarf and probed him to locate a lesser house door. Following me, Kadarf stretched himself outside the door to wait.

Inside was a short hall branching in two directions. I took the left way, leading to Kella and Pavo, noting the other way would bring me to stairs leading down to Jik's level. Passing numerous closed doors, a slight farsense probe was all I needed to warn me if anyone was coming.

My limp had grown worse, but there was no time to rest. Turning warily into another hall, I jumped at the sound of voices, but no one was visible.

I could hardly believe I was creeping through a dread Herder cloister. I would not have imagined I would have the courage, but Jik's fear of being taken to the Isle and my own fear of having to erase his mind spurred me on. I stopped abruptly, realizing I had found them. A brief straining, and the lock clicked. Kella and Pavo looked up, relief flooding their faces.

"There's no time to talk," I said, forestalling their questions. "I'll take you to an outer door. There is a dog there who will lead you to the stables where Avra is kept. Avra said you can get out of the stable to an exercise yard, and from there to the street. Leave at once, and get straight out of the city. You might have to bribe the gatekeeper. Head for Murmroth until the lights of Aborium dim. Camp on the beach. I'll find you. Now let's hurry."

"I will slow you down," Pavo said faintly. I was shocked by his ravaged face. He seemed to have aged years in a few hours.

"Help him," I said to Kella brusquely. She looked hurt at my tone, but some of the dazed horror had faded from her eyes.

Moving back down the hall, I was puzzled to note how awkwardly Pavo moved. Had the disease begun to affect his limbs? Then I saw a bloody streak on one ankle and understood. He had been interrogated.

For a second, I was overwhelmed by a black tide of hate. This dissolved into fear as my senses warned that a priest was approaching. There was no door near enough to offer refuge, and the hall was long and straight with no turnings. Neither Pavo nor I was capable of running fast enough to get back inside the cell before he came round the corner.

Desperation gave me an idea.

"Get close to the wall and face it. Don't move, no matter what happens," I whispered. I blew out the candles on either side of us, throwing our hall into shadow. Flattened to the wall in the dimness, I mustered my strength and sent out a fine coercive probe. I let it mesh with the priest's mind. The alignment was perfect, and for a time, I simply mirrored his thoughts about the power-hungry manipulations of an ambitious senior priest. Then, gently, I began to exert my own force beneath the conscious level and into the semiconscious region of the mind.

My brother, Jes, and I had played hide-and-seek as children, and I had always won when he searched, no matter how bare the boundary we set, because I could make his mind look everywhere but directly at me. Our only hope was that this child's trick would work on the priest.

He came around the corner, and Kella quivered with fright. I willed her to be still as he came nearer. It would only work if we were completely motionless. Pushing the priest's mind fractionally, I made him turn his head absentmindedly to the opposite wall where the candles were extinguished. He passed us looking steadfastly the wrong way, entirely unaware of us or my subtle coercion. I did not dare release him until he had turned the corner, then I slumped back, exhausted.

"He didn't see us," Kella whispered incredulously. "How could he not?"

"Quickly," I snapped.

Outside, I bade Kadarf take them to the stables and prevent their harassment by any other dogs. I did not stay to see them go. Time was running out for Jik. Nearly hobbling now, I sent my mind ahead to let the boy know I was coming.

To my dismay, he was not alone. There were two priests in the room with him. I was too late!

Agitation made me careless and Jik perceived me. "Elspeth?" His mind groped for mine. I was filled with remorse at the terrible duty that lay before me. I dared not let them take him without erasing all of his knowledge about Obernewtyn. No matter how brave he was, in the end they would make him talk, just as Brydda's friend had been made to talk. But I knew I had neither the heart nor the strength for such an operation.

I had another idea.

Hobbling back into the garden, I called to Kadarf. He followed me back to the fence and watched me struggle to climb it. "I'm sorry you are going," he sent.

I waved a brief salute, then dropped to the path on the other side of the wall. Kella and Pavo were nowhere in sight. I hurried around to the ornate double gate Kadarf said was used for most coming and going among the priests, praying they would bring Jik out that way.

I waited, sitting cross legged in the shadows beneath a bush to give my feet a rest. It was some minutes before I saw any sign of life. One of the guards brought a large cart out and harnessed up a white horse. Then a group of priests came out, carrying boxes and parcels. Peering from my hiding place, I saw Jik between them, looking small and frightened. My heart ached for him, but I turned my mind resolutely to the horse. My only hope was to create some sort of diversion to give Jik the chance to run.

Suddenly a hand touched my arm. Whirling, I stifled a scream of fright as I looked into Brydda Llewellyn's face.

"How . . . ," I began, only to be interrupted by the sound of horses and a carriage.

Frantically, I tried to collect my thoughts, but I was too slow. With a cry of despair, I saw the carriage draw away and knew I had failed. I had a brief glimpse of Jik sitting upright among the grim-faced priest masters.

Then he was gone.

✦ 17 ✦

I STARED DOWN the empty street, knowing I had failed Jik—and all of Obernewtyn.

"Quickly," Brydda said. "We will have to move fast if we are to catch them."

He half dragged me across the street and around a corner where a grinning Reuvan sat behind the reins of a carriage embossed boldly with the gleaming Herder seal.

"Courtesy of the Herder Faction," he said with a mock bow.

Dazed, I let myself be lifted in. The cart lurched as Brydda climbed in behind me. Reuvan shook the reins, urging the horse on to a wild pace.

"You are hurt?" Brydda shouted over the clatter of hooves on the cobbles. He nodded at my feet.

"Old wounds," I shouted back. "You followed me?"

Brydda shook his head. "You were gone before I realized, before we could talk of ways and means to rescue your friends. But I knew where you had gone."

"You said helping them was impossible," I protested.

Brydda shook his head. "I said only a madman would attempt such a rescue. I forgot you did not know me well enough to realize that I am just such a man."

I was struck dumb at his words.

"Besides," Brydda said, "you had not meant to come to Aborium, except to deliver my parents' message. Therefore, I am the direct cause of your troubles and honor-bound to help you. And if the Herders are so keen to have your friend, I am just as eager to stop them." He grinned. "We were waiting to see you arrive, never dreaming you had already magicked yourself inside. . . ." He hesitated, obviously curious, but I said nothing. "A lad and a girl came out stealthily leading a horse. They fit the description you gave, so we stopped them. It took us a minute to convince them we were trying to help, and then they told us you were inside. I sent one of my people to show them a safe way out of the city. I wanted them to take the cart, but I have never seen a pair more attached to a horse."

"I don't know how to thank you . . . ," I began, but Brydda held up a hand.

"No need for thanks among allies. Now, the Herders will be going to the wharf. The girl said they want to question the boy. . . ." For a moment, his face really did look like stone, and I understood that Brydda Llewellyn would be a savage enemy. "There's no time for subtle planning. I meant to leave town tonight anyway, so it does not matter if the Herders think I freed the boy. It will madden them trying to under-stand the connection. Was he really a Herder novice?"

I nodded. "What can we do? There are five priests in that cart," I said as Reuvan suddenly reined the horse to a slow walk. I could smell the sea and the sour odor of old seaweed.

"We're nearly to the wharf," Reuvan said over his shoulder.

"Go softly, then," Brydda said. "We can handle five be-tween us, six counting the shipmaster."

I nodded, praying they would succeed, for I knew I couldn't wipe Jik's mind clean of his dangerous knowledge.

The clatter of stones ceased as the wheels ran onto board. We had reached the wharf.

The waning moon broke through the clouds but shed a

wan light, and all was darkness. The smells of oil and spices mingled with that of sea and fish scales. Moored vessels bobbed in the dark, gurgling water, bumping occasionally into their mooring posts with a dull thud.

"The Herders cast off from there," Brydda whispered, pointing to the very end of the wharf. Lanterns swung from either end of a long, slim boat moored there. Illuminated fitfully in the gritty, shifting light was the carriage that had brought Jik. It was empty, and there was no sign of him. Priests were moving between the ship and the carriage, transferring boxes to the vessel.

"Why do they travel at night?" I whispered as Brydda signaled for Reuvan to draw the carriage into a shadowed corner.

"They are a secretive lot, and night suits their fell purposes. Most ships go out at dawn or just before. Folk know the Herders come here at night, and that is enough to discourage anyone else. People who seem too interested in Herder business have a way of disappearing. There's the boy."

Jik was standing between two priests, half obscured by their flapping gray cloaks. His hands were bound behind him, and his shoulders slumped hopelessly.

"Jik," I sent.

His head jerked in surprise, but he subsided when one of the priests gave him a hard look.

"Careful," I warned, and sensed him make an effort to maintain his dejected pose.

"Elspeth," he sent in a powerful wave of gladness that twisted my heart.

"We are at the other end of the wharf, in the shadows. We're going to help you."

I broke contact, feeling Brydda's hand on my arm. "It's no

good. There are at least seven priests down there. And there is the shipmaster. Two of us might barely overcome the lot, and I'd take the risk but for the dogs. They are trained by the priests to tear a man's throat out on command," Brydda said.

I blinked at him, trying to reconcile the savage picture his words evoked with Kadarf's simple kindness. "But you said . . . we've got to get him away from them. I . . . I . . ." I stopped, gulping back tears.

"It's not possible, lass. You see that, don't you?" Brydda asked.

"You don't understand. He . . . he can tell them about us, and about you and your parents."

Brydda shook his head. "That's bad, but there is no way to help the boy or silence him. Getting ourselves killed trying won't help anyone."

I threw caution to the wind. I felt I had no choice.

"Brydda, I am a Misfit," I said. "I can stop those dogs from attacking. You think—everybody does—that Misfits are only true dreamers and defectives. Useless. But there are other kinds, too. Misfits like me and my friends. I can make those dogs do what I want, and I can talk to Jik from here, inside his head. If you can handle the men, I can deal with the dogs."

I could hardly believe myself revealing so much. Reuvan was staring at me as if I had gone mad.

"I'll prove it," I said desperately. "Watch Jik. I'll make him look toward us and nod." I sent a message to Jik, asking him to respond as obviously as he could without alerting his guardians. He turned his head slowly and nodded with a subtle wink. Reuvan hissed in astonishment.

"You can hold the dogs?" Brydda asked.

I nodded, hoping they would be as easy to convince as Kadarf. "Help me save Jik. Please."

After a long tense moment, Brydda grinned. "Well, I'm probably finally going mad, but we'll have a go at it. Seven men—we can handle that many between us, eh, Reuvan?"

"Seven men, yes. But those dogs . . . ," he said doubtfully.

Brydda clapped him on the back. "Come, man, you heard the girl. Those dogs will be all bark and no bite."

Reuvan looked at me warily, as if I myself might bite, but such was the strength of Brydda's personality that he nodded.

"Good lad. Now, Elspeth, tell the boy to run for it as soon as he gets the chance. Don't wait for us. As soon as you have him, get out of the city as fast as you can. There is a gate back near the cloister. Go out that gate and no other. Wait with your friends, and I'll find you."

"What about you?"

"I'll worry about me. Make sure you do as I said."

I reached out and touched his arm. "It was a glad day when I first heard the name of Brydda Llewellyn," I said.

He smiled. "Life is an adventure, is it not?"

They melted into the shadows and began making their way toward the Herder vessel.

I groped about until I found the mind of the shipmaster. He was in the hold, organizing the loading of the cargo. I pinched a nerve experimentally and he groaned and doubled over. I grinned, catching his thought that he must have eaten a bad fish stew.

I tweaked the nerve again, more firmly, and this time he groaned loudly enough to be heard by the priests on the wharf. They looked at one another. One stepped onto the deck and climbed down into the hold.

Taking advantage of their preoccupation, Brydda and Reuvan attacked with wild cries, brandishing knives. One of the priests standing on the edge of the vessel fell overboard in fright. Another Herder, with stronger nerves, reached down to unloose the dogs he had on leash. Quickly, I beastspoke to the dogs, asking for help. I had no strength left to coerce more than very slightly, but they agreed to help. I saw that the dogs had no love for their masters, for all their savage training. As soon as they were loose, they began to bark wildly and snarl, jumping and running in circles. The look on the Herders' faces would have been funny if there had not been so much at stake.

Then Reuvan jumped onto the deck, delivering a stout blow to the emerging priest and slamming the hold shut. That left five. One of the priests held on to Jik while the others divided into pairs to attack Brydda and Reuvan. Brydda was more than a match for two men. A blow from his fist and the first priest crumpled at his feet like a wet cloth. The other had drawn a knife and tried to sink it in Brydda's belly, but the big man was agile for his size and whirled on his toes like a dancer before dealing a blow with the haft of his sword. He stepped over the unconscious priests and turned around.

Reuvan had dispatched one of his attackers and was busy with the other. Brydda turned menacingly to the priest holding Jik. Calmer than his brothers, he drew a long knife from the folds of his cloak and let go of Jik's arm.

"Run!" I sent.

He lurched forward, stumbling, hampered by his bound hands. Panting, he fell as he reached the cart.

"Quick, get in," I whispered. His nose was bleeding and his breath came in sobs, but he clambered awkwardly into the cart and fell across my feet. I gathered up the reins. I hated to leave Brydda, but he had struck me as a man used to having his orders obeyed.

I beastspoke the surprised horse, and we rode away from the wharf.

I was afraid someone would spot us crossing the dark city in the Herder cart and slung a bag over the side to obscure the insignia. As we drew up to the gate, my heart was thundering. But the gatekeeper barely looked at me before letting us through. There was not a soldierguard in sight.

Incredulous, we found ourselves outside the city.

Sheer relief made us both hoot and laugh like madmen the moment we were out of hearing. I laughed till my stomach hurt and tears rolled down my face.

"Who were those men?" Jik asked when the laughter had died away.

"The big one was Brydda Llewellyn," I said, and tried to untie his wrists, but they were too tight. They would have to be cut off.

I beastspoke the horse again, telling her where we wanted to go and promising freedom once we got there. She was a beautiful creature. I was interested to learn that she thought of her masters as jahrahn, the cold ones. She appeared unconcerned at the strange events of the night and even at leaving the walled city.

It seemed the Herders often rode out at night beyond the city limits to meet with funaga on the seashore. Sometimes they brought men and women and children, bound as Jik was. These were always left behind. *Slavers*, I thought bleakly.

I thought I saw a faint flicker of fire in the distance. Closer, we could see it was a shore camp, but we were almost on it before a figure jumped up and Kella's voice rang out gladly.

After the first excited greetings, Kella introduced me to a tall blond youth called Idris, who cut Jik's bonds and left us to unharness the horse. Jik and I warmed our hands and explained Brydda's role in our escape.

Pavo looked pale and fraught. His feet were freshly bandaged, but he refused to talk about what had been done to him, save that his tormentors had made no real attempt at questioning him—they'd only meant to assert their dominance.

Our talk reminded Kella of my feet, and she insisted on examining them.

My shoes and stockings had to be soaked and cut away from the wounds. I was dizzy with pain before a grim-faced Kella had finished her ministrations. Then she looked up, not with the reproof I had expected but with tears in her eyes.

"I don't know how you walked so far on them, yet . . . if you had not . . ." She stopped abruptly and hurried down to the sea to wash her instruments.

I looked at the others with faint embarrassment. "Anyone would have done the same."

Pavo smiled wanly. " 'Would do' and 'have done' are two different things."

I felt my face redden and was glad of the darkness. To turn attention from myself, I asked Idris how he had come to know Brydda.

The boy said his father and two sisters had been taken by the Herders. One night, he and his mother had returned from a visit to find their house a charred ruin. Neighbors said the Herders had come and taken the husband and daughters away, but the priests claimed Idris's mother was mad with grief and that her husband and children must have burned to death in the fires.

Idris had never seen his father or sisters again. He met Brydda after his mother had gone to the rebel for help. She had died shortly after learning her husband and daughters had been sold to slavers. Brydda had taken the shattered boy in, and though Idris did not say it out loud, it was clear he worshipped the big rebel.

It was near midnight before Brydda and Reuvan found us. They had dealt with the Herders quickly, binding and locking them into their own hold before setting the ship adrift. Brydda said in casting off he had offered up a fervent prayer that the ship would be seized by slavers. They had gone back to Brydda's hovel for supplies since they would not be returning to Aborium.

Hearing my amazement at the ease of leaving the city, Brydda grinned and said the real gatekeeper and three soldier-guards had been tied up securely and uncomfortably in the watch hut to ease Brydda's departure. All we had to do now was wait for a message from the city to tell us how the Herders had reacted and if it was safe to move.

We were all weary, but Brydda's suggestion that hot food would do us more good than sleep was met with enthusiasm. We deferred serious talk until after we had eaten. "It is bad for the stomach," Brydda said with a comic roll of his eyes. Kella and Idris unpacked and prepared a meal, and Brydda regaled us with stories of his travels on the sea and his adventures as a seditioner. He made it sound like a game. I suspected he was telling only the brighter side of the tales, but even Pavo laughed at some of his more absurd stories, and we sat to eat at last in good spirits.

With shining eyes for his rescuer, Jik asked shyly how Brydda had come to spend his time fighting Herders. Brydda said it was a long tale and refused at first, but finally, when we all pleaded, he agreed to tell his story.

"I traveled to Aborium as a lad to get a trade as a seaman. Like many a boy, the sea called me. While I sought work, I heard rumors of slavers. I thought them no more than another salty tale at the time, but as I grew and worked on different ships, I learned that there were indeed slave boats that called at our shores. No one said openly how the slavers got their cargo, but it was whispered that the Herders filled their moneybags by selling prisoners and innocent folk they brought in for questioning.

"I pitied those taken, but I thought it was none of my affair and meant to mind my business," Brydda said.

"Then a lad who was the son of my landlord, and very dear to me, was taken. He had simply been in the wrong place at the wrong time. I had no hope of doing anything, for I did not learn of it till days after when I came back from a fishing trip.

"I swore then that I would never again stand aside and let some injustice happen simply because it was none of my business. From that, it was not far to the next step, finding others who thought as I did and were prepared to fight back.

"And so we have done these long years past, stealing their cargo and silver when we could, disrupting their festivals and plans, rescuing prisoners and spiriting them away. And we have bided our time, longing for the day we might be strong enough to revolt openly."

He looked at me speculatively. "If I had a hundred like you, I would dare to try it."

"Don't you fear and despise me for my deformed mind?" I asked so coolly that Kella gasped.

Brydda spat into the flames. "If the Herders are normal, then let me also be called Misfit. As to fearing you, I fear no man—or girl. Even if she can talk to dogs."

Pavo and Kella exchanged a quick look, and Idris regarded Brydda in confusion. I took a deep breath. "Then maybe one day you'll have your wish."

Brydda's eyes flashed. "What do you mean? Your people would fight with me?"

I shook my head. "You go too fast. I'm not the one to decide."

Brydda looked angry, then he laughed aloud. "That's me all over. My mother always said I was like a wild bull at a fence. Yet I think we will one day be allies." His eyes had a familiar faraway look.

I was more convinced than ever that Brydda had some sort of Misfit ability, a combination of empathy and future-telling—just enough to make him an infallible judge of character and a lucky guesser. But if he wanted to think of it as a "knack," past experience told me to say nothing of my theories.

"I have always thought of Misfits as unlucky mutants, but maybe I was wrong," Brydda mused. "Life is too short for all there is in it. A man with his eyes open learns something new every day," he added so ironically we all laughed.

Gradually, the others dozed, but Brydda and I stayed up talking far into the night.

The rebel organization was very large, extending throughout the Land. By comparison, Obernewtyn was a very small operation. But Brydda was far from dismissive, saying more like me might shift the tide of a battle. He was taken aback to discover how young most of us were but still believed we could help one another. I agreed to advocate a meeting between him and Rushton, but I was not sure the extent to which our aims coincided.

"At the bottom of everything, we are Misfits, and few men would have reacted as you did. Can you say for certain all your people would think as you do? Not be disgusted by us or frightened?"

Brydda looked thoughtful at this. "I don't know. Maybe the thought of someone who can talk inside your head or make animals do anything they want *would* seem frightening. Yet if people are frightened, it is because of their ignorance and the Herders' lies about mutations. They could learn," Brydda said at last.

"Maybe, but we have to be sure," I said. "There is no good in our exchanging one kind of tyranny for another."

The others rose, too anxious to sleep for long, and we discussed our plans. Brydda asked Pavo where he thought we would find the Beforetime library. He frowned at the teknoguilder's mention of ruins.

"I don't know about a library, but there are ruins of an old city near here."

Pavo looked excited. "That must be it," he said, then his face fell. "But if it is near and common knowledge, the library is sure to have been found and ransacked."

Brydda shook his head. "No one goes there."

"Why?" Pavo asked in a puzzled tone. "It's not in Blacklands territory. It is not even tainted badlands."

"It is haunted by ghosts of the Beforetime," Reuvan said.

Pavo gaped at him, then burst out laughing. "But there are no such things."

Brydda looked at him without smiling. "So I once thought, but these are real enough. I have seen them."

"And I," Reuvan said with a shudder. "Terrible, monstrous faces twisted in mortal agony."

"Ghosts?" Pavo echoed, confounded by their joint testimony. I stared from one to the other, just as astounded.

"Ghosts," Brydda said decisively.

✦ 18 ✦

WELL BEFORE DAWN, a man rode out from the city with news for Brydda. The Black Dog's attack on the Herder ship and the escape of three dangerous seditioners were the talk of the town. Huge rewards were being offered for information leading to their recapture. There was also a reward for a girl, escaped from custody at the Inn of the Cuttlefish, believed to have been an associate of the Black Dog.

The Herder ship had been found floating aimlessly, and those on board had described Brydda's attack as ruthless and bloody, claiming thirty cutthroats had descended without warning.

"Now you see where I came by my terrible reputation," Brydda said.

He was delighted with the way the Herders had linked the events. "How they will sweat wondering what a Herder novice has to do with the Black Dog," he crowed.

More disturbing was the messenger's report that a search party of soldierguards was combing the town. "It will only be a matter of time before they come upon the unguarded north gate and realize you have got out. There are enough of them in Aborium that they would attempt to pursue you into the plains," the messenger said grimly.

After he had ridden away, Brydda turned to us. "There are four watchtowers with a clear view together of the plains.

They will be scanning for any movement away from the main roads, and all roads will be guarded. We must go at once, while it is dark. I have no desire to visit your ruins, but right now it is probably the safest place for us."

We packed up the camp and left immediately. Reuvan and Brydda rode the two horses they had stolen to leave the city, I rode Avra, and the rest went in the cart with Idris at the rein. We could not gallop or trot because although most of the west coast was plains, they were stony and pocked with holes that a horse might stumble into in the darkness.

To while away the time, Brydda asked me to help him devise a method of signaling that would let him communicate directly with the horses. He was intrigued by their intelligence. "I always liked animals better than people," he confided.

Later, he asked Jik to demonstrate his empathy. He was amazed to find his emotions swayed by the boy. "Imagine such an ability in battle. He could shatter the nerve of a dozen good men without firing an arrow."

"It wouldn't be very fair to make brave men act like cowards," Jik said.

Brydda gave him an incredulous look.

Pavo spotted the ruins first.

He had always seemed ageless to me, but now he looked ancient, shrunken with pain; Kella told me the illness raging freely through his body had progressed more quickly than she had anticipated. Yet he seemed untouched by his physical transformation, in better spirits than anyone, apart from his perplexity over Brydda's ghosts.

We had been riding in silence, each busy with his own thoughts, when Pavo stiffened and pointed.

At first we could see nothing. Then I saw the square

shapes of buildings barely distinguishable from the dark night. Up close, they were in far worse condition than the ruinous buildings we had seen under Tor. Here the walls rose only slightly above our heads, the stone cracked and grown over with a weedy beard of green scrub and moss. The faint moonlight gave the buildings an intangible look, as if they were a mirage that might dissolve any second.

We were within two lengths of the first building when Brydda called a halt. "We'd better stop here. The ghosts will rise if we go nearer. I think it will be safe enough. No one would dream of us taking refuge here."

I looked at Pavo's determined face. "Pavo and I will be going in to look for the library. The rest of you may wait here with Brydda or come, as you please," I said.

Idris said he would wait with Brydda, but the rest, even Reuvan, said they would come. We left all the horses except Avra, who would draw the cart to bring back the books we found. Pavo and I rode while the others walked. The teknoguilder held his precious drawings and maps tightly but did not even look at them; he had pored over them so often that he knew them by heart. Occasionally, he led us to a road that rubble had made impassable, then he would frown and take us another way.

I did not believe in ghosts, but the deeper we went into the dark maze of stone and crumbled walls, the more uneasy I became.

It was clear some disaster had befallen the ruins, for there was far more damage here than to other ruins I had seen on the Blacklands fringes. In one place, pale moonlight glimmered on a charred wall that showed the burned, black shape of a man running. I did not know what it could mean, but I felt a deep chill in looking at it.

I began to think of all the stories I had heard of the Beforetime ghosts, how vengeful they supposedly were when their territory was invaded. The cold crept into my bones, and I wished we had waited until dawn to begin searching. My apprehension increased with each step, though there was no overt reason for it other than the strangely compelling atmosphere of the city.

The others were showing signs of disquiet, too. Kella's breath was coming fast despite our slow pace, and Jik stayed very close to the side of the carriage. Even Pavo's enthusiasm gave way to a distracted frown.

Then there was a faint moaning noise, and we all froze, looking around nervously.

"What was that?" Kella whispered.

"The ghosts," Jik said in a high, frightened tone.

"The wind," I said, but my voice sounded uncertain. I looked at Pavo.

"I don't understand it," he said. "I am afraid, too, but what have I to fear?" He reached out and took up a brush torch and set a flint to it. The flame flickered and blazed, throwing light onto his bony face. "We are not far from the library now. Just down here."

Yet the lane ended in a mass of twisted metal and rubble.

"We'll have to clear this," Pavo said.

I looked at him in dismay. "It will take weeks."

He frowned, then climbed out of the cart with an energy that belied his illness. Taking the torch, he clambered over the rubble.

"It doesn't matter about the light," Reuvan said gloomily, mistaking my look of concern. "We often see ghost lights moving around the city. No one will come to investigate."

Watching Pavo peering about, then scrambling higher, I

found myself unable to believe anything could have survived the devastation that had overtaken the city. Nothing was left but enduring stone, and even that was greatly weathered with time. Paper was a thousand times more vulnerable. But Pavo seemed undaunted by the look of the city.

My neck prickled, and I had the queer feeling we were being watched. With shaking hands, I lit another torch.

"Here!" Pavo shouted, disappearing over the crown of the rubble mound. "The entrance is over here."

I had no desire to go into the dark alley, which waited like a toothless mouth. But Pavo was alone and calling for me. I climbed after him, the pain in my feet a welcome distraction from the fear. The mound did not extend very far into the alley, and Pavo was kneeling on the ground beyond it, scrabbling in the dirt and muttering to himself.

He looked up excitedly. "This is the entrance according to my maps, but the lock is strange. It seems to be locked from the inside. Do you think you can open it? It will be complicated." He described the mechanism, which was indeed complex. I wondered why such a lock would be wanted to protect books when they had been so plentiful in the Before-time.

I looked around, not liking the way the dark seemed to crouch just outside the wavering circle of torchlight. Pavo had marked out the squarish shape of a door. There was a great deal of earth layered over it, but he assured me it would make no difference. I let my mind feel out the lock until I understood how it worked. It was as much a seal as anything, more secure than any door I'd encountered—all the more so because the mechanism had malfunctioned, jamming so that it could not be opened from either side.

After a long moment, I had it. There was a distinct

whirring sound, and the door swung inward. The mounded earth near our feet seemed to drop, sliding away into the revealed space, showering dirt onto the metal steps that ran down from the opening. I had expected the air to smell bad, but it was odorless, dry, and cool.

I knelt and peered in, instinctively raising my hands in defense, certain something was about to leap out at me.

"I'll go first," Pavo said impassively.

"Wait for me," I said.

Climbing back to the top of the rubble, I told Reuvan to stay with Avra. Kella and Jik came to help, carrying their own torches.

"Warn us if there is any danger," I sent to Avra.

We descended into the dark with as much joy as if it were our own grave. Except for Pavo—he went first, fearless. I came next, and behind me, Kella and Jik holding hands. As soon as my head was below ground level, I realized the ground was slightly tainted—enough to prevent me from staying in contact with Avra.

The steps took us down to a long, dark corridor.

I was struck by the smooth sameness of all the surfaces. There was no hint of the owner's personality, no feeling that human beings had ever been there. Now that we were inside, my attack of nerves had faded, and I found myself curious about the library. Why would a library be built like a secret fortress?

"What is this place?" Jik whispered.

"Why are you whispering?" Kella whispered. They stared at one another, then exploded in a fit of nervous giggles.

"It was more than just a library," Pavo said in a normal voice. "The Oldtimers eventually used machines to store their knowledge, and books became less important, even old-fashioned. Luckily for us they never fell completely from favor. This place was an historical storehouse. Among other things."

I did not like his tone, but before I could ask what he meant, we rounded a bend in the corridor.

Pavo stopped dead ahead of us with a hiss of indrawn breath. I looked over his shoulder and gagged. Kella screamed, and Jik looked close to fainting.

Before us, leaning against the side of the hall, were a number of human skeletons. One was small, the size of a young child. Almost certainly the skeletons of Beforetimers.

"They're dead. They can't hurt you," Pavo said, but he sounded shaken, too.

"What . . . what happened to them?" Kella whispered.

Pavo sighed. "There was evidence that this storehouse . . . was meant to store more than just books. The Oldtimers actually wrote about the possibility of the Great White, which they called 'First Strike.' This place was supposed to be a possible shelter, because it could be completely sealed off. They must have survived the holocaust only to be trapped here. And there was no one alive on the outside to help them escape."

"They . . . they were trapped?" Kella said, aghast.

Pavo patted her arm, and we passed single file and ashen-faced.

There were no other unpleasant surprises, although we walked down the corridors leading to the main storage area with as much trepidation as if skeletons might wait around every turn. Eventually, we came to a series of solid and immovable doors. Pavo explained the locking mechanism. I rested my hands on the cool metal and went to work on the locks. Each time a door opened, there was a hiss.

Opening the last door, we found ourselves in a gigantic storage room filled with endless rows of books on shelves, reaching high above our heads and running away into the shadows.

For a long time, we simply stood there and stared. Even Pavo, who must have anticipated such a find, was struck dumb by the scale of the storehouse. Surely all the knowledge of all the ages of man before the holocaust must be contained in the thousands of books we saw before us.

Then Pavo stepped forward and laid his hand reverently on one of the books. "Just think of it," he said in a voice that trembled with excitement. "We are the first in hundreds of years to come here. The first since the Oldtimers." He gathered himself visibly.

"The books are old and frail. Only the dry air has preserved them. Handle them lightly and as little as you can. Look for books on Oldtime machines like the Zebkrahn and books on healing. Also any showing maps of the old world. The Beforetimers were very orderly. If you find one map book, you will have found all such books," he said. "We will each take a different section. Bring anything worth looking at to me, but mark your place so you don't forget where it came from."

I padded to the far end of the vault, amazed at the scale of it. Despite the orderly arrangement of the books, the sheer volume made it hard to find what we wanted. And though I understood the words, many of the books made no sense to me, being filled with references to things I did not understand. Some of those I *could* piece together offered up bizarre notions and ideas.

One book claimed there had once been midget races of various kinds—squat, wizened men with huge axes and tiny people with wings. Another book talked of a land where there were men and women taller than skyscrapers. Kella came hurrying down to show me a book she had found showing drawings of people with fish tails instead of legs.

I began to feel bewildered. If there had been so many different kinds of races, what had happened to them all?

Jik gave a shout. He had found a book showing wonderfully clear pictures of a Beforetime city. Pavo stopped his sorting to explain that the remarkably lifelike pictures had not been drawn by artists but were actual images of reality, somehow preserved by a process designed by the Oldtimers.

Jik's book seemed to be composed entirely of such images showing a number of Beforetime cities in all their glory. Here were the dark towers we had seen in the city under the mountain but lit by bright lamps, thousands of them. "Cities of light," Kella whispered, awed. It was hard to reconcile the dark, decaying city under Tor, or the rubble above us, with the sheer beauty of those images.

Jik was the first to find a map, though whether it was real I couldn't say. It's fringes showed beasts unlike any I'd seen, lizard-like and menacing. "Here be dragons," it read.

"And that was before the mutations of the Great White," mused Pavo.

Soon after, I came across a section containing books on machines. They meant nothing to me, but Pavo went through them carefully, rejecting this, keeping that.

He waved away the books of half-fish people, saying the creatures must have been of a race that had become extinct before humans came. However fascinating, we did not have room for such things, he said.

There were hundreds of books on very trivial subjects—books that told how to dress your hair or make a garment, books on how to set flowers in a jar, and even a book show-ing how to fold paper into the shapes of animals. It struck me that the wondrous Oldtimers had possessed a silly, trivial side.

There were books on every conceivable subject. Books on machines that carried men and women over land, over sea, and even up to the stars. The more I read, the more I under-stood that the old world really had passed away forever. So much had changed; so much knowledge lost that could never be regained. The teknoguilders' fascination with the past suddenly struck me anew as pointless. The future was what really mattered. And perhaps the past was better lost, if it had led the Beforetimers to the Great White.

"It is such a waste," Pavo lamented, wrapping books in waxed cloth to be carried by Jik to the foot of the stairs. "Now that we have broken the seal, the books will decay quickly. You must tell Garth to send another expedition soon, before they are lost to us." I felt a chill at Pavo's calm acceptance that he would not be there to do the telling.

I was about to turn into another aisle when my gaze fell upon a particular title.

Powers of the Mind.

I stared at the book as if it had eyes and might stare back. Breathing fast, I took it down. I let it fall open where it wanted, then struggled to read the tiny script.

Every mind possesses innate abilities beyond the five known senses. For most people, these abilities remain hidden and untapped. Sometimes, they are used accidentally or im-perfectly and called hunches, insight, *or* inspired guess-work.

Even those who have demonstrated these mental abilities,

*or extrasensory perceptions, are barely touching the edge of
their true potential. It would take some immense catalyst to
break through the mind's barriers and allow men and women
to use and develop that hidden portion of their minds . . .*

I felt hot and faint, for what could it mean but that the Oldtimers had speculated about Talents? I trembled at the revo-
lutionary idea that the powers we had always imagined to be
caused by the Great White might have existed before the
holocaust—that they were not mutations but some natural
development of the mind.

I flicked a few more pages and read.

*For time eternal, some men and women have exhibited
flashes of future knowledge and been called* fey. *But who is
to say they are not simply the forerunners of some evolu-
tionary movement, destined to be scapegoats and ridiculed,
tormented and even killed for their strangeness, until the rest
of the human race catches up. . . .*

My eyes flew down the page. Flicking back and forth
feverishly, I found the book mentioned many of the abilities
I knew to be real and even some I had not encountered.

My head ached with the tremendous feeling of having
made a discovery that might well change our future. If the
Council saw such a book, they would have to admit Misfits
were not mutations. But the Council called such books evil
and burned them.

And the discovery might only make things worse for us; if
our kind was the future and not some freakish sideline, what
were ordinary people but a dying breed?

I shivered and read on more soberly.

The Reichler Clinic has conducted a progressive and serious examination of mental powers and has produced infallible proofs that telepathy and precognitive powers are the future for mankind. Reichler's experiments have taken mind powers out of the realms of fantasy and set them firmly in the probable future.

I shivered again, knowing in my deepest heart that the truths contained in the book would not make us more accepted.

"Elspeth?" Jik asked. I started, instinctively closing the book. "Are you all right?" he asked curiously.

I nodded. "What is it?"

"It's Reuvan. I was taking books to the stairs, and I heard him call out," Jik said.

I bit my lip, slipping the book into my pocket and cursing the unyielding tainted earth that would not let me reach Avra mentally. Then I told myself to be glad the taint was not lethally strong, as in the Blacklands. I left Pavo to his books and returned to the stairs, climbing up to poke my head aboveground. It was nearly dawn, and pink light showed faintly in the east. I sent a query to Avra.

"He has gone," the mare sent perplexedly. "I could not find your mind. The funaga ran away."

"Why did he leave?" I asked.

"I saw nothing. There was nothing," she sent.

Bewildered, I lifted my torch and climbed out, wondering what could have frightened Reuvan badly enough that he would desert us.

I opened my mouth to call down the steps, but the words died in my throat.

Fear had seized me.

My heart pounded and the night was suddenly ice-cold as I watched the air before me shimmer and smoke in a way that could not be natural. The smoke coalesced into a spectral face so grotesque and malevolent that only some Herder hell could have spawned it. Almost reptilian, it watched me from the end of the alley, a shadowed creature of roiling smoke and razor-sharp teeth.

Terror flooded my mind; the lantern slid from my nerveless fingers. I screamed then, barely registering the footsteps coming up the metal steps behind me. I heard Kella cry out before I saw her, falling at my feet in a dead faint. That shook me enough to break my trance. I dashed the books from Pavo's arms and half dragged him and Jik out of the doorway. They stared at the specter in astonished wonder.

"Ghosts . . ." Pavo moaned.

I grasped his shoulders and shook him to make him help me lift Kella, all the while keeping an eye on the creature. It did not advance but opened its mouth menacingly. Then there was a savage growling, but not from the monster—it came from the far side of the mound of rubble and was followed by a high-pitched scream.

Then, just as abruptly as it had appeared, the smoky demon vanished.

"What just happened?" Pavo asked.

Jik looked at me, his face transformed. "That growling. It was Darga!"

I thought fear had deranged him, but there was barking nearby, and this time I recognized it. I sent out a probe and immediately encountered Darga.

"There you are," he sent imperturbably. "Come to me."

Startled, I told the others to wait inside and picked my way over the rubble, tracing his probe to what remained of a building fronting the alley. It was little more than four walls, and in one corner a growling Darga held a thin, ragged figure at bay.

I was beside him before I realized it was a girl cowed against the wall, her skin as black as if she had rolled in the mud. To my bewilderment, she hissed and bared her teeth at the sight of me.

All at once, fear assaulted me.

Darga growled again, and the fear vanished.

I stared at the girl in wonder. "*She's* doing it!"

"I learned from a dog that you had left the city. I followed your scent," Darga sent. "Then I saw the child-funaga's mind making you see things. I frightened her enough to break her grip on your mind. She does not know how to speak to my mind, so she cannot make me afraid."

The urchin snarled at me, pressing herself deeper into the corner.

"She is like a wild wolf pup," Darga sent.

I looked at the girl. "Well," I said aloud in a gentle voice, "if you are wild, then I will have to tame you." I backed away, telling Darga to follow. The girl suspiciously watched us withdraw, then ran forward and slithered through a hole in the wall, swift as a snake.

I reached out but could find no trace of her mind.

There was a joyous reunion between Jik and Darga. The others were astonished and relieved that the demon we had seen was no more than a vision. Pavo suggested returning to the library, but I decided we had better find Reuvan, Brydda, and Idris.

"It's been a long night. And we have plenty of time to go through the books. We'll have to stay until I can tame our wild girl."

We found Reuvan unconscious, having run into a jutting piece of stone in the darkness, then returned to Brydda. He was fascinated to hear the truth about his ghosts and, though still wary, agreed to cross into the city. But he was skeptical about my intention to tame the girl.

I shook my head wearily. "I can't give up. I have to win her trust."

"Why?" Brydda asked. "What does it matter?"

I looked at him. "Don't you understand? *She* is the one I came all this way to find. She's one of us. And I have a feeling she needs us as much as we need her."

✦ 19 ✦

WE CALLED HER Dragon, after the picture I had seen in the library.

We had set up a comfortable camp inside the roofless shell of a building with a clear view of Aborium and the surrounding plains. Each night, I set food out, hoping to make her understand that I meant no harm. But though the food had been gone each morning, we did not catch sight of her. Sometimes I sensed her watching us but could not reach her. After a few initial attempts to instill her particular brand of fear into one or another of us, and being fended off by me, she had given up trying to frighten us away.

The third night fell, and I was silent and preoccupied with thoughts of the ragged urchin girl. Kella was trying to force Pavo to set his notes aside and eat. Finally, losing her temper, she shouted at him.

"If you don't eat, you'll be dead before you have the chance to get your precious books out of their hole in the ground!"

She broke off, looking horrified at herself. But Pavo burst out laughing. "Kella, what would I do without you? All right; you win."

We all laughed at the martyred expression he gave the flushed healer.

"No luck with the girl?" Pavo asked me over nightmeal.

"Have you given thought to what sort of powers she has?" Pavo said.

I frowned. "Empathy and coercing, though I have never encountered that combination."

Kella gave me a quick look. "It's more than coercing. Domick can't make things appear in the air."

I shook my head. "The creature she conjured looks so like the ones on the map. I think she took the image from my unconscious and somehow projected it into all our minds."

Brydda yawned. "Whatever she does, it's kept the soldierguards from looking for us here. And I saw no patrols out on the plains today. I think they have moved the search to Half Moon Bay or Morganna. I doubt they will bother with Murmroth or Port Oran, given the distances involved. As soon as you've finished with the books, we can leave."

Pavo nodded absently. "I feel as if I could never be finished, but I'll have as much as we can safely carry by tomorrow."

No one looked at me, but I knew they were thinking of Dragon.

Time was running out, yet I seemed no closer to reaching the girl than when I had begun. I went out with a pot of stew and sat down to wait, determined to make some sort of contact. Hours passed, and I was beginning to drift off to sleep when I heard a faint sound.

Snapping wide awake, I sensed her trying to drive me off. Frustrated and baffled, she paced outside the light like a hungry, wild cat.

"Hello?" I called softly. The wind hissed in scorn, but there was no answer. I took up the pot of stew and held it out.

Still no answer, but instinct told me she was watching. I sighed, feeling suddenly defeated.

Then I heard a movement, and she was there, the half-moon shedding a wan light on her grubby face. I was careful not to make any sudden movements as she crept forward, never taking her eyes from me. She reached out abruptly and snatched the pot from my hands, turned, and ran into the night.

I sighed heavily and went back to the campfire. Reuvan sought to comfort me, saying he thought sheer curiosity would make Dragon follow us when we left. That and our food offerings. I was not so certain, but we had no more time to spare.

That night, we left the city after concealing the entrance to the library under rubble. If Dragon did follow, the city would have lost its guardian, and we did not want the books and all their secrets to fall into the hands of the Herder Faction.

There was no sign of Dragon as we left, but I sensed her eyes watching us from some dark corner of her lonely city.

I sent out a broadspan beckoning call, but there was no response.

Brydda had said that we ought to reach the sparse, distorted trees of the fringes before the moon rose, if we did not stop, for once again we were not able to move at more than a plodding walk. I asked what he would do if we could safely cross the Suggredoon.

"To begin with, I will ride to Rangorn to see my parents. Then I will return to Sutrium and join the group of rebels working against the Council there. I have already been in contact with their leader," Brydda said.

Pavo, Jik, Kella, and I traveled in the cart with the books, and the others rode. Brydda had become adept at communicating with the horses through gestures and spent more time conversing with them than with his human companions. Pavo looked pale and ill, the energy of the last days having deserted him as soon as we left the city. He lay back against his precious books and slept.

Huge flies plagued us by day, and the unseasonable heat made me long for the cool of the mountains. I consoled myself by thinking the weather was good for my feet, which had begun to heal again.

I felt weary when we stopped at dusk the second day. The others talked and sparred while setting up the camp and nightmeal, but I could not help thinking of Dragon and wondering if she would go on as she had before our departure. I had given up hope of her following us and wondered if Maryon's prediction meant that all aims of the expedition had to be achieved to avoid whatever disaster she foresaw. If so, then everything we had done was for nothing, because I had failed to bring the Talent back to Obernewtyn.

Remembering how Dragon had cowered back against the wall, I was filled with self-reproach for my failure to reach her. I ought to have tried harder. Under all the dirt and savagery, she was little more than a child. Depressed, I went to bathe in a stream after summoning Darga to assure me that it had not flowed from Blacklands. The air had a misty mauve tone, and in the west, streaks of dusky sunset ran across the horizon.

Darga's mind broke abruptly into my thoughts. "She follows."

My heart leapt, understanding instantly whom he meant. "Where?"

"Behind the trees," he sent.

I forced myself to walk naturally to the stream. Darga sniffed the water and pronounced it clean. Stretching himself out on the bank, he pretended to sleep. I stripped off my clothes and slid into the icy water with a gasp of delight. Rubbing sand against my grubby skin, I reveled in the coolness, but only half of me was enjoying the bath. The other half was searching for the slightest evidence of Dragon's presence. I was forced to concede that without Darga, I would never have known she was there.

I took up a handful of sand and rubbed it against my scalp until the tangled mass of my hair felt clean, then I ducked under to wash it out. Floating beneath the surface and holding my breath, I opened my eyes and looked up.

To my astonishment, Dragon was leaning over the stream, staring with openmouthed terror into the water. Gasping and spluttering, I bobbed to the surface. She sprang back, and gently I fended off the waves of fright she was generating. I reached for her mind but again was unable to penetrate her shield.

"It's all right," I said softly, realizing she thought I had been drowning. "I'm Elspeth," I said slowly, extending a dripping hand.

She cringed away.

"She fears water," Darga sent.

Dragon looked at him uneasily, though he had not stirred. I gathered up my towel and dried slowly.

I looked up to find her looking at my naked limbs with a hint of bafflement. I stood very still as she reached out one blackened finger and touched my pale belly. Her finger left a dirty smear, and she stared at it, frowning.

Very slowly, I reached out a wet finger and touched her bare stomach. A rag twisted around her body exposed most of her skin, but rag and skin were indistinguishable, merged together in uniform grime. She suffered my touch, then

431

looked amazed at the clean streak my finger had made. She gazed from the dirty mark on my stomach to the white mark on her own flesh, as if our skins had rubbed off on one another.

"Elspeth," I said, pointing to myself. I bent down to put my clothes on. My trousers were worn to shreds, but Kella had given me an old skirt and underskirt to put on.

I saw Dragon's eyes flicker toward the blue underskirt, and impulsively, I held it out to her. Eyes shining, she reached out, then froze, mistrust clouding her expression. I did not move, and finally, she reached out and grasped the underskirt, folding it into her arms and stroking it as if it were an animal. I went on dressing, pulling on Kella's knitted stockings, my shoes, and a cloak.

"Esspess?" she said suddenly in a rusty whisper.

I gaped, for I had begun to suspect she was mute. I had even thought this might be why she had been abandoned.

I pointed to myself. "Elspeth," I said distinctly. "Elspeth." Then I pointed to her.

"Elspess," she said obligingly. I grinned, wondering if my name was the only word she would say. I pointed to myself again. "Els-peth." I pointed to her. "Dragon . . . Dra-gon." Later, when she could talk, she could choose a more suitable name.

She frowned. "Drang-om."

I nodded. She pointed to me. "Elspess." She pointed to herself. "Drangon."

"Close enough," I said. "Food?" I asked, rising slowly. Alarm flared in her eyes. I mimicked eating, and hunger replaced her fright.

Summoning Darga and warning him to move slowly, we made our way back to the camp. Whenever Dragon stopped,

I would mimic eating. I sent a probe to Jik, telling him to warn the others not to do anything to frighten her.

Approaching the light of the fire that glimmered through the trees, Dragon hesitated. I had to coax her the last few steps with exaggerated mimicry of how delicious the food would be. When we were close enough to smell Kella's stew, she sniffed at the savory odor like a hungry animal. The others were sitting very still around the fire, fascinated, for this was the first time they had seen her. To my surprise, she barely looked at them. Her eyes darted about hungrily. Kella had set a pot to the side, and I took this up and held it out to Dragon.

The firelight showed her as an emaciated scarecrow with a mop of filthy hair, clutching the blue underskirt to her chest.

Taking the pot, she squatted unceremoniously and plunged her filthy fingers directly into it, scooping the stew to her mouth with ravenous dexterity.

Kella grimaced and softly wondered aloud whether she had not already poisoned herself with dirt. I was filled with compassion rather than revulsion. I had never imagined that the Talent I had come so far to find would be a half-wild savage who could barely speak. I had imagined a calm discussion ending in an offer of a refuge.

No one spoke while she ate with much lip smacking and slurping, and when she was finished, she licked out the pot, sighed gustily, and sat back on her haunches.

"Well," Kella said faintly. Dragon's lambent eyes turned to her.

"Meet Dragon, our newest recruit," I said with a broad smile.

For the rest of the night, Dragon sat close by my feet, listening to our talk as if to exotic music. She had the disconcerting habit of staring fixedly at first one, then another of us, as if she were trying to memorize our faces. She would not allow any of the others to come near her but eventually fell asleep against my knees.

The next morning we crossed the Suggredoon at dawn. I had expected it to be difficult, but the hardest part was persuading Dragon to hide with Brydda under his enveloping cloak in back of the cart. Jik, Idris, and Reuvan rode the horses, and Kella and I led Avra aboard the ferry. It took only a few coercive pushes to ensure that our papers and the cart were given the most cursory inspection before the soldierguard turned to the few other passengers. I had found a description of myself and Jik in the soldierguards' minds, as well as a far clearer picture of Brydda, but a coercive push ensured that we did not fit any of those descriptions. Once we had left the ferry on the other side, we took a rutted path straight up the banks of the Suggredoon, which Brydda said would bring us right to the ford. But the road was full of potholes and great stones, so the cart fairly crawled along. Even when the rest of us got out and walked, Avra could not move much more swiftly. Pavo alone remained in the cart, though its jolting must have hurt his poor, weary body.

Brydda grew more silent as the day wore on and seemed increasingly preoccupied. Finally, I asked him if anything was wrong.

"I don't know," he said. "I feel uneasy about my parents. And we're moving so slowly." He looked down at Dragon with mingled pity and frustration.

"Why don't you go ahead?" I suggested. "We can't be more than a few hours away at a fast gallop."

Brydda bit his lip and looked thoughtful. "I think I will. Reuvan can come with me." Thinking of his "knack," I worried that his fears could be well founded.

The triumphant mood of the day occasioned by Dragon's presence evaporated with Brydda's departure. He told us to wait at the ford until he returned to tell us the way was clear. He refused to say what he was afraid of, but his elaborate precautions only served to heighten my apprehension.

As if to mirror my thoughts, a heavy, dark bank of cloud looming on the horizon billowed in to veil the sun near the end of the day, and we reached the ford just as a light rain began to fall.

There was no sign of Brydda or Reuvan, so we decided to make camp behind a copse of trees within sight of the ford. It proved nearly impossible to light a fire with the damp wood, but finally we managed and sat around it shivering in the chilly wind. No one felt like talking. Pavo was nearly blue and shivered constantly, but Kella said these were also symptoms of advanced rotting sickness.

Dragon had reacted to the sight of the Suggredoon with real terror, and it had taken all my strength to reassure her. I was afraid she would run off and be lost. Her reaction to the river and to my submersion seemed to indicate something connected with water had happened to her, but I could not penetrate her mind, and she was unable to explain, only clutching at me in mute plea. In the end, I found myself patting her as I would pet Maruman.

"At least she doesn't stink," Jik said earnestly when I wondered aloud to Kella what might have caused her fear of water. We laughed, but oddly this was true. Dragon smelled like rich, dark dirt after rain. She had not used her remarkable illusory powers since joining us. I hoped she would not tame to the extent of forgetting them altogether.

All at once I heard the drumming of hooves in the distance.

We all stood, the underlying fears that had gnawed at us since Brydda's departure showing clearly in our faces. There was one rider, coming fast. Idris gave a shout of joy as he recognized Brydda's horse, then he fell silent, seeing the rider was Grufyyd, whose face he did not know.

Reining the horse in, Grufyyd dismounted. He looked pale and there were dark shadows in his eyes. After a brief greeting, he urged us to pack up quickly and come with him to the cottage.

The serious note in his voice warned us something was badly wrong.

"Brydda?" Idris began worriedly.

"My lad is fine," he said, then once again urged us to make haste.

Not until we were approaching the great forest of trees at the foot of the mountains did he say, "Soldierguards have been to Rangorn. It was fortunate that ye dinna come sooner, else they would have taken us all."

"They were looking for Brydda?" I asked. But Grufyyd shook his head.

"They said they were looking for seditioners. A small group of young gypsies," he added significantly.

I stared. "But why? How? No one from the Council knew we even existed, and the disguise was all but washed away before we left here."

"Henry Druid an' his folks kenned ye were about," said Grufyyd.

"But how could he . . . ?" I stopped, thinking hard. "They said in the encampment that he has a friend in the Council. Someone influential who sends him all sorts of expensive delicacies. Maybe the Druid told his friend about us." I chewed my lip. "But why go to so much trouble over a few gypsies?"

"Perhaps he no longer believes ye were just gypsies," Grufyyd said. "One of the soldierguards said the gypsy attire might be a disguise and that the seditioners were more dangerous than most."

Uneasily, I remembered that I had been forced to reveal my power in the escape. The gatewarden would have woken with a strange tale of the gypsy girl who had rendered him unconscious with her touch. It had been wishful thinking on my part to assume his testimony would be dismissed as ravings or excuses.

Katlyn met us at the door of the cottage with smiles and talk of a hot meal and warm beds. Despite everything, it was a happy reunion but for Pavo's obvious deterioration.

Wrapped in a blanket and shivering from a chill no fire could abate, he was clearly in great pain. His neck and arms were now covered in bruises, a symptom of tissue degeneration. The slightest bump left a livid mark on his skin. Katlyn did her best for him, feeding him decoctions to numb the pain, but they were only temporary measures. Pavo was dying.

"He is content," Darga sent from where he lay on the hearth. "He is not afraid to die."

After we had eaten, Katlyn managed to do what we had failed and persuaded Dragon to wash.

Jik, Idris, and Reuvan went off with Grufyyd to organize sleeping quarters in the barn, and Kella went to sort out blankets.

I was glad to find myself alone with Brydda, having had no chance to question him about the soldierguards. His first words took my breath away. "I don't suppose you come from Obernewtyn?"

I gaped at him.

He nodded. "It was a thought I had earlier, for I guessed you weren't quite telling the truth when you said you came from the highlands. Then my father said one of the soldier-guards had asked about Obernewtyn, and everything came together. I had heard the place was near destroyed by a firestorm."

"A lie to keep people away," I admitted. "But useless now."

"I don't think they knew anything for sure."

"They couldn't have managed to connect us and Obernewtyn at all, unless the Druid . . . this confirms he's part of this. We already feared that the Council had been questioning what Rushton was up to. But the Druid is the only one who could have informed them about our disguises." I blanched. "And if he *has* guessed we are not real gypsies, he would question all that I told him about Obernewtyn being in shambles. I must warn Rushton."

Brydda nodded. "It might be safer for your friends to leave Obernewtyn before any investigation. I would be happy to have your people join me. I am sure Bodera will be glad to have you join his rebels."

"Rushton will have to decide that," I said. "He is our leader."

Idris opened the door and asked Brydda to help shift the books from the cart into the shed, because it had begun to rain again. Left alone except for Pavo, I forced myself to accept that he would not survive the journey back.

His eyes fluttered open, and he saw the pity in my face. "Don't be sad for me, Elspeth." His voice was barely audible. "I have lived free in a world where freedom is rare. I have pursued work that I love. I have learned much, and I have had good friends and perilous adventures. What man who lives three times my span can say as much?"

I blinked hard and found I could say nothing without crying. I was glad when everyone trooped back in, laughing and talking. Kella called out that she was warming some fement. This prompted Brydda to sing a rollicking song about a drunken seaman. In the midst of uproarious laughter, the door opened and Katlyn entered with a stranger.

The room fell into an astounded silence. The unknown girl was slender as a willow wand, with creamy pale skin and a thick silken mop of flame-colored curls.

Slowly, it dawned on us who we were looking at.

It was Dragon.

"I don't believe it!" Jik gasped.

I was stunned. Who would have suspected what lay under the dirt? Even clad in a rough hessian shift dress, she was extraordinarily beautiful. And such hair! I had never seen hair that color—like gold and flames entwined. Later, Katlyn told me it had broken her heart to cut it, but it had been so matted and fused with dirt that she'd had no choice.

Dragon's eyes, blue as the summer sky, flickered round uneasily.

"Don't stare at her. She doesn't understand," I said softly.

Though unable to stop looking, the others sank into more natural poses. Beaming with pleasure, Katlyn ushered Dragon around to my side. Reaching out, I tugged at one springing fiery curl.

Dragon took the strand of her hair and pulled it round to her eyes, then she let it loose. She lifted the shift to show the blue underskirt I had given her.

Reuvan burst out laughing. She looked up at him, startled,

and bared her teeth. That broke the spell woven by her dramatic transformation. "She may be a girl," Reuvan said, "but she is still dragon-natured and had better keep her name as a warning to anyone who might think otherwise."

Brydda patted his mother's shoulder. "Well, I always knew you were a witch."

Even Pavo smiled at this absurdity.

Over steaming mugs of fement, we talked of ways and means to reach our various destinations. I told Katlyn and Grufyyd the whole story of Obernewtyn, deciding it was better to take them fully into our confidence. If Obernewtyn was under investigation, we would have to leave it anyway. And if not, I had an idea that Katlyn and Grufyyd might be glad of a reason to return to the highlands. The trouble was that the chance of reaching Obernewtyn before the mountain pass froze was dwindling.

"If only the Olden pass had not been poisonous, we might have gone that way and cut off days of traveling time," I sighed.

"Poisonous . . . ?" Brydda began.

Suddenly Darga growled, and Dragon jumped to her feet.

"What is it?" I said, but Brydda hissed. In the silence, we could hear a horse galloping toward the house.

I farsensed the rider and breathed a sigh of relief. "It's Domick," I told the others. There were steps on the porch, and the door was flung open.

"You are here!" cried Kella, leaping up to embrace him.

"Thank Lud you're here," he said, keeping Kella close in his arms. "You must leave tonight, all of you."

"What is it?" Brydda asked sharply, rising to tower over the coercer. Domick's face changed as he noticed Idris, Reuvan, and Dragon.

"It's all right, Domick. They're with us," I said quickly. "They know about Obernewtyn, about everything."

The coercer looked less disapproving than I expected. He glanced at Brydda speculatively. "I guess you must be Brydda Llewellyn, better known as the notorious Black Dog. It is good to meet a man whose name I have heard so many times as one who ferociously opposes the Council."

Brydda met this with a curious look. Domick sighed. "It's a long story, but I'll give you the meat of it."

He threw off his dripping oiled coat. "I first heard the name of Brydda Llewellyn here, but I heard it again before I had even reached Sutrium. Soldierguards were watching the ferry, looking for you. I overheard them saying Brydda Llewellyn's network of seditioners had been exposed, and he was on the run. I wanted to come after you, Elspeth, to warn you, but I knew I couldn't get to you before you reached Aborium." An expression of suppressed agony crossed his face, and I realized what a struggle it had been for him to proceed with his mission.

"The first thing I noticed about Sutrium was the number of Herders about. They seemed to outnumber Councilmen, and there was a definite feeling of fear whenever they were around.

"I mingled with people wherever there were crowds. I had the feeling I was safer that way. I let people understand I was a trading jack whose cart had been burned in a firestorm. That explained my ignorance about customs lowlanders take for granted. And it let me ask questions as I sought work to amass coin enough to replace my cart and tools. I knew I had to get close to the Council, but I couldn't think how.

"Then one night in a drink hall, I overheard two men talking to a third man who was to take up a job at the Councilcourt. They were laughing and warning their friend that his new job was dangerous. The third man was beside himself with fear by the time the other two left. I struck up a conversation with him by offering him a mug and learned that he had come from the highlands to work in Sutrium. He had been recommended by a Herder, and though he neither wanted nor liked the idea of going to Sutrium, he dared not refuse. In the end, I managed to persuade him to let me take the job." Domick flicked a look at me, which told me what sort of persuasion he had used. "I turned up in his place and was accepted at once, since they were expecting someone from the high country.

"At first I heard nothing useful. It was a menial job, and I began to think I would have been better off applying to be a soldierguard. Then I realized I could not have found a better way to spy on the Councilmen. Once my face was familiar, it was as if I were nothing more than a broom or a mop, and they talked quite freely in front of me.

"I heard them talk of a sweeping investigation of the highlands planned for next year, after the first thaw, to flush out traitors and seditioners. I heard enough to make me certain the Council knows the Druid is alive. I also heard much talk about the Black Dog and his efforts to undermine authority and plunge the Land back into chaos. They think of you as a terrible threat, Brydda, and hunger to get hold of you. They were expecting word of your capture from Aborium. My guess is that news has come by now but that it was bad news." He grinned at Brydda.

Domick paused to drink thirstily from a mug Katlyn had given him.

"What about the Druid's friend? Did you learn who he is?" Kella asked.

Domick looked grim. "Almost from the start, I heard talk

442

of a special agent who worked for both the Herder Faction and the Council, getting information to help expose seditioners. He had masterminded the capture of the man who betrayed your network, Brydda. And he forced him to talk when he refused to betray you. The agent was said to be brilliant and completely ruthless."

"Then you heard no talk of Obernewtyn?" I asked.

Domick shook his head. "I had heard no mention of Obernewtyn—until two days ago. I overheard a conversation between two Councilmen about this special agent and his certainty that something was going on at Obernewtyn. One Councilman said he didn't think there was anything in it, and the other reminded him that the agent had seldom led them wrong. I became certain then that this special agent and the Druid's friend were the same person."

"That sounds right to me," I said. "The Druid befriended Rushton at one point, and maybe his agent resented this. It may be why he decided to play Druid for a fool."

But Domick frowned. "That's what I thought, because what other reason would this agent have for wanting Obernewtyn investigated?" He looked so stern, I felt suddenly frightened of what he was about to say.

"I never saw the agent," he went on slowly. "Though I often heard him spoken of, there was never any mention of his name. But I was curious. Someone told me he came only at night to make reports, so I managed to get myself assigned to night duty.

"I was able to catch glimpses of him, but he always wore a hooded cloak that concealed his face. When I heard him talk, I had the strangest feeling I had heard his voice somewhere before. That made me more determined than ever to see what he looked like. Last night, I hid in a cupboard in the meeting room. I watched him through a crack in the door, but he kept his hood on the entire time he talked. I could not see his face, but I could hear him clearly.

"He told the Council he had been torturing more suspected seditioners in Aborium. Most knew nothing, but one seemed to think Brydda had family in Rangorn. A mother and father. Apparently, the poor man had only overheard that, because everyone else believed Brydda an escaped orphan. The agent said soldierguards had been in the area recently, and their report showed only one couple fitting the description. He wanted Council permission to bring them in for interrogation.

"The Council voted to send a troop of guards to Rangorn. They are on their way here now."

Brydda's face was pale and tense. "I did not think anyone knew. I was too careless."

I said nothing. Something in Domick's manner warned me the story was not finished.

"I was desperate to get away to warn you, but I had to wait until the room was empty. At last the meeting ended, and all the Councilmen left but this agent. Only then did he take off his hood, and I saw his face."

"You . . . you recognized him?" Kella guessed.

Domick nodded.

"Ariel," he said. "It was Ariel."

PART III

◆

THE KEN

✦ 20 ✦

WITH SOLDIERGUARDS ON their way, it was too risky to proceed as planned. We decided to hide at the foot of the mountains until the danger was past. No one would guess we would deliberately trap ourselves in a cul-de-sac.

"The soldierguards aren't subtle enough to suspect we would do anything other than the obvious," Brydda said. "When they don't find us here, they'll think we have escaped by going around Glenelg Mor, because that's what they would do in our place."

Brydda knew of an area at the foot of Tor where we could make a safe camp, a narrow valley running into the foot of the hills and concealed by a thick copse of trees. From the other side, no one would suspect the trees continued for just a few steps before reaching the steep mountainside. Brydda had played there as a boy and remembered it well despite his long absence.

We had spent precious time packing Katlyn's invaluable store of dried herbs. Almost everything else had to be left behind, and tears coursed down her face as Brydda threw a flaming torch on the roof of the cottage.

"It is only stone and mud and straw, I know, but all the memories of happy years are in those walls, and now they burn," she sobbed.

Jolting through the darkness and chilled by a damp, blustery wind, I thought bitterly of Domick's news. Obernewtyn was in danger. With Ariel to force the pace, I had no doubt the soldierguards would appear in spring, immediately after the thaw. Ariel, of all people, would know that Obernewtyn was at its most vulnerable then. If we failed to get back in time to warn Rushton, they would be completely unprepared, defenseless against an onslaught of soldierguards.

But it was a matter of days before the pass would be snowed shut. Domick must have known when he came to us that he was losing the last chance of warning Obernewtyn. But if he had not delayed and ridden to warn us, the soldierguards would have taken us all.

I could not imagine how Ariel had survived or what course had brought him to the Council, but I had no doubt that his primary motive was to revenge himself on Obernewtyn and Rushton.

He could not know for sure that the firestorm story had been a lie, but he might have guessed it was a ruse to keep the Council away from Obernewtyn, for he knew that Rushton had befriended me. But how had Ariel inveigled himself with Henry Druid and then the Council? The most obvious likelihood was that he had stumbled into the Druid's men in the White Valley, and he had somehow won the old man's trust. But how had he reached Sutrium from the highlands, and how he had gained the Council's trust?

It did not take us long to reach Brydda's hiding spot. It was as good as he had led us to believe. We could even see the cottage burning in the distance, while we were invisible behind a thick girdle of eben trees. Brydda bade Kella, Jik, and his mother to organize supper in order to occupy the older woman's mind. He asked me to walk with him to collect firewood, leading the way purposefully through the trees. The ground sloped up steeply, offering a sweeping view of the area.

"This is a sight I remember well," Brydda said softly. Over the treetops, I could see the dense darkness of the Blacklands in the moonlight like a shadowy stain across the Land.

Pavo had once said the Blacklands would recede in time, but I could not imagine anything growing on the black, stinking soil. I shuddered, and for a moment, it seemed to me Ariel and the Blacklands were symptoms of the same evil.

Beyond the hills was the silvery rush of the Suggredoon and the huddled village of Rangorn. I could even see the mists that hung above Glenelg Mor. Behind me were the towering bulks of Aran Craggie and Tor. So many ways to go, and none fast enough to get us to Obernewtyn in time.

The wind in the treetops sounded like the whispering ebb and flow of the sea. Brydda stirred as if the same wind had blown through him, ruffling his thoughts like so many leaves. I bent to pick up a stick for kindling, but Brydda touched my arm and drew me aside.

"I want to talk to you alone," he said in a low, serious voice. "I think you should consider coming back to Sutrium with me, all of you, and especially Domick. Very few people have managed to work their way into such a position as he has attained on the Council. He will be valuable to both our causes." He nodded toward Pavo. "He is certainly not up to a hard, long trip to the high mountains. And he needs Kella with him. I can organize a safe journey for you all to Obernewtyn after winter."

I shook my head. "It would be too dangerous to have Jik in Sutrium after what happened in Aborium. Especially if there are as many Herder priests about as Domick said. And

Dragon could not be confronted with a city. I would be grateful if you would take Kella and Pavo for the time. But one of us must try to reach Obernewtyn before the pass freezes. I will go and take Dragon and Jik with me."

"Why can't you speak to this Rushton with your mind?" Brydda asked.

"The mountains between the high country and Obernewtyn are badly tainted and thick enough besides to form a barrier that my mind cannot broach," I explained.

"But is it wise or sensible for *you* to go, Elspeth? What about your feet?" Brydda protested.

"My feet will take me where I need to go, and I am better equipped to deal with trouble than any of the others."

To my surprise, Brydda grinned. "If you are so determined, I might have a way to shorten your road back to Obernewtyn. Let's get some wood and go back to camp. I have an idea I want to put to you all."

It was after midnight by the time we had eaten and Brydda laid his plan out. Pavo, Kella, and Domick were to go to Sutrium under Brydda's protection. In exchange for shelter and the setting up of the safe house Rushton wanted, Domick would share all he learned with Brydda, unless the coercer believed it would jeopardize Obernewtyn. "Elspeth, Dragon, Darga, and Jik will travel to the highlands, through the Olden way, and go straight across the White Valley to the mountain pass, being careful to avoid the Druid's encampment," Brydda said.

"The Olden way is poisonous," Domick objected.

In answer, Brydda pointed to Darga. "I grew up in this district, and I know of this pass. It is badly tainted in some parts, but there are parts that are tainted so little as to be harmless.

And that is where Darga comes in. I have seen with my own eyes that he can tell poisoned substances from clean ones. Therefore, he will be your guide. Only you have to go on foot. The Older way is passable only on foot."

"If you are right about this pass, it is a good plan, and it may be our only opportunity to reach Obernewtyn in time to warn Rushton before snow closes the pass."

"I'll go," Domick said.

I shook my head. "You have an important job to do. Find out as much as you can of the Council's intensions, but keep out of Ariel's way. If you remember him, you can be sure he'll remember you."

"What about the Druid?" Kella asked.

I grinned. "We know that the settlement is some distance away from the encampment. I will farsense to make sure we do not encounter anyone. And if we find our way blocked, I'll have Dragon frighten anyone away."

The others laughed, including Dragon, who, though she did not understand what we were saying, seemed to find laughter itself funny.

"Rushton will never forgive me for letting you go into danger," Domick groaned.

Ignoring this, I suggested we set off at first light. Brydda would take us to the start of the Olden way, and then he would return to the others and wait until the soldierguards had searched Katlyn and Grufyyd's farmstead before going to Sutrium. Brydda gave me careful instructions about how to contact him in Sutrium, and then we parted in the cold, gray light of the very early morning. It was painful to say good-bye to Pavo, knowing it might be the last time I would see him. I could not hug him, because any sort of pressure was unbearable for him. He was delirious most of the time now, and he blinked at me in a puzzled way, as if his memory were disintegrating.

"He is content," Brydda said gently when we had left the camp behind.

"That's what Darga said. But I'm not content. What a world this is that someone like Pavo has to die so young," I said.

"People will always be dying too young, whether in the Beforetime or now. That is the way of the world."

It took less than an hour to reach the fall of rocks that Brydda said concealed the opening to the Olden way. My feet were already hurting, though we had traveled at an easy pace.

Before leaving Brydda hugged us all tightly. Dragon, who liked the big man, cried unself-consciously. Darga wagged his tail slowly. Last of all, Brydda looked at me seriously. "Be careful, little sad eyes; your trials are not yet over. But I expect to see you in the spring."

After he had gone, I straightened myself, determinedly throwing off a wave of depression. I took a deep breath and started to climb, instructing Jik and Dragon to stay close behind Darga. Once we reached the top of the rockfall, I was disheartened to realize we would have to climb down the other side before we could begin the ascent to the pass entrance.

It took us a considerable time to get down to the opening, and we were all dirty, grazed, and exhausted before we reached the narrow slit in the rock, which would barely fit a full-grown man. Thick vines had grown across it like a net, and some sort of spider had made a web in them. It was years since Brydda had last gone there, and I suspected nothing had passed that way since, for the webs were intricate and many layered, and covered in thick dust.

Dragon would not go through until she was certain none of the cobwebby tendrils would touch her.

It was late in the morning when we finally stood inside the Olden way. Darga sniffed, saying he scented no poisons in the vicinity.

Dry reedy grasses made a papery, whispering noise as we made our way up the incline. It was not as steep as the rockfall, but my feet ached with the strain of digging in for purchase. The trees growing in that early section were stunted, with spiky grayish leaves and stonelike buds, but ahead we could see a dark-green belt of trees. On either side of us, the mountains soared straight up, pitted gray walls.

It was an arduous climb to the tree line, and we were all puffing by the time we reached it. I was disappointed to find the ground did not level out—the trees had only given that illusion. It was darker beneath the canopy of entwined branches and leaves, and an eerie silence reigned that reminded me of the Silent Vale, where I had gone to collect whitestick as an orphan.

Jik worked to teach Dragon to say his name as we walked. I listened with only half an ear, preoccupied by a sudden feeling of unease. When we came out of the trees, I noticed the sky had darkened.

After a short distance, the now sparse trees gave way to a high, thick kind of bramble running before us in a solid barrier. It offered no natural paths and was filled with stinging thorns. That meant we had to use knives to hack our way through. The severed branch ends leaked a defensive odor that made our eyes sting.

It took more than an hour to bypass the brambles. On the

other side was a narrow, very deep gorge cutting directly across our path; at the bottom ran a tumultuous course of water. The stream and the gorge appeared to run all the way from Tor to Aran Craggie. I thought it quite likely the stream was a tributary of the Suggredoon, escaping through some crack from inside the mountain. It was too wide to jump; the only way to cross was to descend into the trench and swim the stream.

We wasted another hour trying to find a less steep descent but, in the end, returned to the original spot to climb down. The stream was overhung with a thick, trailing fringe of creepers and vines, but the bank on both sides proved treacherously soft. I stared into the water, glumly wondering how we would manage to get across safely. Up close, the water ran very fast, and Dragon eyed it fearfully.

"I will swim with a rope in my teeth," Darga sent. "On the other side, I will pass the rope around a tree and hold it tight. Jik can cross first since he weighs little; then he can tie it."

I looked at the opposite bank doubtfully. "All right. But I'll tie the rope around you and hold the other end so that I can pull you back if you get into trouble."

At first, Darga disappeared completely beneath the roaring water. But a moment later, he bobbed to the surface and struck out for the other bank. The current was so strong that he had to swim at an angle that made it look as if he were trying to make his way upstream like a salmon. He crept forward, drawing fractionally nearer the opposite bank.

By the time he reached the edge, he was clearly tiring badly, but the ordeal was not over. I watched in consternation as he tried to scale the soft edges of the bank. Time and again the earth gave way, plunging him back into the raging water.

"Pull him back," Jik cried fearfully. "He's drowning!"

"No," Darga sent, his mind an exhausted whisper. The soft banks were deeply gouged before he managed at last to get a firm footing. I could see his body trembling with weariness as he dragged himself over the lip.

"Darga!" Jik shouted through his tears. Darga flapped his tail weakly twice, then lay like one dead for a long time.

When he had recovered, Darga walked around a tree several times and braced himself. I tugged my own end to test the strength of Brydda's rope, then fastened it to a stout tree trunk, pulling the rope taut.

Jik went across hand over hand. The rope creaked and sagged until he hung waist-deep in the water, but it held. He reached the other side safely and gave a triumphant yell before untying the rope from Darga and fastening it around a rock. I had thought I might have to knock Dragon out and somehow pull her across, but watching Jik seemed to have given her confidence. She was pale but surprisingly calm, and when I saw her cross, I realized it was because she had thought of a way to make sure the water did not touch her. She, too, went across hand over hand but with her legs hooked around the rope, too. She had been less frightened of the crossing than of the water itself.

I went last, half sorry I could think of no way to untie the rope. It was the only piece we had and might be needed again.

I was further disheartened at our lack of progress. Unless the way became easier, we were wasting valuable time negotiating endless obstacles. Climbing out of the trench was harder than getting down into it, and at the top, I decided it was time to rest and eat.

Jik lit a small fire, and I set a pot of soup to cook over it. While we waited, Jik softly sang a strange song the Herders had taught him about the Blacklands. He had a remarkably sweet voice and at my request sang songs until the food was hot enough to eat.

Renewed, we went on.

Not far ahead were more trees. The bandages on my feet were filthy, and I suspected the wounds were bleeding again, but the pain was less intense.

We trudged the remainder of the day without stopping. The trees proved less dense than they had been in the first belt, and gradually, the slope became slighter and walking less arduous. Darga assured me we were still some distance from the poisoned region, which was close to the other end of the pass. Obernewtyn still seemed far away. I could hardly believe that in a few days we would be home.

I looked up through the trees at the dim, bleary afternoon fading into a smoky twilight, and shivered, glad of the blankets Brydda had insisted we carry. Winter had begun. It struck me that the first falls of snow would have blanketed the higher mountain valleys. Very soon, snow would fall at Obernewtyn, if it had not already. I shivered again and pulled my cloak around my shoulders. The moon had begun to fatten in its cycle and should have lit our way clearly, but though visible, it produced a wan, strained light, and we were forced to set our torches to flame. We halted momentarily at Darga's warning that we were on the verge of badly poisoned ground.

"Can you find a safe way across it?" I asked him.

He sniffed. "I can smell clean ground ahead," he assured me. We both knew it would be safer to wait until daylight to go on, but I had the queer feeling the delays were bringing us close to some disaster.

I looked over to where Jik was continuing his language lessons with the bemused Dragon. "Ready?" I asked.

Jik looked across at me unsmilingly, and for an instant he looked suddenly old and frail, as near to death as Pavo. Then he smiled, and the impression vanished.

We walked single file from then on, Darga leading the way through a stand of giant trees with monstrously gnarled and misshapen trunks and thick, dark roots writhing up out of the ground. I thought I had seen such trees beyond the compound wall in Matthew's vision and hoped it meant we were nearing the other end of the pass.

At the same time, the ground beneath our feet became wet and soft. Our feet made sucking noises that echoed in the silence. The torchlight flickered on dark, odorous puddles of water that seeped into the slightest depression of earth. There seemed no source for the dampness. The light made a bizarre shadow play on the twisted tree trunks, making them look like the faces of ancient men and women. Dragon eyed them doubtfully as we passed.

After a time, the wind rose, and leaves flapped sluggishly, heavy with moisture. We waded through a thick blanket of them, and the smell of the festering layers of leaves below filled the air with a sweet, rotten scent that made us all gag.

Darga sent a constant dialogue of instructions as the way became more fraught with danger, and I began to regret not stopping. He warned against certain plants, trees, and even areas of bare ground, guiding us through the poisonous labyrinth. Without him, we would have been helpless, for there was scant outward sign of the poisons other than the distorted sizes and shapes of the trees and bushes growing all around us.

In the end, the dog called a halt, saying he needed to rest. We went on until he found a patch of ground relatively clean of taint. My feet no longer gave me any trouble, for an ominous numbness had deprived them of all sensation. I felt I could walk over flames without feeling anything. I did not dare undo the bandages, afraid of what the loss of feeling might mean.

We ate the last of our store of perishable foods and sipped at the meager remnant of water. I had wanted to fill the containers along the way, but Darga had pronounced all water in the pass tainted enough to make a person sick. We would have to ration what was left of the water to make sure it would last us out.

I was drifting into a light, troubled sleep when a terrible, savage growling rent the air around us.

✦ 21 ✦

THE GROWLING SEEMED to vibrate in the air, even after it had ceased. Nothing stirred in the silence that followed except for a faint breeze tugging at our blankets.

"What was that?" Jik whispered.

I set my mind loose, searching, hampered by the static given off by the poisons. I found nothing. "Do you know what that was?" I asked Darga.

"Some kind of animal," he suggested unhelpfully.

Dragon was crouched near a tree, her eyes wide with fright. I opened my mouth to reassure her, but another of the blood-chilling growls cut off my words. My skin puckered into gooseflesh.

Again the growl faded, but still there was no sign of the creature that had made it. Neither Jik nor Darga were any more successful at locating the mind pattern of the monster. I encountered a number of barely sentient minor patterns, but these were mere flickers of instinct rather than thought.

We gave up and sat around staring uneasily into the darkness around us.

Five more times the eerie sounds shattered the night, and I began to suspect that it was not, as we had all feared, a signal for attack or a hunting cry. Even so, I could not help thinking that a creature who could make such a noise and conceal its mind might be clever enough to hide its intention.

But there was no attack.

Morning found us bleary-eyed and ill rested, for the sounds had seemed to grow nearer and more frequent as the night wore on. In the end, we decided there was more than one of the creatures, or one was circling us. Either prospect made for uneasy slumber.

To our further dismay, we had not been walking long the next day before the giant stand of trees gave way abruptly to a seemingly endless mire reminiscent of the blighted Berryn Mor. Here the few trees that managed to grow in the sodden ground were thin and sickly looking, bereft of leaf and shrouded in a furry gray mold.

The only reassuring thing about the spindly skeletons looming out of the mist was that they told us the water was quite shallow. The ground lay only a few handspans below the surface and, though soft, was firm enough to walk on. Darga went ahead, warning us to step exactly where he did, since there were holes and trenches all through the swamp. He said the water was tainted but only slightly.

Tired and thirsty, we plodded doggedly after Darga. There was no possibility of resting until we reached dry ground. Soaking through my boots and stockings, the swamp water was tepid. An evil-smelling mist hung low over the surface of the water and swirled about our feet as we passed.

We walked in silence, concentrating on keeping our footing and moving as quickly as we could, until Jik ventured a question.

"If I fell in this water or touched one of those poisoned plants, would I die at once or slowly like Pavo?" he asked gravely.

Repressing a flare of anguish at the thought of Pavo, I said, "I don't know. I guess it depends on how potent it is. If it's strong, it could work quickly. But if weak, like in the places we find whitestick, you have to be exposed to it over long periods of time before it does any harm."

He nodded thoughtfully, his brow furrowed. "What is whitestick, anyway?"

I smiled. "Your guess is as good as anyone's. Pavo says it is what was left by whatever caused the Great White, like ash from a fire. Once cleansed, it's used for everything from starting fires to making medicines. But surely you know that much?"

"I heard that the Herders make a kind of gas with it that makes your skin burn," Jik said.

I looked at him curiously. "I've never heard of that."

He shrugged. "It's a secret. I heard them talk of experiments. A man who they tested it on was said to have gone blind from the gas, and then his skin blistered. It was terrible. I think he died."

The thought of whitestick being used for such a purpose disturbed me deeply. But perhaps it was only a story.

"The Herders told us Lud sent the Great White because the Oldtimers were evil. But the Teknoguilders say the Beforetimers made the Great White happen on their own. Why would they do that?"

I smiled at his insatiable curiosity for taboo subjects. "I doubt anyone meant to cause the Great White," I said. "I believe it was a kind of accident. But no one knows for sure. Not even the Herder Faction, even though they think they know everything."

"Did weapons make the Great White happen? Pavo told me some of the Oldtime weapons and poisons might still be hidden someplace, like the skyscrapers under Tor," Jik said seriously.

I forced myself not to react. "It's possible," I said slowly.

"What would happen if someone found that kind of weapon? Someone like Ariel or the Druid? There might be another accident. . . ." His voice trailed off.

"This is a bad place for such talk," I said.

The water bubbled all around us now, issuing clouds of colored gas. I noticed a greenish vapor first and pointed it out to Darga. He told me it was a poisonous gas but too weak to harm us. One virulent yellow gas was dangerous enough for Darga to give a wide berth, while a sickly blue shade made him backtrack hastily.

The region of gases was narrow but seemed to take hours to negotiate. My nerves felt ragged by the time we left the mists behind. Suddenly, right in front of us, a bluish gas coalesced. Jik almost fell over in his effort to back away from it. I sent a quick command, and he steadied himself. "It's Dragon," I said. "She's mimicking the gases." Jik nodded, staring at the apparition unhappily. Noticing his expression, Dragon's triumphant smile faded and the mist vanished.

"Bad?" she asked contritely.

"Good," I said firmly. "Very good."

"More?" Dragon asked eagerly, waving her hands to indicate that she would make something huge and mysterious and complex.

"Uh . . . maybe later," Jik said sheepishly.

As soon as the sun set, the dim day gave way to a starless night, and the air resounded again with the mysterious growling noises. They sounded much closer, and I could not get over the feeling that we were being stalked, despite another fruitless mind search.

We were all relieved to stand on solid ground, though the darkness kept us from seeing what sort of land lay ahead. I decided we needed a break, having been unable to stop at all while crossing the swamp. We drank the last of our water with a feeling of recklessness. Already light-headed from lack of food, I prayed we were close to the compound.

Lying with my back against a tree, I heard Darga beside me sniffing delicately, tasting the various scents of the night. I could smell nothing but the noxious swamp gases and my own filth. The dog was proving an invaluable member of our company. I wondered if his presence was the real truth that lay behind the vague futuretelling of Jik's importance.

A slight breeze ruffled my hair, and Darga lifted his head. "A storm comes," he sent.

I nodded impatiently. "But can you smell any funaga yet?"

"I smell them," Darga sent, confirming that we were nearing the end of the pass.

I decided we would rest for a time and leave the pass in the very early morning hours. I slept heavily and dreamlessly. I woke only once to the sound of Jik's laughter echoing in the darkness.

He explained that he had been walking around to keep himself warm and alert on his watch, when he had nearly stepped on a small, lumpy-skinned swamp dweller with bulging eyes. Immediately, the frightened creature's neck had blown up to three times its diminutive size, and it had let out the incredible growling rumble that had so mystified us. We had seen dozens of the creatures since leaving the area of bubbling mists, sitting on logs and blinking sleepily at us, but we had not connected the giant noises with such harmless life-forms.

Jik's suggestion that the dreadful calling was a kind of love song made me laugh until my stomach ached. I lay back to sleep finally, with a smile on my face. It was good to laugh. I had been doubly amused to find that Darga took Jik's guess quite seriously. Beasts lacked only one funaga virtue that I regretted, and that was a sense of humor.

"You may call it a lack," Darga broke into my thoughts. "So might I lack a pain in my head." That made me laugh again.

I had intended to stand last watch, but Jik had not woken me, saying he had felt wide awake and thought I might as well sleep while I could.

I stretched, feeling oddly lethargic. I threw the blanket away from me, realizing it was hot. At once, my feet began to ache with a new pain, and my head and neck felt damp. I looked down at my feet uneasily. Standing carefully, I could not stifle a gasp of pain at the hot fire shooting up my legs.

"What is it?" Jik asked.

"Nothing," I said. "My feet have gone to sleep." It was not easy to lie to an empath, but Jik was young and untrained.

I turned away from him to hide the fear in my eyes. The numbness that had enabled me to climb the Olden way had been too good to be true. I forced myself to face something that I had known for a while. My feet had become infected. Fighting off a dull drowsiness, I roused the others, deliberately isolating the awareness of the pain.

This was a dangerous thing to do, and Roland forbade it in all but the most extreme need. Pain suppressed was pain in waiting. Eventually, it had to be endured, and the longer it was allowed to accumulate, the more devastating its final effect. It was possible to suppress minor pain for so long that the accumulation, when released, could stop one's heart. I knew I would pay dearly for my suppression, but if I could suppress it until we reached home, Roland could have the healers siphon off some of the pain.

Resolutely, I went on, refusing to allow myself to think about the consequences if I failed to reach Obernewtyn before the pass was closed.

We had been walking less than an hour when Darga stopped abruptly, his fur bristling. "Funaga. Just ahead," he sent.

I told the others to wait and limped through the trees. Catching sight of a low wall, I had to fight back tears of relief. This was the last obstacle between us and Obernewtyn.

I peered over the wall warily.

Three or four armsmen stood talking near the diggings. The yellow sky cast an ivory light on their faces, turning their flesh a sickly, sallow hue.

On the other side of the clearing, nearest the gate, an armsman was deep in an argument with a white-robed Druid acolyte. The acolyte looked angry. A few steps away stood another armsman, leaning on his spear and yawning. There was a lot more open space than I remembered from Matthew's vision and no way of passing over it unnoticed without a diversion.

Jik brought Dragon up to the fence just as a low rumble of thunder sounded in the distance. Dragon shuddered from head to toe, pointing at the sky and gibbering fearfully. I patted her arm, realizing she was afraid of the storm. That was all we needed.

I turned to Darga, who was looking up and sniffing the wind.

"We'll have to go straightaway. Dragon's frightened of the storm, and she might not be able to make a vision if she gets any more agitated."

As if to underline my words, lightning flashed directly overhead, and Dragon cowered to the ground, hands over her ears. I had a sudden impression that time was folding back on itself. My general sense of apprehension had increased to the point where it bordered on premonition, but I knew the suppression of pain could confuse the other senses. And Dragon's growing agitation made it imperative we move at once.

I stroked her face gently, and slowly she relaxed. It took some time to make her understand what was needed, but in the end she nodded.

A moment later, the man leaning on his spear gave a muffled shout, and another man actually screamed with such terror that my hair stood on end. Then chaos broke out across the compound. For a moment, there was a hail of cries and panicked shouts. Peering through a crack in the fence, I could see no sign of any apparition and wondered what Dragon had conjured up. I watched until the clearing was deserted, then hissed at the others to run.

Lightning flashed as we thrust aside the barrier of stakes, but no one cried out. I saw a lone man running frantically for the huts; everyone else was already inside.

Lightning flashed with lurid brilliance, and for a second, our shadows ran before us, elongated and sharp edged, merging with the tree line just before us.

We had reached the White Valley!

Thunder crashed again, and this time the air vibrated with its force.

As soon as we reached the trees, I urged the others to run ahead and slowed to a limping walk. There was no more need to run, and I did not want to aggravate the suppression any further. Preoccupied, I failed to notice a rock in the grass and tripped, sprawling on the ground. Hearing my involuntary cry, Dragon turned as if to help me. Then she froze.

I looked up at her, puzzled, and my heart jerked with sickening force. Her face was a grotesque mask of terror. She began to shriek hysterically. I looked over my shoulder to see what she had seen.

Less than fifty spans away ran a wall of fire, and there was no mistaking the greenish tint of the flames or the blue crackle in the air. I had seen it before—the miscolored sky, the dull, bleared light—but I had not recognized it.

A firestorm, and we were out in the open!

✦ 22 ✦

"GET UP AND run, girl, unless you want to die!" cried a voice.

Wrenched violently to my feet, I found myself half dragged, half carried along by a tall, brown-faced youth. Dragon ran ahead of us, wild with terror.

"That way. There are caves," he shouted, pointing. Dragon swerved the way he indicated, disappearing into the trees. The acrid smoke billowed around us, and dimly, I heard the muffled crash of thunder in the distance. A wave of heat flowed over us. I dared not glance over my shoulder to see how near the flames were. All I could think of was the burning of my mother and father. The screams and the dreadful smell.

"Thank Lud!" the youth said harshly as the trees parted to reveal a rough hill of granite knolls.

"Inside, there," he said, thrusting me unceremoniously into a shallow cave in the side of the steep, stony hillock. "This is not deep enough, but there's no time to search further. Pray the wind changes, or we'll fry." He had to shout over the roar of the flames bearing down on us.

I turned to watch the fire racing across the countryside. Black smoke rose above the trees, blotting out the sun. The youth pressed me into a depression in the deepest section of the cave and forced himself in beside me. Our breathing sounded unnaturally loud.

The wall of fire came to less than a span from the hill before sweeping to the left and away. I found myself trembling from head to foot at the thought of how close I had come to following my parents into the purifying flame.

"That was hellish close," the youth said shakily, wiping sweat from his face. Though we were no longer in immediate danger, the heat was intense, since the firestorm still raged all around us. "If we'd been caught in that, we'd be charcoal now."

"Dragon!" I gasped, starting for the entrance. "Jik and Darga!" My rescuer dragged me back into the cave.

"Are you mad? The girl came this way. There are many caves she might have taken refuge in," he said.

"You don't understand. There were others—a boy and a dog," I cried.

He shook his head. "Either they found shelter and are safe, or . . ." He looked at the fierce orange glow of the flames, still uncomfortably close.

I sank to my knees, realizing there was nothing I could do until the firestorm ended. Abruptly, the youth leaned down and twisted my face to the firelight.

"You are not from the camp. Who are you?" he demanded in a queer tone. Through a haze of smoke, brown eyes surveyed me from a craggy, tan face. His hair was brown, too, and worn longer than lowland fashion dictated. He was about Rushton's age and wore the unmistakable garb of a Druid armsman.

Recapture by the Druid meant trouble. But that was overshadowed by my fear for Jik, Dragon, and Darga. I tried to farseek them, but the air was filled with static generated by the firestorm.

The young armsman dropped to his knees beside me.

"Look at me!" he commanded. "Don't you know me, Elspeth?"

I looked at him properly for the first time and, incredibly, realized I did know his face.

"Daffyd?" I whispered.

He sat back on his heels. "Lud save us, it is you, grown into near womanhood. I met you only that once, yet I never forgot your face."

I sat up too quickly, and the world tilted crazily out of focus. I leaned forward and vomited on the ground, heaving until my stomach ached. Gently, Daffyd wiped my mouth with a piece of cloth. I felt no pain, and the nausea was swallowed up immediately by the suppressing barrier.

"I think you'd better stay still," Daffyd said. "You must have breathed in too much smoke. You're lucky I came along when I did."

I looked at Daffyd searchingly. "You may call it lucky . . . unless you mean to turn us over to the Druid."

He smiled. "Gilaine spoke to me of you and your friends. This is one Druid armsman you need not fear. I was surprised when she called you a gypsy; then I realized you must have escaped from Obernewtyn when it changed hands and had somehow ended up traveling with gypsies."

Daffyd screwed up his eyes, and I was astonished to feel a clumsy probe seeking entrance to my mind. The weakest shield would have held him off. It was like watching a baby trying to walk. He sighed. "I'm not very good at it. Gilaine showed me how to think outside Lidgebaby's net, the way you showed her. It is odd to think we were both Misfits when we met in the Councilcourt that day, though I did not know it then."

He coughed as a thick cloud of smoke blew directly into

the cave. "Gilaine and the rest of us thought you were dead. Gilbert saw your raft go into the mountain, but all the same, the Druid had everyone out searching for you when I arrived. He was convinced it was a trick and you too crafty to raft to your deaths." He frowned. "Was it a trick, then? Have you been hidden in the valley all this time?"

"The raft carried us through the mountain and down to the lowlands, though I would not want to take such a passage again. I came back through the Olden way," I said. "It's less poisonous than the Druid thinks. We were trying to cut through the compound when the storm struck. I saw everyone taking cover, but I thought . . . I didn't realize a firestorm was coming."

I looked at the cave opening worriedly. "I hope the others are safe. I pray this firestorm ends quickly." I made to rise, but all the suppression in the world could not make useless limbs work.

Daffyd laid a gentle hand on my arm. "Be patient. Even when the storm front passes, there is the rain. We can't brave that and live."

As if his words were a signal, it began suddenly to rain with great force. For a moment, we both looked outside, watching steam hiss and billow from the dying fires. I bit my lip and hoped Dragon understood the danger of being out in the stinging rains.

The cave we were in was no more than a shallow scoop of erosion, and if the rain had been slanting from the opposite direction, it would have filled the cave. As to the fire, the blackened ground showed that it had come to within a single span of the rocks. I shuddered. The area visible from the cave was devastated, and some of the trees were still aflame with their eerie blue halo. The beat of falling rain was curiously soothing amid the sight and smell of destruction, and my eyes drooped. The suppressing was draining my reserves.

"Elspeth, Gilaine said you were trying to reach the coast. If you did get through the mountain, why did you come back?" Daffyd asked.

Forcing myself to full awareness, I looked at Daffyd squarely. I had always found it hard to trust people, but this time I did not hesitate. My infected feet rendered me useless as a messenger. Providence had brought Daffyd to me.

"The Druid's friend on the Council," I said. "What do you know of him?"

Daffyd looked at me closely as if trying to judge if I were delirious. Then he turned his gaze out at the teeming rain and shrugged. "A couple of years back, a boy stumbled into the camp one winter, more dead than alive. The Druid had him looked after, no doubt hoping for some useful information, or at least another set of hands. When the boy regained consciousness, he claimed to have lost his memory. Eventually, the Druid decided to let him join us.

"Though fair faced, he was not well liked. And yet he had a charm, when he chose to use it. The old man grew fond of him, began to think of him as a son. In the end, he was privy to the armsmen councils. Then he came up with a daring plan to infiltrate the Council and feed information back to us. It was a dangerous proposition, but he is an insidious sort of fellow. If anyone could carry out such an audacious plan, it was he. So he went off to Sutrium." Daffyd shrugged. "A lot of us thought he would disappear as soon as he was out of the Druid's sight, maybe even betray us, but he did as he had promised, supplying us with luxuries and information, working for the day the Druid comes out of hiding to challenge the powers that be."

"Ariel," I murmured, not believing for a minute he had lost his memory or that he truly had the Druid's interests in mind.

"It's strange to hear him named openly," Daffyd said. "The Druid has forbidden us to speak of him by name. How did you come to hear it?"

"We met before he came to the Druid," I said bleakly. "He is a Misfit, from Obernewtyn. You have heard of the seditioners there, Alexi and Madam Vega, once enemies of the Druid? He was their pet creature.

"Daffyd, I did not leave Obernewtyn and fall in with the gypsies. I and my friends came from Obernewtyn *disguised* as gypsies. The new master there, Rushton, has made it a secret haven for Misfits like us. I could not tell Gilaine the truth, but I wanted to return to offer you a place with us at Obernewtyn when Lidgebaby is old enough to leave the Druid encampment."

"Then Obernewtyn was not ruined by a firestorm?" Daffyd said.

"No. It's quite safe—so far."

"But, why are you telling me all this now, if you would not speak of it to Gilaine?" Daffyd asked.

I sighed. "Because I need you to go to Obernewtyn and warn Rushton that Ariel is behind the Council's interest in us, before the pass is closed with snow. Tell him soldierguards will arrive at first thaw, and they will find no firestorm-racked ruins. Maybe Rushton can evacuate, take everyone higher into the mountains. Maybe they'll decide to fight, defend the pass. But if I don't get word to Rushton, they'll be defenseless. Ariel will have won."

Daffyd looked pensive. "Ariel always seemed fanatical about Obernewtyn, now that I think of it. He has convinced the old man that Rushton was a threat to us. He was up here just days ago, and when he heard that a group of gypsies had seen Obernewtyn with their own eyes and then slipped through our fingers . . . Well, he was very interested in you and your friends. He cursed when there was no trace of your bodies and swore you had not died. If not for him, the Druid would have called off the search much sooner. Does he know the truth about Obernewtyn?"

"I'm not sure what he knows, but it seems to me he has guessed that Obernewtyn is undamaged. And he wants revenge," I said bitterly. "He must also realize that Rushton can expose him to the Druid, or to the Council, as a Misfit and a seditioner. Daffyd, will you go to Obernewtyn for me?" I asked, too weak for pretense.

Daffyd's eyes flicked to my legs.

I nodded. "They're badly infected. So far I've been able to block the pain so it wouldn't slow me—one of my more useful Talents. But stopping the pain can't make these legs carry me any farther."

There was a long pause. Finally, Daffyd spoke. "I can do as you ask. But what about you and the girl and boy you spoke of?"

"We'll be fine. Rushton can send help for us. The storm is interfering with my farseeking, but once it's over, I'll call Dragon and Jik and Darga to me."

I looked out of the cave. There were no more flames, and a gray curtain of firestorm rain obscured the outside world. Carefully, and remembering Daffyd had no love for the Council, I related all that had befallen us in the lowlands. When at last the rain ceased, I urged him to leave at once.

"You must go now—" I began, when an anguished cry shattered the stillness.

It took a moment for me to understand that it was Dragon screaming, the grief in her voice tangible and terrifying. Daffyd gave me one startled look, then plunged out into the open.

Long moments later, he returned carrying the prostrate form of Dragon.

"She's not . . . ," I began, but he shook his head.

"Fainted," he said stiffly as if his lips were frozen. His face was very pale as he laid her on the ground inside the cave and wiped the wetness from her bare skin.

"What is it?" I asked, sensing disaster.

He looked up bleakly. "She had found a body. Burned beyond recognition. It might be one of the people from the compound," he added unconvincingly.

He reached into a pocket. "She was clutching this." He held out a hand, and something glinted dully in his palm. It was the small empath novice token that Dameon gave to new members of his guild.

I felt the suppressing barrier weaken with shock and revulsion.

Jik. It was Jik.

I was filled with a guilt deeper than anything I had ever imagined possible. I was responsible for his terrible death. I might as well have killed him with my own hands. If only I had left him with Brydda. If we had not brought him away from Obernewtyn, had not brought him out of the cloister. My teeth chattered, and I felt dizzy with horror.

Daffyd knelt beside me and made me drink water from a tin jar. "Drink," he said, and his eyes, filled with honest pity and compassion, were my undoing. I wept then, great choking tears that seemed to take pieces of my soul.

Jik's face rose in my mind's eye, sweet and grave with eyes

always a little too old for his years. He had hardly joined us before we had set him on a path to this horrible death. And what had bringing him achieved? I was now certain Jik's presence had been necessary on the expedition only because it ensured Darga's. Maryon had admitted her prediction was unfocused. I could not recall any vital action of Jik's, but without Darga, we would never have found Dragon or completed our survey of the library; we could not have come through the Olden way. But even if Obernewtyn was warned in time, was even that enough to justify Jik's death?

"There was no sign of the dog," Daffyd said quietly. "It might have escaped." I shook my head, knowing Darga would never leave Jik in danger by choice.

I wept myself empty of tears.

Daffyd went to bury what remained of Jik's body and returned looking pale and weary.

"Daffyd," I said. "You have to go now, while the pass is still open, or it will be too late. Take Dragon."

"I'll carry you," he said. I shook my head. I would slow them to no purpose. Not even Roland could help me now. I was sure too much pain had accumulated.

Dragon was less easy to convince when she woke. She only agreed when I told her Daffyd's friends would be coming to help me. Jik had told her about Obernewtyn, and she had built it up in her mind to be a place of endless happiness where everyone was always safe. Her horror at the manner of Jik's death made her vulnerable, and I exploited this shamelessly.

I made them go immediately, maintaining a calm façade for Dragon's sake. I shook Daffyd's hand, pressing my armband into it. "This will make them believe you," I said softly.

"Is there anything . . . anyone . . . ." Daffyd hesitated.

I thought of Rushton as I had last seen him, his hand raised to me through the driving rain. There had always been a strange, prickly affection between us, a bond of sorts. It was hard to believe I would not see him again.

I smiled. "Tell him . . . tell them, goodbye . . . ," I said.

When they had gone, I sank gratefully into a black feverish sleep filled with dreams, but I did not release the suppressing. At the end, life and sanity were too sweet to give up voluntarily. I knew it would not be long before the barrier gave way of its own volition.

I dreamed a horse with wings came and carried me to the mountaintops. I dreamed Darga was there and singing to me in Jik's high, sweet voice. I dreamed of Maruman, his fur ruffled by the winds. I dreamed of a voice inside my mind calling and calling.

I dreamed . . . of birds.

✦ 23 ✦

THE SOUND OF a breaking branch in the silence of the devastated valley dragged me from my feverish drowsing. I had imagined myself beyond fear, but the notion came to me that the sound had been made by a predator seeking easy prey in the aftermath of the firestorm.

I stared out of the cave, craning my neck as far as I could to keep from using my legs. I dared not overload my mind with any more pain. Miraculously, the suppressing was still intact, although my vision and hearing seemed distorted.

I could see nothing outside but blackened trees and earth and a drifting haze of smoke. There was no sign of life anywhere, but I felt I was being watched. My scalp prickled, and I groped for a rock to use as a weapon.

"Who's there?" I called, my voice a dry, frightened croak.

Letting my mind loose in desperation, I was surprised to find myself listening to a mental dialogue.

"What do you think it is?" one mind asked.

"A funaga, of course. What else makes such ugly noises?" came the response.

Astonished at the strength of minds that were clearly nonhuman, I projected, farsending my own thoughts. "Who/where are you?"

"It spoke!" came a third mental voice. Younger than the others and less controlled, I thought. There were quick shushing thoughts from the other two, who recognized the significance of my mental questions.

I gathered myself, trying to decide if I was dreaming.

Forcing down a mad urge to giggle hysterically, I made an effort to sound normal. "I know you're out there. There are three of you, and I can hear your thoughts!" Nothing. "Answer me!"

I heard a faint movement and craned my neck, trying to farsense them.

A shudder of branches caught my eye. Squinting, I realized there were birds in the tree. I let my eyes follow the trunk to the ground, thinking the three Talents might well have disturbed them.

No one.

The branches rustled again, and I looked up, wondering what had brought the birds to such a place. Animals generally avoided firestorm-devastated areas for months after, sometimes years. There was no small prey, no insects, and no plant life. No reason—yet there they were, just sitting and staring.

One of the birds extended its wings, and I drew in a sharp breath at the flash of red on its plumage. Guanette birds. I had seen one up close only once, a stuffed trophy. Even dead, the bird had possessed a quality that had enthralled me, a wild sort of nobility.

Looking more carefully, I could tell one of the three was a male, with a straighter beak and smaller body. The two larger, with curved beaks, were female.

I sent a questing probe to the birds. After a moment, the smallest began to fidget, shifting weight from one claw to the other like a sheepish child. I sent a more aggressive inquiry. The male flexed his wings and gave a faint chirrup.

"Will you answer?" I sent directly to him.

There was no response, and I was unsure I had reached the bird. Its mind was oddly opaque, and I felt light-headed and weak. Then I felt a probe in my mind. It had entered with such precise delicacy I had not even been aware of being broached. The finest shield I could create would not bar entrance to such a fine-tuned probe.

"Greetings, funaga," came the thought shyly, but with undeniable grace.

"I am Elspeth," I sent. "What name/shape may I call to you?"

"Do not speak to it!" came a sharp, intrusive probe, no less delicate than the first. I wondered if the infection were somehow weakening my natural defenses.

The first hesitated, then spoke again, its presence the merest cobweb in my thoughts.

"My name is Astyanax," he sent. I heard a brief aside directed to the other mind. "And 'it' is a *she*."

The two females, still side by side on the topmost branch, exchanged a doubtful look, and the effect was so like two old women conferring that I laughed in spite of everything.

All three looked up at the sound of laughter. One of the others addressed me. "Funaga, we of the Agyllians do not give our names lightly. But answer this: Are you a male or a female of your kind? It is not easy to tell your sort of creature apart. You all look so much alike, plucked and naked as an eggling."

"I am female. What are Agyllians?" I sent, wondering why the strange word sounded familiar.

No one seemed ready to answer, and the two females looked at one another for so long, I sensed they were communicating on some unknown level.

Without warning, the silent communion ended, and the

largest of the three birds dropped from the tree and glided to land near the cave entrance. The bird was much bigger up close, standing higher than a tall man. I drew back nervously, wondering if Guanette birds were carnivorous.

"Is it the one?" the bird mused, apparently thinking to itself. It eyed me intently with beady black eyes.

"I wouldn't taste very good," I sent uneasily. "My wounds are poisoned."

"Wounds! Did you hear what it said?" sent the other female. I was beginning to be able to tell them apart.

"She is the one," Astyanax sent with sudden certainty. Both females looked at him pointedly; then the first returned to its inspection of my limbs.

"It is dark. . . . Hard to tell," murmured the bird on the ground. It came closer in a curious drunken gait. My fingers closed around a rock.

"Funaga," it sent. "I am Ruatha of the Agyllians, and my companions are Illyx and Astyanax. Do you truthtell about these injuries?"

Bewildered, I nodded. "I was burned a long time ago. The scars have become infected. I'm sure I would taste horrible. I might even be poisonous," I added earnestly.

The bird made a dry croaking noise. "We do not wish to eat you, funaga. Agyllians are not eaters of flesh."

I relaxed slightly but not too much. The bird hopped lopsidedly closer. "Injuries are common after the firestorms. You do not look very important," it added thoughtfully. "But perhaps Astyanax is right, and you are the one we seek."

My involuntary withdrawal had jarred my legs, and I heard this through a red mist of pain. I fought against faintness.

"Are you Innle?" the bird asked.

481

The mist cleared for a moment in shock at hearing Maruman's old title for me. Innle meant "seeker" in beast symbols. And hadn't I heard that name more recently? The effort of sustaining the suppressing stopped me thinking clearly. I concentrated, shoring up the barrier, and slowly, the tides of pain ebbed.

The bird had not moved, but the other two had flown to the ground and hovered some way back.

"Why do you call me that?" I asked.

"The eldar sent us to find Innle," Astyanax said, "the Seeker, who lay mortally injured in this valley. Many are dead nearby, but the eldar told that you would be alone, wounded and waiting to die. It is hard to know if you are the one. The eldar said there was no time for a mistake."

"What is an eldar?" I asked, fear giving way to puzzlement.

This time Astyanax answered. "Eldar is the name of the high council of the Agyllians. Eldar are the wisest of our kind, and the wisest of the wise is the leader of the council—the Elder."

Now I was sure I was dreaming or delirious with pain. A council of birds? Even the dogs and horses who were organized had not gone that far.

"What is this Seeker?"

"Are you the one we were sent to find?" Illyx demanded with waspish exasperation.

"Peace," Ruatha sent gently. "She cannot know she is the one. We will take her."

I blinked, forcing back a wave of nausea. "What do you mean?"

The bird ignored me. One last searching look from ice-colored eyes, then she thrust her head beneath one wing and appeared to be trying to pick out the feathers there. Instead she withdrew a pouch in her sharp beak, dropped it on the ground, and pecked at it until the woven edges parted. Inside was a net.

"No!" I struggled to maintain the suppressing.

"The Elder cannot leave the Ken, so we will take you there," Ruatha sent calmly, reaching for my leg with one strong claw.

Pain.

More pain.

Darkness.

I fought against consciousness, frightened of what I would find.

"You will not die . . . ," sent a voice, as soft in my mind as a falling leaf.

Slowly, I let myself be drawn, opening my eyes to a sky so pale and clear it was more white than blue. The wind fanned my cheeks with icy fingers, and puffs of cloud burst from my lips and dissolved with each breath exhaled.

Dreaming . . . , I thought vaguely. *All a dream . . . but so real.* Another puff of cloud floated from my mouth. I turned my head slowly to follow it and froze.

I was having one of those horrible dreams where I seemed to be right on the edge of the highest cliff in the world. Below, visible through a veil of drifting cloud, was a vague grayness that might have been sea or land.

Piercing the cloud rose numerous stone columns; I seemed to be lying atop one. First there had been winged horses, then giant birds that thought more clearly than any human, and now I had been transported to the top of the world. I wondered dizzily if these were the dreams that came to the endless sleep called death.

Guanette birds wheeled and flew and skimmed all about in an intricate airborne dance. It was one of the loveliest sights I had ever seen.

I heard the rustle of wings and turned to see one of the birds come to ground. It was a male.

"You have woken, funaga. Welcome to the Ken. I am of the eldar. My name is Nerat. Among your kind, I would be called a healer." It sent these thoughts past my shield without effort, with the same scything ability the other birds had demonstrated.

He moved closer but slowly, as if his bones were stiff. Just as Ruatha had done, the bird reached under a wing, withdrawing a pouch. Balancing precariously on one foot, it took the pouch into its talons, plucking it open with delicate pecking motions. A few grains of yellowish dust drifted on the wind.

"The infection in your body is bad, but not so bad that Nerat cannot draw it. The real difficulty will be in finding a way to drain off the pain you have allowed to build up behind a mental block. Open your mind to me," he commanded.

I flinched at the hint of strength, for here was a mind easily as powerful as my own.

The bird tilted its head quizzically. "You find it hard to open your mind? Dying would be harder. Understand that there is only so much we can do from without. Your body must be taught to repair itself and build its immunities. That is a simple matter and can be done even as I drain the mental poisons. But you must open willingly to me. If you resist, the block will crumble. You will die. Let me in and sleep. Trust me."

I swallowed dryly, wondering why even in the midst of a dream, I could not bear the thought of opening my mind completely.

"That is a question you will answer for yourself in time," Nerat sent. "Now, do as I say, before the poison flows too deep. I can do many things, but I cannot bring the dead back to life. And you must not die with so much left undone," he added cryptically.

I saw a sudden vision of Rushton's brooding face and felt the curious ache his memory always evoked.

"He thinks of you, too," Nerat said absently; then he made a choking sound and regurgitated a grayish lump of paste onto the stone.

"This comes from the substance the funaga call *whitestick*," Nerat sent. "We call it *narma*. I have mixed it with various salivas and acids that I have generated to fight the poisons. Narma rose from the ashes of the Great White and is ever a reminder that the poisons now in the earth fade. Next time, there will be no narma."

I shivered, imagining all the world fused smooth as glass, and black.

"That is how it will be, the next time," Nerat sent. He stared into my eyes. "Come now, ElspethInnle, for it is not only your life that hangs in the balance. Open to me, but leave the block in place until I command you to release it."

Slowly, I let my head fall back onto the stone, trying to make my mind a passive vessel.

Nerat's probe was inside then, swift as a snake, smooth as a single strand of silk. "Relax," he sent. "Dream, and I will do my work. I am not interested in the longings and secret thoughts of a funaga."

Once Nerat commanded me to release the suppressing, I drifted between excruciating pain and numbness, burning heat and freezing cold.

And the pain in my legs. The pain. The pain.

For a time, I forgot who I was, and it seemed all my life had been spent in a dream of pain on the top of a mountain.

Occasionally, I was aware of Nerat's mind weaving a pattern in my thoughts as complex and intangible as smoke in the wind. Sometimes I smelled flowers and herbs, and sometimes acrid, choking smoke.

And then I floated for a very long time.

"She wakes," came a thought bound with weariness and satisfaction.

I opened my eyes and found myself looking into pale avian eyes. The bird was so close I could see the fine crack in his beak, thin as a hair. I felt his mind like tenebrous fingers at the edge of my thoughts; then he gave a strangely human bob of his head and hopped away.

I did not move for a long while, waiting to see where the dream would take me next. Idly, I wondered if I would feel myself plunge into the mindstream when I died. I thought I would like to hear that glorious siren song once more.

Astyanax appeared. "You are well, ElspethInnle. You can get up now. Or do you wish to lie there longer?" he sent with all the politeness of a host not wanting to upset a guest. Urged on by the eager expression in his eyes, I lifted my head carefully.

It is a dream, I told myself. *That is why there is no pain.*

Slowly, I sat upright. I made myself look down my body, prepared to see ruined, evil-smelling flesh and black infection. My legs seemed to rise at me from a dark mist.

Below the skirt they lay before me, pale as cream and utterly without blemish. Even the old childhood scars of skinned knees had vanished.

My heart sounded like a drumbeat as I reached for the

laces. They were stiff with congealed blood. The socks were the same, but when I pulled them down, they came away from the skin easily. The flesh beneath was as flawless as that on my calves. Unable to believe my eyes, I reached a hand out. The skin felt smooth beneath my questing fingers. I wriggled my toes experimentally, watching the movement as if it were an exquisite dance.

I laughed, and my laughter seemed to reverberate off the mountains. No one could heal that fast, and I knew enough of healing to know it was impossible to heal poisoned flesh or banish old, deep scarring.

"Well met," Astyanax sent pertly. "You are now to see Atthis—Elder of the eldar."

I climbed warily to my feet and let myself be led across to a cairn of stones and around to face an opening in the other side.

"Greetings, funaga," came a thought from within the cairn, so clear and gentle it was like a song in my mind. There was the sound of shuffling movement, and slowly, a very old female Guanette bird emerged, her feathers less red than dusty brown with bald patches of pink. The end of her beak was broken right off. But strangest of all were her eyes. There was no pupil, and they were white and milkily opaque.

She was blind.

Looking at the ancient bird, a mist of terror crept through my veins at the sudden certainty that I was not dreaming.

The old bird stopped, eyes turned unerringly toward me. The movement reminded me of Dameon's blind grace. "So, now you are come, just as was foreseen. You may call me Atthis, and I will call you ElspethInnle, as does the yelloweyes."

I blinked, startled. Did she mean Maruman? Then

something else struck me. This was the voice that had called to me in the old cat's mind.

But I'm dreaming, I thought dazedly.

The old bird stepped closer, and a suffocating odor of dust seemed to surround me.

"Why do you pretend? You know this is no dream."

I felt as if someone had kicked me in the stomach, and I was nauseous and breathless all at once.

"You made Maruman sick!" I said indignantly, remembering what had been said to me inside Maruman's mind.

"It could not be helped," Atthis sent gently. "We could not reach you otherwise, at such a distance."

Something else occurred to me. "You told me I had to go on a journey. Is that why I'm here?" *A dark journey,* she had said.

The bird sent nothing for a long moment, but I had the uncanny feeling she could see from those white orbs.

"I did not know we would meet so soon when first I called to you in my dreamtravels through the yelloweyes' mind. I did not foresee then that the Agyllians would have some other part to play. Even the wise are sometimes pawns."

The old bird came closer, her tattered wing brushing one of my feet. I looked into her blind eyes with faint dread.

"You do not like the look of my sightless eyes? Well, sight is a facile thing," Atthis sent.

It was nearing dusk, and a fleeting final sunbeam bathed the old bird in crimsons for a moment. Beyond the cairn lay the rim of the world. On one side, the sky was night-dark, and on the other, the sun shone its final rays. In the west, the moon was rising flat and bright. I looked back to see that the avian face had not looked away from mine.

"ElspethInnle . . . the Seeker," the old bird sent.

"I don't know why you call me that. It's just a name Maruman made up. I don't call myself by it," I sent.

"Not all names are chosen," Atthis sent. "Some names are bestowed."

"What is this all about?" I sent briskly.

"You know," the bird sent, unperturbed. "Have you not wondered at the coincidences and chances in your life? Have you not felt that there were great forces at work about you—forces for good and for great ill? Have you not felt the purpose in your life burning?"

Unwished, a vision came to me of the black chasm I had glimpsed while being tortured by the Zebkrahn. I thought of Jik asking if it were possible for it to happen again and of the Druid and his insane search for Beforetime weapon-machines, his greed for power and revenge blinding him to all else.

"You know," sent Atthis. "You have always known."

"Who are you?" I whispered.

"You may call me a chronicler and . . . what do your people call it—a futureteller. Long ago, I foresaw that the machines that made the great destruction lie sleeping. I saw that a second and greater destruction would come to the world if these machines were not destroyed. That will be no easy matter, for the machines have a kind of intelligence and will protect themselves. But I dreamed one would be born among the funaga, a Seeker to cross the black wastes and ensure that the deathmachines can never be used again.

"Very recently, I foresaw a faltering in that life—a moment when you might easily die. I saw that you would suffer such mental and physical injuries as only the Agyllians could heal. And so I sent out my egglings to find you."

"I'm grateful," I said. "But why seek the machines at all? If they're so far away—if they're truly in the Blacklands— might they not be useless by the time anyone found them?"

"The machines are beyond the Blacklands, but they have slept without harm for hundreds of lifetimes. The danger of their discovery alone would not be enough to make me act. But I have foreseen that there is another funaga whose destiny is to resurrect the machines. Your paths intersect. You are the Seeker, the other is the Destroyer. If you do not find the machines first . . ."

I felt sick. I wanted to tell myself that it was too ridiculous, that I must be dreaming, that prophecies belonged to stories. But too much had happened. I had seen and felt too much, and in my heart, just as the bird said, I had known for a long time that I would find the chasm from my vision. The burning of the maps on Obernewtyn's doors had only been the beginning.

"Why does it have to be me who finds them?" I asked. "Don't I have any choice?"

"There are always choices."

I shook my head, feeling suddenly bitter. "If what you say is true, then the future is set out, and I *have* no real choice."

"The future is a river whose course is long designed but which a flood or drought might easily alter. Whatever choice you make will have its own consequences. If I had not chosen to interfere and have you healed, your death would have been a kind of choice."

The sun sank, and suddenly it was night, the old bird no more than a dust-scented shadow.

"What do I have to do?" I whispered.

"For now, only live," Atthis sent. "What else comes will come."

"You . . . you brought me here to say that?" I asked, incredulous.

The old bird seemed to sigh. "The time is not yet right for you to travel that black road. You were brought here to be healed, and so you are healed. Return to your home and friends. Help them in their struggle, for it is worthy and they have need of you. But do not forget that your true path lies away from them and their quests."

"Have you . . . foreseen that I will succeed on that path? Will I destroy the machines if I go on this journey?"

Atthis shifted slightly and dust filled the air. "That, I have not foreseen."

A wave of weariness flowed through me, and a kind of hopelessness. I sensed compassion in the mind of the old bird. "One day, you will learn that it is not always safest to be alone. Until then, happiness will elude you. But perhaps it is best for you to be alone with this secret burden."

"I don't understand," I sent.

"I know. You are tired. Sleep, and while you sleep, my egglings will transport you to a place where one waits to carry you back to the mountain valley of Obernewtyn."

The old bird's eyes stared into mine, and I felt myself falling into them, sinking into the soft whiteness as if it were a feather bed.

✦ 24 ✦

THE COLD WOKE me.

I was freezing, and I wondered if it had snowed in the night. I felt a sharp stab of grief and was puzzled by it. Then I remembered Jik.

I opened my eyes.

It was night. I frowned, wondering at the icy chill of the air. Perhaps winter had come early to the White Valley. Even so, it felt too cold for the highlands. I doubted it had ever been so cold even at Obernewtyn in the dead of winter.

With a shock, I realized something else. The suppressing barrier was gone from my mind, and so was the pain!

The only answer seemed to be that I had slept off the pain somehow, but if that was the case, the infection in my feet would have worsened, being untended. The pain would come, and it would be dreadful. Better lie still.

Then something warm and moist touched my face, and I gasped in fright. Gazing down at me with dark, troubled eyes was a black horse—unmistakably Gahltha.

"It is I, funaga," he sent in answer to my thought that I was still dreaming. "I am Galta who was once Gahltha."

"Galta?" I echoed stupidly. My eyes drifted past the horse, and questions about his change of name were swept aside in an even greater shock.

I was no longer in the cave in the White Valley, with its

pervasive reek of smoke and the blackened skeletons of trees standing outside like silent sentinels.

I was lying on a flat, narrow stone ledge jutting out from a massive cliff face. I had taken the cliff for the wall of the cave, but there were no walls around me and no roof. Running in all directions from the gray-pitted cliff face was a vast, flat plain covered in snow, glittering in the moon's cold bluish light. There was not a single tree or bush in sight. In the distance, I could see the darkly defined shapes of mountain spurs and outcrops of cracked stone.

The ice and snow, the lack of trees, and the incredible brightness of the stars told me I was in the mountains. Except that it was impossible.

I thought fleetingly that the suppressing barrier had shattered, and the accumulated pain had destroyed my mind. Madness seemed the only rational answer. I giggled at the paradox but shivered when the sound echoed.

The black horse watched me patiently, his dark coat almost blending with the pelt of the night.

I opened my mouth to speak, then closed it with an audible snap, thinking of the queer dream I had fallen into after Daffyd had gone. If it had been a dream.

Carefully, I levered myself into a sitting position. There was no pain in my feet or legs. I looked down.

My legs were bare and unscarred. I touched them reverently, remembering I had done that in the dream. Only it had not been a dream. Thin legs with knobbed knees and rather long feet, but at that moment the most perfect legs in the world.

"Where are we?" I asked my feet.

"In the mountains," the horse answered gently. He looked down at me with grave serenity, and I wondered at the change in him. The last time I had seen him, on the banks of the Suggredoon, he had been almost insane with terror and frustration. The violent impatience and scorching bitterness that had characterized his behavior had disappeared as completely as my own wounds.

"Come," he sent. "If you are too weak to walk, I will carry you. Soon the storm will come, and it must not find us in the open."

I looked up at the cloudless sky, wondering why he thought there was going to be a storm. But I left my doubt unspoken. So much had happened that was impossible to explain that a clear sky might easily hide a storm. I pulled my socks and shoes back on and slid from the ledge, tensing myself for the pain that had been part of my life for so long.

There was a faint jarring but no pain. I stared down at my feet in fresh wonder.

"I have found a place nearby," he explained. "There is wood. You will light a fire for us, and perhaps we will live."

I looked up, startled, and realized with a faint shiver that he was quite serious.

"It will be a bad storm," he sent.

I stepped forward, sinking up to my knees in powdery snow. The black horse went ahead, forging a wide track. I followed in his wake, marveling at the pleasure of walking without pain.

The wind whipped my hair and skirt around now that we were away from the buffer of the cliffs, and the cold stole into my bones long before we reached the shelter. It turned out to be a cave at the end of a narrow cleft. I sighed, thinking I was in danger of becoming accustomed to living in caves; I had seen the inside of so many. This one was quite big, dry, and surprisingly warm, being cut off from the wind by its awkward position in the wedge-shaped cleft.

"We must block the mouth or the coldwhite will come in," the horse sent.

Under his direction, I labored for more than an hour, piling stones at the mouth of the cave, shivering in my light dress and coat. When I had finished, there was nothing but a narrow slit I could barely squeeze through.

"Now the fire," Galta instructed.

Fortunately, I still had my hand flint, and there was a pile of wood and twigs. I managed to burn myself twice before setting them alight. I crouched over the flames, trying to warm my fingers as smoke curled up to the roof of the cave. Outside, the wind had reached a shrieking intensity, and snow fell in a dense curtain. I looked at Galta searchingly, but he only stared into the flames as if mesmerized. "How long do you think the storm will last?" I asked humbly.

He answered simply that he did not know.

I bit my lip. "How did you get here?" *Never mind about me,* I thought.

The horse looked up. "The funaga must know everything," he sent, but without his old contempt. He looked into the fire as if it were a window, and miniature flames leaped in his eyes.

"I spent many days in the place where the mountain ate you. I thought you must be dead, and I was tortured by my cowardice. I believed then that I did not care what happened to me, but when the funaga tried to trap me with their nets, I fought them and ran away. I did not go to Obernewtyn, but higher, to the fields where I once ran with Avra. But I could not stay. I went on and on to the high places where the old

495

equines go to die. I meant to abase myself before their spirits. I hoped I would die, that they would demand it of me.

"I did not eat or drink, as is the custom among equines seeking a vision. I waited and day after day, there was no answer. I thought the old ones were deaf to me and had cast me out. I called myself Galta—nothing.

"Then one night I slept, and in my dream I saw a vision of a high mountain valley, where a lake lay yet unfrozen in the midst of ice and snow. A voice told me to find that place. It promised that I would find absolution there. When I woke, I began to search.

"It was hard, and many times I despaired and thought of giving up. But every night in my sleep, the voice came, reassuring me, urging me higher, promising an answer to the pain in my heart and a purpose for my life. It told me many things for my ears alone, and a blackness, one that had been inside me all my life, began to melt as easily as coldwhite before the sun. I could have gone back to Obernewtyn then, for I understood that pride and arrogance, rather than true grief, had kept me away. But the voice urged me always to go on.

"At last, I found this valley. Then the voice came again, telling me I had been drawn to the mountains to take part in a quest whose end would concern not only equine and funaga, but all living creatures. This was to be my life's most important work, above any other glory I had imagined." I could feel the faint sense of awe that marked his thoughts.

"The voice told me a funaga would be brought here, one whom I must keep safe. One day, this funaga would fight a great and perilous battle whose outcome was unknown even to the wisest of the wise but which might mean the destruction of all life on the earth forever. I must carry this funaga wherever it wishes to go and protect it with my own life if it were needed.

"It was strange and ironic that I, who had so despised the funaga, should find myself bound to such a task. There was a time when I would have refused, believing your kind to be a blight on the world. But the voice had helped me see that no life-form is greater than another and that all are bound up in an intricate and delicately balanced pattern of coexistence.

"In the daylight, I found this cave. And then I waited. Many weeks passed, yet always the voice told me to wait. So I waited. Two moons passed, and still I waited, wondering if it was my punishment to wait forever in these cold lands for one who would never come," he sent bleakly.

"Two moons?" I whispered incredulously. I remembered how I had imagined time passing in my sleep. If he was right, winter was near ended. I felt a stab of despair at the thought that Obernewtyn was yet unwarned, unless Daffyd had got there in time.

"Then I found you, lying on the ledge. At first I could not believe you were the funaga the voice had spoken of. But why else would you be there? And how could you have come there, when there was not a single footprint in all the un-touched snow? Then I thought you were dead, for your skin was like ice. But your heart was beating, and you woke."

There was a long silence in the wake of his strange tale. Outside, the storm winds howled derisively, and tiny whirl-winds of snow blew through the cave opening, falling in a white drift against the stones. The fire's orange light danced silently upon the walls.

"Only someone insane could believe your story. Or mine," I said softly, but my words sounded hollow. I had fallen

497

asleep, half-dead, in the highlands and had woken completely healed, sixty days and thousands of spans distant, on the highest and loneliest of mountain peaks.

I felt a ghostly echo of the dangerous weight of pain that had pressed against the feebly erected barrier in my mind. I shuddered.

The fire crackled, and I turned my face to the glowing embers, drinking in the warmth.

"When this storm is over, we will go back to Obernewtyn," I said.

But outside, the storm winds shrieked.

HOPING THE SUDDEN silence was not merely a lull, I used a stick to clear the snow and rocks from the entrance of the cave. We had lost count of time, and the firewood was nearly exhausted.

Coming out of the narrow crevice, I was cold and hungry, but I forgot physical discomfort in the dazzling sight that met my eyes. The world was blanketed in pristine white, reflecting the sunshine with painful intensity. A delicate lace of icicles hung from the ledge on which I had slept until I'd been found by Gahltha—for that, I'd decided, was a far more appropriate name for the formidable black horse than "Galta" could ever be.

Unaccountably, I remembered sitting at the Kinraide orphan home with Maruman, dreaming of the fabled world of the Snow Queen, a forbidden Oldtime tale my mother had told us.

"It is a hard trek to Obernewtyn," Gahltha warned. "It will not be safe to go too quickly. The coldwhite will hide crevices and rocks. We will have to put our feet down carefully."

"Life has always been a matter of putting one's feet down carefully," I said. Even the prospect of a long hard trek through frostbitten country with an empty belly and scant clothes could not quell my joy.

We left at once, for there were no preparations to be made.

Gahltha led, forging a path; even so, my shoes and legs were quickly soaked. I was glad to walk, since the exertion kept me warmer than the dazzling sunlight could on its own.

Gahltha warned me to shade my eyes with a piece of cloth to avoid being snow-blinded.

I looked back once at the mountain in whose skirts we had sheltered. It sloped backward, outjutting rocks and drifts of snow adhering to the flat surfaces, making it look like the stern face of a very old man. The slant made it impossible to see the top, and I wondered if that was where the Ken of the Agyllians lay.

We traveled across the ice lake, and the land beyond seemed to go right to the horizon. This puzzled me until Gahltha said the distance was an illusion. We were on a large, flat plateau and would shortly reach its edge.

The wind, which had howled for days and nights, seemed to have exhausted itself, and the air was clear and still. The only sounds to break the silence were those of our footsteps and breathing. We could have been the only beings alive in all the Land. I felt as if the air were a kind of fement that one might become drunk on, and hunger increased the heady feeling. At the same time, I felt I could understand anything and everything very easily there on the roof of the world.

It was nearing dusk when we reached the edge of the plateau. I was within a single handspan of the edge before I realized. Only a sharp warning from Gahltha stopped me walking off the edge. I looked over, and a cold, freshening gust of air blew up into my face. What I saw below took my breath away.

Clouds were strung out across the sky like skeins of wool—below my feet!

Seen from above, the clouds were fluffy mounds of cream

or sea foam shot with glorious sunset colors—a fairy realm. The Land was barely visible through the woolly curtain. And between the Land and the plateau there were rank upon rank of mountains, jagged as upturned teeth, streaked with snow and lacking the slightest touch of color or softness.

Some of the mountains were dense and dark, unmistakably Blacklands. Few dared travel through mountainous terrain, because a snowfall could hide lethal, poisonous ground. Yet Gahltha seemed unperturbed, saying only that the voices had told him where to walk safely.

I had often gazed at the distant mountains, but I had never had any real idea of the sheer size and barrenness of them. Gahltha's lone trek to the heights had been an incredible act of faith.

Something glistened on the far horizon. Squinting, I realized I was looking at the great sea. For a moment, I seemed to smell the salty wetness of waves on the shore. All the world lay spread at my feet. The one thing I could not see was a way down. The plateau stood apart from the other plains and mountains. I looked at the black horse and found him watching me inscrutably.

"I brought you here to see the world, funaga. I wondered if it would move you as it once moved a proud and bitter equine. It was here I saw my own smallness and understood how stupid and arrogant I had let pride and hatred make me," he sent.

"Not many could see this and be unchanged," I sent gently. "But you haven't said how we can get down."

"Patience," Gahltha sent.

He made for the opposite side of the plateau, and there I looked out, aghast. Again the plateau was high, but there were no clouds to hide the dreadful vision from us.

Stretched out like a charred skin were hundreds of spans of Blacklands, lifeless and still. I had thought the snowy slopes barren, but this was a terrible stretch of obsidian, flecked here and there with dark, gleaming pools reflecting a tarnished sky. A stretch of mountains, breaking away from the main mass, ran across the nightmarish terrain and out of sight. It was the Land, dead and without hope of life. Looking at that, it was impossible to share Pavo's assurance that the Blacklands would not last forever.

Even as I watched, night crept like a dark shadow across the bleak plains, and though the heights were still bathed in sunlight, I felt strangely cold. I had wondered why the Agyllians left me in the mountains when it would have been so easy for them to carry me down to Obernewtyn. Now I thought I understood.

"I did not know it went on so far. So much land poisoned . . . ," I whispered.

"Perhaps there are many lessons to be learned in the mountains," Gahltha sent gravely.

I could not take my eyes away.

I thought of the Oldtimers and wondered whether they would have built their weaponmachines if they could have foreseen what would come to pass. And why create machines that would outlast a hundred lives? Had they been so enamored of war and destruction that they had to make it immortal?

For the first time, I felt I could understand the original Councilmen and their tyrannous rule. Farmers and children of the Oldtimers, they had seen firsthand the will to destroy and the hunger for power that knew no boundaries. Perhaps they had even known the deathmachines existed and had hoped to ensure no one would ever use them again. No wonder they had forbidden delving into the past.

They had been afraid.

Unfortunately, the repressive philosophies had become a different sort of threat. I doubted the present Council understood the real dangers any better than those who had made the weaponmachines in the first place. I had only to think of Henry Druid and Alexi to know there would always be men and women prepared to pay any price for power. Even our own Teknoguild would risk agonizing death to revive the knowledge of a lost age.

The Elder was right. It was inevitable the machines would someday be unearthed and used. And Atthis had said I was the only one with any chance of destroying them. If that made me the Seeker, it was a responsibility I was finally ready to accept.

Resolutely, I thrust the machines and the Agyllians from my mind and looked at Gahltha. "I will be glad to go from this place and its foreboding lessons."

He blew air from flared nostrils. "I did not bring you here for lessons. See, there is where we will go down."

I followed his gaze and saw a natural stone path leading unevenly to the next plateau, cleaving to the edge of the slope. The path began not far from where we stood, moving this way, then that, ever lower, across the face of the cliff.

Gahltha looked at me. "You are weak still. Ride on my back and we will travel more quickly."

I looked at him curiously. "You want me to ride?" I asked.

"One warrior will carry another, if the strength of one proves greater. Each has his own strength but also his own weakness." He spoke with the air of repeating a well-learned lesson.

"Wise words," I said simply. "I am glad to ride on your

back if it will help us move more quickly."

We traveled that day and the next through the monotonous snowbound terrain of the high mountains, and on the third day, we came upon a few scant green shoots, thrusting their tips through the snow. "It will be more dangerous now that the thaw has begun," Gahltha said. "But I think tomorrow we will reach the valley of the barud." *Barud* was the equine word symbol for "home"—it seemed Gahltha had come to miss Obernewtyn.

Snow clouds gathered overhead, and with the bleak afternoon came unexpected doubts. I began to fear Obernewtyn had changed and that I would find there was no longer a place for me there. My whole life had been spent as an outsider, and even at Obernewtyn, I had felt misplaced until the journey to the coast. Ironic if I discovered too late where my own barud lay.

Just at dusk, for the first time, we encountered another creature. A wolf.

The wolves that frequented the mountains were savage, pale-eyed wraiths with coats the color of mist and snow. They were nearly impossible to spot deliberately, and it was sheer luck that I saw this one. I had been plodding along, shivering and staring aimlessly into the distance, when the landscape appeared to shift fractionally. I realized I had been staring right at a wolf without seeing it. It had been watching us, but now it turned, melting back into the white landscape.

Later I heard several desolate calls in the distance. I was tempted to try communicating, but the wild keening calls across the frozen wastes made a desolate song of the night and did not invite a response.

The calls went on for hours, then abruptly ceased.

I was glad of the respite, but Gahltha seemed more disturbed by the silence than by the bloodcurdling howls. I was too tired to worry and slept leaning against his warm flank. Gradually, I felt him relax, too. Exhausted and half-starved as we were, we needed sleep. Initial hunger pains had long since given way to an empty ache that was easier to bear. If sleep was all the comfort that remained for us, then that would have to be enough to get us home.

Suddenly Gahltha stiffened, and I was jerked awake. Dense clouds obscured the moon. I looked around in the pitch darkness fearfully.

"What is it?" I sent.

"The Brildane," Gahltha responded.

I laid a gentle hand across his back, wondering if there was danger.

"What or who are Brildane?" I asked.

"I do not know what name is given them by the funaga, but Brildane is the name they call themselves. We call them gehdra, because they are invisible. They have no time for any creature but their own kind. But they hate the funaga, because your kind trap and slay their young."

"Are they hungry?" I asked, trying to understand what sort of animal it could be.

"If they were, we would already be dead," Gahltha sent. "You heard their calls throughout the night? The mountain equines know a little of their strange speech. Their calls concerned us. They wonder what we are doing here. The gehdra claim the high mountains as their own world. Here we are intruders."

"Wolves! The Brildane are wolves!" I cried. I looked at Gahltha. "Are you telling me they're just curious?" I asked.

"The curiosity of the gehdra is as savage as its hunger," Gahltha sent quellingly.

I looked around uneasily, wondering how he had known of their presence. I had heard not a sound. And even now, I could sense no minds but our own. The wolves must have some ability to cloak their minds.

"Would it help if I sent a greeting?" I suggested.

"No!" Gahltha sent urgently, as if he expected me to leap up and rush into the night with a cry of greeting on my lips. "It is impossible to predict what they will do. Speaking to them would not stop them eating us, if that was their desire. And if they wanted to confront us, they would have done it. But I think they came to look, not to feed or speak. Better to do nothing. With the gehdra, that is always safest."

Gahltha's warnings were underlined by a sense of tangible fear. Bleakly, I realized these may be the very wolves Ariel had hunted and trapped. He had driven them mad to ensure their ferocity and had used them to guard the grounds, hunting and killing runaways. We had hoped to heal the beasts once Ariel had gone, but his sadistic treatment had made it impossible. In the end, the best we could do was give the wolves back their freedom.

I dared not stir a limb until Gahltha reported that they had gone, fading back into the night as mysteriously as they had appeared.

"Are you sure you didn't imagine them?" I asked.

"In the morning you will see," was all he would say.

It was hard to go back to sleep, but after a while I fell into a light, troubled slumber. I dreamed of Ariel as he had been, a boy with almost unearthly beauty and a sadistic turn of mind that delighted in causing pain. I woke disquieted. The night grew steadily colder, and even Gahltha's considerable body heat could not keep me warm. Eventually, I gave up trying to sleep and lay waiting for the horse to wake.

With relief, I felt Gahltha stir at dawn. It was barely light before we were off but light enough to see that Gahltha had been right the night before. The snow all around us was covered in paw prints, some a mere handspan from where my feet had lain.

The Brildane.

I shivered, and suddenly it began to snow. Just a few flakes at first, but blown with stinging force into our faces by a hard, icy wind. The snow was already thick underfoot and made walking tiring. Gahltha offered to carry me again, but he could only walk a little faster than I and was easily as tired, so I refused. I knew neither of us could go much farther without proper rest and food.

Near to dropping, I was trying to remember how long it had been since I had eaten when Gahltha neighed loudly. Squinting against the wind and flying snow, I realized he had rounded a spur of rock and was out of sight. Forcing weary limbs to hurry, I caught up.

"What is it?" I sent, wondering if I had strength enough left to deal with another obstacle.

"We have reached the valley of the barud."

I blinked stupidly. Barud? "Obernewtyn!"

All weariness fell away from me then. I was close enough to send a questing probe, but something kept me from it, a desire to have my first glimpse of Obernewtyn unhampered by greetings and explanations.

I had just begun to recognize some of the hills and stone

hummocks when the wind fell away and the snow stopped, making our first glimpse of Obernewtyn clear and unmistakable.

A cry of happiness died in my throat, stillborn. I stumbled to a halt, unable to believe my eyes.

All that remained of Obernewtyn was a charred ruin.

✦ 26 ✦

ONLY A FIRESTORM could have done so much damage.

Little remained of Obernewtyn but rubble. The walls of the main building were no more than jagged, blackened stumps of stone. The windblown snow adhered to the crevices, and a rambling kind of thorn brush thrust its roots deep into the cracked rubble.

It looked like a ruin of years rather than moons. How had it degenerated so quickly? I blinked, for when I stared hard, I seemed to see the ghostly shape of Obernewtyn as it had been.

Tears blurred my vision, and the wind froze them before they could fall. It was bitter cold on the hillside, but I scarcely felt the chill. To have traveled so long and far only to find Obernewtyn destroyed was beyond a nightmare.

"Come," Gahltha sent.

I stared at him incredulously.

He asked doubtfully, "Do you not want to go to the barud? I am sworn to take you wherever you will."

I shook my head, disturbed by his lack of emotion. Perhaps he had changed less than I realized and welcomed the downfall of any funaga institution. I looked back at the wreckage and wondered whether any had escaped the firestorm. What a tragic irony that the lie that had protected us for so long had come so horribly true.

Stumbling forward, I prayed I would find some clue as to

where everyone had gone. The ground was sodden from the melting snow, and fresh flakes fell soft as ashes on the dark, wet earth.

Abruptly, I stopped and stared, squinting against the cold wind blustering across the valley. I thought I had seen a smudge of smoke.

It had come from somewhere on the far side of the valley, near the pass to the highlands. My heart beat faster as I made out a number of dark shapes that might be buildings. It seemed to me I was looking at a small settlement.

Gahltha offered to carry me, though he seemed puzzled at my instruction not to pass too close to Obernewtyn. It occurred to me that equines might not know that a poisonous residue was left behind by a firestorm.

Some obscure instinct of caution stopped me riding directly into the camp. I asked Gahltha to take us into a clump of trees a short distance away. With the mountains behind and on one side and the ruins of Obernewtyn on the other, we were safe from detection.

Peering through the greenery, I could see several roughly constructed stone-and-thatch huts, set in a circle and surrounded by a wall of stripling branches. Even at a distance, it was clearly a poor settlement, and an air of hopeless dilapidation hung over it.

Two men emerged from one of the hovels. I bit my lip. Soldierguards!

They could only have come through the pass. That meant the thaw had already opened the way. At least the Council would have no more cause to doubt Rushton's word . . . if he had survived the firestorm. A strange feeling of despair filled me at the realization that he might be dead.

I felt Gahltha's restive movements and looked at him.

"Perhaps we should go to Obernewtyn to find out what has passed here," he suggested.

I shook my head impatiently. "What good will that do? Besides, it would be dangerous to go there now. I want to get a better look at that camp. The soldierguards can't have built those huts. I want to know who did. We'll go back the way we came and right around to the other side."

Before I could mount, Gahltha sent a warning that someone approached.

To my horror, it was three soldierguards. Fortunately, they stopped in a clearing several spans from where we were hidden. Grumbling about the cold, they sat on logs, rubbing their hands and faces.

"I tell you, I am weary of this hellish place," said one man resentfully. " 'Get wood,' the captain orders, but what is the use of it? Quick as the fire warms you, the wind chills you to the bone."

"That fellow Rushton does nowt seem to feel th' cold," said a big burly man with a highland accent, and I was glad to hear Rushton's name despite the circumstances. "It whistles through th' holes in his clothes, an' he nary shows a shiver. His blood must be as cold as th' snow."

"There is a madness in him," said the first. "No sane man could wish to stay up here, yet the fool claims he will rebuild Obernewtyn once the taint is faded."

The big man nodded. "I heard he was offered a billet in th' lowlands but chose to come back here."

"He is proud enough to want his inheritance rebuilt," said the first speaker, rising and stamping his feet. "But what does any of this matter to the Council? I swear this is a fool's errand. Three suns have risen on this barren valley since we came here. And why?"

"Why indeed?" asked the third man, who had not spoken yet. He had an unpleasant hissing sort of voice and quick, sly eyes. "We are to find out if Obernewtyn is truly destroyed and if there is truth in rumors of sedition here."

"One look answered those questions," said the first man.

"Did it?" asked the third in an insinuating tone. His two companions eyed him curiously.

"Do ye say there is sedition here? I have seen no sign of it," said the big highlander at length.

"I say neither yes nor no to it. But the captain is no fool. He would not stay here for pleasure. Perhaps he knows something we do not."

"What do ye mean?" asked the highlander.

"Just this—captains, as a rule, are told more than rank-and-file soldierguards. I heard he had his orders direct from the Council's agent. Who knows what information he has," said the hissing man.

"There *is* somethin' strange about these mountain folk," opined the highlander after a moment of thought. "I dinna know what it is, but when I am among them, my skin creeps."

"Mine too," said the first man. "Ariel spoke certain of sedition, and he's seldom wrong."

"Call him not by name!" snarled the third man, glancing about as if he feared immediate reprisal.

"His name is not so secret," sneered the first.

"Well, then call him by it when next you see him, fool. *There* is one to make a man's skin crawl."

"I say we mun just as soon kill them all, miserable creatures," the big highlander pronounced. "Then we need not trouble ourselves with findin' out if they be seditioners."

"Usually, we are told to bring back prisoners alive. But I have heard it whispered the Council's agent wants none to come alive from the mountains. I wonder if it is true, and why," pondered the first man.

"Indeed. I wonder what he suspects . . . or fears," said the third soldierguard.

After a long pause, the highlander shook himself like an ox. "I wonder only how long before my head rests on a real bed an' my tongue tastes a sweet fement," he sighed plaintively.

"Never, if I catch you idling again when I have given an order!" came a new voice, so close my heart skipped a beat. Cautiously, I moved and saw that two more men had entered the clearing. From the markings on his collar, the tall, sallow-faced newcomer was the captain.

But the person behind him was no soldierguard. I stifled a gasp at the sight of Rushton!

Clad in shabby trousers and a ragged jumper, he was grim-faced and gaunt. The wild, dark gleam in his eyes told me why the soldierguards had judged him mad. He looked like a man possessed, and deep lines of suffering and despair made him appear far older than he was. There was a bitter twist to his lips that I had never seen before, and I was filled with pity at the thought of what the destruction of Obernewtyn had meant to him. He must have loved it more than life for its demise to mark him so.

As if he sensed my scrutiny, his head turned; he seemed to stare straight into my eyes. I shuddered at the emptiness in his face and was glad when he turned aside to follow the captain and his men from the clearing.

I slumped back, aching all over from tension. I could not forget Rushton's face, for it warned me worse might have happened than I could even imagine.

I went afoot as we made our way back along the valley,

but this time we went more warily and stayed close to the walls of Obernewtyn where trees grew thickly, offering shelter. I noticed fumes of faint blue smoke rising from the ruins and was struck by the feeling that I had seen them before.

"Elspeth?" came a voice from behind. I whirled in fright and found myself looking into the astounded face of Daffyd. Gahltha, who did not know him, moved aggressively between us, until I reassured him.

Daffyd came forward slowly, as if he thought I would disappear. "By Lud, it *is* you!" he cried. "I thought I was dreaming with my eyes open. We thought you dead. Your feet . . ." He looked down.

"Are healed," I said firmly. "I coerced you to think them worse than they were, because I knew I could not make it back to the mountains before the pass closed. But what has happened here? Was Obernewtyn like this when you arrived? Were any hurt in the firestorm? And when did the soldier-guards come?"

Daffyd burst into laughter. "It must be a powerful illusion if it fools even the guildmistress of the farseekers. But they do say little Dragon is as strong as you were . . . are," he added ruefully.

I felt my mouth drop open, and a great joy welled up in me. "Then . . . this"—I waved a trembling hand at the ruins—"this is all an illusion?"

"Of course," Daffyd said.

I sank to my knees, weak with relief. "No wonder Gahltha behaved so oddly. Dragon's illusions do not work on animals." I sent an explanation to Gahltha, who still looked puzzled.

"Then everyone is inside?" I asked.

Daffyd shook his head. "Rushton thought that too much risk. We are using the Teknoguild cave network as a base.

514

Only a few live in the camp, for appearance's sake. Rushton, of course, and Ceirwan, Dameon, and most others trained in farseeking and empathy."

"Not coercers?" I wondered.

"They are in another hidden camp very near the pass," Daffyd explained. "They are our insurance, in case this sleight of hand fails to deceive the soldierguards and open battle is needed to stop them carrying tales to the Council." He frowned. "But how is it they did not see you come through the pass just now?"

I shrugged, realizing it would suit me to have everyone think I had come from the highlands, rather than from the high mountains. "I came very stealthily. And I have some coercive Talent. The soldierguards didn't see me either, but I saw them. And I fear we might have to fight despite this illusion." I told Daffyd what I had overheard.

"It is true the soldierguards have stayed longer than we hoped," Daffyd said worriedly. "Tonight Rushton will come here, and you can tell him this news." He gave me a quick look. "He will be amazed to see you here. I think your death was a grievous thing to him."

I nodded absently. "I heard one of the soldierguards say they have been here for three days. How is it Dragon can sustain an illusion so long?"

"She has practiced all wintertime," Daffyd said. "Even so, it is a strain, and she does not maintain it in the dark hours. Luck has made them come in the waning of the moon. The blue fumes are an added touch to give credence to Rushton's story that the ruins are contaminated. That stops the soldierguards wanting a closer look." He glanced at the ruin pensively. "I wonder what keeps the captain suspicious."

"From what I heard, it has to do with Ariel's insistence."

"You were seemingly right about his haste for revenge. As you feared, the soldierguards arrived the moment the pass thawed," Daffyd said. "We have kept Dragon out of their sight. It is easier for her to hold the illusion away from the distraction of people. Matthew stays with her to protect her during the day. At night, we three camp not far from here, for no one would dare come so close to Obernewtyn. They will be back soon. In the meantime, what about some food?"

"I'm starving," I said fervently. "And so is Gahltha."

As we walked to the campsite, I explained to the black horse all that I'd learned. It did not take Daffyd long to make a small fire and warm some stew. Gahltha preferred grass to the bags of horse feed. I sat gratefully by the fire and accepted a cup of strong fement once I had eaten.

"I meant to go back down to the Druid camp after delivering Dragon and your message, but that very night, snow fell thick and closed the pass," Daffyd said, sitting beside me.

"I suppose you're worried about Gilaine and the others . . . ," I began, then faltered, seeing the grim look on the armsman's face.

"I don't know if they're still there. One of the soldierguards said the firestorm had all but burned out the White Valley."

"Oh, Daffyd," I said, aghast.

Again he shook his head. "I don't believe they are dead. Rushton has pledged Obernewtyn's help to find them when the soldierguards are gone." He sipped his drink as if it held a bitter draft.

We both froze at the sound of running feet. The brush parted, and Roland burst into the open. "Where's Matthew?" he cried. "We need him to farseek the camp! Something has gone wrong. All contact has been severed, but we dare not go down there with the soldierguards . . ." He stopped dead, catching sight of me. "Elspeth?"

"Yes, it's me," I said impatiently. "I'll see what's happened."

"But you . . . ," he said, dazed.

I waved him to silence, closing my eyes to concentrate. I sent my mind flying toward the makeshift camp, seeking out any familiar pattern. It was as if all there slept.

At last I located a weak consciousness. Focusing in, I discovered it was Ceirwan.

"Who . . . who is that?" he sent groggily, barely discernible.

"It is Elspeth," I sent. "What has happened there?"

There was a pause. "Elspeth . . . impossible."

I felt his grief but could waste no time on it. "I did not die. Now you must focus. I can hardly understand you. What has happened?"

I sensed his struggle to concentrate. "I . . . They drugged us. The soldierguards think we hide evidence of sedition in the ruins. You must stop them from getting to Obernewtyn . . . get coercers . . ." He faded out again, and this time it was impossible to recall him.

I opened my eyes. "They're okay, but they all sleep," I said. "The soldierguards have drugged them and are about to go and examine the ruins firsthand."

"We'll have to fight," Daffyd said.

I shook my head. "I have a better idea, Daffyd. One less likely to escalate into violence. You ride Gahltha and bring back one of the coercers. The guildmaster, Gevan, if you can. Also, get a group of them to go down to the camp as soon as the soldierguards leave." I outlined my plan quickly.

"It might just work," Roland said.

"And it would explain why Rushton was so anxious to keep them away from the ruins. But will the captain react as you expect?" Daffyd asked.

"It's my guess they'll prove a craven lot, more worried about their own skins than their duty. But if not, Gevan is a coercer, and so am I, at need."

"You, a coercer?" Roland asked sharply. I ignored him, giving Daffyd a leg up onto Gahltha. The black horse allowed Daffyd to mount, then sped off, keeping close to the tree line.

"Come. We'll meet Gevan in front of Obernewtyn," I told the Healer guildmaster. "We'll have to make sure they don't come too close to the buildings. Now describe to me the symptoms. . . ."

It was dusk when the soldierguards appeared, riding along the entrance road leading up to Obernewtyn. Catching sight of Gevan and me, the captain reined his horse.

"Who are you, girl? I've not seen you before. What trickery is here?" he shouted harshly.

When I did not answer, he ordered one of his men to bind us. The man dismounted, but he paused when he was close enough to see my face clearly.

"Captain . . . I think there's something wrong with her . . . ," he called uneasily.

I lurched toward him, and he backed away hastily. "Help me!" I moaned. "Help me. I am ill."

The captain dismounted, staring at me suspiciously. "Ill? What do you mean? I won't stand for . . ." He stopped, having come close enough to see the black blisters on my lips. Gevan moaned loudly, making the man jump. His face changed, contorting with horror, and he spun away. "Lud's curse! These creatures have the plague!"

The soldierguards murmured in dismay.

"Shut up and let me think!" the captain snarled, mounting his horse. The other soldierguards did the same.

"What are we goin' to do, Captain? We won't be allowed to live if anyone finds out we've been in contact with the plague!" said one soldierguard.

"We can't stay here. I don't want to die of plague!" wailed another man.

"We won't," said the captain tightly. "Now listen to me, all of you. It will take closed mouths and a tight story to save us from being burned. We will tell the Council all was as Rushton had claimed—Obernewtyn a poor ruin, the valley tainted. We will tell them we found no one here. No one must ever know there was plague here. Even a whisper would be enough to see us dead."

The men nodded, ashen faced.

"But are we not already infected?" asked one of the men.

"Thank Lud we made our own camp and did not sup or dally with these wretched people. 'Tis said plague spreads by close living. We should be safe if we leave at once."

"What about these two and the people in the camp? We can't leave them here alive," said another of the soldierguards.

The captain shook his head grimly. "There must be no witnesses. If anyone ever does come up here, it must be exactly as we have said. Do not bother with these half-dead wretches. The wolves will finish them. But while the others are drugged, we will burn the camp. Now let's ride. I want to be quit of this cursed valley as soon as possible."

It was growing dark when the soldierguards torched the camp.

As I had hoped, they did not trouble to make sure their victims were inside, else they would have found the settlement deserted. The coercers had carried all the unconscious out and set them under the trees.

From the distance, we watched the huts blaze. Silhouetted in orange light, the soldierguards let out a hoarse cheer before mounting and riding out of the valley. None looked behind him.

"Are they all right?" Gevan asked, watching Roland lift Rushton's eyelid.

He nodded in satisfaction. "Only drugged, though I have not seen this kind of drug before." He moved to look at Ceirwan.

I leaned over Rushton and stared into his ravaged face. In repose, he looked so terribly sad.

Unexpectedly, his eyes fluttered open, flamed with longing; then he shook his head and groaned. "Ah, Elspeth, love," he sighed; then his eyes fell shut.

I stared down at him in wonder.

✦ 27 ✦

"I AM THE Master of Obernewtyn. Who among you will choose a guild this night?" Rushton asked.

Those prepared crossed to stand in line facing him. "We choose our places," they spoke in unison.

Rushton handed each of the candidates a candle and then lit them all from his own, the flame guttering slightly. Fortunately, the wind was low. "May you choose well," he murmured.

"I am Merrett. I choose the Coercer guild," said the first, a thin, dark-eyed girl.

There was a predictable buzz of surprise, since her mother was a healer. Merrett crossed to the table and set her candle amidst the Coercer token.

Zarak, grinning with pride, held up his own candle. "I am Zarak, of the Beastspeaking guild. With permission, I choose anew: the Farseeker guild." There was a burst of applause as he crossed to the Farseeker table, and I smiled inwardly at the success of Ceirwan's negotiations.

There were no other surprises, and when all had chosen, the newly guilded led a toast to Obernewtyn.

Able to escape momentarily from his affectionate guilders, Dameon came to sit beside me. I was amused and flattered to hear some children sing an idealized version of my own first journey to Obernewtyn.

"I had no idea how brave and wise I was," I laughed.

Dameon smiled. "I think they are already at work on the epic of your journey to the coast. But I doubt anyone will ever sing the complete story."

I looked at him. Dameon had always been able to see more than most people. Like Atthis, his judgment lay in some keener place than his eyes. I had not told anyone what had happened in the mountains, but for a moment, I was tempted to confess to the empath. Such a secret burden made me feel lonely, even in the midst of my friends. Then I remembered Atthis's warning that I must tell no one of what I was to do.

Behind my seat, Gahltha stirred, as if he, too, heard an echo of the voice that had changed his life. The black horse had become my shadow whenever I moved outside Obernewtyn's halls, regarding himself as my special guardian. Fortunately, this was not too noticeably odd, since he and Avra had become the first animals to attend guild-merge. Rushton had decided to make use of the direct entrance from the outside that had once been a secret passage; the horses used it proudly.

Dameon patted my hand. "Some secrets are safer kept."

I smiled wanly. "I'm glad to be home, but I can't help worrying about what will happen next."

Dameon shrugged. "The battle is won, but the war goes on. Do not dwell too much on yesterday's struggles. Take things as they come. Today is a day for singing and celebration." He laughed. "Do you suppose Kella and Domick will bond before they go back to the safe house in Sutrium?"

I stared at the empath. "They told you?"

Dameon smiled. "I am an empath master, but the greenest novice might guess as easily. They might as well announce it and get it over with."

I grinned. "They're working up courage. It will rock their two guilds on their heels. Merrett's choosing will be nothing to that."

"It is well done. Such divisions are not good for Obernewtyn," Dameon said approvingly.

"I hear Dragon is doing well as an empath novice," I said, catching sight of the red-haired beauty.

Dameon shook his head. "She is a handful, that one. I do not envy Matthew her violent affections. Yet I would like to know more about her past."

Lina ran up, grinning. "Dance with me, master?" she cried, taking his hands. I opened my mouth to rebuke her, but to my surprise, Dameon let himself be coaxed to his feet. As if sensing my surprise, he cast a smile over one shoulder. "Remember, today is for dancing, not worrying about the future."

I sat back in my seat. So much had changed subtly at Obernewtyn, as if winning one battle, even if by trickery, had given everyone bolder hopes.

It was spring, and the choosing ceremony had been the high point of our own moon fair. It was the wrong season and the moon had waned, but the brief, lovely season and an increasing feeling of hope for the future ensured its success. There had been a merry feast. After the choosing, there were tests of skill between the coercers, a vision demonstration by Dragon, and various entertainments by the other guilds as the musicians played their instruments.

Daffyd appeared beside me with a mug of fement. I motioned him to sit as the musicians tuned between songs, and strains of discordant music filled the air.

Daffyd smiled, but his eyes were sad. "Gilaine would love this," he said wistfully.

"Is there any news of them?"

He shrugged. "Nothing definite. You might remember Gilbert, the leader of the armsmen? He devised a plan some time back in case there was a need to evacuate the camp in a hurry. It was meant to be used in case of soldierguard attack, but it would have served well in the firestorm. If Gilbert survived to put it into operation, he would have kept the survivors together."

"Have you spoken to Maryon? She might be able to help pinpoint them."

"The Futuretell guildmistress thinks they're alive, but 'tis hard for her to get a definite reading, because she dinna know them." Daffyd was sunk in thought for a minute. "I mean to leave when Domick, Kella, and the others go. I'll travel with them as far as Sutrium and then . . . well, I'll keep lookin'. Rushton has offered help, but until I find some clue as to where they are, I'm better working alone."

I felt a shadow touch my heart at the thought that each had his own deeds to do, his own battles and quests. Mine lay in a dark chasm across endless Blackland plains.

I caught sight of Rushton deep in conversation with Brydda and Gevan, apparently oblivious to the music and laughter. As ever, he treated the festivities as yet another guildmerge, going from one group to the next in his effort to have everything organized before his departure. He was going down to the lowlands with Domick and Kella when they returned to Sutrium with Brydda. The big lowlander had been vastly impressed with all he had seen at Obernewtyn, and he and Rushton had taken an instant liking to one another. Brydda was eager to have Rushton meet his allies.

Addressing a guildmerge, Brydda had made it clear that though he had no prejudices about Misfits, he could not speak for his allies. But he was certain that, in time, the book

I had found about mind powers would convince them that our Talents were not evil or mutations caused by the Great White but were a natural development of human abilities that had existed in the Beforetime.

Brydda had brought Katlyn and Grufyyd to Obernewtyn to stay. His parents had hated the city and had been only too glad to be invited to live at Obernewtyn. Katlyn had already begun to replant her collection of herbs, much to Roland's delight.

The news of Pavo's death had saddened me, though I had expected it, and the Teknoguild, still mourning his loss, had mounted an expedition to the city under Tor in his memory. I felt the loss of Jik even more keenly.

Maryon had told me she'd foreseen his death soon after we had departed, though not Darga's. "It is true the predictions focused on the boy, but I think the dog would not have gone without him," she explained. "Futuretelling is inexact at the best of times, and I regret that. But there is no sense blaming ourselves for Jik's death. Who knows what would have happened to him if he had not left the cloister or if he had not gone on your expedition and Obernewtyn had fallen. Dwell not on this death, but on his last happy days with us."

Brydda whirled Kella past me in a dance, rousing me from my memories. I smiled, already regretting that Brydda had to leave. He had a heartening manner and a cheery way of making everything seem possible.

As with all coming and going at Obernewtyn, they would travel across the now barren White Valley and down the Olden way. Few dogs were as sensitive to poisonous taints as Darga, but with care, it would be possible to find a suitable path, retracing our own journey. It was no longer safe to come openly along the main way, as our mountain valley was

525

supposed to be deserted and barren. Domick had gleefully informed us that this was the report made by the soldier-guards. It had been accepted by the Council, and Ariel had lost some credibility over the matter. With this and the dis-appearance of the Druid and his people, Ariel was no longer in a position to threaten us.

From the corner of my eye, I watched Rushton. No emo-tion showed on his features. It struck me suddenly that he had spent a lifetime hiding his thoughts and feelings.

The memory of his words as he lay dazed after being drugged by the soldierguards came back to me with a queer thrill. No one had heard those words but me, and it was clear from Rushton's behavior afterward that he did not remem-ber having said them. Yet, in the light of them, many things seemed suddenly clear: Kella's cryptic scolding about my in-ability to see the truth of things, for one, and Rushton's re-luctance to let me join the expedition to the lowlands.

I turned to find Rushton standing beside me and flushed at my thoughts, glad he had no ability to deep-probe.

"You are always alone, even when there are people about you," he observed.

I shrugged. "Matthew tells me I'm too gloomy. But I find it hard to forget all the bad things. All this is wonderful . . . but sometimes it seems like a pleasant dream that can't last. So many have died. And Jik was so young. It's a high price we pay for our place in the world."

"If we did not fight, there would still be deaths, because Misfits will continue to be born. We want to stop the killing, and that means fighting."

"War to end war? It doesn't sound very sensible," I said. We stared at the dancers for a moment in silence; then I felt his eyes on me.

"I could scarcely believe it when I heard you were alive," he said remotely. I did not know what to say. When I looked up, embarrassed by the long silence between us, his expression was stern and unsmiling.

"It will take much to convince me to let you go away again," he said gravely. "Yet I sense you don't really belong to us or to Obernewtyn. There is something in you that holds you ever apart. You are like a piece of smoke in my hand."

"I am glad to be home," I said, not knowing what else to say.

A wintry smile lit his dark features. "Home? This is the first time I have heard you call Obernewtyn that."

I smiled. "You would be astonished at how often I thought of it that way and longed to be here. What is that saying Louis has?"

"The greenest grass is home grass . . . something like that." He gave me a long look. "You are a strange one, Elspeth. Everything you do is mysterious and unexpected. Roland is sadly puzzled over the healing of your feet. He tells me even the scars have disappeared—something he assures me is impossible. The coercers talk of nothing but your ability to coerce as well as Gevan, and the healers praise your miraculous healing of Maruman. Not to mention the change in Gahltha. And what of your sudden appearance when we had thought you dead? How much more is there about you that you choose to keep hidden? I would swear you tell more to Gahltha and that cat than to any of us."

I suppressed an urge to smooth the frown from Rushton's forehead. I had never imagined loving anyone, and I had always believed Rushton incapable of doing so. Perhaps I was wrong in both cases. But something stayed my hand and tongue.

My life would not be fully my own until I had fulfilled my vow to destroy the weaponmachines. Until that was done, I could not truly belong anywhere or to anyone; I had no right to think of Rushton as anything but the Master of Obernewtyn while my dark quest lay before me. That secret set a tiny chasm between us. And until that was gone, I did not belong even to myself.

"Tomorrow you go to the lowlands," I said, wanting to distract him.

He looked out beyond the walls of Obernewtyn. "Maryon said the time to take our stand is not far away. I want to meet Brydda's friends and see how they regard Misfits. There is no good our making allies of bigots, and despite his optimism, I think not all his friends will welcome us with open arms."

"What about Ariel? Domick said he has taken vows to become a Herder," I mused.

Rushton shrugged. "We have nothing to fear from those dabblers in dresses. But Ariel has much to fear from me. I'll deal with him once I have dealt with the Council."

I looked at him, hoping he was right.

"We have come far, but the road is not yet ended," Rushton said.

I sighed. "Don't you think of anything but fighting battles and winning? There must be more to life than that."

"More? Perhaps," Rushton said. "But life is a battle just the same, whether you fight it with weapons or with words. You have to fight for what you believe in and for the things you want."

Abruptly, he held out a hand. "Dance with me."

I stared at him, astonished. I had never seen Rushton dance, and I did not dance myself. I opened my mouth to say so, but the words died on my lips.

His arms went about me, lightly and impersonally as one might hold a piece of soap.

"I have always fought for what I want," Rushton said with calm determination.

✦ EPILOGUE ✦

IT WAS RAINING.

"Soon the coldwhite will come again," Maruman sent.

I looked down at him, marveling again at his recovery. His appearance was as disreputable as ever, but his eyes shone with their old stringent light. We were in the Futuretell hall, waiting for Maryon.

"The time of cold is the time when Obernewtyn is safest, secure behind a barrier of snow and ice," I sent.

"There are some things no barrier can hold away," Maruman sent.

I stared at him, suddenly uneasy. "What do you mean?"

"When the others come, it will be time to make the dark journey," he sent.

I shivered, knowing at once what he meant, though we had barely spoken of it since the day I had returned from the mountains. "What others?" I sent.

"You will not go alone," Maruman responded. "The oldOne has promised." I received a vague mental picture from Maruman of what looked like many dogs. One, I knew.

"Darga?" I whispered, wondering if it was really possible Darga had survived and, if so, where he was. And what did he have to do with my quest?

"He will come, and when he returns, it will be time. Best to forget until then," Maruman sent.

I dared not ask him to explain. Maruman had only ever told what he wanted and no more. Besides, I thought morosely, I would know soon enough if what he said was true.

If Darga returned . . .

I wondered suddenly if this had anything to do with Maryon's request for me to call on her. I was aware she was more likely than anyone else to see what lay ahead for me. Already I had appeared in her dreams, but as yet she had not fathomed the meaning.

Abruptly, I felt cold with premonition. Unlike Maryon and those of the Futuretell guild, my ability to see the future was restricted and infrequent. Most often, my premonitions were no more than a strong feeling of danger, but I had become accustomed to trusting them.

Sensing my mood, Maruman looked at me, his yellow eyes gleaming in the dull evening light. "Fear or no, you must do what must be done. You are the Seeker."

"That's what scares me most," I sent. "If I fail . . ." Strangely, Rushton's face and his words on the day of our moon fair came into my thoughts.

Life is a battle. You have to fight for what you believe in. . . .

"Even the funaga have their times of wisdom, rare though these come," Maruman sent with oblique humor.

I laughed.

*What will come of the Misfits' alliance
with the rebel forces?*

THE REBELLION

Includes two complete novels
ASHLING • THE KEEPING PLACE

THE NEXT BATTLEGAME to be played was called "the Ride."

"I am for this," I told Rushton, for a swift probing had told me there were horses in a corral just behind a clump of trees.

For a moment, our eyes met.

"Yes," he said. "But, Elspeth, we have to do more than win this with speed and grace. We won the last game, I am sure, but we have to show some aggression. It sounds as if these Sadorians value that in the rebels, and we're losing because of it."

"I'll try," I said.